LOVERS
LIKE US

BOOK 2 IN THE **LIKE US SERIES**

KRISTA & BECCA
RITCHIE

Cover Image © Stocksy
Cover Design by Twin Cove Designs

ISBN: 978-1-950165-02-5

CHARACTER LIST

Not all characters in this list will make an appearance in the book, but most will be mentioned.

Ages represent the age of the character at the beginning of the book. Some characters will be older when they're introduced, depending on their birthday.

The Hales

Loren Hale & Lily Calloway
Maximoff - 22
Luna – 18
Xander – 14
Kinney – 13

The Cobalts

Richard Connor Cobalt & Rose Calloway
Jane - 22
Charlie – 20
Beckett – 20
Eliot – 18
Tom – 17
Ben – 15
Audrey – 12

The Meadows

Ryke Meadows & Daisy Calloway
Sullivan - 19
Winona – 13

The Security Team

These are the bodyguards that protect the Hales, Cobalts, and Meadows.

SECURITY FORCE OMEGA

Akara Kitsuwon - 25
Thatcher Moretti - 27
Farrow Keene – 27
Oscar Oliveira - 30
Paul Donnelly – 26
Quinn Oliveira– 20

SECURITY FORCE EPSILON

Banks Moretti – 27
J.P. – 30s
Ian Wreath – 30s
…and more

SECURITY FORCE ALPHA

Price Kepler – 40s
…and more

PROLOGUE

Maximoff Hale

OCEAN SPLASHES AGAINST a docked yacht. I stand on the crowded deck and tune out the rowdy end-of-summer bash behind me. Everyone in swimsuits, taller people knock into low-hanging pineapple streamers on their way to the bar.

Torches light up the night.

I tighten my grip on the yacht's railing. And I just stare out at the dark horizon. My eyes narrowed and unblinking.

I made a *colossal* mistake only twenty minutes ago. It plays on repeat in my brain. Like a fucked-up radio station that I can't shut off.

I descended the boat's stairs to the cabins. I meant to use the bathroom, but I solidified at a familiar voice. Coming from a cracked door to the master cabin.

"I have to tell you something while Moffy is gone," Jason Motlic said, a senior on the high school swim team. Four of us graduated recently, and college is beginning in a week. So I invited them to my family's party. Hanging out one last time.

I'd even *driven* them here, volunteered to be their sober driver because I don't drink. And they wanted to get hammered.

So I stood there, hand frozen on the bathroom door. Not moving. Not entering. Just listening to the voices in the nearby cabin and waiting for an inevitable, metaphorical gunshot to pierce my chest.

"I was over at Moffy's house yesterday—"

"Bullshit," Ray said, also a swim team graduate. "Moffy never brings anyone to his house."

But I did. One time. Yesterday.

I let Jason inside my family's house, and he waited in the living room while I searched the kitchen for my car keys. Just for ten *goddamn* minutes.

"We're friends," Jason countered and then lowered his voice. "His mom was there. I'm telling you, she had *fuck me* eyes. So I got a little closer."

I strained my ears.

"Then she went at me, horny as fuck. She gave me a blow job right by the microwave." *Fuck you, Jason.*

Fuck you.

I couldn't move. Barely breathed.

"No way."

"I'm not lying." They all laughed together, called Jason "the man" and their hands slapped together in a congratulatory shake.

My skin crawled, blood boiled—and just so we're clear, I believe *zero* percent of his story. Sex addict and all, my mom is just like any other normal mom.

She'd never do that.

Ignore them. Use the bathroom. Forget them. I stayed still, my hand fisting the bathroom doorknob.

"You think his mom will blow me too?" Ray asked.

"I bet she'd do more than that—"

I snapped and *bolted* into the master cabin.

All three of the swim team guys were there. Frozen and wide-eyed at the sight of me and my red-hot rage.

I don't want to hate people. I *don't* want to be calloused and bitter and angry. But these moments make it so goddamn hard.

"Moffy?" Jason said. "I was just joking."

Some fucking joke. I expected that shit from trolls and assholes. Not people I mistakenly considered "friends"—and I wished for a time machine.

Take me back to yesterday. Don't invite him inside my house.

Take me back to twenty minutes ago. Don't overhear him in the yacht's cabins.

Then maybe I could keep up the fantastical charade of believing that I can have *real*, honest to God friends from school. I barely even trust people to begin with, and what little I gave Jason, he shit on.

"You're just joking?" I said, my voice hollowed out. "Are you fucking serious?"

Jason glanced at Ray. Then back to me, their smirks etching. Like I was the butt of a joke. Like I was the famous nineteen-year-old that should take the beating.

Like all those times we'd been on two-hour bus rides to swim meets and talked and laughed had been a damn lie.

I should've left the cabin. Right there. *I should've left.*

Instead, I threw the first punch. Ray and Clark jumped me from behind. Three on one, and I would've fought them until I couldn't breathe. Until they choked the life out of me.

Maybe they saw that I wouldn't end it, and after a while, they just left the boat cabin. One-by-one. I picked myself off the ground, steady as a statue. With a stinging lip, aching jaw and festering rage.

And now here I am. On the deck, gripping the railing. Knuckles reddened.

Not able to stop *thinking* or remembering.

I breathe, my ribs throbbing, muscles burning. I blink and blink to push past the moment.

But part of me wants to rattle this yacht railing. Then climb over and jump into the restless ocean below. Just to *scream* beneath salt water.

But I don't.

I stay stoic.

I turned nineteen in July. I'm the oldest guy to too many cousins that look up to me, to siblings that need me. Like I'm Captain America. Their superhero.

Dear World, how many times have you seen Captain America jump into an ocean and throw a pity party of one? I'm asking for a friend. Sincerely, just a human.

So I can't have a public breakdown. I can't cry bitterly and angrily.

I can't scream.

Just move on.

I swallow my feelings.

"Moffy."

I turn as Dr. Edward Keene sidles next to me, a lime mojito in hand. He's in his early fifties, ash-brown hair tied in a small pony, strong jaw and nose. I always thought he resembled Viggo Mortensen, circa *Lord of the Rings*.

I'm not surprised my family's concierge doctor is at the summer bash. The Hales, Meadows, and Cobalts invited peers, employees, security team, their friends-of-friends—pretty much anyone we'd shaken hands with and said *hello* to.

I'm more surprised that he's nearing me. And lingering. Dr. Keene sips his mojito and eyes my raw knuckles, abs and chest.

I release my tight grip off the railing. "Hey."

"If you were hurt fighting, I should take a look," he says, curt and to the point. "I won't tell your parents."

Doctor-patient confidentiality. Plus, I'm a legal adult. All of that, I understand. Still, I don't want help. Not like that.

I glance at a row of baby blue lounge chairs along the yacht deck. About twenty feet away. Adults, teenagers, and kids congregate around them and eat tiny plates of meats and cheeses.

The infamous *Loren Hale* sits on the edge of a lounge chair. Hand on the back of his neck. Jaw sharpened like ice. Sometimes he tries not to be a helicopter dad, but his amber gaze flits to me. Overly concerned.

Uncle Ryke and Uncle Connor take a seat on either side of him.

I'm not going to be the one who burdens my dad or my mom. Add in the media and three more kids under fourteen, they have enough shit to deal with.

I stand straighter. Taller. Shoulders squared.

I face Dr. Keene. "I'm okay. I think I cracked a rib or two, but I don't want pain meds. I can just take Advil."

Dr. Keene nods, not pushing further. "Are you excited for Harvard?" He sips his mojito again.

I think about tonight. I think about Jason and how much trust I gave and lost. I'm pretty sure I won't be able to trust anyone on campus. Except for my cousin. That has to be enough.

I nod to myself.

"Really excited," I say honestly. "Charlie and I are rooming together, so it'll be cool." I wish Janie chose Harvard too, but she dreamed of attending the same alma mater as her mom. *Princeton*.

Dr. Keene rests an elbow on the railing. "Have you both picked a major yet?"

"Philosophy for me, and Charlie decided on History of Art and Architecture—" A multi-colored beach ball sails high towards us.

"Moffy! Get it!" Eliot Cobalt calls out, running but not fast enough.

I extend my body halfway off the railing, and I catch the inflatable ball for my fifteen-year-old cousin.

When my bare feet hit the deck, Dr. Keene gives me a brisk smile. "Take care." He leaves towards the bow of the yacht.

Eliot slows to a stop, and I hand him the ball.

He's about to run back to his brother Tom, but he pauses. And he turns, pats my shoulder, and tells me, "Thanks for this and for earlier—"

"Earlier?" Charlie magically appears.

I jolt, "Jesus Christ."

He's *right* next to me. I grab the railing, one small step from a heart attack. *Don't go into cardiac arrest on this boat.* I'm so not fucking prepared for mouth-to-mouth from Dr. Keene.

Charlie laughs and relaxes on the railing. He lowers his Ray Bans over his eyes. Dressed in black slacks, a halfway unbuttoned white shirt—he looks like he's ready to slouch in the back of a college lecture hall.

In reality, he's almost seventeen and a full-blown genius who lives life unlike anyone I've ever known.

Maybe because I have no clue what he does half the fucking time. Some moments, he's just gone. And then he sneaks up on me.

Literally.

His laugh dies as Eliot explains, "*Earlier,* Ben was crying on the swim deck."

"Ben?" Charlie frowns at the mention of their ten-year-old brother.

"Yeah," Eliot starts backing away from us as someone calls his name. "Don't worry, brother. Moffy fixed it!" He scampers off.

"You were in the right place at the right time?" Charlie asks, his voice abnormally tight.

I rake a hand through my thick hair. "No, Eliot found me in the galley and asked for help. What happened, it wasn't that serious," I add so he won't be worried. "Some asshole threw Ben's shirt in the water. I just jumped in and fished it out. He should be fine. I talked to him for a bit."

"How heroic," Charlie snaps…almost scornfully.

I flinch. "What?"

His yellow-green eyes pierce me.

"I just did what your brother asked me to do." I lick my lips. I get that I haven't always been on good terms with Charlie. There were moments, when I was eleven, maybe twelve, and we clashed.

He disappeared a lot, went off on his own, and I didn't understand him.

A lot of times, I still don't. But in high school, he was there. Every fucking day for the last four years, he was by my side. By Janie's side. The three of us combatted any harassment in Dalton Academy together. And we just graduated *together.*

He could've been homeschooled like his twin brother Beckett and our cousin Sullivan. He could've left Jane and me out to dry and do his own thing. But he didn't. He chose to stick around.

So actually, I'm really goddamn confused by him right now.

Charlie messes his already messy golden-brown hair. "We should talk."

"Okay, yeah, let's talk."

We leave the crowded yacht for a little bit of privacy. When we reach the second deck, we pass a packed hot tub where Jane chats loudly with her younger sister.

I share a quick glance with Janie. And I nod towards the next set of steps. She nods back like, *we'll see each other later.*

Once Charlie and I are off the yacht, we stand on the wooden dock. The boat towers next to us, looming and constantly reminding me of our familial wealth.

I never forget what and where we come from.

Paparazzi are nowhere in sight, thanks to the private marina. I crack my knuckles. And I just watch Charlie stuff his fists in the pockets of his slacks, his sunglasses hooked on his shirt.

"You planning on rocketing to some planet?" I banter. "Want me to come along with?" I flash a dying smile, my lips down-turning fast off his stone-cold glare.

"Not everyone wants you next to them."

Ouch.

My frown darkens. "I never said *everyone*. I just meant you."

Charlie lets out a short, irritated laugh, his smile almost pained. "Stop assuming I want you by my side."

Jesus…I shake my head over and over. I keep licking my lips like I'm on the verge of the right words. I'm not sure what the hell they are, but someone, give them to me. "What did I do? Is this about Ben—"

"You're on your own."

I feel whiplashed, not following. "What—"

"You're on your own. At Harvard."

"Wait—"

"There's no waiting, no talking me out of this," Charlie says so assuredly, so confidently. "I'm not going to Harvard. I'm not going to be your roommate. Find another one."

I rest a hand on my head, muscles contracting. "College is in one week."

"And the whole campus would just love to live with Maximoff Hale."

What the fuck is his problem? "You were the one who wanted to go to Harvard." My voice starts to rise, but I'm not yelling yet. "I would've been *fine* to attend somewhere closer to Philly, to be near our family, but you said, *let's go to Harvard together*. Now you're just bailing?"

"Yeah." Charlie lets that word linger.

About five feet separate our bodies. But for the first time in four years, an ocean swells between us. Pushing him further and further away from me.

I take a step towards him. "Why?"

"If I tell you *why*, you'll want to fix it like you always do, and did you ever contemplate, ever think, that not everything needs to be fixed?" His angered yellow-green eyes burn me. "Let alone by you."

I open my mouth, but words stick to the back of my throat.

"Why are you so upset? You're *Maximoff Hale*," he practically spits out my name. "You can do anything by yourself and then some."

I think about Jason again. I think about how I was holding onto Charlie at Harvard like a familiar lifeline. If he wants to bail on college…that's fine. I can't trap him, but I just don't understand *why* he's doing this all of a sudden.

And yeah, I want an answer.

Is that so fucking bad of me? "Just tell me why—"

He nears, bridging the distance, but not in a good way. "I can't stand to look at you. To be around you, and I'd rather bathe in peroxide than suffer four years of college with you." Charlie watches my face contort. "Can't handle the fact that someone dislikes you?"

"Oooh," an audience says, ogling us from the yacht. They push up against the railing and stare down at the wooden dock where I combat my cousin.

"*Fuck you*." I glare. Charlie knows classmates have hated me. Just not family. I point at him. "You're just an immature sixteen-year-old *kid* who likes pretending he's an adult, but you're one of the most irresponsible, self-involved—" I see his right hook, and I slip left, dodging the blow.

I'm on autopilot, a reflex, and I swing at him. My fist lands with a thump against his jaw.

Shit.

I raise my hand, not wanting to seriously injure him. I'm more muscular, stronger. Even if he's an inch taller. "Charlie—"

His narrowed eyes drill into my skull. And he launches another punch. His knuckles smash into my cheekbone.

"Ohhhh!" the audience clamors.

I wince and shove him back hard. He tries to nail my ribs. I shove him again.

"Isn't this what you're good at?!" he yells. "Hit me!"

I'm wound up, about to snap, and when he comes at me for a third time, I seize his shoulder. I slam a fist into his abs, and he barrels his weight into me. Until we're on the dock. Wrestling with one another. Spit flying, fists digging, and pulses pounding.

I bust skin on his cheek.

He pummels my already battered ribs. Some kind of hate brews like acid between us, and I can't end it. I don't know how.

I'm on my back. And right as I turn my head towards him, he launches an uppercut. His knuckles bash my chin and catch my nose—*goddammit.*

Blood just pours out of my nostrils. Charlie stands off me, and I sit up, cupping my hands to my face. Breathing heavily.

I try to ignore the cacophony from the damn yacht, the "oh shits" and "fuuuucks".

I rise to one knee, my muscles on fire.

Wanting to *scream.*

But I look up. Charlie touches the wound on his cheek, his whole body as badly beaten as mine, and he inhales a strong, sharp breath.

"Don't do this, Charlie," I say, voice muffled with my bloodied nose. I don't want us to be distant. I don't want to return to what we were when we were younger.

Charlie sways, but he catches his balance, then steps closer. Towering. "You want the cold-hearted truth?" His voice is a deep, pained whisper, so only I hear. "I'd be better off if you never even existed."

My eyes burn. A hurt I've never felt before plunges through me like twenty knives to my lungs. Worse than any punch or kick.

Charlie turns and leaves for the marina's restaurant.

Blood seeps through the cracks of my fingers, dripping down my bare chest. My pulse is lodged in my throat. But I try to distract myself by focusing on the blood. Not Charlie, who disappears out of sight.

I try to staunch my nose with my bicep, and then a wadded up black shirt suddenly lands by my knee. I glance at the yacht, looking for the person who threw it at me.

The audience already starts dispersing. Faces too hard to recognize from down here. I gratefully ball the shirt and press the fabric to my nose. And I rise to my feet.

Back on the yacht, I manage to bypass most people. I make my way to the empty bow, darkened since all but one torch is snuffed. Beige cushions form a sunbathing pad, but I don't sit.

I squat, slightly wincing, and rifle through a blue cooler. Ice all melted, cans of beer and soda float in lukewarm water.

I stare faraway. Charlie's words ring in my ears. *I'd be better off if you never even existed.*

You can do anything by yourself and then some.

Have you ever felt like you need something or someone? Just for one moment.

Just one damn second.

I'm rarely alone, but I'm not talking about Jane or my parents or any of my siblings or family. Have you ever felt like you're missing something? Like a void exists, and you're not sure how to fill that space?

Maybe it's not supposed to be filled. Maybe this is it, and I have to be satisfied with this carved out chunk, this hollowness.

I'd be better off if you never even existed.

Yeah.

"Move, wolf scout."

My head swerves abruptly towards the only guy who calls me that. The concierge doctor's twenty-four-year-old son.

Farrow Redford Keene.

Black swim trunks hang low on his muscular waist. I almost drink in his body. He's lean-cut and sculpted, but instead of a swimmer's build like mine, his stature screams *MMA fighter*.

What's more, his bleach-white hair is pushed back, nose pierced, and the *sexiest* tattoos crawl up his fucking neck and down his chest. Inked pirates, skulls, ships, daggers, sparrows and swallows.

I'm trying my hardest not to give Farrow an obvious once-over. But he hovers close. Like actually right beside me while I'm frozen in a squat.

How long has he been there?

Farrow raises his dark brows at me. Like I'm not catching on fast enough, but he chews a piece of gum with a sense of unhurriedness. Then he rolls his eyes and just squats beside me.

I watch him rummage through the cooler.

Fuck, he wanted me to *move* out of the damn way.

I rake a hand through my hair, waking up out of a dark stupor. "What do you need?" I ask, licking my lip a few times, tasting iron from blood. I keep the black shirt wadded in my hand.

"Don't worry about it." Farrow grabs a couple of beers and then glances at me for a short beat. "You look like shit." He stands.

I stand. "Thank you," I say, sarcasm thick. "For a second there, I thought *blood* was an attractive accessory. You know, like a hat, a scarf, a goddamn lightsaber."

His lips upturn. "You would find lightsabers attractive."

I almost groan, trying not to crack a smile. He's irritating four-fifths of the time. The one-fifth makes me *almost* break into a weird grin. I give him a look. "Did I say that lightsabers were attractive?"

"In so many words." Farrow stacks his beer cans in one hand, like he's about to leave. But he hones in on my bloodied chest from my nosebleed.

I lick my lips again, inhaling a deeper breath. Something powerful surging into me. *Stay.*

"Farrow!" a guy calls from inside the galley. Farrow keeps his gaze on me.

I keep mine on him.

Then he walks backwards to the yacht door, towards that voice. "Need anything, wolf scout?"

Yeah.

I shake my head. "No."

His gaze drops to the black shirt in my hand, and his smile stretches wide. "Keep it."

"What?"

"My shirt. I don't need it back."

Holy…shit. I have no time to protest or offer to return the shirt— he already exits into the galley.

You'll never believe this, but I'm smiling. I laugh to myself, my chest swelling with a better, lighter feeling. I glance back at the shut door, then the dark horizon. Ocean ripples below, calling me, to free me.

Fuck it.

I run. Onto the sunbathing cushions, and I leap and dive off the bow. Water cocoons me like a hug and a welcome home.

1

Maximoff Hale

HURRYING, I PULL ON a plain green shirt in a lake house bedroom. My elbow catches a bear-shaped lamp—I reach out too late. *Fuck.*

Glass crashes on the hardwood and shatters.

I quickly squat, barefoot, and pick up the larger shards. All things considered with my family issues, a broken lamp isn't a big deal.

I can handle it.

As I gather the pieces, Farrow lowers to a crouch and helps collect the sharp glass—also while fitting in his earpiece. A radio is already clipped to his black pants.

I open my mouth to protest. To say, *I got it.*

But I stop myself and just watch him. My tattooed-childhood-crush-turned boyfriend. We were just watching *The Fast and the Furious* on my laptop. I paused the movie only fifteen minutes in

Because both of our phones rang unceremoniously. I should already be halfway downstairs. But I'd much rather be dealing with a broken lamp with Farrow.

He sweeps the tiny slivers into his palm, his focus on the fragments near my feet. And the more I watch him, the more I think, *lucky me.*

Seriously, I'm damn lucky.

A few hours ago we hiked the top of a mountain.

I told him I loved him.

He said he loved me.

Adrenaline still pumps hot in my veins from the moment, but the current fallout from the media clings to me like a backpack of cement. He's the only one I'd even *consider* unbuckling the backpack for and passing half the weight.

When I eye his silver-ringed fingers, he catches me staring. I lift my gaze higher to the tattooed swords on his throat, then his strong jaw and amused lips.

His brows spike.

I stay quiet. My pulse pounds hard. But my mind speeds in undiscovered directions—I can't stop *thinking* about everything and anything, past and present—and I'm not even sure how to start speaking.

Farrow waits for me to say something.

Anything.

When I don't, he stands. "Watch your feet, wolf scout." He scours my tensed build. Reading me well.

"I got it." I stand and we dispose of the broken glass in a small trashcan.

Farrow brushes his palms clean before combing his hands through his dyed-black hair. "You going to tell me what you're obsessing over?" He leans casually on the wooden dresser.

I'm a rigid statue in comparison. I'm not used to unloading on people, but for some godforsaken reason, I want to unload on him. I know he can carry it.

I take a short breath, and I blurt out, "What about you? How are you doing?"

Jesus.

Christ.

That's not what I meant to tell him.

"At the moment," Farrow says matter-of-factly, "I'm watching my boyfriend deflect by asking me how I'm doing."

I nod, arms crossed. "He sounds like a real keeper."

LOVERS LIKE US // 15

"He's something," Farrow teases and checks the time on his phone. He steps away from the dresser and walks backwards to the door. Away from me.

I have serious déjà vu from the yacht four years ago.

"Last chance." His voice is deep, rough but paradoxically smooth.

Last chance to speak about what's on my mind. Phone calls summoned both of us downstairs. Me, by Jane. Him, by Akara.

Farrow looks straight into me. His strong gaze clutches me tight while caressing me. Silently prodding me to speak but softly reminding me that he's always protected my thoughts and feelings.

"Wait," I say.

He stops and lounges his shoulders on the door.

"I'm thinking about how Jane just called and said, *come downstairs to the kitchen. We need to talk, Moffy.*" I gesture to Farrow. "I get that I'm not an expert on relationships, but I know friendships and *we need to talk* is never a good fucking thing."

His mouth starts rising in a *drop-to-your-knees* smile. "Or she could just want to talk."

I hone in on his piercings: the hoop around his lip, his nose ring, and dangling earring—I'm dating a twelve out of ten. For more than just his looks. He's standing here, entertaining my hang-ups, and I know he'll only give me honesty in return.

"Or Jane wants to move out."

"You're overthinking."

"I'm preparing for the worst," I rebut and motion to the door. "Since that stupid fucking article, she's been spending most of her time with her brothers. I have no clue where her head's at." For the first time in… maybe forever, Jane and I aren't on the same page of the same book.

"You're about to find out," Farrow reminds me and checks the time on his phone again. "And you're going to be late."

"So," I say without thinking. Such a genius. I rub my sharpened jaw.

"*So,*" he draws out the word and nears me, his knowing gaze raking me from head-to-toe.

My muscles contract and burn, fucking aroused. Everything about him has become a turn on. I'm happy that he's only two feet away now, but a bit irritated that I didn't initiate that movement first.

"You're stalling, Maximoff. *So* either you're really nervous to hear Jane out," Farrow says in a deep, rough whisper, "or you're obsessed with me."

For Christ's sake. His words fist my cock.

His satisfied smile stretches from check-to-cheek. Somewhere in some alternate universe, I'm a philosopher writing dissertations on that fucking smile. And its sheer effect on me.

Farrow says, "I'm flattered."

I groan out my agitation. Blood pumps south, my cock still not understanding. "I'm mildly, somewhat attracted to you," I tell him. "That's so far from *obsession*, I can't even reach the word in five millenniums."

"Mildly, somewhat," he repeats softly, his gaze dancing across my features. He runs his tongue over his bottom lip and silver piercing. The air is headier.

My chest rises in a deeper breath, and I close the two-foot distance.

Farrow clutches my sharp jaw, his large palm warm. I clasp the back of his neck, my hand rising to his black hair. Our mouths teasingly close but not touching.

I walk him backwards. Until his muscular shoulders hit the door again and our legs thread. He lets me take the lead for now.

I breathe, "Did you hear the part where I said I'm not obsessed with you?"

His brown eyes flit to my mouth, then back up.

Kiss me, man.

"Did you hear the part where I said you're nervous?" His graveled voice wraps me up like safety.

I nod. "Yeah." *I'm kind of fucking anxious.* In a lot of ways, I want this guy by my side, but reality slams hard.

And I pull back.

Our hands drop.

We both look disappointed, but I just tell him the truth, "You shouldn't be late to your SFO meeting."

He rolls his eyes. "It isn't a formal meeting. If you need me, I can be with you while you talk to Jane—"

"No," I cut him off and take another step back, a knife in my ribs. "You shouldn't bail on Akara after he stuck his neck out for us. Not because of me." I quickly add, "I'm fine on my own. I always am." I cringe at my choice of words, ones that remind me of *Charlie* on that yacht.

Fuck.

Farrow notices. "Your face says you're not fine."

I try to pull my features. "Then stop staring at my fucking face."

Farrow tilts his head back and forth. "No."

I rock at the firmness of that *no.* "What?"

"You heard me." Farrow taps the doorknob with his thumb ring, the *click click* filling our short silence. "You're smiling."

Fuck me. I rub my mouth a couple times. Yeah, I was smiling like a damn idiot. "I don't know what you're talking about."

"Sure you don't."

I swear he's one second from pushing his tongue against the inside of his cheek. I breathe hot breath through my nose, and my muscles almost unconsciously flex.

I'd like to say that my body isn't listening to my brain, but both have bought and made *Team Farrow* T-shirts against better fucking judgment. There's some place in me—a pinky…a microscopic nerve-ending in my frontal lobe—that tries to resist.

I backtrack the conversation. "I promise you, I'm fine. I can survive *two hundred* decades without you."

His smile is out of fucking control. "With or without me, you're not going to survive to be two-thousand-twenty two years-old."

"I didn't realize you could see the future."

Farrow laughs once. "Such a smartass." He shakes his head in thought. "*Need* wasn't the right word then." He holds my gaze. "Do you want me with you?"

Yeah.

Something wells up inside of me. I let go of any and all emotional barriers, and he sees that affirmation a thousand times across my face.

Farrow steps off the door. And in a swift, seamless move, he clutches the back of my head—and he kisses me. *Fuck.*

Me.

I part his mouth, hunger driving my tongue against his, and our bodies instinctively thrust together. Like we've been teasing for a damn century. Every explosive kiss detonates my body. My brain.

I grip his hair in a tight fist; his low groan barrels against my mouth.

"Fuck," he breathes and nips my lip.

Christ yes. Heat sweltering, building, scalding—he stops first, drawing back.

Farrow fits in his earpiece that must've fallen out. "You want me, you have me. Let's go, wolf scout."

I'm still winded, my head on a tilt-a-whirl. I lick my stinging lips. I feel like he just fucked me in multiple positions.

He combs his hands through his ruffled hair, his mouth curving upwards. "You need a minute to catch your breath?"

"Not if you don't," I retort and stop breathing heavily. "Follow me."

I can feel his eye-roll and grin behind my back, and I rub my mouth again and realize I'm smiling. Even in the face of what could be a serious, *real* doomsday.

2

Maximoff Hale

SURPRISE, I'M NOT THE late person here. Jane texts that she'll be in the kitchen in a second.

Proactively *waiting* isn't my thing. I can admit that. So when Farrow unwraps a piece of gum and tugs open the fridge, I ask him, "Need help?"

He chews his gum slowly and glances at me in a way that reminds me he's twenty-seven. I'm twenty-two, and he's more than capable to do shit himself.

Farrow starts to smile. "It's cute that you think I need help getting eggs." He grabs a carton and kicks the fridge closed.

"You could've dropped the fucking eggs." I'm fighting a stupid battle. And I grimace-smile which makes me want to poke my own eyes out.

Farrow pops his gum. "You mean *you* would've dropped the eggs."

"Did I? Pretty sure I meant you could've."

Farrow sets the carton by the sink. "I have steadier hands than you." He leans close and whispers huskily, "You're not beating me at this."

I shake my head on instinct. When it comes to Farrow, boyfriend or not, I don't want to concede that fast. "It's not proven yet."

He rolls his eyes into a smile. "Hold out your hand."

I extend my hand, palm-down. Wondering how he can discern any shake just by sight.

Farrow rotates my wrist. "Like this." And then he smashes an egg right in my palm.

Don't smile at him. Don't smile at him. "Thanks for that," I say sarcastically, hand dripping in broken eggshell and yolk.

"Anytime." He laughs, and I act quickly and wipe the runny egg onto his black V-neck, feeling the ridges of his six-pack beneath.

Farrow props his elbows on the sink and actually lets me use his shirt as a towel, even while he's wearing the thing. *Christ.*

He's a Grade A sexy asshole.

"Sorry for being late." Jane crests the doorway in an out-of-breath pant, and our heads turn. She's dressed in coffee-print grannie jammies. A binder tucked beneath her armpit.

She sees Farrow. "Oh, you're both here—" Her cat slippers slide on the slick hardwood, and she almost face-plants.

Binder drops to the floor.

I sprint to reach my best friend, but by the time I catch her elbow, she already steadies herself with outstretched arms.

My lips almost rise. "Bonsoir, ma moitié," I whisper. *Good evening, my other half.*

Her big blue eyes smile weakly up at me. I wait for her to say *it's just you and me, old chap*—or any kind of variation of that phrase. Just so I know we're alright.

We're the same as we always were.

Nothing's changed.

She's still Janie. I'm still Moffy. And we're best friends until the bitter fucking end.

"I'm glad you're here," she says and rubs her runny nose. Smothering her emotions. She picks up the binder. "This is for you. I need to talk with you about something important. Something I've already discussed with my brothers."

I've always been the first person she turns to and vice versa. With secrets, personal struggles, *something important*, anything—Jane Eleanor Cobalt is my number one.

My ride-or-die.

But she talked to Beckett before me. And even Charlie. Though, I'm highly aware that someone is in my corner and currently in this kitchen.

Farrow pulls his dirtied shirt over his head and then washes his hands. His earring sways as he shifts around the kitchen to cook eggs. And his protective gaze meets mine in a stronghold.

He's here for me. If I need him.

It feels more than good.

I know it's no longer just me and Jane anymore, but I also don't want the best parts of our friendship to change because of our other relationships.

I take the binder, and Jane lingers. I linger. Before the media blowout, we'd hug in greeting or I'd kiss both of her cheeks. Now, she hugs onto her arms, and I stand uncomfortably rigid.

God, I hate this.

"Tell me what you want to do," I whisper.

"I will." She nods assuredly and peels a piece of wavy hair off her freckled cheek. "That's why we need to talk."

"Alright." I stretch my arm and head to the fridge. "Need anything?"

"No, I'm making coffee." She's already halfway to the pot.

I open the fridge and grab a Ziff sports drink. The label is a Z with the words *Ascend* beneath, a limeade flavor and a Fizzle product. The lake house is stocked with Fizz sodas, Lightning Bolt! energy drinks, and lots of Ziff.

I flip open a binder on the island counter and find blank white sheets of paper. "It's all blank?"

Jane fills up a mug. "Since my handwriting is dreadfully hard to read, I thought you'd want to take some notes."

I find a pen in the binder pocket. "No problem." *What the fuck am I about to write down?* Being kept in the dark—not my favorite feeling.

But you know that.

I rest my elbows on the counter. "Are we planning a funeral, a trip to Jupiter, or the reinvention of the Invisibility Cloak?"

"She said 'important' things," Farrow says and puts his frying pan in the sink.

I give him a look. "So funerals aren't important to you? Great. Never plan mine."

"We've been through this. You're not dying before me," Farrow says matter-of-factly. He grabs his bowl of scrambled eggs and sidles next to me. "Give up that dream."

"No," I say, voice firm.

A smile edges his mouth, but we both fixate on Jane.

She cups a mug between two hands. "I told my brothers and Sulli that you and I don't want our friendship to change, but inherently, the media and paparazzi will put pressure on us to split apart. And how do we stay the same, Moffy?"

I gesture to the door like the paparazzi are on the other side. They're not. But somewhere in Philadelphia, they wait like desperate vultures. Hungry for our carcasses. "We ignore them, Janie."

"Can we?" She sips her coffee. "Every time we're together, they'll be in our faces. I don't care what they think, but they're gnats and we'll both crave to swat them away. To do that, all we have to do is add distance, stop being seen out together, don't look at each other—"

"*No*, fuck no." I shake my head.

Janie starts smiling.

Realization sinks in. "You have a plan?"

"THIS IS INSANE," I MUTTER, STILL STARING AT THE binder. Now crammed full of notes, some of which are lyrics to a *Semisonic* song. Farrow apparently shelves *notes* with *rules* in the "fuck it" category.

He leans against the island. Eating his eggs slowly. "You agreed to this insane plan."

"It took me thirty fucking minutes." I glance at the doorway, but Jane left to tell Charlie, Beckett, and Sulli that I agreed.

"All five of us are going on tour," I say aloud. Letting this reality sink in.

No, it's still a-hundred-million-percent bizarre. All five of us together. Sleeping on a tour bus with our six bodyguards. A total of eleven people on one bus. Driving across America.

How'd I agree to this fucking mayhem? I skim my notes.

The plan: book meet-and-greets at various cities. People will pay to take photos with us and get autographs. Television actors do convention circuits all the time. I even jotted down *short Q&A panels*. The whole FanCon will be run by H.M.C. Philanthropies. All proceeds go to charity.

I'll be working, but that's not exactly why I agreed.

Farrow swigs a glass of water. "You'll be out of Philly for a while."

I nod. I was never planning on isolating myself at the lake house forever. Eventually we'd have to deal with paparazzi in Philly, but it'll be easier dealing with cameramen on the road. Not all of them will want to follow us.

Our parents still live in Philly.

Our parents are still more famous than us. Many cameramen will choose to stay in the city with them.

People always say, *just leave if you hate the media that much*. I always reply, *my family and my work are here, and I don't hate the paparazzi. We coexist.*

Since I was born, I've dealt with their sometimes friendly and sometimes frustrating presence. I don't even know what it's like for cameramen not to trail me.

I take a bigger breath. It's *still* sinking in.

I flip a page in the binder and then glance at Farrow. "From an outsider's perspective, do you think the tour will help with the rumors?"

Farrow considers this for a second. "All five of you haven't been publicly together in years. That tour will be front-page news and bury any other shit." He scrapes a spoonful of eggs. "I'd take the risk, but my laces aren't triple-knotted like yours."

I blink. "Thank you for that last-second, unneeded addition."

He smiles into his bite of eggs. "You're welcome."

I flip another page. His presence is like a magnet that says *look at me* and then I veer off track. I'll relax too much, and I need to *think*.

"I can't let him fucking do this," I say aloud, reading a sentence I underlined five times: *Beckett has taken a temporary leave from the ballet company.* As a principal dancer, that's a big deal.

Farrow barely skims the page. "You forgot to write *the tour is his idea.*"

Yeah, I still can't believe Beckett Cobalt concocted this plan. To help Janie, his sister, most of all. It's why his twin brother Charlie agreed. Heaven and Earth and every air particle knows Charlie didn't signup for a 4-month tour just for me.

He may be at the lake house out of support, but the seeds of our relationship are still rotted. They have been since that night on the yacht. Nothing good can grow overnight.

And Jane said that Sulli talked about the moments where I'd been there for her. Like the time when she thought she broke her foot on a desert hike. I carried her in a piggyback for eight miles, and I kept trying to calm her. Saying she was a kickass human being and strong. I gave her my canteen early on, and her tears soaked my shirt. She kept telling me her swim career was over, and for Sulli, *swim* was synonymous with *life.*

Even at twelve.

I was fifteen, and I remember how when we reached the end of the primitive trail, her parents found us. Uncle Ryke and Aunt Daisy immediately drove their daughter to the ER, and I felt responsible for Sulli getting hurt.

For eight miles, I wished that'd been my foot.

I keep shaking my head, and I grip the counter. "Everything I've ever done," I tell Farrow, "it wasn't to cash in for a favor later. I never thought I'd be in a position where my *younger* cousins feel obligated to put their careers and lives on hold." For Jane.

For me.

Fuck. "We're the ones who've protected them," I explain to him. "We even used to take their phones and block numbers of porn producers who had called us. Just so they wouldn't be able to fucking reach them."

Farrow shuts the binder. "Look at me."

I can barely rotate my taut shoulders. I want to open the fucking binder and reread everything. Again.

"Maximoff—"

"I get it. I'm overthinking." I'm white-knuckling the counter, and finally, I look at my boyfriend.

His eyes carry complete understanding. And somehow he still looks like he'd *love* to undo my tight-laces. "I'd be irritated, too, if my younger cousins decided to pay it forward when I didn't want to be paid. But it's happening, and you have to deal."

I nod, my neck stiff. I want to be the kind of guy who can thank them, but I'm not there yet. I recognize the power in family, in that willingness and sacrifice, but just having this conversation, I feel like I failed Sulli and Beckett and even Charlie.

I reopen the binder. I circled the date *December 14th* a billion times. The start date. It's soon.

"What are you thinking?" Farrow asks.

"None of us will be here for Christmas." My family normally stays at the lake house for Christmas—a pretty secure place—and our personal bodyguards are allowed to leave and spend the holiday with their families. "I'm thinking about how you and the rest of SFO will feel—"

"We don't care," Farrow cuts me off.

I frown. "You sure?"

He smiles. "Man, most of us are in our late twenties. No kids, no spouses, no other obligations. We're fine to spend holidays where our work takes us." He lifts his spoon to his mouth. "We know what we signed up for."

I nod again. My little brother turns fifteen on Christmas day. I'll miss his birthday, and I don't want to hurt him. I think it might.

Me being in a serious relationship—it's new to my family. Cousins and siblings have been blowing up my group chats since they found out I'm dating a bodyguard.

Kinney texted that I'm uninvited to her funeral until I go on a double date with her and her future girlfriend. Luna keeps sending me confetti and thumbs-up emojis. But Xander…

He hasn't said anything at all.

Maybe my little brother is thinking back to the hickey on my neck. And how I could've confessed the truth then. Maybe he thinks we're not as close as he believed we were. Maybe he's questioning everything.

I tried calling him multiple times today, and he never answered. I'd rather eat a bowl of nails than be out of touch with my brother. So I'm hoping I can reach him soon.

All the thoughts about my relationship sidetrack me. I crack a knuckle. "How is this going to be…for us?" I ask Farrow.

He cocks his head slightly. "What do you mean?"

"I've been thinking a lot—"

"No shit."

I almost smile. And he notices. *Fuuck*.

Farrow stares at me like I blew him. Way too satisfied.

I pull my face, brows scrunched. Scowling. "Like I was saying," I tell him, "how am I going to survive being on a bus with *you* for four months. Plus my family, plus SFO, and again, *you*. Sounds like hell."

His mouth upturns. "Sounds like fun."

"My hell is your fun," I realize.

"Wow." Farrow grins. "When you put it that way, I love it more."

I give him two middle fingers, but his hand slides around my waist. We draw closer. His chest against my chest, my bicep instinctively curves around his shoulders. We're almost eye-level, almost exactly the same height.

In the past thirty minutes, I've thought about every small moment.

The private hours I spend with Farrow. Every drive in Philly. Nights where we're alone in my bedroom. The morning wakeup calls where we whisper about stupid ordinary shit.

It'll all change slightly, and he may like *change*—but I don't know what our relationship looks like when we start moving pieces. And I'd be lying if I said the unknown didn't scare me a bit.

Farrow breathes, "We're going to be…" His voice trails off, his fingers touching his earpiece. "Those fuckers."

We detach, and before I ask, he tells me, "SFO knew about the tour before I did. Come on." He heads into the hall with his bowl of eggs.

I follow him, my stride lengthier than his. Easily, I catch up to his side.

We're step-for-step.

He's not running. He's not alarmed. Farrow eats and walks, looking more unconcerned than concerned, and his tattooed fingers comb through his hair.

"You're still in hot water with SFO?" I question.

"I'm always in hot water." Farrow eats a spoonful. "It's where I do my best work." The sexiest smile inches up his mouth.

Fuck me.

We turn a corner, and as soon as I open the door to the study, I spot three bodyguards. Lounging on dark leather furniture. Ceiling-high bookshelves landscape the forest-green walls.

Their heads automatically swing in our direction.

And Thatcher, Oscar, and Donnelly are only looking at *me*. Appraising me like I've intruded into an exclusive *Bodyguards Only Club* and I'm not allowed inside.

3

Maximoff Hale

BY NOW, YOU KNOW that the security team is both strangely elusive to me and close like family. Thanks to Farrow, I see glimpses of how security works and how they actually perceive us: the Hales, Cobalts, and Meadows.

Since I'm a celebrity and a client, I probably would've excused myself and let them work out whatever they need to alone. But they're now aware that I'm Farrow's boyfriend, and these aren't just his coworkers.

They're the closest guys in his life. *His friends*. And if he's all-in on my world, I think I should be all-in on his.

So I'm staying.

I approach Thatcher Moretti. "When'd you get here?" I ask.

In my peripheral, Farrow nears Donnelly on the couch and lightly kicks his ankle, both speaking under their breaths. Donnelly gestures with his head at me. So they're talking about me.

If only I had bionic hearing.

Thatcher stands, five inches taller than me. "I drove in about four hours ago."

We shake hands. I'm sure to most people a six-foot-seven, unshaven Italian-American man with a perpetually stern gaze would be intimidating.

For me, he's not even close.

Thatcher used to protect my little brother, and talking to him in the past, the topics never diverged from security. He's as professional as they come and also the biggest thorn in Farrow's side.

Now he's a secondary bodyguard to Jane and unofficial chaperone to me and Farrow. A small price to pay to keep Farrow as my 24/7 bodyguard. If the public finds out that I'm dating a bodyguard, it could cause all of SFO to become famous by association.

That can't happen, and Thatcher said he'd ensure it doesn't.

"Thanks for voting to keep Farrow as my bodyguard," I tell Thatcher. "It meant a lot."

He nods. "I was voting for what you'd want. Personal grievances aside, I'm here for you and your family."

It reminds me that he wasn't the only vote. "Where's Akara?"

"Out for a run with Sulli." Thatcher twists a knob on his radio. "Last night, Akara and I agreed we're going to share the lead position in Omega. If you need to inform security about anything, it's still Akara, Price, and me you should contact."

The Tri-Force is still intact then.

I bet it's all the same to Farrow since he's not a rule-follower anyway.

"Hey, Moffy—" Donnelly is cut off by Farrow's hand over his mouth.

"Excuse Donnelly," Farrow says to me, really at ease. He sits on the armrest of the couch. And his bowl of eggs skillfully balances on his thigh. "He has an undiagnosed condition called *verbo-emesis.*"

My brows furrow.

Oscar swigs a Lightning Bolt! and translates, "Word vomit."

Huh.

I have no clue what "Hey, Moffy" was about to morph into, but with the surface of my childhood nickname, I'm *unfortunately* more aware of my age difference between all of them and me.

"Security should only call me Maximoff," I state here and now.

Farrow lowers his hand from Donnelly's mouth, and some of the bodyguards exchange furtive glances. And Farrow tries to restrain an amused laugh, but as he looks to me, his eyes almost caress mine in affection.

Alright, I must've sounded like a dick.

Or a conceited dick.

An entitled prick.

All of the above? Probably.

Thatcher tells me, "I'll let the whole team know."

I nod and try to loosen my shoulders. Just to appear somewhat less domineering.

Boundaries here are blurrier than usual, and I don't want to be just the client in their eyes. But two milliseconds ago, I made a declaration that sounded more like a dickish celebrity requesting a special menu than a regular guy asking to be treated fairly.

I try to figure out a better plan of action. One that doesn't include me leaving this damn study. Retreating—that's not an option.

Suddenly, Farrow stands. Nearing me, but he speaks to Thatcher. "Did you put me on temporary probation from security meetings?"

"No."

"Then why the hell didn't I hear about the one where Omega discussed the tour?" Farrow stops beside me and offers me his bowl of eggs.

I shake my head. "I'm good."

He only peels his eyes off of me when Thatcher responds.

"You were in the bedroom with Maximoff." He ends there. Like that explains everything.

Farrow glares at Thatcher.

Thatcher glares back, not relenting. This is the equivalent of a silent pissing match.

I gesture to the co-lead of Omega. "Is knocking not in the body-guard handbook?"

Neither of them moves.

Oscar unwraps a Honey Bun. "You're still a client who prefers privacy."

"And you were with your boyfriend, Mof—*Maximoff*. Fuck," Donnelly mutters.

They left Farrow in the dark because of me. *That's not fucking happening again.* "Thatcher," I say, and he breaks the glare to acknowledge me. "Farrow's job comes first."

"His job is *you*," Thatcher emphasizes. "This is complicated—"

"Then let's un-complicate it," I say simply. "Anything related to security, you can disrupt me and get him. I'd prefer it. And if there's any other confusion, just ask."

I swear I hear Farrow mutter an impressed, "*Damn*," beneath his breath.

The whole talk screeches to a halt as the door creaks. Jane and Beckett slip inside. Carrying trays of coffee for everyone. Jane hands me a mug of hot tea, and we all scatter around the study.

Farrow and I are the only two standing. While he leans on a bookshelf—absentmindedly fiddling with a handheld wooden puzzle that he's already solved twice—I grip my mug of tea. And listen to the conversation veer off into FanCon territory. Logistics.

How the fuck it'll all work.

Thatcher motions to Jane on a rocking chair and to Beckett on the couch beside Donnelly, and he says, "If you have any acquaintances or friends or…" Thatcher pauses for the word.

"NSA," Oscar clarifies.

"What?" Beckett looks to Donnelly, his 24/7 bodyguard.

"No strings attached," I tell my cousin.

"A fuck buddy," Donnelly explains.

Thatcher cringes a bit, obviously hoping to avoid that word. "If you want them on the bus," he says to Jane more than Beckett. "I need a list. Names. We have to clear them before they're allowed on tour."

A cold draft wafts into the study, snow falling heavier outside.

Becket zips his leather jacket over a black *The Carraways* band T-shirt, half tucked into ripped jeans. His brown curly hair is artfully styled, and he's lean and tall, built perfectly for dance. A warm smile toys at his pink lips. He looks older than when I last saw him.

Like he's met more parts of the world, and he came out better. Tougher.

You know Beckett Joyce Cobalt as a principal dancer of an elite ballet company in New York City. His tattoos and extracurricular activities cause a stir for tabloids. But they also fill seats for shows. You call him *the bad boy of ballet* and he doesn't bother proving you wrong.

I know him as my twenty-year-old hard-working, extraordinarily talented cousin, the most calm and the least dramatic of the Cobalt Empire. He has no room for bullshit, and he'll be the first to say you smell full of it. If he weren't Charlie's fraternal twin, maybe we'd find common ground. But if there really are sides in my family, Beckett will never be on mine.

Fair Warning: if you fuck with Beckett, I won't hesitate to team up with Charlie and rip you limb-from-limb.

Beckett extends an arm. "No fuck buddies for me."

Donnelly rocks back. "You sure?"

You've definitely seen Beckett pick up random girls at NYC nightclubs. You don't know that he sometimes goes to private sex parties—the only reason *I* know is because he once told Eliot, who then let it slip to Tom. Who told Jane. Who then told me.

Gotta love family.

"Positive," Beckett says. "If I'm going to hookup, it'll be with someone I meet on the road."

I take a larger sip of tea, and I notice how everyone's zeroed in on Jane.

She's quiet and tucks a pink throw blanket around her body. Maybe she's thinking about her options. I'm about to ask, but Thatcher beats me to the question.

"Do you want to bring Nate?" he asks.

Her blue eyes meet me. "I don't know."

Farrow messes with the puzzle. "You can't smuggle him on the bus, Cobalt. If you want him, we're all meeting him."

"What do you think, Moffy?" she asks.

"I think it's your choice." I dunk a tea bag a couple times. "But if I have to share space with your Asshole With Benefits, there's not a chance I'll be able to hold my tongue."

She could do light-years better than that fucking douchebag. He cares more about expensive things than about her. I swear he's complained a million times that our townhouse lacks a pool, hot tub, six-car garage, private guesthouse, etc.—and he's told Jane that she should move out ASAP.

Beckett eyes me. "He's that bad?"

I see-saw my hand like *so-so*. "AWB #2 was definitely worse."

Jane shoots me a strong look. "Je regrette d'avoir demandé ton avis." *I regret asking for your opinion.*

I touch my chest. "Tu connais mes sentiments à propos de Nate." *You know my feelings about Nate.*

Beckett turns to his sister. "Est-ce qu'il t'a frappé?" *Did he hit you?*

Oscar whispers in Donnelly's ear. I quickly realize that I have no idea which bodyguards are fluent in French. Farrow definitely isn't.

Jane shakes her head adamantly. "No. Never."

"He's just an asshole." I finish off my tea in one gulp. Literally every bodyguard trains these narrowed, pinpointed eyes on me like I'm withholding *security* info. "That's it."

Farrow tilts his head from side-to-side, considering my words. "Okay, but there's a range for assholes, and most of us want to know where Nate falls."

Oscar spreads out two hands to demonstrate the range. "There's the likable asshole over here." He waves his left hand before lifting up his right. "Then there's the abusive motherfucker that deserves to eat cow shit."

"And die," Donnelly adds.

"Painfully," Farrow finishes.

"Funny," I mutter and notice Jane and her pissed off face: brows pinched, lips pursed, not as terrifying as she wishes she could be. "Junie can tell you where he falls on the asshole range. She knows him better than me."

"He's a likable asshole," Jane announces without a beat, fierce blue eyes pinging to everyone. "He's only treated me with respect. For the sake of my future orgasms, leave him be."

Donnelly smirks. "Farrow knows a little something about protecting and *serving* orgas—"

"No." Thatcher shuts that down.

Christ, my neck is burning. I'm not embarrassed. No—that's not a feeling I feel often, and I'm not letting it creep into me.

Farrow studies my reaction, and I try to recover with a sip of nonexistent tea.

Yeah, my mug is empty.

He's near-laughter.

I'd combat him, but Thatcher speaks. "Back to the main issues." He focuses on Jane. "About your cats—"

"I've taken care of them," Jane begins with urgency. No emotion attached. Like she's discussing bus mileage and the trip route. "My sister already agreed to watch all six while I'm gone. My oldest cats and youngest kittens love Audrey, and she loves them fiercely. It all works out well."

My brows scrunch. "It's *four* months, Janie." She's never been away from her cats for that long.

"They're in good hands."

Thatcher types on his phone. Taking notes. "How's Licorice doing?"

Jane almost blushes. "Um," she says, frazzled by the question. "Still skittish from being stuck in the crawl space, but I'm glad you found him."

"Me too." Thatcher checks notes on his phone. "The tour should help with the incest rumor."

Jane clears her throat. "I propose we ban that word." She means *incest*.

I grimace. "I second that."

Heavy silence falls, and Thatcher pockets his phone before looking to Jane, then me. "I don't know if it'll mean anything to you two," he tells us, "but I understand what you're going through. Years ago, when I was in high school, Banks and I got the gamut of twin questions. Most were harmless but others…" He trails off, and we can easily fill in the blanks.

Banks Moretti is his identical twin, and also the 24/7 bodyguard to Xander.

Beckett nods strongly, also a twin. Also understanding.

Jane and I don't have to ask for examples or specifics. I stare off for a second—for Christ's sake, I should've realized sooner why Charlie would be at the lake house in support.

Why he'd understand like Thatcher and Banks. Like Beckett.

With zero evidence, the media tried to twist my close friendship with Jane into something perverse. But Charlie dealt with that all the time too.

I was there in high school. I heard guys ask Charlie harmless questions like *can you read your twin's mind* and then they'd veer into shitty things like *do you sleep with your twin?* They'd snicker as they prodded *how many three-ways have you had with Beckett?* And weird shit like *if you're naked, are you confused about who's who? Have you touched each other's…?*

Charlie would wear his annoyance. I remember that and how he'd just walk away. Move on. That's all he could do.

And I know that's all we can do now.

"Merci," Jane says to Thatcher.

I nod, appreciative of the support. The rumor will die sooner or later. It has no merit or validity, so I think we'll be fine.

Jane rests her chin on her fists. "I couldn't care less what the media or public thinks of me anyway." Her gaze lowers though. Clearly caring about something.

I know she's still upset that our parents doubted us for a split-second. I've been trying to understand their perspective so it'll make more sense, but it's not that easy. For either of us.

"Mom was crying," Beckett tells his sister, "and you know, Mom. She says she only sheds tears for the ones she loves. She really felt like shit for not believing you."

"Good," Jane snaps.

Beckett continues, "She also told Dad they needed to cut out their hearts for the betrayal and gift each to you in a glass jar."

Jane tries not to smile. "Encore mieux." *Even better.*

Farrow glances at me. "Did your parents say anything?"

"Yeah." I nod. "Just that they'll be here tomorrow."

4

Farrow Keene

"WEATHER REPORTS A WHITE-OUT blizzard at zero-nine-hundred hours." Thatcher's voice resounds through comms.

I pull out my earpiece while I ascend wooden stairs to the second floor. It's pushing 5 a.m. after a never-ending Omega meeting where we all planned security for the tour. I thought I left Thatcher in the fucking kitchen.

Now he's in my eardrum. With the volume high, I still hear him. "Be alert if you're driving to the lake house—"

I swivel my radio's knob, and his voice cuts off. Security agreed to spend the night at the main house and not security's cabin a mile out. There are plenty of vacant rooms, but I choose the one with Maximoff.

Quietly, I slip inside the bedroom and expect to find him sound asleep. He's upright, leaning against the log headboard. Maximoff types relentlessly on his laptop. Dark crescent moons shadow his eyes.

He looks spent, but he's still forcing himself awake.

I frown and slam the door shut behind me.

"Hey," he greets, not flinching. Not looking up. He props his phone beneath his ear. Listening to a voicemail or something equivalent since he doesn't speak.

I sidle to the bed and unclip my radio from my waistband. I wrap the earpiece cord and set it on the night table. "A call or notification wake you up?" I ask and rest a knee on the bear-printed quilt.

Maximoff lowers his phone and returns to his laptop. "Never went to sleep." He tries to catch a yawn and fails.

"Okay, enough." I push his computer closed. He rubs his eyes and doesn't try to reopen the laptop.

I step back, keeping an eye on him, and I find black drawstring pants in my duffel.

When I unzip my pants, Maximoff hones in on my tattooed fingers. Especially as I fish the button through. *He likes that.*

My lips rise.

He tears his gaze off me, neck slightly reddened, and he rotates his strained deltoids, computer still on his lap. "You've been awake for just as long," he says.

"And I'm not the one that looks like shit."

Maximoff bites down to fight a small smile, which sharpens his jawline.

I skim his striking features from afar, my blood hot, and then I step out of my pants and into the drawstring ones.

"We're not the same," I remind him, lifting the elastic band to my waist. "I'm used to vigilant nights. Sometimes they even excite me." I kick my duffel aside. "But clearly, sleeplessness isn't your thing. Let go and just sleep."

Maximoff rakes a rough hand through his thick, dark brown hair. "If I'm going to be out of the office for four months, I have a million-and-one things I need to take care of and schedule."

His work ethic is admirable and insane.

I sit on the bed. "Plan tomorrow. It's not going anywhere. And your parents are trying to beat an incoming blizzard right now. They'll be here earlier than you think."

His muscles flex, readying himself for that shit storm.

I put his laptop on a night table, and I edge closer to Maximoff. When I lean back against the log headboard, our shoulders brush.

Close. Both of us on top of the quilt and shirtless. His charcoal gray boxer-briefs cling to his toned build.

Maximoff fixes his messy hair. A knockout sexual tension grips us both, his muscles flexing. My jaw clenching, hot breath brewing at ninety-degrees inside of me.

He probably wants to make the first move. But I reach out and massage his taut shoulder.

His breathing heavies, and our tough gazes bore into each other.

Maximoff leans forward, allowing me to go lower. For a guy that doesn't trust easily, his permission to "go lower" is absolutely priceless. I want to give him more.

And more.

I knead his muscles, using my whole body to massage deeper. I run the heel of my palm down the length of his back.

"Fuck," he mutters, blinking repeatedly to keep his eyes wide open.

If he weren't tired, he'd flip me over by now. I like how hungered he usually is, but there's something extremely fucking sexy about how he's trying to battle his exhaustion.

I pull him between my legs to massage his back with two hands. I brace more of my weight against him, and my thumbs knead the base of his neck.

He swallows a wolfish groan, the noise almost fisting my cock.

I grit down and shift slightly.

Maximoff glances back at me, his *fuck me, kiss me* eyes in full blood-boiling effect. Before I even make a move, he rotates his body to take charge. And he yanks my leg, pulling me down—my head hits the pillow.

Damn.

My pulse hammers in my throat as I lie beneath him.

I clutch his neck and bring his mouth to mine. The starved kiss turns deep and heady as his tongue parts my lips. *Fuck, Maximoff.*

The way he uses his mouth is fucking killing me.

He falls to his elbows. Lowering his pelvis against my pelvis, thin fabric separates us, but he's grinding while deepening a kiss.

Hot friction hardens him and me. Veins throb in my cock, and his dick pulses against mine. *Fuckfuck.* A gruff noise cages inside my lungs.

Maximoff shifts his head and scans me in a slow, thundering wave. One that clearly reads *I want to fuck you.*

His voice is more hollowed out as he says, "I don't want to fucking sleep. Not yet."

With him above me, I run my palm down his hard chest and the valleys of his abs. Our stinging lips brushing, I whisper strongly, "You want to fuck me?"

His mouth crushes against my mouth, and his hips buck against my waist before he grows more against my thigh. Fuck, I *love* feeling a guy harden.

Our muscular legs tangle; my ankle rubs his calf, and I grip his hair with one hand, our tongues wrestling. I could flip him to his back, but instead, my other hand travels to the waistband of his boxer-briefs. Dipping under them, I cup his perfect bare ass.

He grumbles an aroused curse against my mouth.

Huskily, I ask, "Did you like that?"

His gaze narrows in want.

I test something and edge my fingers towards his—he tenses. Badly. Enough to where I draw my hand back to his shoulder, and he stays rigid and catches his breath.

I have to ask. "You still want to try to bottom?"

Maximoff lifts his body off me a little more. His palm on the quilt by my shoulder. His eyes trace an inked skull pirate on my ribcage. "Yeah," he says with a heavy breath. "I do, but I keep thinking about the tour bus and how the fuck this'll work."

"We'll figure it out," I say, confident about this.

He waits for me to add something else. A strategy or a plan. Maximoff likes to pack his survival gear, and I'm basically saying, *just trust me with what we have on our backs.*

He makes a face. "So we'll figure it out in a million light-years."

I roll my eyes into a short laugh. "I meant we'll figure it out in the moment, not when we're both buried six feet under the ground."

His phone rings and then buzzes somewhere on the bed.

He sits up. "I could be immortal."

I sit up too. "You're definitely not humble." I find his phone beneath his pillow and toss it to him. "Here you go, beautiful."

Maximoff catches his cell and looks thoroughly annoyed by me. Job well done. "Thanks," he says. "Now I'm eternally sterile."

"That's not how that works," I say. "Looks like you need elementary biology."

His next words are garbled in a long yawn.

"And sleep," I add as he pinches his tired eyes—he drops his hand, glowering. His forest-greens flit to my rock-hard bulge, then his bulge.

"I can tell you who's bigger. And it's not you."

He tries hard not to break into a smile. "Funny."

"It wasn't a joke."

He glares. "Now I'm fucking limp. Thank you."

I tilt my head. "Do I really need to point out the lie here?"

He ignores me by pulling the quilt over our legs. Then he unlocks his phone. "It's probably Dari." *His assistant.* "I emailed her about the tour." A frown crests his face. "I missed a call. Maybe a butt dial since it didn't ring that many times…and a text from the same person." He straightens up.

I rest my elbow on my bent knee. "It's not Dari," I assume.

He flashes his cell, a text on the screen.

Can we talk when you have time? – Dr. Keene.

Fucking hell. My father is texting him. On a subject unrelated to his health.

Someone among the Hales, Cobalts or Meadows must've told my father that I'm dating Maximoff. It makes the most sense.

And instead of contacting me, his son, he's reaching out to Maximoff. I sense the strain between me and my father all the time, but it seems to yank tighter.

Maximoff cracks a knuckle. "What do you want me to do?"

"I don't care." I'd rather he just lie back down and try to sleep than deal with this shit.

"You do fucking care," he rebuts, "or else you wouldn't look ready to uppercut a punching bag right now."

"If that were true, then it'd mean my father pisses me off." I'm about to swing my legs off the bed. "And when it comes to him, I feel nothing."

Maximoff catches my bicep before I move away. "You seriously feel nothing?"

"It's irritating that he's texting you and not me, but that's it. I didn't start the cold war. It's all him." My father wants me to join the family legacy and be a practicing doctor. I have the MD, but I'm never finishing my residency. It's just not what I want, and he hasn't accepted that.

Maximoff nods. "I'll call him back later."

I try to slide off the bed again.

Maximoff pulls me back for a second time. "Where the fuck are you going?" he asks.

My lip quirks. He really doesn't want me to leave him, and I struggle to look anywhere else but at him. *Consumed.* "Need my hand?"

"No," he says firmly. "I just want you."

That hits me hard. I almost crawl back. *Do your motherfucking job, Farrow.* I grit down and then tell him, "I have to get my phone. I haven't checked social media threats tonight."

Security's tech team spends more time doing this tedious shit for us. But personal bodyguards are still supposed to "stay updated" and "aware" of the discourse about our client on social media.

With the media fallout, it's more important for me to gauge the climate surrounding Maximoff.

"You can do it on my phone," he tells me, handing me his cell. Trusting me with it.

I can imagine the envy of girls and guys everywhere. And he chose me. *He loves me.*

Damn.

My chest swells for a second.

Maximoff lies back, smashes a pillow and then places his head down. He yawns. "I think I'm going to…" He yawns again.

He's going to pass out. Exhaustion starts drawing his eyes closed. *Good.*

He needs that.

I've slept in the same bed with him enough to know that he's typically not a cuddler until a couple hours into sleep. It's a private, personal fact that tabloids would crave and reprint a hundred times. And it's all mine for safekeeping.

I stack a couple pillows and lie flat. I'm not about to click into his texts. Privacy is already hard for him, and I've never been a nosy little bastard.

I download a program to his phone. It filters certain words on all social medias, and I select a time range. Basically from the last time I did this yesterday to now. Then I type out variations of phrases I need searched like:

kill Maximoff Hale
die Moffy
murder Lily & Lo's son

Results pop up, 99% just hyperbolic bullshit or slang. I scroll and scroll for two hours. Long enough that Maximoff turns on his side towards me, and our legs interlace.

He rests his head on my shoulder, his arm splayed across my abs. A small smile edges my mouth, and I rub his back before holding him against me.

With my other hand, I still scroll. I have to reach the bottom of the list. About finished, I hover over a search result: @maximoffdeadhale

Usernames like that one are rare. I click on @maximoffdeadhale to find the origin. An Instagram account: 3 posts, 0 followers, 1 following.

I go very still, and my gaze narrows on the oldest photo.

Posted 8 hours ago, the user photoshopped Maximoff reading a comic at Superheroes & Scones into a gory death scene. Eyes crossed out, swords impale Maximoff's chest, and blood gushes. In the comments, the user posted only one thing: #DeservesToDie

Motherfucker. I grit my teeth, my nose flaring. Distaste runs into the back of my throat. I pop up a second photo, posted 7 hours ago.

An altered photo of Maximoff in his Audi. Where he's halfway out of the windshield. Blood soaking the glass. My stomach roils. I swallow a rock, and I remember to view this horrific account as his bodyguard.

Not his boyfriend.

Right now, I have to separate the two. My job description says, *scrutinize visual deaths of your client with rational thought and care.* But I'm scrutinizing visual deaths of the guy I love. I may as well slap a hot iron at my face. Painful—and it's pissing me off.

I grind my teeth a few times.

Be his bodyguard. I can't lash out in the comment section of an anonymous internet user. I can't be overly sensitive to idiotic fuckers. I'm the shield that protects Maximoff Hale, and I'm never going to break and leave him defenseless.

See, I have to practice a great deal of restraint. Especially now.

I examine the photo closer. *Real threat or fake threat?*

It could be a troll account. I don't have enough information yet.

Third and most recent photo, posted 5 hours ago, shows Maximoff outside of the nightclub Tidal Wave. And he's *decapitated.*

Fuck.

My chest constricts, and Maximoff shifts his jaw more in the crook of my neck and shoulder. He's only vulnerable like this with me, and usually, it happens when we're alone. Shit, I just want to protect the fuck out of him.

Staying motionless, I try my best not to wake Maximoff.

And I force myself to analyze the third photo. Searching for anything to help determine if it's a real or fake threat.

Seems fake. But my heart rate elevates. Because I recognize it's not 100% confirmed. With the slimmest chance, someone out there may truly want Maximoff Hale to die.

Enough to make it happen.

"Farrow?" Maximoff lifts his head groggily.

"Go back to sleep," I whisper and click his phone screen to black.

He squints and rubs his eyes roughly. "Your whole body is flexed…" His gaze lands on the black-screened phone, and he readies himself like a soldier for combat. Immediately sitting up, alert and awake.

"Maximoff—"

He steals the phone out of my hand. Basically, I let him have it. I'm not here to cultivate secrets and lies between us. Do I wish he wouldn't have to see that account? Yeah.

Will I willfully keep him in the dark? Never.

Maximoff swipes out of the lock screen, and the @maximoffdeadhale Instagram account is already popped up. Almost instantly, his head swerves to me. "It's a fucking troll account." He tosses the phone on my lap. "It's not a big deal."

I cock my head, watching him smash the pillow again to lie back down. "You just saw visual depictions of your death, created by someone out in the world, and you feel fine?"

He yawns into his bicep and then clutches my gaze. "I get death threats every damn week. They've never been serious."

"Someone took the time to photoshop your head off your body, and that doesn't seem serious?" I honestly wonder if he hears himself. When I was his mom's bodyguard, I saw plenty of fucked-up graphics.

Like pie charts poorly estimating Lily's sex partners, her head photoshopped on rabbits, slut typed a hundred times on her face—but not her being murdered.

Not like this.

Maximoff brushes a hand through his disheveled hair. "Sounds like a normal Sunday through Saturday to me."

I nod a couple times. "At least now we know you're desensitized to your own death."

Maximoff rubs his jaw. "Maybe I am, but you don't need to worry about troll accounts and my plausible death with no sleep at whatever a.m."

"It's my job," I remind him. I deal with this so he doesn't have to. "I'm flagging this fucking account to be taken down." And that'll be the end of that. My gut instinct says differently, but I let it go for now.

Just as I report the account, an aggressive knock raps the door.

Maximoff slides off the bed at the exact same time as me. The knock practically electrocuted him into action. We exchange a look that says, *I'm answering the door. Stay back.*

He's too stubborn to listen, and I love seeing him try to catch up to me too much to let him go ahead.

We bolt to the door and race to be the first. I'm already out in front. "I thought you planned to sleep," I say, about to grab the doorknob.

His arm bangs into mine, but I clutch the knob first, smile widening.

Maximoff barely steps back, squeezing his build against my build. "I thought I told you that I open my own doors."

"Number 52 on your list of rules. I remember." I lower my voice to a whisper. "I remember everything…but see, this is *our* door."

His forest-greens drop to my mouth and my lip piercing. He also layers on a half-hearted glare. "Pretty sure for *my* things to become *your* things, we'd need a legal binding agreement."

Shock ratchets up my brows. "Marriage?"

"*No,*" he says definitively, shutting that down.

I roll my eyes. I know he's exaggerating his point, but he's more defensive than usual. "Technically, you don't own the lake house," I tell him. "So it's not even your door."

Maximoff groans and sends a daggered glare to the ceiling.

"Was that glare meant for me or the light fixtures?"

"The lights," he says. "This is for you." He gives me a middle finger.

I laugh a short laugh, and just as he tries to reach for the knob, I turn it and swing the door open.

Oscar Oliveira stands on the other side, brown hair curly and damp like he just showered. He steadies a cream cheese bagel near his mouth.

Arms crossed, eyes narrowed, Maximoff looks ready for hell and back. His resolve is fucking sexy.

I tell Oscar, "I didn't sign up for the Oscar Oliveira Wake Up Call."
I lean on the door frame.

Oscar's eyes drift from me to Maximoff, who stands rigid only
one-foot away in boxer-briefs. His muscles are front-page-worthy,
his defined V-line disappearing beneath his waistband. His lips are a
little reddened from earlier, and his usually combed hair is wild and
unkempt.

Mine isn't much different. I smooth my hair back with two hands.

Oscar fastens his gaze on me, not able to restrain a smile. "It's
almost growing on me. You two…together." He bites into his bagel.
"Though I didn't realize you like them young, Redford—"

"You don't realize a lot of things, Oliveira," I cut him off, "still, we
try not to hold it against you."

He laughs into another bite.

Maximoff stands sturdy, layering on authority like he's commanding
a boardroom. "I'm not young or naïve," he says, his firm tone instantly
quieting Oscar. "And if you're here just to shoot the shit, tell me.
Because I could be sleeping."

Okay, that was hot.

Oscar wipes cream cheese off the corner of his mouth with his
thumb. "I'm here as a courtesy."

"What do you mean?" I ask.

Oscar licks his thumb, but his expression is more serious. "Lily and
Lo just got here." He looks at Maximoff. "Your parents said they'd
wait until you woke up to talk, but I thought you'd appreciate an extra
warning."

"Thank you," he says, grabbing his jeans from the floor.

"No problem." Oscar flashes a wince at me. "Boyfriend's parents
are already pissed at you, Redford. I don't envy your position."

I'd say *parents love me*, but I'm not a liar or a kiss ass. And I'm
painfully certain that I've fallen onto Loren Hale's permanent shit list.

5

Maximoff Hale

WHATEVER I PLANNED TO SAY, whatever I thought I'd feel—it all just disappears when I see my dad. He paces from the living room fireplace to the window. Pauses. His hand balls in a fist. He glances towards the kitchen.

Looking. And *longing* for something.

Not someone.

I've seen that craving before. A look that screams, *just one drink*. For as long as I've been alive, he's never fed that demon. Never sipped alcohol.

Never broke sobriety.

But he's looking again.

I stand on the second floor balcony that oversees the living room with vaulted ceilings and skyscraping windows. Sunlight pierces leather furniture and wooden floors, and outside, snow dumps hard in the cold morning.

I can't help but think about *everything* I unloaded on him at the Charity Camp-Away. When he didn't believe me about the rumor, I yelled at him in a way that I never do. I showed my disappointment. I iced him out.

Wounds are still open. Freshly cut. And what if I pushed him? What if I caused him hurt so deep that he'd want to numb it with whiskey?

My chest is on fire.

I death-grip my phone, and I loosen my clutch at the sight of a rugged and brooding Ryke Meadows. My dad's half-brother who's one year older.

Any anger I had at Ryke's reaction towards my boyfriend—it takes a backburner right now. I'm glad my uncle is here in case my dad needs him.

Connor Cobalt saunters confidently past the leather couch to reach my dad and Ryke. I didn't think my uncles would join my parents at the lake house, but as they place a hand on my dad's shoulder and speak toughly but calmly—I realize they're here for him.

They're his support. And my dad isn't okay.

"Moffy," Connor says and angles his body towards the balcony. All their eyes meet mine.

Spotted.

My dad rubs the back of his neck. His cheekbones as sharp as ice, and brows pinched in a multitude of tangled emotions. "Can we talk?" he asks.

I nod. "Yeah."

We all agree to take a short hike to the hot tub. Apparently the blizzard is moving east, so we just have to deal with five inches of snow and counting.

After putting on winter gear, the four of us trek up a snowy ridge. Weaving through skeletal maple trees. Ryke and I gain a good amount of distance on my dad and Connor. Both out of earshot.

So I ask him, "Did he relapse?" I should've kept my phone on. I should've talked to my dad. I should've called him and not acted like a fucking punk—

"No," Ryke says, our gazes attached for a painful second.

"He almost did," I infer, my breath smoking the air. Guilt crushes my ribs.

"It's not your fucking fault," he tells me. "Your dad would never put this on you." I feel his narrowed gaze, but I just stare straight ahead.

I lick my chapped lips. "I keep thinking about what happens if I accidentally break my dad down. I keep thinking of how it'll tear apart my mom, my sisters—God, Xander…"

"Stop here." Ryke clutches my arm. And he means to literally stop. Fir trees flank a log hut, visible on the ridge's highpoint. The hut covers an eight-person hot tub.

My dad and Connor reach our spot on the trail.

"Everything okay?" Connor asks us.

"Go ahead." Ryke motions to the hot tub. "We'll catch up in a fucking second."

I can't even look at my dad, but I sense them nodding in agreement. When they leave, Ryke faces me.

I pull up the hood to my green Patagonia jacket. He wears a similar style but a darker shade of green. Right now, I don't give a fuck. The media isn't around to write up articles about our similarities, but even if they were, I don't care anymore. Compared to what else is on my plate, it's insignificant.

I don't care if you know how much I love him.

How much he means to me.

How much he influenced and shaped me.

I am who I am, and I'm not changing. I can't change for anyone. Not even for my own dad.

"Look," Ryke says, "you have to be honest with him, even if it fucking hurts him—"

"No—"

"Moffy." Ryke grips my shoulders until I stare him in the eye. "You can't be afraid to hurt him. It's going to fucking happen."

It already happened.

I'm rigid and cold. "You know what I think?" I take a tight breath, my gaze hardening. "I think the Hales are a line of dominos, and when my mom or dad falls, my siblings topple with them."

Ryke doesn't refute.

I nod a few times. "And I already pushed them down. I'm *never* doing it again."

"That's your fucking choice, but I'm telling you that I'll keep your dad and your mom standing. If you need to be upset—"

"I don't." I make a plan. I'll be honest with my dad, but not enraged or overly emotional. I'm not coming at him with guns blazing.

Ryke lets go of my shoulders. "They can handle a lot."

"But you know I still have the power to hit them where it hurts the worst. And they'll relapse."

Ryke brushes snow off his dark hair. "But here's the thing, Mof. You'll never hit that place."

"How do you know?"

"Because you're the furthest fucking thing from callous and vindictive." He gestures with his head to the hot tub. "My brother raised a good man."

I inhale stronger, and in a silent beat, a lot goes unsaid in our eyes. Less about my parents. More about him and me. And his aggression towards me dating a bodyguard.

"Later?" Ryke asks.

"Yeah." One thing at a time.

We rejoin Connor and my dad at the hot tub. Steam rises off the water, and my uncles decide to take a walk and make some phone calls.

Leaving me and my dad alone.

Not saying much of anything, we shed to bathing suits and then quickly lower into the hot, soothing water. Snow flutters in the horizon, and I watch white powder cake on the mountainsides and frozen lake.

I hear a splash, and I turn my head.

Across from me, my dad slicks his hair back with his wet hands. When he was in his twenties, he modeled for a single day and then quit. But he could probably still model if he wanted to.

Why the fuck I'm hanging onto this—out of everything—I try not to overanalyze. *Yay me.*

"I was wrong," he says. "That's the first thing you need to know."

I already knew that. My words aren't even close to surfacing. I just stare at the one man who means the most to me in my life. I teeter between worry and hurt. I fear saying the wrong thing, but I wade in this murky pain from our blowup.

My dad rubs the back of his neck again. "At your charity event, I made a mistake." His amber eyes lift to my forest-green.

I cradle all my words before I let them loose. I speak with ten-billion times less emotion than I really feel. "This isn't a normal mistake, Dad." I rest my arm on the hot tub edge. "This isn't forgetting to sign a field trip slip or missing a birthday. You sided with the…" I pause to avoid a curse word. "You sided with the media over me."

His brows cinch. "I didn't side with anyone. I didn't know what to believe."

My muscles burn. *Don't get angry. Don't get fucking angry. Hear him out.* I hold his gaze. "But you couldn't fathom believing me."

I'm starting to wonder if he brought me to the hot tub because it'd be twice as hard for either of us to just walk away.

My dad squints as the sun brightens. "What do you remember about your grandfather?" *His dad.* He died of liver failure when I was a little kid.

Most of my memories are good. He always bought me a new toy when I saw him, and he tried to give me life lessons: *listen to your parents* and *be grateful.*

But I was also aware that my dad would never leave me alone with him.

"I remember he had a loud, distinct voice. Pretty forceful, but I was never scared of him." My shoulders stiffen. "I guess he was nice to me." I know the history.

I know my grandfather verbally abused my dad.

A quick Google search says as much, and I've seen a few clips of *We Are Calloway* where my dad and Ryke talk about their father.

"Nice…" My dad mulls over that word, and then he shakes his head. "He wasn't that nice. I still loved him, but he was a terrible father. Just… goddamn awful. And it took me *years* to come to terms with that."

He leans his neck back, gazing at the hut's wooden rafters as he says, "Living with someone who tears you down every goddamn day—

it's like living with a constant monster. You start believing his words. That you're a piece of shit. *You're* the problem. Until you just… become him."

He tilts his head towards me, strength in his amber eyes.

"For the longest time," he continues, "I thought I was as awful as my father. Some parts of me were. And I believed that those parts would make me an equally terrible dad…it's why I *never* wanted kids."

I didn't know that.

I rub my lips, hand warm from the water. "What changed?"

"You," he says. "You weren't planned. As you know."

"Yeah." The media loves toting around that fun fact about the surprise pregnancy and my subsequent birth. It's not a big deal to me.

My dad stares at the snow-capped mountainside. "When Lily said she was pregnant, I told myself that if I fucked up, I'd ruin everything good and pure in my life. I made a promise to stay sober. To do better. I hung onto something that made me feel like I could."

I hesitate to ask, "What?"

"I hoped for a girl."

I bottle something inside. What's the feeling I feel? I don't know. I won't let it rise, but it amasses inside me like a cement block.

"I was afraid to raise a boy," he explains. "I was afraid to find out decades later that I raised someone just like me." He lets out a dry laugh. "I don't know why I thought I'd get what I want. I was such a shitty person back then; I didn't deserve any kind of shortcuts or easy outs."

I stare at the water and force myself not to defend his character. I didn't know my dad in his early twenties, and I need to stop protecting someone who's gone. My dad isn't that guy anymore, and he knows it, too.

"Maybe three months after your birth," he tells me, "I started actually believing I could be a halfway-decent dad. But that fear never really went away. It's still there. I've been terrified that you'd make the same mistakes as me. The same mistakes as my father."

This is where we diverge.

"You know me," I refute. "You know I would *never*—"

"You haven't lived in my house for four years, Moffy," he interrupts with quick-paced words. Eyes on mine again. Intensity laces his voice that silences me. "We talk, but you're not around all the time. I've been more concerned with Luna, Xander, and Kinney. And I know who you are. You're kind and compassionate, and I'm so goddamn *proud* of the man you've become."

My eyes burn. I know there's a *but* coming.

"But I thought somewhere in those four years you could've become someone different, and I missed something. People change." He gestures to me. "You can change."

I shake my head. "I don't feel like I can."

My dad looks like he wants to reach a hand out, but his face twists as he keeps to himself. He shakes his head once. "You're stubborn like Ryke. He thought that too, but he's not the same as he was at twenty-two. You have *years* to grow and be someone different. Someone you like more or less, and it's terrifying. I know it is. Because at twenty-two, I was shitting myself thinking about it."

I don't blink as I take it in.

"I know you're a lot like my brother. But you're still my son. You have all the best parts of Lily—thank God for that. But there's a chance you could have the worst parts of me."

I open my mouth, but everything I'd say next to appease him would be a lie.

"You know it, too," he says. "If you didn't think there was a chance, then you wouldn't be as careful around alcohol."

A chill bites my exposed skin, maybe by the weather or his words. I drop my shoulders beneath the hot water, and I listen intently as he keeps going.

"The thing about addiction is that it changes you," he tells me. "You don't care about the people you love. All compassion and kindness dissolve in the face of your own wants and *needs.*"

He extends an arm in the freezing air to point towards where Ryke disappeared. "I was that person lying to my brother. To my family. To your mom, a woman who has half my *soul.* That's how bad it gets.

And when we confronted you at the summer camp, all I could see was myself."

My stomach knots.

"I wish I handled it differently," he says. "In hindsight, I should've given you more time to speak, but if I never questioned you, I would've hated myself every goddamn day. Because I was raised by a father who didn't give a shit where I was. And your mom was raised by parents who couldn't care less about her."

He sits forward. Closer to me. "The moment I held you in my arms, I vowed to always care. In my world, that means questioning you when I sense something's wrong. Even if I turn out to be the jerk in the end."

I stay completely still.

My dad has always been candid with me, but this is different. How he's speaking—it feels like he's reaching to a place he rarely touches and he's splitting himself open.

He's fallible. Imperfect. He's been telling me that since I was little, but my dad had always been a superhero in my eyes.

He's so human. It hurts.

"Me and your mom, your aunts and uncles—in almost every circumstance, we wouldn't trust the media over your word. But security's intel about your NDAs and the 'mystery girl' that we wouldn't approve of—it aligned with the media. Something wasn't adding up. We thought it could be anything, not just the rumor. You could've been drinking or..." He takes a giant breath.

I was lying about Farrow.

I take fault for that.

"Interrogating each other," he tells me, "it's how we deal with lies. Your aunts and uncles have done it to me, and I've done it to them." He pauses. "We were all worried you and Jane were in trouble...and I just needed..." He turns his head away, but I catch sight of his pained face. "I'm sorry."

"It's alright." A lump lodges in my throat, and a question gnaws at me. I ask as carefully as I can, "What would your dad have done if he were in your position?"

He drops his head.

"You don't have to answer—"

"I can. Easily." His jaw sets sharp. "The Jonathan Hale damage control handbook. First, he takes away your trust fund. Then he conducts a meeting where he lists all the steps you have to follow to rebuild your image. Mainly for the sake of the family companies. The trust fund is collateral."

"Fuck."

"He's not done," my dad says. "You're broke now. That is, until you complete those necessary steps. One of which, you're getting married. In his timeframe. And definitely *not* to your bodyguard. But at least in Jonathan's handbook, he talks to you face-to-face. You pick up the Calloway handbook, Lily's parents, and they'll just send the lawyers to deal with you."

I stare haunted. "Something like this happened to you and Mom?"

His face says *yes*. "I love you more than you'll ever realize, and I hope one day, you can see that our reactions at the camp were out of fear and love. Nothing else."

I'm starting to see now.

Before, I couldn't comprehend why and how my parents could doubt me, but he just gave me their viewpoint. I wanted automatic loyalty, but my dad cared enough to question me. They all fucking did. They took the chance of being wrong and dealing with this fallout because if they'd been right and did nothing...

I could be drowning in alcohol. I could be hurt and floundering alone. I could be silently screaming for support and no one's there to answer the call.

So I get it.

I wish that doomsday could've been avoided altogether, but if it had to happen, at least I have parents that love me enough to be there for me.

I nod stiffly. "About Hale Co...." We haven't talked about the billion-dollar baby product company, built by my great-grandfather. The rumor about me and Jane doesn't exactly help sell bottles and diapers.

Hale Co. stocks dropped, and I'm sure it's made my dad's job as the CEO even harder.

He frowns. "You think I care about the company? You could drive my business into the ground, bud, and as long as you're breathing and alive and happy, I wouldn't care."

I nod again. Thinking about everything he's said. *Forgiveness* isn't that hard for me—maybe it even comes too easily—but when faced with love or a pointless grudge, I'm going to accept love.

Once I find the words, I tell him, "I wouldn't trade you for any other dad. No bullshit." I figure he'll think I'm tiptoeing around him because he's in a bad place. I kind of am, but I still mean what I say.

He usually has a response for everything, but he grimaces in thought. Maybe he can tell I'm overly praising him.

I run my hand across a hot tub jet. "How's mom?" I still regret snapping at my mom at the camp. I've never yelled at her before, and it may seem like a stupid comparison, but I feel like I kicked her.

"She's sad," my dad says, "but I've seen her sadder."

Great.

He gives me this weird look that's been forming for a while. Like I've floated into outer space halfway through our conversation.

"What?"

"You're worried about us, and we're the people that hurt you. Jesus Christ, it's *strange.*"

"You're my parents—"

"And we fucked up." He winces and then flashes his iconic half-smile. "Where's the condemnation and the tantrum and the *I hate you so much, Mom and Dad*, huh?"

He wanted me to put up a fight and knock him down at least once. I actually think there's a part of him that felt like he deserved it—and fuck that. "I guess I'd just rather love you than hate you. Sorry," I say with edge that matches his.

His face scrunches. "When's the last time you've cried?"

I almost shake my head. "Why are you asking that?"

"*Concern.* I told you it's okay to cry growing up, didn't I?"

LOVERS LIKE US // 57

"Yeah, you did. All the time."

He would say, *you can cry, bud.* But I must've been thirteen the last time I really cried. Someone kept stuffing notes in my locker like *your mom sucks a lot of dick* with penis doodles. There I was, sobbing into my pillow, and my little brother knocked on my bedroom door. Wanting me to read him a fantasy book.

He was super fucking young, and I remember rubbing my face until all the tears dried. I didn't want Xander to be afraid of bullies. I realized then that if I showed my cousins and siblings that I couldn't handle the world—young kids who saw me as a role model, their leader—then they'd never believe they could.

"I was thirteen," I tell my dad. "There just hasn't been a lot to cry over since."

Twigs rustle in my peripheral. I crane my head over my shoulder. Two figures hide poorly behind leafless maple trees. Only about twenty feet away.

85% chance of eavesdropping.

My dad gapes in mock surprise. "Christ Almighty, I wonder who the hell that could be."

Connor and Ryke emerge and glare at each other, shirking blame for being discovered.

My dad touches his heart. "I had no idea."

I almost smile. As they dip into the hut, Ryke removes his gloves and stomps snow off his rubber soles. "Cobalt wouldn't move his ass any higher up the fucking ridge."

Connor unzips his navy blue jacket. "I lost cell signal. Of course, you wouldn't understand the importance of needing to be reachable because not many people need to reach you."

"Fuck off." Ryke throws a glove at Connor's face, but without even looking, Connor dodges the glove and it plops in the hot tub.

I grab the soaked glove and toss it back to Ryke. "If I remember correctly, you both were also at Camp Calloway *doubting* me and Jane."

Ryke sheds down to his bathing suit. "We were also there trying to fucking protect you—"

"Is an *I'm sorry* that damn hard?" I ask.

His frown darkens, and he climbs into the hot tub. "I'm fucking sorry." It sounds sincere, and he wraps his arm around my shoulder. Giving me a side-hug.

Connor places his jacket on a wooden table. "I apologize for hurting you."

"I accept," I say, "but Janie's gonna need more than that."

Connor nods. "I'm aware. She already asked her mom and me to write a three-thousand word essay on why we love her." His lips pull upward, admiration for his daughter clear in his eyes.

My dad flashes a dry smile. "That's what happens when you raise a bunch of geniuses and make your family motto: *loyalty to the death.*"

Connor grins a billion-dollar grin.

I lie back, but my shoulders won't unwind. "Isn't the Cobalt motto, *'let me play the lion too: I will roar'* and whatever else Eliot says?" My younger cousin always recited that Shakespeare quote from *A Midsummer Night's Dream*, and it's weirdly become the unofficial Cobalt rallying cry.

"We have many mottos," Connor says and finishes undressing to his blue bathing suit. He joins us in the hot tub, sitting closer to my dad while Ryke stays next to me.

Connor sets his phone in a cup holder, and I remember what I've been meaning to tell all three of them.

"I've been working with a tech & security company." I capture their attention. "The engineers are updating all of our electronics and the security team's to ensure no hacks from any outside sources. Phones, computers—everything will be safer to use. It was supposed to be my Christmas present to everyone, but I'll roll it out before the tour starts."

Connor looks marginally impressed. Which is more than he gives most people. He nods repeatedly. "This'll allow you to text Farrow without fear of a public hack."

Sudden mention of my boyfriend/bodyguard heavies the air. "Yeah. It's an added benefit." I start to unconsciously smile when I imagine us texting like we're together, for real.

I've never had that before.

Connor reads my features. "You like him."

"I love him," I correct.

Ryke scratches his unshaven jaw.

"Say it," I tell him.

"Look, we hired these fucking bodyguards. All of our kids trust them. You lower your guard around them, and it feels fucking *wrong* for security to take advantage of your vulnerability—"

"I'm an adult," I remind him for the millionth time. "It was my choice, and it wasn't fucking easy for me." I can't lie to my uncle and say that trust wasn't a factor.

Inherently, I need to trust someone before I can be completely myself with them, and I trusted Farrow. But I also knew him before he was a bodyguard.

Ryke digests this. Silent.

"If you're worried about your daughters or the little kids with security," I say, "you don't have to be. The team is professional, and all they want is to keep everyone safe. You all know that."

"I do," Connor says like Uncle Ryke is being dumb.

Ryke rolls his eyes.

My dad watches me, but he stays quiet. I can't tell where his head is at regarding Farrow, and maybe he's not even sure.

I feel the need to defend my relationship. "I know you want me to be in an uncomplicated relationship," I tell my dad. "Some guy or girl I met in a coffee shop or at some damn comic book convention, but that was never going to happen."

My dad twists his wedding ring.

I solidify.

Then I try to straighten up, water lapping the ledge of the hot tub.

I follow his gaze that drifts down the ridge. Someone bundled in gray faux fur hikes towards the hut, and as my dad relaxes more and more, I know it can only be one person.

I climb out of the water. Cold bites every inch of exposed flesh. I shiver and quickly put on my pants, shirt, jacket—the works. I bet they know what I'm about to do. No one protests as I leave and run down the slope, snow past my calves.

I skid on a patch of ice but keep my balance. Wind slaps my face, and right as I round one corner, I startle the gangly, fur-clad figure.

"OhmyGod!" she shrieks, wide-eyed, and then catches her breath as she realizes it's just me.

"Hey, Mom." I lean down and wrap my arms around her bony shoulders, hugging her tight. "I'm sorry."

"Nonono," she says rapidly and pushes my chest.

I back up, lungs cemented in my throat.

Tears just stream down her round cheeks. "Why are you apologizing?" Her voice cracks.

I yelled at you. I hurt you. "Mom—"

"I had a whole *I'm sorry* speech planned." Her chin quivers. "*I* wronged *you.*" She jabs a finger at my heart, but the longer I look into her glassy green eyes, the more fragile she seems—the more my resentment just depletes.

"I forgive you—"

"You can't," she cries but hurriedly wipes at her tears.

"I just did." My chest is on fire again.

"Well, you shouldn't." She hiccups and then lowers her fur hood to shield her splotchy, reddened face from me. "Ihavetogo," she mutters.

"Mom." I catch her hand. "I love you, you know that." With every word, I do more harm than good. I'm fighting for the right thing to say and do.

She rubs her face with her forearm. "I love you too…I'm so sorry. I'm doing this all wrong again." She releases her grip, then treks further up the ridge and embraces my dad.

I turn my head.

Last night, the tour seemed like an okay idea—complicated, fucking risky—but in this moment, I love the whole concept.

Because I feel like I should be anywhere but here.

6

Farrow Keene

"PRICE TO SECURITY TEAM, everyone stay out of the study," the Alpha lead orders through comms, the lake house abruptly packed with all three famous families. While Maximoff is outside with his parents and uncles, I hit the basement gym.

Four bodyguards from Security Force Alpha are working out, all of which I ignore. Because I hate side-eyes just as much as I hate cliques. And they're side-eyeing the fuck out of me since I broke their golden rule about sleeping with a client.

Akara is the only one from Omega here, and while I do my twentieth pull-up, sweat suctioning my black shirt to my abs, he kicks a boxing bag in quick spurts.

"What's happenin' in the study?" Donnelly asks through comms.

Price's voice booms in my earpiece. "Jane and her mom are talking."

On the weight bench, an older bodyguard says, "I heard them *crying.*" And then he side-eyes me again.

I make eye contact, and he diverts his gaze and grumbles something under his breath. *That's what I thought.* I grit down and lift my chin above the bar, ankles crossed.

Akara kicks the bag hard. "I looked at the Instagram account you sent me."

I drop and take off my hand wraps. See, typically I wouldn't even bring this to a lead of any Force, but the @maximoffdeadhale account is still active, and the user posted another photoshopped picture about a half hour ago.

This time, Maximoff is falling off the side of a mountain.

Akara wipes sweat off his brow with his bicep. "It's a troll account."

"That's what I thought." I pop the cap off my water bottle. "But no tabloid has run a story about the Hales heading to their mountain lake house, so why would the user post a picture where he's falling off the side of one?"

Akara snaps his finger to his palm. "Coincidence."

"There's a chance the user could know Maximoff personally." I swig my water, and my gaze narrows as Akara gives me a pitying look. "It has nothing to do with him being my boyfriend. I'm still his bodyguard, and as his bodyguard, this shit isn't flying with me."

Akara picks up his towel. "I'll send in a request for our tech team to trace the IP address. Until then, don't check that account." His voice is strict. "That's not friendly advice; that's an order."

I roll my eyes. "Aye aye, captain." My phone rings in the pocket of my track pants. Caller ID: Kinney Hale. Maximoff's thirteen-year-old sister almost never calls me.

I answer, "Hey?"

"We need you now. Don't tell anyone. Hall bathroom near the kitchen. Be fast or die." She hangs up.

I KICK THE BATHROOM DOOR CLOSED, AND KINNEY

bombards me, green eyes shadowed in heavy black liner, dressed in knee-high socks, a black skirt and top, and a choker necklace. She puffs out her chest, but her bony build makes her appear comically tiny.

"We have problems," she snaps.

I raise my brows. "No shit."

"*Real* problems, you turd." She crosses her lanky arms. "You need to drive us somewhere."

"No," I say and unpeel a piece of gum. Stepping past Kinney, I discover the "we" here.

By the toilet, Luna runs in place and then shimmies her arms and hips. I'm positive she's dancing to no music, and if I should question the weirdness in that act, I don't.

Kinney confronts me head-on. "We're your boyfriend's siblings."

I pop my gum and notice Xander lounging in a claw-foot tub.

He pulls his bulky red headphones to the collar of his *Winter is Coming* shirt. "Save your breath, Kinney. He doesn't give a damn—"

"Wow." I slowly chew. "You really believe I don't care when I'm here, entertaining a fragmented phone call that said absolutely nothing."

He slumps further down the tub and lifts his headphones to his ears. "I think you'd rather bang my brother."

My jaw muscle tics, but I lean casually on the granite counter. I didn't imagine that dating Maximoff would affect his relationship with his brother, and I'm not happy about this at all.

"He didn't mean it," Luna says, panting as she runs in place.

Xander tugs down his headphones again. "Yeah, I did."

I unpocket my phone to text Maximoff. "Your brother's been trying to get ahold of you."

Xander sits up, elbows on the lip of the tub. "He could've convinced someone to keep Thatcher on my security detail, but no, he wanted to fuck his bodyguard, and now I *lost* mine so you two could have a stupid chaperone."

He's fourteen-going-on-fifteen. He's upset. I'm not about to tear into the kid, but I'm fucking irritated that he keeps referring to me as his brother's fuck-buddy.

I loosely cross my arms. "If you think your brother would risk everything just to 'fuck his bodyguard'—" I use air quotes "—then you don't know him that well."

His gaze hits the floor.

"Man, if Maximoff or I had the power to return Thatcher Moretti to you, we would in a fucking heartbeat. I want him around me like I want gangrene and a root canal."

I recognize that Thatcher voted for me to remain Maximoff's bodyguard, but I can't even feign obedience. I'm not accustomed to being indebted to anyone either. I'd rather buy him a bottle of booze and call it even, but knowing Thatcher, he'll want my firstborn and my coronary artery.

Xander mutters under his breath, "Moffy could've made it happen if he wanted to. He can do anything."

I'm fucking glad Maximoff isn't here. If he heard that, guilt and pressure would crush his shoulders. Then he'd make himself sick trying to fix this for his little brother, but he has no power over the Tri-Force.

Security switches happen, and Xander has to accept that Thatcher isn't his bodyguard anymore.

"He can't do everything," I tell Xander. "Right now, he doesn't even have a license."

Xander gives me a weird look. "Shouldn't you be his number one supporter? You're dating him."

He didn't say "fucking" him. *Getting better.* "And I'm not over-estimating his abilities and putting him in a shit bind. I call that…" I start to text Maximoff. "…love."

Kinney lunges to steal my phone. Reflexes quick, I raise my cell in the air and then put a hand on her forehead. I use minimal strength to keep her back.

"You can't tell anyone we're here," she sneers and flails for the phone.

"I'm texting your brother."

Her thrashing ends, and she suddenly acts blasé and uncaring, sitting on the tub ledge. "Fine. He can join. As long as we leave soon." She rolls her eyes at me. "God, stop looking at me like I'm a moron. I know things."

I pop my gum and smile before texting: Come to the hall bathroom by the kitchen when you can. Xander is here with your sisters. I tuck my phone in the back pocket of my track pants and then swivel the volume of my radio.

"Wherever you need me to take you three," I say, "I'll need to call your bodyguards to join—"

"Uh-uh, *no*," Luna pants, swinging her arms left and right in a retro dance move. "Just us, Farrow."

I rest an elbow on the sink. "I can't, Luna."

"Excuse me." Kinney gawks. "You're a rule-breaker. Break the rules."

I'm not a fan of Epsilon, but the guys in SFE will want my head on a platter if I take three of their clients on a joy ride to fuck-knows-where without them.

I shake my head. "I bend rules for the benefit of my client and his privacy. You three aren't my clients—"

"But my bodyguard is a nark," Kinney says. "Luna's bodyguard is a bigger nark, and Xander's bodyguard—"

"—is cool," Xander interjects, "but Banks will tell Thatcher, who'll tell—"

"I'll stop you there," I say, my brows spiked. "That's the definition of a nark."

"Banks and Thatcher are still cooler than you."

My smile stretches. "That must be why you asked them here instead of me."

"Burn," Kinney deadpans.

Xander flips his sister off before putting his headphones back on.

Luna twirls in a circle. "Can't you poach some trustworthy bodyguards from SFO, then?"

"That's not how the security team works." If I asked to bring Oscar with me over Luna's bodyguard, J.P. would act like I nail-gunned his feet to the floor. I watch Luna spin six more times, and my concern elevates. "How serious is this?"

She blows out a breath. "To be determined, but it's not looking great…"

It's about Luna, I deduce. "Okay. If you need something, I can go alone—"

A knock pounds the door.

I let Maximoff inside. He's still wearing his wet Patagonia jacket. Our gazes latch for a strong second, and then I lock the door while he skims his siblings.

"What's going on?" He nears his brother.

Xander lowers his headphones to his neck again.

"Hey." Maximoff has this empathetic expression that screams, *I care. I care. I love you.* "I've been trying to reach—"

"I know." Xander climbs out of the tub and clasps his older brother's hand. Maximoff brings Xander into his chest, and they hug.

Out of the corner of his eye, Xander sends me a pleading look. As though saying, *don't tell him I was upset.*

Unless Maximoff asks, I won't bring it up. They pull apart, and Maximoff says to his brother, "I heard you got your door back at home."

Xander shrugs. "I only lost it for a day."

Maximoff told me that Xander has a *no locking doors* rule. Whenever he breaks it, their dad takes the door off its hinges.

I prop the back of my boot on the cupboard, knee bent, and I watch Luna run in place for the third time. I don't ask because I'm about 99.9% sure Maximoff will.

He breaks focus from his little brother and zeroes in on Luna with a hardened gaze. "What the hell are you doing?"

She pants, "I read on *Celebrity Crush* that if you dance a lot, you can possibly, maybe, somewhat make your period appear."

Shit.

Silence hangs heavy.

"You missed your period?" he asks, voice firm. He taps into big brother mode with ease, his body rigid, and he shoots me a glare. As though I didn't inform him of the scenario where his eighteen-year-old sister may be pregnant.

"I didn't know," I say, and then I look at Luna. "You can't make your period appear by dancing, but nice try."

Kinney scoffs. "You're a guy. You know nothing about periods or the female anatomy. You haven't even touched a vagina."

"*Kinney*," Maximoff growls.

My mouth curves upward. Because it's cute when he defends me, but I can handle this shit. "I graduated medical school," I tell her, "but I don't need an MD or a high school diploma to know that medical advice from *Celebrity Crush* isn't accurate or even good advice. It's just bullshit."

"That's what I said," Xander says, taking a seat on the tub ledge next to Kinney. "I mean, it's the same tabloid that rumored Jane and Moffy to be—"

"Too soon," Maximoff cuts him off and then hones in on Luna again. "How? When? Where? Why?"

Luna falls flat to her feet and tugs at the sleeves of her baggy star-printed sweater. "Sex. Last day of school before winter break. In the back of his car. Because I was digging him." Her amber eyes ping from me to her older brother. "I'm only a few weeks late, and I know I screwed up already because of school. Mom and Dad can't know about this. Not until I figure out if it's real."

Before Maximoff even knew, I heard from the security team that Dalton Academy said Luna has to be homeschooled for the remainder of the school year—or else she won't graduate on time.

Luna places her hands on her head. "Maybe I can go on tour with you."

"Me too." Kinney stands.

Maximoff pushes Kinney back down until she sits. "No, and no." His muscles contract, and he gestures to Luna. "Did he not wear a condom?"

"I didn't think about it." She twists a piece of light brown hair around her finger. "It was my first time, and I thought the probability was low."

I rub my temple, almost cringing.

"Jesus Christ," Maximoff mutters. "Our mom is a *sex* addict, Luna. You should know better."

She looks to me for an out, but she forgets that I'm a hardass too.

"You should've listened in sex ed."

"Lay off her, you turds," Kinney says.

"Stop, Kinney," Maximoff says harshly.

Luna swings her head to Xander. "I told you I should've asked Tom and Eliot for help."

Xander stands. "They may be your best friends, but they would've told all the Cobalts, Luna. Moffy and Farrow are going to fix this. Right?" In unison, all three of them rotate and set their gazes on me and Maximoff.

I'm still casually leaning on the sink. Maximoff stands like he's currently supporting the world on his shoulders.

And I already understand why they called me here in the first place. I tell Maximoff, "Luna needs a pregnancy test."

Kinney steps forward. "Farrow is taking us to the convenience store."

"No, I'm going alone," I say.

"I'm coming with you," Maximoff rebuts.

Always stubborn. "You're staying in the car." If someone catches him buying a pregnancy test, he'll stoke the rumor he's trying to extinguish.

"We'll talk about it on the way there."

I roll my eyes, but this isn't an argument I need to win right now. Especially in front of his three siblings. "Let's go, wolf scout."

7

Farrow Keene

BEAR CLAW ONE-STOP SHOP is the nearest convenience store, a fifty-two mile drive on windy and icy roads. We chained the tires of Omega's Range Rover before leaving the lake house, and we safely reached Bear Claw. Only a Jeep in the parking lot. Most likely the storeowner.

I make a quick choice and agree to let Maximoff join me inside. The tiny, outdated store has no security cameras, and half the shelves are bare. We'll be lucky if they even have a pregnancy test. We both notice the old gray-haired man sleeping at the cash register.

While we peruse the aisles, Maximoff's shoulders stay tense and neck stiff. Always a knight prepared for a looming war.

He checks a bottom shelf, finding jugs of water. "Bet you didn't think you'd be doing this today."

"Technically, I never thought I'd be doing this any day." I grab a pair of aviator sunglasses off a rack and slip them on, price tag hanging off the rim.

Maximoff glances back at me, and he almost lets himself check me out, *almost*. His gaze stops at my chest, and then he unzips his Patagonia jacket, hot, and rounds the corner with me.

Aisle number two carries mostly junk food: beef jerky, Pringles, and popcorn. Then random fruit. Oranges, bananas—I take a red apple.

And I place a hand on his chest. Stopping him mid-aisle because he's been too quiet. Even the whole ride here. I lift the aviators to my head, pushing my hair back. "The talk with your dad went that badly?" I finally ask.

"My dad kept twisting his wedding ring." He purposefully buries his emotion, his face blank. "That means—"

"I know what that means," I say, even if the fact isn't public knowledge. I spent three years around Lily and Lo, and anytime Lo was in a bad place with his addiction, he'd twist his ring.

Maximoff blinks a few times, his guard descending. Letting some kind of emotion break through.

My hand rises to the back of his neck, and he suddenly clasps my shoulders, his muscular arms wrapping around them. At the same time, we both step into a hug. Chest against chest. I stroke the back of his neck, and he holds us together in a strong embrace.

I feel his heart thud hard and fast.

Against his ear, I whisper, "I'm sorry." I know how much he loves his parents, and not being able to fix this must be killing him.

His chest collapses in a deeper breath, and we tilt our heads back, our eyes skimming each other. I'd say I lean in first, but he'd tell you the exact opposite.

I kiss him tenderly like I'm the saint, and go figure, he full-bodies the kiss like he's the sinner. Meaning, he pulls our builds even closer together while our mouths meld deeper.

Damn.

I step him towards the back of the store, and he wrestles for the lead and spins me into a shelf—*shit*. My shoulder blades knock into a tower of Moon Pies, and they start falling onto the linoleum floor.

We tear apart, and I push the Moon Pie box back on the shelf while Maximoff picks up the fallen packages.

I eye the old man at the cash register. He lets out a long snore. Not waking. Even if he did, I doubt he's in touch with celebrity news.

I peel the sticker off the red apple, and Maximoff fixes his disheveled hair. He also keeps licking his lips, like he still feels me on them.

Our eyes meet, and he asks, "Did my mom talk to you?"

I didn't expect that divergence. "I just kissed the fuck out of you, and now you're thinking about your mom?"

He feigns confusion. "Let me get in my time machine. Look at that, I just kissed the fuck out of *you*. Not the other way around."

I roll my eyes and then smile. "And I'm a hundred-percent positive you dreamed of my tongue in your mouth at sixteen." I toss my apple in my hand. "That's a true fact."

Right on cue, he gives me two middle fingers, and his eyes drift to my mouth.

I whistle. "And he wants me to kiss him again."

Maximoff glances at the storeowner. Dead asleep. Then me. "Seriously, Farrow, did my mom talk to you?"

"No," I say easily. "I didn't expect her to."

He frowns. "Why not?"

I pause, apple near my mouth. "It has more to do with me than you. When I was on her security detail, I built a lot of trust between me and your parents. By lying to them about you, I basically obliterated all of that. They'll patch things up with you because you're their son, but I expect a four-month cold shoulder, at least."

He nods, tensed again.

"Don't worry about it. It's my shit to deal with." I bite into the apple, and he looks at me like I've just stolen half the store—which, to be honest, contains nothing valuable to steal.

"What are you doing?" he asks and checks on the sleeping old man again.

Maximoff. "Eating." I extend the apple to him. Just to piss him off. "Want a bite?" I walk nearer, and he makes a point to cross his arms, biceps bulging.

"You're stealing."

"And you're so pure." I take a larger bite.

He growls out his irritation, but his lips start to slowly rise. "Farrow."

"I'm going to pay for it. Relax. *Relax.*" I widen my eyes and then lower my aviators.

He exhales a bigger breath, and we peruse the next aisle. Some stocked over-the-counter medications.

I squat and shift boxes of cold medicine. I give him my half-bitten apple so I can reach further back. I feel him fixating on the movement of my hands. I smile and find only one pregnancy kit.

I flash him the box. "I'll check out with cash and rip up the receipt."

He looks surprised that I have a game plan.

I rise. "I'm still your bodyguard, wolf scout. And I'm still taller too."

He laughs shortly and backs up from me. "By one fucking inch." He lets his gaze drop all the way down my body.

8

Maximoff Hale

WE'RE LEAVING.

It's time, and this isn't some alternate universe. This is actually, in real life, happening. Six inches of snow blankets a deserted parking lot. Right outside of a Food Lion. I shove the tenth suitcase into the storage bays of our parked tour bus.

Security Force Omega darts around and coordinates through their mics, carrying cases of water, beer, soda, and other supplies.

My four cousins hop on and off the black sleeper bus, bringing in snacks and pillows.

And paparazzi—they're gone. Vanished. They trailed our families back to Philadelphia, and they probably believe we're with them. But me, Jane, Sullivan, Beckett, Charlie, and six bodyguards are still in the Smoky Mountains.

It's weird—not having a cameraman up in my face.

I keep thinking about that. And how I'm more used to their invasive presence than the unadulterated peace without them.

My family also decided to extend the hiatus for *We Are Calloway*. I called Jack Highland, an exec producer of the docuseries, and he agreed to push film dates until after the tour. So those cameras won't be around for at least four months.

"Moffy?" Jane steps off the bus into the snow.

I heave another duffel into the bottom bay. "Bonjour, ma moitié." My voice is tight. Because we haven't talked without a peanut gallery—her brothers, my boyfriend, or any of the security team—in fucking forever.

And by *forever*, I mean *days*.

For us, that's practically a century.

She nears. "Regarde-moi s'il te plaît." *Look at me, please.*

I stand straighter and lift my gaze. Wind whips her tangled brown hair, and her outfit is classic Janie: furry pink boots, cat-stitched mittens (gifted by me years ago), a chunky zebra sweater, and a mint-green tutu over knit leggings.

Just seeing my best friend, my mouth aches to rise.

Jane touches her mittens to her rosy cheeks. "It's just you and me, old chap, and a tour bus full of beautiful people. Friends and family."

I start to smile. I can feel us finding footing in our friendship again. And I think we're going to land upright. "You sure they're beautiful?"

"You're right. They're *dreadfully* gorgeous." A cheery smile overtakes her face, and we notice Quinn and Donnelly lingering by the rear wheels. Watching our exchange.

So Jane and I walk over to a curb that landscapes a skeletal tree. Grass probably hidden beneath snow. We're out of earshot from the bus but still in view.

Jane ties her hair into a messy pony. "My little brothers keep calling this the Damage Control Tour, but to me, it's something entirely different. It's the Preserve Jane and Moffy's Friendship Tour, and I miss you…terribly."

I pull Jane into a hug, and she immediately wraps her arms around my waist. This is home. This is safety and love.

She is my *best* goddamn friend, and I don't want anything to ever come between us again. I kiss her cheek and whisper, "I missed you too, Janie, and we're going to get through this."

"Ensemble," she whispers a Cobalt declaration in French. That means *together.*

Together.

We part, and she props her chin on her knuckles. "What'd I miss?"

A lot, but I start with the first thing that crashes against me. "I told Farrow I love him."

Her hands touch her mouth, and her bright blue eyes only grow brighter. "You did? And what'd he reply?"

My smile overwhelms me for a second—just feeling her happiness for me. "He said that he loves me too."

Janie shakes my arms, elated, and then we catch each other up. Apparently the younger girls—Audrey Cobalt, Winona Meadows, and my sister Kinney—protested about not being able to join the tour. They made a PowerPoint presentation, and when our parents said *no*, they locked themselves in a lake house bedroom.

"It was dramatic and passionate," Jane finishes, "but they lost."

"Good. We don't need the youngest kids on the tour with us."

"Je suis d'accord." *I agree.* "The meet-and-greets are already very spontaneous," she says, "and Beckett and Sulli aren't as used to the spotlight as us. Having the teenagers here would be twice as chaotic."

My assistant just emailed me the schedule for the first leg of the tour, and I organized a crew to follow our bus. They'll set up the meet-and-greets at each convention center. Taking care of the tech aspects.

The H.M.C. charity team and I decided on an *unstructured* tour. We'll announce each FanCon city only the day before the meet-and-greet. It'll create more buzz and social media interaction. Fans will try to guess which city we'll be in next, and they'll keep checking to see if we'll be near them.

It also helps keep our location more anonymous on the road. And hopefully, more paparazzi will lose track of us.

I already know what else I need to tell Jane. "My sister thought she was pregnant," I let that bomb drop.

Janie's eyes widen. "Merde."

"Shit is right." I brush snow out of my hair. "She's not. Thank God." The test came back negative, and Luna just broke down sobbing in relief. "I thought about what you would've done if you were there."

"You did?" Jane clutches her elbows, cold.

I unzip my outer jacket. "I put on *The Fifth Element*—"

"One of Luna's favorite movies," Jane says, already knowing.

I nod. "And I made her a Pop-Tart."

Jane smiles. "She's lucky to have you as a brother."

"No, she's lucky I tapped into Jane Eleanor Cobalt's *Best Sibling Guide*." I shrug off my Patagonia jacket and hand it to her.

She sticks her arms in the holes and zips it up. "Merci."

I glance at the twelve-bunk sleeper bus. More of Omega lingers outside on purpose. Maybe they're taking bets on the status of our friendship. Weirdly, I'm kind of glad they care.

I ask Jane, "How are you and your parents?"

"We're not speaking really. I need time," she says. "You?"

I think back to the talk with my dad and mom. "Honestly, I don't know. They're not ready to forgive themselves, and there's not much I can do."

She asks about their feelings on Farrow, but my parents didn't even reach that topic. Maybe it's what Farrow said. It has less to do with him as my boyfriend and more to do with him breaking their trust as a bodyguard. Those weeds are too tall for me to crawl in, and so I don't start.

"What about your passion?" I ask, realizing that I haven't even brought this up. Not once. "You're supposed to be finding what you want to do."

"I will. Just...not now."

"Janie."

"I brought knitting." She crinkles her nose because she's tried knitting and she's not good. "It's something, but I don't think I'll have time...don't look at me like that. Our friendship comes first."

"You come first."

Jane pinches her eyes. "Don't make me cry. My tear ducts are in pain. They haven't been in this much use in ages."

I hug her again, and we chat for about ten more minutes, then we walk back to the bus—*fuck*. "I need to make a call," I tell her, our bodyguards reanimating and shoving the last of the supplies in the outside-accessible bays. "I'll tell you about it later."

A smile pulls her freckled cheeks. "Let's never fight again."

"Deal."

I step away from the bus and trek back to the curb. Searching for a number in my contacts. Cold drives through my gray sweatshirt, and my arms shake a bit.

Farrow rounds the bus, black boots crunching snow, and our eyes latch. He combs a hand through his *bleach-white* hair. He dyed the strands early, early this morning.

His features pop a billion times more. A barbell pierces his brown eyebrow again, and he stands like no stress on planet Earth could weigh him down.

God, I am colossally, uncontrollably attracted to him. I motion Farrow over to me, 100% subconscious. My brain zeroes in on him and just computes one word: *closer*.

Farrow hikes over, his masculine stride so casual and unhurried.

My muscles contract, blood pumping in my veins and rushing down. In one blip, I imagine us tangled together. Legs, arms, bodies welded—I want him all over me. His hands, his eyes, his emotion, his mind.

I solidify at one jarring thought.

I want to be smothered by my boyfriend.

Fuck.

Me.

"Maximoff." Farrow waves his hand at my face, pulling me from a somewhat-fantasy. His smile expands to James Franco territory.

Jesus. "I'm great. Thanks for asking."

"I didn't ask." His barbell rises with his brows, and my neck heats. "Where'd you go?"

"Neverland," I quip.

He rolls his eyes, but his *knowing* gaze drips down all six-foot-two of my build. "Next time," he says, "take me with you."

You were already there.

I swallow the words and my infatuation. Because I'm too apparent. He looks like he's about to catalogue this moment, frame it, and gift it to me. "I was thinking about the weather and tour route," I explain.

"Sure you were." His teasing smile strokes my cock. *Fuck me.* He notices my phone. "Making a call?"

"Yeah." *Focus.* "I'll put it on speaker." I scroll back through my contacts, and a large gust blows through the parking lot. Without my outer jacket, I shake way more than I want to.

Farrow suddenly moves behind me.

I lick my lips, pulse heightening in anticipation of the unknown.

He drapes his arm over my shoulder, then he clutches me around my collarbones. And he draws my strong back to his hard chest.

His warmth sheaths me, the embrace more intimate than I'd allow *anyone else.* With Farrow, I almost ease back, letting myself sink against him.

"Separate!"

"*Fuck,*" I curse and rip apart from Farrow. I run my tongue over my teeth. Fucking A. Thatcher is hawk-eyeing us from the damn tour bus. I stand more rigid on the curb and try to refocus on my phone.

Farrow is nailing the coldest glare into Thatcher, and then he clicks his mic. "We weren't even kissing."

From afar, I notice Thatcher clicking his mic and speaking.

Farrow unhooks his earpiece, letting the cord dangle on his shoulder, and he raises the volume on the radio.

Thatcher's voice filters through the earpiece speaker. "You look like a couple. You want to do that, do it on the bus. The windows are tinted."

Farrow is about to click his mic.

I hold up a hand. "Just drop it," I say. "We're in public right now, and we can't get caught." Thatcher thought we'd be less cautious now that family and security know we're together—and I'm starting to realize he was right. I didn't even think twice, and I should've.

Farrow's jaw muscle tics. "We're in the middle of fucking nowhere at eight a.m.—the risk is nonexistent."

"Not to him." I gesture to Thatcher. "And I don't want to burn that bridge. Not after he helped us."

Farrow combs two hands through his bleach-white hair. His nose flares, and then he half-heartedly nods. "Fine." He watches me scroll through my contacts. "Who are you calling?"

"Your father." I find Dr. Keene's number. "He keeps texting me to call him." *Now's the time.* I press the green button, and Farrow props his shoulder against the skeletal tree. He looks unconcerned but as curious as me.

"Moffy." Dr. Keene answers on the first ring. "I've been trying to reach you."

"Sorry." I lift the speaker to my mouth. "It's been hectic."

Farrow mouths, *don't apologize.* As though I'm being too nice.

I give him a middle finger.

Farrow almost smiles, but he eyes the phone as his father says, "That's not a problem. I heard you've been busy planning a meet-and-greet tour."

"Yeah." I turn my back to the roaring wind. "And I get why you're calling, but Farrow and I are happy, we're adults, and I hope you can respect our decision to be together. Even if it involved some risks."

The line goes quiet.

Farrow pushes off the tree, brows knotting, and he comes to my side. My voice is firm. "Dr. Keene?"

"You're together?" he questions. "As in…dating?"

Holy. Shit.

I'm in a slow-mo car crash. I find myself sinking into a crouch, my face buried in one hand. Why the hell did I assume he knew?

Dear World, can you die from embarrassment? Sincerely, a dying or possibly already dead human.

"What happened?!" Donnelly shouts from the bus.

I quickly cup my hand over my phone's speakers.

Farrow speaks hushed in his mic. "Shut up, Donnelly." Then he crouches in front of me.

"I think I'm dead." I grimace.

"You're breathing. You're alive." Farrow rests a hand on the curve between my shoulder and neck. "Come on."

I have to let this car crash happen. I crack a knuckle, then I uncover the speakers. "Dr. Keene?"

"I didn't know you and my son were together," he says, his voice unreadable.

I rise at the same time as Farrow. My muscles are set to broil. "I thought my parents told you," I say, my tone even-keeled despite my body *frying alive* from my fuck-up. I rarely make these kinds of mistakes. "And I assumed that's why you were calling." Stupidly. I glance at Farrow and my hard gaze carries a million-and-one apologies.

He mouths, *it's fine.*

"I'm calling," Dr. Keene says, "because you haven't had an STD screening in months. That didn't seem like you." He clears a tight ball from his throat. "Now I know why."

I'm fucking his son.

Dammit. I don't know what to say. This is the first time I've dealt with a significant other's parent. I'm not a normal human being either. I'm a celebrity from birth, American royalty, so I have no idea the correct protocol for any of this.

First thing that comes to my head, I tell Dr. Keene, "We're safe."

Farrow chokes on the brittle air, and he shakes his head vigorously at me and mouths, *no.* Like he doesn't want his father in on his sex life. I get that now.

He's twenty-seven. I'm sure he stopped talking to his father about that shit eons ago. That is, if he ever talked to him about it at all.

"Farrow is still your bodyguard?" Dr. Keene questions. "How?"

"Our relationship is staying secret from the public," I tell him, and Farrow fixates on the phone in deep thought.

"Right. Be safe on the tour. Have a good rest of the day."

After I say my goodbye, we hang up.

Farrow shakes his head a few times. "That's not good." He points at my phone. "That fucker has the strongest motive to leak our relationship to the public."

I rub my sharpened jaw. "You really think he'd try to get you kicked off security?"

"To force me back onto a medical career path, yeah. I do."

I start thinking about avenues we can take. "I'll fix it." *I can make a call—*

Farrow steals my phone.

"*Farrow*—"

"Wolf scout, you can't patch bullet holes before the trigger is pulled. Take your own advice, and just drop it."

I crack a crick in my neck. "The doing nothing thing—I'm not good at."

"No shit." He laughs when I glare.

I fight a smile. "Shut up."

He leans towards me and lowers his voice to a sexy whisper, "See, every time you try to fix unfixable things, just imagine me pounding you so hard you cry when you come."

Fuck me. My cock stirs, and I look at his mouth. *Kiss me, man.* "Sounds like fan fiction."

Farrow watches me drinking him in, and his smile widens. "Trust me, it can easily be reality." We somehow drift closer. Nearer. Hands on each other's shoulders, slipping to the back of his neck, my neck—and my body thumps for more contact.

Mouths inches away, I breathe, "Bite me."

He kisses me hard and then nips my lip, *fuck yes*—

"Separate!"

We do, and Farrow fits his earpiece in with the shake of his head. "If he does this the entire trip, I'm going to strangle him."

9

Farrow Keene

FIVE HOURS AND TWENTY-THREE minutes into the drive—
the tour bus rolling along the interstate towards the first convention
stop—and someone is already bleeding.

Instantly, I stand and guide my boyfriend into the small bathroom,
his hands cupped under his nose. The luxury tour bus is split into four
sections, from the front to back:

Driver seat and passenger seat.

First lounge: two gray couches, chair and booth, television, granite
counter with a coffee pot, sink and microwave; ice chest and fridge,
and then a door leads to the bathroom/shower.

Sleeping bunks: on either side of a narrow hallway includes two
rows of bunks, stacked three high. Twelve total.

Second lounge: a U-shaped couch, tabletop, and a television and
game console.

Almost all of us were playing poker in the second lounge, and
really, when you put that many people in a confined space, this shit is
bound to happen. But out of eleven people, the one person I'd choose
not to be bleeding is gushing blood right now.

"Pinch your nose," I instruct and chew my gum.

"Fuck," he curses, his palms crimson from the steady nosebleed.
He starts to tilt his head backwards on instinct. *Come on, wolf scout.*

"Maximoff." My hand rises from his shoulder to neck. "Stay bent forward. Turn to me." I need to see if the bone is fractured.

Before he does either, a voice distracts him.

"What…in the ever-loving-fuck," Sulli curses in the doorway, jaw unhinging. "I'm so fucking sorry. I just get so competitive and…*fuck*." She won the last hand of poker, and she sprung up in excitement and accidentally elbowed Maximoff in the face.

He keeps his hand cupped beneath his nose. "I'm alright, Sul."

She inches inside as Donnelly and Beckett fill the narrow hallway to watch. Only three bodies max are able to fit in this cramped bathroom. Jane would be here, but she's sleeping in a bunk with earplugs.

Blissfully unaware.

But the more onlookers, the more Maximoff turns his back on them, just to decrease their concern.

Shit, I need him to bend forward, pinch his nose, and face me. He sort of corners himself by the faucet and pretends like he has everything under control.

In one motion, I hop up on the counter. Sitting, but I'm still a few inches taller. And I seize his waist and draw him towards me. "Pinch your nose or I'll do it for you—"

I smile at his immediate reaction, his fingers automatically pinching his nose and forest-green eyes automatically narrowing.

The guy doesn't like being coddled any more than I do.

I hold his jaw and guide his head forward and a little downward. I can feel him watching me as I examine the bridge of his nose.

By sight alone, the break isn't clear. His nose isn't sitting crooked on his face, but it swells. Skin in the corner of his eyes also reddens, the start of bruising.

His voice is stuffed as he tells me, "It's not that bad."

I pop my gum. "That's cute that you think I can't tell if it's serious or not." I glance at the three spectators. "Get me ice."

Sulli darts out. "Kits, where's the ice?"

Beckett slips further inside the bathroom, clutching the neck of a beer, and he scans the trickles of blood along the stone tile.

Maximoff pulls out of my hand. "I'll clean it later. Watch out, Beckett."

"I've seen worse." Beckett puts his beer to his lips. "You've forgotten that I've lived on my own in New York for the past three years. I've grown up. Independent and free." He outstretches his arms before looking at me from head-to-toe. Sizing me up for the fourth time, and that's just counting today.

See, what I know of Beckett Cobalt is mostly based on bodyguard-talk, and Donnelly told me that Beckett is anti-relationships from trust issues being a celebrity.

He's cautious of me. Either he believes I'm going to fuck and chuck Maximoff or toy with his emotions. Both of which, I'm not subscribing to.

But I'm not about to convince a twenty-year-old that I'm "here for the right reasons" and prefer long-term relationships.

I raise my brows at him. "Question?"

Beckett licks beer off his lips. "Not at the moment." Then he shakes his head at Maximoff. "She was one elbow away from me, and you were hit. You have the worst luck."

"It's the Hale Curse," Donnelly says, propping his tattooed arm on the door frame and drinking a beer.

I roll my eyes and gesture Maximoff closer.

"The what?" Maximoff asks, his brows knotted, but he edges nearer and stands between my legs. I clutch his jaw again and inspect his nose.

"Don't ask him," I tell Maximoff. "Donnelly tattooed *Cobalts Never Die* on his knee. He'd create imaginary curses for any family but that one."

Beckett grins into his swig of beer. "That's true."

Donnelly ignores his client and motions his bottle to Maximoff. "The Hale Curse. If there's a Hale in the room: what could go wrong, will go wrong to the Hale. Statistically proven."

The security team basically loses their shit whenever Beckett makes the face that he's making now. It's a scrunched-up, un-replicated *you idiot, that's utter bullshit* face.

"Statistically proven," Beckett says, "zero percent of the time."

Maximoff starts smiling, even covered in blood.

I barely glance at Donnelly. "Looks like your client is smarter than you."

Donnelly pats Beckett's back. "Learned from the best. Me." *Such a buddy-guard.*

Oscar squeezes through the hallway. "That's a negative thing, Donnelly." He skids to a halt by the door and winces at Maximoff. "*Ouch.*"

Quinn peeks his head in. "God, I know how that feels." He points at the scar along his crooked nose. "Two years ago, right hook in the ring."

"What's that scar from?" Sulli wedges in and points at the tiny scar below his eye, and she tosses the ice baggie wrapped in a towel to Beckett. He catches it.

I'd really love for this unnecessary audience to evacuate the bathroom and hallway and stop distracting Maximoff. Who at this point has completely rotated his head away from them, and he stares at the wall.

"Skin split from another boxing match," Quinn says. "I KO'd the other guy."

Oscar and Donnelly start clapping in jest, and normally, I would've joined the mock applause, but I need these fuckers out of the bathroom.

"Okay." I chew my gum. "I can't do my best work with you bastards shadowing the light." I'm not about to say, *hey guys, Maximoff has trouble being vulnerable in front of people, so please kindly exit.* No. I gesture to the Omega bodyguards. "Get the fuck out."

As Donnelly leaves, he blows me a middle-finger kiss, and Oscar makes some remark about me being territorial. Quinn asks if I need anything, and Oscar sticks his head back in, just to mouth, *my brother loves you.* He bats his lashes.

I pop my gum and just tell Quinn, "Ibuprofen for Maximoff."

Once they disperse, Beckett stays in the bathroom with Sulli in the doorway.

I train my focus on Maximoff. "I need to touch your nose and feel for a fracture."

His joints lock up.

I'm not going to hurt you. I express that through my eyes, and then he nods. I lightly skim my thumb down the swollen bridge before pinching a little.

He shuts his eyes for a moment, the only sign of pain. "I'm fine," he tries to assure me.

I concentrate on a centimeter of bone, adding almost no force as I run my finger back and forth. *Shit.* I drop my hand when I'm 100% certain.

"He's prone to nosebleeds," Beckett tells me. "This happened years back at that yacht party, and the bone didn't break."

Maximoff holds my gaze strongly, both of us remembering that moment. I was there. I stood on the yacht deck and saw him fight Charlie on the dock below.

He was nineteen.

I was twenty-four, on the very, *very* cusp of a career change from medicine to security. Even back then, I found myself investing my interest in Maximoff Hale.

I wanted to intervene on his behalf. Fuck, I would've loved to pull him out of that fight. But a silent Hale-Cobalt-Meadows declaration always hangs in the air: *do not interject in familial arguments.*

Even me, the maverick on the security team, hasn't bent that rule out of shape, but to come to his aid, I've wanted to.

Many times.

Maximoff breaks eye contact and fixes a narrowed look on his cousin. "Thanks, Beckett," he says dryly.

"I didn't bring it up to be an asshole," Beckett clarifies. "Farrow should know your medical history."

Maximoff growls in frustration and tries to roll his head backwards.

I tighten my grip on his jaw, keeping him bent forward. "Don't move."

"Just tell me the diagnosis," Maximoff says, still pinching his nose. "I need facial reconstructive surgery, right? A brain transplant tomorrow? Probably a full-body cast and a coffin fitting?"

I smile while chewing my gum. *This guy, man.* "You can keep going."

He glowers. "I'm done."

"That's too bad," I say seriously and slide off the counter, my chest brushing up against his chest. I keep hold of his jaw. "I love watching a Harvard Dropout self-diagnose a nosebleed as a full-body injury."

He'd flip me off if he could.

My hand descends, and I rub the back of his neck. My other fingers hover by his wrist. "Bleeding looks like it's slowed." I draw his hand down so he stops pinching his nose. No blood dripping. That's good.

"And?" he asks.

"No surgery, no X-rays. You only need ice and pain meds. It's just a small break." I've seen several minor nose fractures in the ER like his. I take the ice from Beckett. "Keep the ice across the bridge of your nose and be gentle. It'll help with swelling."

His shoulders loosen, relaxed at the news. I know what concerns him—and it's not pain—it's calling the concierge doctor, scheduling a surgery date, and derailing the meet-and-greet tour where fans, crew, and everyone on the bus are counting on him.

Maximoff splays the ice baggie across the bone, and I wash my hands in the sink.

"I'm so fucking sorry," Sulli says again. "If you want to bail on the ultra marathon, I totally get it."

Maximoff speaks for three full minutes, assuring Sulli that he can easily still run. The race isn't soon either, and regardless, they won't have that much time to train on tour.

Beckett sips his beer and watches me wipe my hands on a towel. Blue and yellow braided "friendship" bracelets are tied loose on his wrists. Identical to the ones on Sulli's ankles.

He has a question for me. I can tell. "Ask," I say and toss the towel on the counter.

"Is Maximoff your first relationship?"

"No."

Maximoff extends his hand. "Beckett, let's not go here, alright?"

Beckett turns on him. "Have you asked Farrow why his other relationships ended? Did he break up with them or was it the other way around? How many guys has he been in love with—"

"Man," I cut him off, "no offense, but I'm not in a relationship with you. If Maximoff wants these answers, I'll tell him, but I'm not holding a public forum."

Beckett skims the length of me for the fifth time now. "Why not? You have something to hide?"

"Stop, Beck," Maximoff warns.

Sulli wavers uneasily, disliking confrontation.

"I'm just looking out for you, Moffy," Beckett says while zeroing in on me. As though I'm prey, but it'd take more than this kid's skepticism to arch my back and reach for a figurative gun.

I lift my brows and chew my gum casually. He stares harder. My nonchalance is grating on him.

"I appreciate the concern," Maximoff says, "but I'm *highly* capable of dealing with my relationship on my own." His voice is firm and unyielding. All alpha.

My smile stretches, roped in for a second, but as I turn, I realize quickly that Beckett mistakes my reaction for arrogance. Like I'm toting a win over his head and smirking, *Maximoff took my side, not yours.*

Not the case.

Not the truth.

"I don't play under the table," Beckett says to me, "so I'm putting this out in the open." He mimics me, raising his brows. "I don't trust you—"

"You don't trust me because you don't know me—"

"Whatever the case," Beckett says.

And I spot Akara in my peripheral, lingering. He whispers to Sulli, and she nods before slipping out.

Beckett continues, "If you betray my cousin, all seven Cobalts will destroy you far worse than you could ever hurt him."

"Fair enough," I say, more so acknowledging Akara who motions me out of the bathroom. As I leave into the first lounge, Maximoff shuts the door and starts talking privately with Beckett.

Most of SFO are spread out on the gray couches, eavesdropping. Oscar stands and whispers to me, "They haven't dealt with siblings or cousins in serious relationships. You're the first."

"I realize that." I comb a hand through my bleached hair. "You know Kinney Hale would've stabbed you in the eye for calling her ex-girlfriend not serious."

Oscar motions from his chest to mine. "You and I know puppy love isn't serious. What is she, nine?"

"Thirteen." I run my hand over my jawline. "She'll 'revoke' your membership to that Rainbow Brigade shit if you're not careful."

Oscar almost laughs, and he reties a rolled bandana around his forehead. "It's not real until she makes pins."

"Tell her that." I glance at Akara who finishes chatting with someone on a bunk. He motions me further down the hall and into the second lounge.

Before I follow, Oscar lowers his voice another octave. "Seriously though, I know Maximoff is one of the hottest celebrities, and I can imagine what the sex is like—"

"No you can't," I say easily.

His mouth parts. "Now I'm gonna need details."

I let out a short laugh and glance at Akara, who's waiting. "Oscar—"

"You have to ask yourself," he whispers, "if dealing with these families on a personal level, not professional, is really worth it. Because I know you, you'll get in the trenches and fight until you die. But now's the time to step out while you still can."

I chew my gum slowly and shake my head. "I'd never commit, fuck a guy, then break up. And I'm not about to crush him because I'm scared of his family when I'm not even a little bit afraid."

"And your lack of fear makes me uneasy," Oscar says outright, "but you do you, Redford. When this crashes and burns, it'll be my turn to take you out for drinks."

I roll my eyes.

He broke up with his long-term boyfriend in college, and I took him to a bar so he'd stop texting Darrien.

And I may've bought him one Corona.

Without another word, I finally make my way to the second lounge. Only Akara here.

He rests against the tabletop and snaps his fingers to his palm. "So first thing, did you read the SFO email?"

"Yeah."

Thatcher sent the email to all of us at the crack of dawn. I barely skimmed the words, but I can recite the entire "memorandum" by heart.

SFO Rules on Tour (not to be negotiated or disputed):
1. SFO will take shifts driving the tour bus. Since Paul Donnelly & Quinn Oliveira failed the driver's test to operate the bus, only Akara Kitsuwon, Farrow Keene, Oscar Oliveira, and Thatcher Moretti will drive.

Thatcher has been behind the wheel for the past hour.

2. The tour bus acts as a "home on wheels" and for this reason, you're considered "off-duty" on the bus. You're not required to wear radios on the bus, but you must immediately wear them once you step off. Keep your phones charged in case Alpha or Epsilon need to reach you.

3. Bus doors must be locked at all times.

4. Alert the driver if your client leaves the bus. Always join your client. Don't leave their side.

5. Any guests must be vetted before allowed on the bus. NDAs are required.

6. We'll drive through nights, so please be respectful of those sleeping. Don't bang doors.

7. Some conventions will include overnight stays at hotels. Bodyguards must stay in the hotel room with your client. It's likely some clients will want to room together (i.e. Sulli & Jane) – make note of this.

8. There are nine men to two women. Please respect their space.

9. Recognize that the tour crew isn't allowed on the bus. You are. Understand this honor, and ensure the protection of your client.

10. Lastly, remember the hierarchy. You have any concerns, bring them to Akara or Thatcher.

"Good," Akara says. "Thatcher wanted to make sure you didn't just delete it."

"Of course he did." I notice the severity in Akara's face. "What's wrong?"

He checks over my shoulder, but no one is eavesdropping. Then he whispers, "Tech team traced the IP address of the Instagram account. The user is from Philly."

I don't blink. "The probability that they know Maximoff—"

"Is a lot higher," Akara finishes. "The user blocked the tech team, and now there's a firewall stalling us."

"Shit."

"Possible motives for someone to make a personal 'death threat' account would be revenge." Akara pauses as the bathroom door swings open, and we both shift. Our backs to the hall. "Omega is going to quietly work on unmasking the anonymous user, and while we gather intel, don't obsess over the account."

I frown. "How is the account still active? We flagged it."

"We need it to stay live now," Akara explains. "If the user really is plotting to hurt Maximoff, that account is the only evidence we can track."

I nod, my gaze searing. Everything inside of me craves and pleads to solve this now and free Maximoff from a threat. To keep him safe. *Protect him.*

But I'm on a bus.

Headed towards a sleepless city, and his fast-paced life isn't stopping for anyone.

10

Maximoff Hale

FARROW DRIVES THE GRAVEYARD shift. On route to Cleveland. I camp out in the passenger seat and keep him company.

I prefer Farrow driving over pretty much everyone else. I can fucking admit that I've been on edge. I'd do just about anything to sit behind the steering wheel, except break the law.

Which leaves me with a bucket load of nothing. Unfortunately.

Lights dimmed, the bus hums. Quiet. Bodyguards and my family sleep in their bunks. The privacy door is slid closed, so we're shut out from the first lounge. And only one paparazzi van has been trailing us. With tinted windows, there's not much cameramen can catch.

Farrow keeps one tattooed hand on the steering wheel, posture all cool confidence. His left foot is perched on the seat, arm relaxed on his bent knee. He constantly glances at me with an ever-growing know-it-all smile.

My blood simmers. I crack a knuckle or two and shift in my seat.

I never thought a lot about *chemistry* or how his unperturbed energy would be compatible with my strong-wired, but something about Farrow just drives me nuts. My pulse pounds harder than my broken nose throbs.

Every damn time I'm with him, it feels like the first time we're together. He's inched under my skin, into my blood stream, definitely my brain—I've been a fucking goner since I was sixteen. And I still haven't fully accepted this fact.

That someone in my life is here for me. Because they love me. A romantic love. Not family, not solely friendship. It still seems unbelievable.

I don't know why.

"What are you thinking?" he asks.

I unconsciously glance at his zipper. Fuck my sexually frustrated brain.

He tilts his head, and then eyes the road with a satisfied smile. "You dreaming of fucking me?"

I give him a weird look while I prop my foot on the dashboard. Trying my hand at relaxing. It feels strange. "Why would I dream about it when I can just fuck you?"

"Because you're not fucking me right here, wolf scout."

He knows I usually get what I want as a celebrity. And him telling me *no*—it just sets my body on fire. I drop my foot, my muscles flexed and abs tight. "Hold on, let me wish upon a star," I say, sarcasm thick.

He glances at me, the road, then the bulge in my jeans. It's a normal bulge. Don't get excited. "How pent-up are you?"

"Not enough to ram my dick in your ass and kill everyone in the back."

He rolls his eyes and then smiles. "Always a precious smartass." He unwraps a piece of gum and steers by propping his knee on the wheel.

"I've seen way too many movies where a couple dies because one is blowing the driver. Death by blowjob—*not* how I'm dying."

"Okay, that's not what I asked." He crumples the foil and tosses it in the change tray. "Time hasn't really been on our side lately, and if you need to jack off without me, I won't be pissed." He focuses on the road as the GPS directs him off the exit. "That's not a hall pass, by the way."

"Wait a minute." I sit up straighter. "You're telling me people stop masturbating when they get in a relationship?"

He checks his side mirror. "I never expect it, but I've been with someone who did."

I grimace. "Fuck that guy."

Farrow starts smiling. "And you do know what a hall pass is, right?"

I blink into a glare. "No."

"Sarcasm?"

"Yes. Jesus Christ." I growl out my irritation.

"Just checking. You seem a little—"

"Don't say it." I'd literally cover his mouth if he weren't driving right now.

"Pure."

I flip him off, and in the next brief glance, he studies the corners of my eyes, the skin beneath bleeding black-and-blue. I've checked in a mirror. I'll need to conceal the bruises with makeup before the meet-and-greet.

I watch his palm and fingers rub his knee before he clutches the wheel again. Talking about sex just sends me down a rabbit hole. An abnormal, really strange abyss that no one would expect, but he can tell I'm drifting somewhere. Mentally.

"What are you really thinking about?" he asks.

I try to lean back. "My mom."

Weight sinks in the air at those two words, but he waits for me to continue.

I inhale a strong breath. "I was just thinking about how difficult a trip like this would've been for her—if she were here at my age, still battling her sex addiction." I lick my lips. "I don't know. It's the small stuff. Like, would she have wanted to stop the bus and screw my dad? Would she be fidgeting or upset? Or would they've just fucked on the couch? Then I start thinking about how fucking weird it is to be casually *thinking* about my parent's sex life."

He opens the cap to a Lightning Bolt! energy drink. "It's your normal," he tells me. "It doesn't have to be everyone else's." He sips the drink, then offers me the slender can.

I take a swig and pass it back, remembering how non-judgmental and open-minded Farrow is—and yeah, I like it. I can't have someone in my private life belittling me for not being perfect. I get that too much online.

Farrow merges onto another freeway. "What would you've done if you weren't rich and famous?" he asks me. "For a career?"

That alternate universe. "You don't know?"

"Why would I?"

"It's public knowledge. Every time press interviews me, they ask that question." It reminds me of something Beckett said in the bathroom. Something that I've tried not to let creep into my brain like a parasitic insecurity.

Beckett told me, *"For every 200 facts Farrow knows about you, you only know 2 facts about him. So what do you really even know about Farrow? I'm not trying to be a dick. Just be careful. You're not the kind of person who lets anyone in, and he's slipped past all your guards, hasn't he?"*

He has, and maybe I haven't grilled Farrow enough or fucking quizzed him as much as Beckett would. But I hate being indecisive or even doubtful about my own actions. I like to move and speak with assuredness, and even this morsel of uncertainty makes me *cringe*.

Farrow is quiet trying to find a memory. "Didn't you joke around in those interviews?" He switches lanes. "Unless you were serious when you said you wanted to be an intergalactic bounty hunter."

"I was serious, and I was four," I say.

He pops his gum, about to laugh. "When I asked, I was asking the twenty-two-year-old in the passenger seat. Not the four-year-old."

"Right." I lick my lips, restraining a smile. "Truthfully, I try not to think about that alternate universe, but sometimes...I know where I'd be."

Farrow holds my gaze for a longer moment, understanding in his brown eyes. "The military," he says with a nod, beating me to the answer.

"Yeah, the military," I say. *He knows me.* Really well. I rake a hand through my hair, my gray paracord bracelet still tied around my wrist. I don't take it off that often. "So your past relationships..."

He checks the directions on his phone's GPS. "I was wondering when you'd ask."

So he knew Beckett's words would seep into my brain somehow. Some fucking way.

Farrow sets his phone down. "Whatever you want to know, I'll answer." He's always said as much.

I instinctively shake my head. "It's not that big of a deal. A huge, colossal part of me hasn't wanted details about your exes, which is why I haven't pried before."

Picturing him with other guys when I have strong feelings for him—I start scowling, then wincing. Almost like I've sprayed Pam or Lysol in my eyes. No, actually, I'd rather spray my eyes with household products than hear in grave-fucking-detail how Farrow fell in love with another man.

My brows furrow with another thought. "I don't know what people typically do in serious relationships." My shoulders tighten. "I don't know…should I ask you and pry? Is that the *right* thing?"

His smile breaks through. "Wolf scout, just do what you feel. There's no right or wrong here. And there aren't any 'best boyfriend' merit badges on the line or even 'worst boyfriend'—I promise, you're safe either way."

My carriage rises in a deeper breath, confidence surging back. I rotate some, just to face him. "I don't need to know any of your exes' names or anything like that. But I'm just curious…did you break it off or did they?"

"One was a mutual break up." He takes a larger gulp of energy drink. "The other three, I ended things first." He glances at me, and I listen intently, interested in his past. "One had to move out of the country for work, and I didn't want to do a long-distance relationship. The other two, I wasn't feeling after a while."

"You grew bored or something?" I ask.

Farrow tosses his head from side-to-side, considering this. "Or something." He places his drink back down. "I never actively looked for a *forever* guy, but at some point, I'd wake up and I'd think, *can I do this for another year, two years, three?* And if the answer was constantly *no*, then I broke it off."

Huh.

I stare faraway for a long beat. "Even if you loved the guy?" Our eyes catch.

Then he focuses on the road again, but his body is still completely relaxed. "I don't think I loved them as much as I could've or else I'd still be with them and not talking in the past tense."

I ease back. I don't need extra reassurance or for him to promise that I'll be the *forever* guy. Because this is fucking brand new for me, and I can't foresee the future either. But right now, he's mine.

I'm his, and there's no better feeling than that.

"Is that it?" he asks, sounding surprised.

"You usually go for jocks or am I an outlier?"

His smile stretches wider and wider. *Fuck me.* I want his mouth wrapped around my cock like yesterday.

"Are you an outlier?" he repeats my words with a husky voice, and his gum chewing habit somehow bolsters his casual confidence to the umpteenth degree. In a boiling glance, his gaze just scorches down my body. "I've gone for jocks before, but not a lot look like you." He motions to my face. "Supermodel." Then points to my abs. "Athlete."

"So you're saying I'm hotter than you."

His smile reaches cheek-to-cheek. "I'm absolutely still hotter than you, wolf scout."

I believe it, but I also want to contest it. Just to prolong this damn moment. "Says who?"

"Your cock."

My muscles contract. We both stare at each other's *mouths*. I want to kiss the fuck out of him. Until his body welds against my body and separating would take a century.

I grab his hand that rests on his knee, and he must sense my next action because he takes control and places his palm on my thigh, jean fabric between his skin and my skin.

He slides his hand towards the inside, closer to my pulsing cock—he's teasing but not able to do anything real while behind the wheel.

We're both used to *no touching* while driving in Philly, but on this tinted bus, it's safer. So Farrow touching me—in any capacity—I'll hungrily take.

He gives me another long once-over before watching the highway. "What kind of guys do you usually go for?" he asks.

"I was only looking for sex, a one-night stand," I remind him. "But I gravitated towards men the same size as me or bigger. Pretty much any guy who looked like they'd want to manhandle me."

Farrow chews his gum slowly in thought. "But you wouldn't let them take control in bed." He knows how aggressive I am.

"Right."

He sucks in a breath. "Damn."

I hear something more in his voice. "What?"

"That's a fine line, especially since you're famous." His eyes flit to me. "They could've easily hurt you."

"They didn't," I assure him.

He nods, and his hand slides towards my knee. He rubs my leg, almost comfortingly. In a way that relaxes me against my seat. *He cares about me.*

I could get way too used to this.

We start talking about nineties bands when he raises the stereo volume. Not loud enough to wake everyone else. Halfway through, he off-handily mentions *Thatcher* being a stick-in-the-mud asshole.

"What's your deal with Thatcher anyway?" I ask and swig from a bottle of Ziff.

"The fucker tased me."

I choke on my sports drink. "What?" I wipe my mouth with the back of my arm. "You're joking."

"I'm not," he says. "We worked an event together a couple years ago in New York—"

"What event?" It had to be related to my family.

"You weren't there," he prefaces. "It was a cover photo-shoot for Forbes magazine, and paparazzi leaked our location."

I remember my parents, Aunt Rose and Uncle Connor, and Aunt Daisy and Uncle Ryke were all on that cover together. "Why was Thatcher there if he was assigned to Xander?"

"We took extra security that day." Farrow looks to me, then the road. "Once we exited the building, all hell broke loose. Paparazzi stormed Lily's car before I led her to the door. Hecklers appeared, and one tried to grab your Aunt Rose's purse." He shakes his head. "By that time, I'd already safely locked Lily in her car without me. I could see this dickhole behind me, messing with Rose. I turned, cold-cocked him, and as soon as I put a hand on Rose's back—I was tased."

"Why would he do that?"

"Thatcher said he 'mistook' me for the shithead I punched. But it just so happens that the only mistake he's ever made sent electric volts through my body. *Sure*." He rolls his eyes. "We're not supposed to take out our weapons in crowded areas. It causes fear, panic—and we're hired to deescalate these situations. Thatcher knew that. Yet, the rule-abider did it."

My mouth parts in shock. "Fuck...I can't believe he *tased* you."

Farrow lets out a short laugh. "My first day on the job, he made me do a 19K in the Poconos Mountains. Alone. In the dark. The first day for Donnelly, a pancake breakfast. I can't fabricate this shit." He flips on his blinker and switches lanes. Letting a speeding car pass.

Since Thatcher is a lead, he has power over Farrow. Just picturing him using his position against my boyfriend—my jaw sharpens. "And now, I want to go kick his ass."

His lips quirk. "That's sweet that you think I need protecting."

"Maybe you do."

Farrow changes radio stations, his smile extraordinarily large.

Before he says, *you're the famous one* or *you can't be the knight in every situation*, I ask him, "Why did Thatcher single you out?"

"Before I was hired to your mom's detail, Thatcher's twin brother was supposed to fill the position. But Lily found out that I finished security training, and she requested me."

Realization washes over me.

Farrow Keene used to just be the son of our concierge doctor, and my parents had always really liked him. So I could definitely see my mom requesting Farrow as her 24/7 bodyguard.

Farrow watches my reaction for a second, his tattooed hand back on my thigh.

I place my palm on top of his hand and twist one of his silver rings. "I didn't know any of that."

"You wouldn't. That kind of information stays in security." He pauses. "Do me a favor? Grab the USB from the—"

I already lean forward and open the glove box. In a quick second, I connect his phone to the stereo and put on his nineties playlist.

He nods a couple times, a smile in his eyes. And I wonder if he's thinking, *Maximoff knows me. Really well.*

I lick my lips. "So you took Bank's job and that put you on Thatcher's shit list?"

"Partly." He uses his left hand to drive. "I wasn't just the guy that took his brother's job. I was the son of the family's doctor, a guy who had little security experience, who hated rules, and who was now the bodyguard to Lily Calloway. In Thatcher's eyes, I was given the position without earning it." Farrow chews his gum with a smile. "Little did he know, I'm the best at everything I do."

My brows scrunch. "It's like one minute you make sense and the next, it's Klingon."

Farrow stares at me for as long as he can, then fixes on the road. "Not ashamed to say that I don't know what the fuck that means."

"Let this go on every record that ever exists: I know something that you don't."

Farrow glances back. "Enjoy this while it lasts because it won't last long."

"I always last longer than you," I retort.

Farrow whistles. "The last time I made you come must've really fucked with your memory."

"Did you make me come?" I feign confusion and shift in my seat. "I'm not sure you did."

He smiles out at the road. "Don't worry, I'll remind you what it felt like."

Fucking Christ. My brain, my body—all the Team Farrow pieces of me *crave* and beg to cash in on that right now.

Then my phone buzzes in my back pocket. It's late for most of my family to be texting. As I unpocket my phone, I think about how Farrow has already proven himself to the security team by keeping my mom safe.

Alpha may complain about him, but I've seen the Tri-Force radio Farrow in high-stress situations. Like during the Hallow Friends Eve incident, Akara turned to him *first*. When push-comes-to-shove, the entire security team trusts and relies on Farrow. Knowing he'll be there and he'll be ready.

If this weren't true, he would've been fired a while ago. And Thatcher would've never voted to keep him around.

I ask Farrow, "Thatcher knows you're good at what you do, so why does he still hate you?"

"Because I haven't proven myself to his standards." Farrow rotates the wheel, taking a sharp exit onto a ramp.

Maybe it has to do with Thatcher's upbringing. "His dad was a Navy SEAL, right?"

Farrow frowns. "How do you know that?"

"Xander mentioned it once." I click into my recent texts.

I AM SUCH A LOSER!!! — Tom

I straighten up because that doesn't sound like Tom Cobalt. Before I even reply, another text pops up.

I'm gonna go die now — Tom

Farrow eagle-eyes me while I ditch texting and just call my seventeen-year-old cousin. I put my cell to my ear and unplug Farrow's phone from the USB. "Call Tom's bodyguard. Something's not right."

11

Farrow Keene

I KEEP AN EYE on the darkened road and use one hand to speak in my phone. *"Call Ian Wreath."*

I'm out of radio-range from Epsilon and Alpha while we drive away from Philly and NYC. And I haven't kept track of the families in the team's daily logs.

I prop my phone to my ear with my shoulder. Streets begin to narrow now that I'm off the highway.

We're a little less than five minutes from the hotel to sleep overnight. Which is about a mile from where the convention is taking place. Maximoff didn't book rooms in the same hotel as the Cleveland meet-and-greet. Because that'd be a security nightmare.

"Tom?" Maximoff lowers the phone, his gaze hardened. "He hung up on me."

My line clicks. "Ian?" I press *speakerphone* so Maximoff can hear. "You out somewhere with Tom?" Drums bang loudly in the background.

"Why do you want to know?!" he yells over the cacophony.

I don't like SFE, and SFE doesn't like me. It's been written in stone. "Man, I'm asking for my client. I wouldn't call you for shits and giggles."

"What does Maximoff want?!"

Maximoff instantly takes over. "Where's Tom?"

Bass and guitar strums through the speaker. "We're at his bandmate's house!"

"Let me talk to him," Maximoff says, not shitting around.

"TOM!" Ian shouts, and after muffled sounds, the bang of a drum, crash of an object, laughter and more chatter, Tom speaks.

"Moffy! What's up, dude?"

Maximoff cups my cellphone. "Have you been texting me? Where's your phone?"

I picture Tom patting his pockets, and his voice fades. "Which one of you douchebags took my phone?" More laughter.

I put two-and-two together: a kid stole Tom's phone and texted Maximoff as a prank. I spit out my stale gum. I'm fucking irritated at Ian.

Maximoff keeps shaking his head, and he tries to stretch his flexed arm over his chest.

See, the mistake is on the bodyguard. Ian shouldn't have let anyone steal his client's phone. If Tom set it down, his bodyguard should've picked it up. Simple as that.

"Sorry, Moffy," Tom says, voice louder. "My bandmate has a bad sense of humor. Phone's back."

"You staying there all night?" Maximoff asks.

I pull into the hotel parking lot, the clock blinking 4:32 a.m., and once I stop in *bus parking*, I switch off the ignition.

"Yeah, I'm crashing here," Tom says. "Wait a sec." I hear footsteps, as though he's walking somewhere more private. Background noise deadens.

Maximoff unbuckles his seatbelt the same time as me. I zip up my leather jacket, and he reaches around the seat and finds his plain green sweatshirt.

Tom continues, "There's this dude here named Freddie, my bandmate's friend of a friend, and he keeps going on and on about how you and him hooked up one night."

I go still, bus keys in my hand. If they did hook up in the past, the fuckwad is breaking his NDA by talking about it.

And since the @maximoffdeadhale user has become a real threat, everyone who personally knows Maximoff is on my radar. I'm beginning to realize that any of his one-night stands could be culpable.

I don't know how many people that could be. I never asked for a number. I never sifted through his old NDAs. I didn't need or want to, but if I need to now…

My nose flares, mixed emotions slamming at me.

Maximoff brick-walls his features. I can't read him. He tells Tom, "I don't remember a Freddie."

"He said you were the best lay he's ever had. I thought you should know in case he's violating a privacy contract, but if he's just lying—"

"Ignore him," Maximoff says and grabs his dark Ray Bans. "Give the phone to your bodyguard."

I re-lace one of my boots and tug on black gloves. Then I stand out of my seat and holster my Glock in my waistband. The most tedious prep for the tour was applying for each state's gun permits.

"One more thing," Tom says. "I've sobered up a lot, but I, uh, took Fireball shots, and during those minutes or hours, I said some things I shouldn't have—but I think they think I'm full of shit. So we're all good."

Fucking hell.

I collect my radio, untwisting the wires to the earpiece, and I descend a few steps to the bus door.

"What'd you say?" Maximoff asks, lifting his hood over his head. He stands too and sheaths a hunting knife on his ankle. He also pockets a tactical switchblade.

He won't need those, but I know he feels safer armed.

"I was trying to defend my sister," Tom explains, referring to Jane, "and to stick up for her, I mentioned that you're dating someone."

Maximoff scowls.

I stay relatively at ease and hook my radio to my black belt. If Tom didn't say my name, we're fine.

Maximoff knows this, too, so he asks, "Did you say who?"

"I told them *Zac Efron*, hence why they think I'm full of shit. If this ends up in *Celebrity Crush* tomorrow, I also know they're all assholes."

Maximoff follows me down the steps. "Thanks for telling me. Go easy on the Fireball—"

"I will—here's my bodyguard." He must hand the phone to Ian.

I hang my earpiece on my shoulder and start unlocking the bus door. Maximoff is one step behind me. If he thinks he's leaving the bus with me, he's mistaken.

"Hey?" Ian says.

"He's *seventeen*," Maximoff growls. "He's a fucking teenager who's in a band, who's not paying attention to everyone around him. That's your job, and if you don't fucking do it, I'll let Thatcher, Akara, and Price know."

"I understand," Ian says quickly. "I apologize. It won't happen again. You don't need to tell the Tri-Force. Please." He's whining.

"Watch Tom." Maximoff hangs up at that curt endnote.

My brows arch with my barbell. "You made Ian Wreath piss his pants."

"Akara would've made him shit his pants."

"He's lucky you're nice." I unlatch the door. "You're not coming with me, by the way." I extend my arm in the stairway, blocking him.

Purplish bruises shadow his eyes. I scrutinize him a little longer, and a pit tries to wedge in my stomach. Shit, I don't like seeing him hurt. In any capacity.

"Why not?" Maximoff combats.

Starting with my thumb, I count off the reasons. "You look like you were in a fistfight." Pointer finger. "You're a severely recognizable celebrity." Middle finger. "Refer to reasons one and two."

On any normal day, Maximoff wouldn't care if people caught wind of his location or if fans bombarded the hotel. He's used to that chaotic shit.

But we all agreed to keep locations as safe as possible for Beckett and Sullivan. Those two were never on the *We Are Calloway* docuseries, and so they were able to foster private lives much easier than Maximoff and Jane. They're not that accustomed to quickly amassing crowds.

Akara wants to ease them in if we can.

As much as Maximoff loves his cousins, he's always risked his personal safety to feel free. Posting his location, in real time, is his norm. Now he's at the mercy of these confining restraints, and unfortunately for him, only *I* can unbuckle them.

"I'm hiding the bruises," Maximoff says, about to slip on Ray Bans—I catch his wrist. Stopping him.

Our eyes never detach.

"That'll hurt," I warn. His sunglasses are going to sit near the fracture.

"I can handle it." He tries to take a breath, but his chest collapses. "Farrow, I'm not staying behind on this bus. I need out. On the chance that someone recognizes me, it's 4-something-a.m. and there can't be that many employees awake." He nods a couple times. "We can deal with one or two people noticing."

My choice directly affects his life and the lives on that bus. I weigh the risks, grappling for a middle-ground where he feels safe and free.

When I release his hand, he gently puts on his Ray Bans. Concealing the black-and-blue marks.

I scan his sweatshirt, hood hiding his dark brown hair. "You'd do better wearing an actual costume."

His shoulders bind. "Clark Kent only wears glasses and a fucking suit."

My brows spike. "Did you just compare yourself to Superman?"

"Fuck off." He almost starts smiling, but he sighs roughly instead. "Seriously, Farrow…"

I block out Thatcher, the rest of Omega, and anyone else who'd say or do differently—and I'm dying to give my client what he needs, and right now, he needs air.

Decision made.

12

Farrow Keene

"WHAT NAME IS YOUR reservation under?" a tiny hotel receptionist asks me. Round glasses fall down her aquiline nose, and wispy red hair curls around her ears. She's the only one in the marble lobby, the elevators in sight.

"Farrow Keene." I pass the twenty-something girl a credit card.

Next to me, Maximoff stretches his quad muscles and cracks a crick in his neck. I know what he needs.

"Is the hotel pool open 24-hours?" I ask her.

Maximoff tries to control himself from looking in my direction, but even with sunglasses, his expression is easy to read. Mouth upturned, neck a little reddened, desire flexing his muscles—it's pure attraction.

Towards me.

Damn.

I swallow hard. His lack of restraint is killing me. I comb a hand through my hair.

"The hotel pool," the girl repeats while typing on the computer and swiping the credit card. "Oh, um…" She pushes up her glasses. "We drained the pool yesterday to fix the lining. I'm sorry, but we have complimentary breakfast and free internet."

"That's perfect," Maximoff says, sounding sincere. If he's downtrodden about the pool, he doesn't let on.

The girl busies herself with key cards, not aware that a celebrity just spoke to her. "Great, great." She slides an envelope across the counter. "Your block of rooms is ready. Do you need help with your bags?"

"We're good." I take the envelope and credit card.

"Thanks for your help," Maximoff tells the girl.

"Oh, wait, um." She raises a finger in thought.

Maximoff solidifies.

I lean against the counter and unwrap a piece of gum. There's a very, *very* good likelihood that she'll recognize him in the next five minutes. I've already accepted this.

"Are you here for business or pleasure? We have an excellent guide-book of Cleveland if you're sightseeing. Let me just…" She crouches to find a brochure in the cabinet.

Maximoff puts his arm on the counter. "We're just here for tomorrow—"

"Izzy!" A girl rushes out of the back *employees only* room, dressed in an identical blue blazer, and she waves her cellphone. Squealing. "Izzy, Izzy, you have to see this!"

Maximoff rotates, his back to them.

Izzy clears her throat and whispers, "We have guests, Sana."

Sana swings her head to me. "Oh my God, I'm *so* sorry…" Her voice trails off, and she eyes my neck tattoos and my lip, nose, and brow piercing, plus my earring. She presses her lips together to keep from smiling. "Sorry, it's just that the H.M.C. FanCon announced its first city." She spins to Izzy. "And they're coming *here*." She bounces on her feet with a grin.

I smile and pop my gum in my mouth. I step back a little from the counter. Just so I can see Maximoff.

His lips rise, and he mouths, *should I tell them?* He realizes it's only a matter of time, too.

I shake my head and mouth, *not yet.*

"The FanCon is in this hotel?" Izzy asks.

"Not here *here*," Sana clarifies and speaks to me. "It's in the Regala Hotel, much larger and more convention space. It's one mile from here. I can give you directions if you need them."

I suck in a breath and decide to irritate Maximoff a little. "Never heard of an H.M.C. FanCon."

He shoots me a look.

My smile stretches.

Sana gawks. "Have you not been online in the past twenty-four hours?"

"I've been working," I say easily. "Is it about comics or something?"

"No, it's the biggest meet-and-greet tour of the past decade." Sana rocks on the balls of her feet. "Maximoff Hale, Sullivan Meadows, Jane, Charlie and Beckett Cobalt will all be in the same room *together*. We haven't seen that…*ever*."

"In years," Izzy corrects. "They've probably been together at least once." She slides over a brochure. "Here's that sightseeing guide I mentioned before—"

"Izzy, this is all the sightseeing he needs," Sana says and then turns to me. "You should look into the FanCon. Tickets will sell out soon."

Izzy nods. "I heard they'll go within the hour."

Maximoff smiles a more heartfelt one. He's dedicated most of his time to raise money for charity, and knowing this tour helps other people means everything to him.

I rub my thumb over my lip piercing. "What would you do if you saw one of them?"

"The five?" Sana asks, hand to her heart. "I *live* for any photographs of them together. Can you imagine the camaraderie? The friendship? The loyalty?"

I can do better than imagine. I've seen the friendship and loyalty with all of them but two. Charlie and Maximoff created a fissure within "the five" that's palpable. They haven't even spoken one word to each other since we started driving.

I chew my gum slower and lean into the counter. "Not a photo. If you met them in real life."

"Like at the FanCon?" Sana asks.

I'm worried she may faint if Maximoff turns around. It wouldn't be the first time. The most memorable was in Philly at Lucky's Diner.

A boy passed out on a plate of pancakes when Maximoff waved to him. Someone shouted for a doctor, and no one stood, so I assessed the kid.

He suffered only from embarrassment.

"Who's your favorite?" Izzy suddenly asks me.

I tilt my head. "Favorite...?"

"Favorite Hale, Meadows, or Cobalt." She pushes up her glasses. "Mine is Lily Calloway. She's..." Izzy just smiles.

I know. Lily is endearing. I miss how she'd text me random shit about tortilla-shaped blankets and superhero memes. But she hasn't messaged me since I broke her trust.

"Mine is Ryke Meadows," Sana chimes in. "He's such a DILF."

Maximoff barely flinches, used to people fawning over his parents and uncles and aunts.

I restrain a laugh. "That's great—"

"And I love *all* the Cobalts," Sana adds, "except for Jane Cobalt."

This took a bad turn. I tap the counter, tentative, and I'm about to interject. But she speaks quickly.

"She's always seemed pretentious and just unmotivated. Everyone in her family has done something extraordinary, and she's just...blah. If I was a Cobalt, I wouldn't be wasting my potential like her."

Shit.

Maximoff mouths, *I can't.*

He can't reveal himself now. He'd crush this girl.

I hold onto the key cards. I can't let him go to a room without me.

Here's some unspoken history catalogued only by security (not public): two men tried to jump Maximoff in a hotel hallway when he was fifteen. Unprovoked. His old bodyguard escorted him to safety, but that shit is why he's stuck with me 24/7.

Izzy asks me again, "So who's your favorite?"

"Maximoff Hale," I say without pause.

His chest lifts in an aroused breath.

My smile is killing me. I rub my mouth a couple times.

"I *love* him," Sana swoons.

Same.

"Well, I used to," she sighs. "I don't know. That article about him and Jane Cobalt made me feel…weird."

Izzy nudges Sana's arm. "It's fake. *Celebrity Crush* already issued an apology, and so did three other tabloids who ran with the *fake* story. I think one of them is even getting sued."

That's the work of the Hale and Cobalt lawyers.

"It's been entertaining," I say casually, "but we need to grab our bags—"

"Thatcher to Farrow." A strict voice blares through my earpiece that hangs on my shoulder. Audible to Maximoff and both girls. "Farrow, are you in the hotel with Maximoff—" I quickly decrease the radio volume, but not fast enough.

Shit.

"Oh…my God." Sana has her hands to her mouth. Both girls stare intently at Maximoff's back. "Is that…?" Tears flood her big eyes, upset. Because she knows he heard every negative thing she said. "I didn't…I…"

I hang back, already knowing what he'll do.

Maximoff hurriedly spins around, drops his hood, and raises a hand. "Hey, it's alright, don't cry, don't cry."

Sana bursts into a sob. "I didn't mean…" Her knees buckle while she cries, and Izzy catches her co-worker's elbows. Maximoff sprints around the counter, and I follow close behind.

I fit my earpiece in, but I don't worry about the volume yet. Instead, I take out my phone and tap into an electronic contract.

Maximoff crouches to Sana. "I know you didn't mean it."

She mumbles something about hurting Maximoff Hale and how Jane Cobalt is his best friend.

He shakes his head. "No, you didn't hurt me. I'm okay. I'm okay. You don't need to cry." She's still sobbing, and that's affecting him.

He glances briefly at me, his chest constricted.

I squat next to him. "Sana, he's smiling. He's not upset."

Izzy wipes her friend's tears with her blazer sleeve. "He doesn't look mad at all, Sana."

She sniffs, but she stares at the carpet. "I'm sorry…I didn't mean…"

"I know. I understand. It's okay," Maximoff says, and he asks if he can touch her. When she agrees, he rubs her arm in comfort.

As Sana gathers her emotions, we all stand.

He hugs the girl, then Izzy. And I describe the NDA in detail that they each need to sign. No photos posted online. No alerting the media that Maximoff and his family are here. After they sign the electronic contracts, Thatcher pushes through the revolving door.

Aimed for me.

We back away from the counter and stop him midway. I open my mouth, but he already cuts me off, "Turn up your radio volume."

My jaw tics. "That wasn't a priority—"

"It is," he snaps, and then raises a leveled hand to Maximoff. "I'm sorry, but I need to talk to Farrow in private. It's security—"

"He can hear," I cut off Thatcher. "I don't give a shit." All three of us head towards the revolving doors, the two girls unable to hear us.

Thatcher towers over me, and I rest my shoulder blades on the wall, uncaring about the whole domineering tactic. He begins to scold me for not waking him up before we left the bus. Apparently that was a rule since he's keeping an eye on Maximoff, too.

"Thatcher." Maximoff draws his attention. "I told Farrow not to wake you up."

"No he didn't," I tell Thatcher and shoot Maximoff a cold glare. He's *never* lying to cover for me. I can't be the reason the best parts of Maximoff change. Ever since we kissed in front of his parents, I promised myself to protect the *good* in him.

His honesty isn't dying by my hand.

Thatcher's strict gaze pings between me and my boyfriend before landing on me. "Try harder or there'll be repercussions for every infraction."

I force myself not to roll my eyes. "Sure."

He leaves at that, and we're left alone in the lobby, the girls disappeared in the back room. Maximoff adjusts his sunglasses. *They're hurting his nose.*

"I'm fine." He lowers his voice. "I guess it's good to know people are still talking about the rumor." His sarcasm is clear.

"It took her ten other comments, including calling your uncle a DILF before she even mentioned it," I whisper. "I'd say that's a success."

"Yeah." He nods, more assured. "I think the tour is going to help."

"Me too." I sweep his tensed build, stress weighing heavier on his shoulders. My muscles burn because I want to step nearer and wrap my arms around my boyfriend. And just hold him for a second.

Maximoff takes one foot forward, but he stops himself. Craving the same thing.

13

Maximoff Hale

FINALLY IN MY HOTEL room with Farrow, I prep in the bathroom for something I haven't tried since I was eighteen.

I'm a pro at sex. But being a bottom is new for me, and there's a pretty good chance I'll be a terrible lay.

I try to shelve any doubts and just focus on the fantasy. Of Farrow Redford Keene—a twenty-seven-year-old sexily tattooed guy—driving his cock into me.

I lick my lips. Goddamn, I crave that.

I exit the bathroom.

A champagne-colored comforter fits a king-sized bed. Nothing else in the modest-sized hotel room besides a desk, chair, dresser, and television.

Farrow winds the wire around his radio and tosses it on the chair. As soon as he turns, our gazes latch like magnets. We inhale the tension, built from constant, nonstop teasing on the bus. The air could snap.

My body says *go, go, get him*.

In a second, we both saunter forward and bridge the distance—our bodies collide, our mouths crush together. Instinctive and starved.

Holy fuck. I hunger for his touch, his love.

I breathe deeply into a kiss. Gripping his bleach-white hair in a tight fist.

Farrow cups my jaw, his masculine grip driving me closer. Nearer. *Fuck me*. We're pushed up against each other. Muscle to muscle. Heart hammering against heart.

The corner of his mouth curves upward *knowingly*.

Newsflash: I'm more aggressive. In a powerful kiss, I walk him backwards into the hotel dresser.

"Fuck," he curses, his gaze rakes my build like hot coals.

Closer, my body demands. *Fucking closer*. I grind forward. Our cocks confined behind the fabric of his pants and my jeans—they rub. Hot friction hardening us.

I pull off his leather jacket, and I yank off his black shirt over his head while he lifts off my sweatshirt and tee. Our mouths return like a firestorm. Wild, crazed. Never ceasing.

When my waist bucks against him, he curses huskily. His large hand drops to my throat, *fuck me*. His fingers add force, and he carefully chokes me. His eyes dance all over my face. "You like that?" he whispers into a kiss.

Fuck yes. Veins pulsate in my cock, and my eyes almost water in desire. *More*.

Fucking more.

I grip the dresser on either side of him, his back digging into the wood. So close, our foreheads nearly press together.

"Harder," I order, breathless.

Farrow tightens his grip a fraction. Air lunges from my head, dizzying me—*fuckyesfuckyes*. My mouth parts, and he whispers in my ear, "You want it hard and rough?"

I could come to his voice, day and night.

He nips my ear.

Desire and need tauten my whole body. "Fuck," I swear and grasp his jaw. I throb for greater, harder pressure.

His silver-ringed fingers dive down the ridges of my abs. He sucks the nape of my neck, bites my shoulder, my bicep—I growl out a guttural noise.

Beyond fucking aroused.

I hook my fingers in his waistband and pull him off the dresser. I watch his fingers unbutton my jeans, moving effortlessly and precisely.

We quickly undress to our boxer-briefs, and we start wrestling for the lead. Hands everywhere, our forceful movements light up my nerves and boil me alive.

Farrow gains an advantage. With a hand to my chest, he shoves me on the king-sized bed. I catch his wrist and bring him down next to me. I top him—he flips me.

Easily. *Fuck.*

Now he's on top, and Farrow puts me in some kind of MMA lock. His forearm across my collarbones, knee splitting my legs open. And he imprisons my hands behind my back.

Our mouths a literal millimeter away, his smile rises. "Never forget," he whispers, "I'm stronger than you."

I try to combat that. And I use my strength and attempt to rip out of his grip. He bears his body down on me, and I practically fucking *melt* under his weight.

Oh *fucking Christ.* This feels better than good.

My chin tilts upward. And my eyes nearly roll back, but I breathe through my nose. Pulse pounding. *Get it together, Maximoff.* Combat him. Wrestle him. Don't *melt* already.

"*Fuck,*" I growl into a fucking groan. *Fuckfuck.*

He kisses me, my groan lost in his mouth. Even without my hands, I slide my tongue along his, always deepening the kiss, and Farrow curses, "Fuck, Maximoff."

His lips descend to my jaw, my neck. Sucking again, and I mutter French and Spanish in his ear. Extremely fucking dirty. NC-17.

And Farrow understands not a single damn word. Still, his muscles contract and a low noise breaches his mouth.

We make out in this same position for a long while. I'm practically bursting through my fucking boxer-briefs. I try to move my hands, but he still cages them behind my back.

I'm too pent-up to untangle and flip him. I let out a heady breath. "I was thinking about jerking you off, and now…"

Farrow runs his tongue over his bottom lip piercing, smiling. "*And now*, I'm taking you in my mouth." He lets go of my hand, and I prop myself on my elbows. Comforter soft beneath my back.

My chest rises and falls in shallow breaths while I watch him suck and bite my flesh. Down to my elastic waistband.

His feet are on the floor, and he pulls me further down the mattress, my legs hanging off the bed. My ass close to the edge. God. *Fuck me.*

His mouth skims the outline of my erection. Boxer-briefs wet from pre-cum.

"*Farrow*," I snap into a groan, pissed that he's teasing. I can't handle it, and I almost fall back off my elbows.

He nearly laughs. Then he pulls my boxer-briefs off—way too goddamn slowly. My cock springs out, and I try to sit up to tear off his black boxer-briefs. But he pushes my chest back.

"Relax," he says in that graveled voice.

I glare. "And you call me bossy?" I reach down to a nearby duffel on the ground and unzip to find lube.

"You are bossy." Farrow is standing and takes off his boxer-briefs. His hardened dick comes into full view, and I pause. Soaking in his chiseled muscles and cascading ink, not to mention the mouth-watering erection that's supposed to be inside of me.

Don't get fucking nervous now.

"Never said I wasn't." I lick my stinging lips for the millionth time. "But maybe you are too."

"Maybe?" he repeats, his barbell lifts with his brow. "I am bossy. Lie back."

I chuck the bottle of lube at him. He catches it with one hand. Jesus.

"Let's do this fast," I say, "because I'm on a fucking ledge, man."

Farrow strokes his length while he lowers to his knees. Then he grips mine, licks the tip, and he sucks me—*holyshitholyshit*. I clutch my thigh with one hand and clench his hair with the other. He devours my reaction, and I bite down, a mangled noise in my throat.

I pay attention to how his lips wrap around me, and the pressure—*Christ*, the pressure. He slows, and he lubes his fingers. *This is it.*

He pops his mouth off my cock. "Lean back, Maximoff." He lifts my foot onto the edge of the mattress. I've done this enough to other people, so I'm highly aware I need to set my other foot on the bed to let him in.

But I'm fucking frozen.

He tries to distract me, his hand rubbing me. And he stands and leans down, kissing me strongly. My heart rate is elevated. I slide back more into the middle of the bed, and I bring him down. Not liking when he's standing and I'm not.

Farrow clutches my jaw. "I'm not going to hurt you. Trust me."

I take a deeper breath. And I try not to tense, but my muscles cut sharp. While he's on top, face-to-face, we make out; he strokes me, I stroke him, and he whispers, "Relax." His voice soothing.

And his other hand descends.

His fingers brush against my puckered hole. I do my best to focus on my pent-up arousal, and one finger slides into me. Deeper, finding my prostate.

He massages, and I tighten, the nerves killer. Almost too sensitive.

"Wait, wait." I put a hand on his chest, and he's out of me in a millisecond.

I'm honest-to-God shaking. And I can't tell if it's from being too wound-up, *teasing overload*, or anxiety.

Farrow studies my body language, his hand holding my waist protectively. "Talk to me, Maximoff."

I rub my face a couple times. Frustrated with myself. "No more edging; I just need to come."

His smile stretches too far. "It felt good then."

"Too good."

"That's the point, wolf scout." He leans forward and hovers over me, his earring dangling. I clutch the back of his head, and I'm about to say what I feel but I lose sight of the words.

He reads me. "I think you're scared."

I think you're right. I'm quiet, not combatting him like usual. Sex is uncomplicated for me. It feels good, and I go full-force. This feels

fucking good, but it's a level of intimacy that I couldn't give strangers.
I tried.

I failed.

And now, as I try to reach this place with a guy I love and trust,
the last guard I've raised will drop. Being that *bare* with someone is
fucking terrifying and exhilarating—and I want it, but can I let myself
get there?

Farrow places a kiss on my shoulder, and he asks, "Have you used
any sex toys before?"

"Yeah, all the time."

His brows spike. "All the time?"

"Sometimes," I correct.

He eyes me. "You're going to have to spell it out."

I give him a look like he's flown to outer space. "I like sex."

"No shit."

I glare, pretty weakly. "So I've used dildos and prostate massagers
before we got together, maybe a few times a week."

A satisfied smile edges across his mouth. "This is good news."

I'm not following. "How?"

"You're going to let me put a dildo inside of you," he says casually,
but I heat from head-to-toe in want. "It's something you're already
used to, so you won't be afraid."

"I'm not that fucking scared," I refute now.

"Sure," he says, eyeing my lips. "Just like I currently don't have a
hard-on for you."

"What gave you a boner then, the ceiling or the floor? No wait, let
me guess, the pillows."

He rolls his eyes. "You're such a smartass." He stares at me for a
long beat, almost asking me if I agree with the plan.

I nod. "Not today though." It'll have to happen during another
hotel stop. I already told him that I'm not bottoming on the bus. I want
more privacy to prepare. He agreed.

Right now, I'm way too fucking impatient to be teased for another
hour or two. I push him to his side, and I turn on mine to face him.

Our mouths meet again and again, bodies grinding. Hands seizing each other, escalating an intense friction.

Then I shift on top, and his muscular legs break apart on either side of my frame. I use lube and tease open his hole with a finger.

He mutters a pleasured curse, and after another deep kiss, I whisper, "I'm going to fuck you."

He seizes the back of my neck, his hot gaze narrowed into me. "Good, *fuck me*."

I find a condom and rip it open. He grips my bare ass while I sheath my length and lube up. I like most positions, but mainly doggy-style. So does he, but every now and then, we'll do missionary. Like now. Mostly because it's easier to look at each other.

Achingly fucking slow, I push my erection into him.

"Fuck," he breathes. His hand tightens on my neck, lips parted, and he strokes his length once, twice.

I rock forward, the pressure and tightness out of this fucking world. I thrust in a hypnotic tempo, in, out. In, out. Deeper.

Deeper.

Our mouths meet, making out roughly, aggressively. The heady sensations flick my nerves. Sweat coats our skin.

He breaks a kiss and grits down. Containing a moan that rumbles his throat. "Fuck," he barely gets out.

I throb inside of him, *fuck yes*, and I arch deeper, our chests pushed together.

"*Fuck*, Maximoff," he curses, mouth broken completely apart. He rakes his fingers down my back, and he clutches my ass in the strongest grip and bucks his hips. It drives my cock deeper into him. Practically fucking *me*.

God.

My eyes almost roll. Nearing a peak.

Hot skin against hot skin, I quicken my pace. Harder, faster—I clasp his face. My ass flexes beneath his palm. He holds me just as strongly. Like he's two seconds from riding me and finishing the job.

JesusChristfuck. I rub his erection, timing my thrusts with my hand. One more hungry kiss later, I drive so fast and deep that we're white-knuckling each other to hang on.

I'm blown to fragments, and he comes in my palm. Breathing heavily, I milk my climax. Slowly, slowly descending with him.

14

Maximoff Hale

"HEY, EVERYONE. IT'S MORNING here in Cleveland." I hoist my phone, camera pointed at my face for an Instagram Live video. Janie films twice as many live videos as me, but I thought I should do one before the event. I smash a couple pillows against the headboard.

I'm buck-ass naked, but I stay beneath the champagne comforter. Plus, my abs are barely in frame.

I slouch on the pillow mound. More comfortable. "My cousins and I are pumped to meet some fans today at the meet-and-greet," I tell the viewers, "and we can't thank you all enough for buying tickets. We sold out of today's FanCon within thirty minutes. You all are amazing. Seriously, this is going to help a lot of people."

I was on the phone with the H.M.C. Philanthropies board this morning, and we all agreed to allocate the money raised to our College Merit programs and LGBTQ+ initiatives.

I yawn into my bicep. "Someone have any hot tea?" I smile tiredly at the viewers. Then I glance at the hotel door, but Farrow hasn't returned. He left about an hour ago.

Hearts flutter nonstop on the right side of the Instagram Live video. Comments scroll fast, new ones pushing old out of view. *94.4k viewers* and counting.

I catch a few comments:

I'll give you tea in bed!!!

wait for me, boo <3

What kind of tea??????

DID YOU GET IN A FIGHT?!

I purposefully didn't put on sunglasses. Bruises are in full black-and-blue glory under my eyes.

"Earl Grey tea," I say and brush a hand through my disheveled hair. "Or green tea. I'm not that picky."

WHAT HAPPENED?!

Are you okay? omg maximoff!!

"So some of you already noticed my face. I didn't get into a fight. Shocker." I lick my dry lips. "It was a total fluke accident. Got elbowed in the nose on the tour bus."

Get better soon!!

Be safe OMG

I love u Maximoff

I wanna be those sheets so bad

"Love you all too," I say with another sleepy smile. I prefer being open. And while I like privacy in my relationship and sex life—I'm more used to being public in every other area. Keeping up some charades isn't worth the headache and trouble.

And telling the truth on an Instagram Live is better than a tabloid creating an elaborate fake story off a paparazzi photo.

Where's the next tour stop?!

"We haven't revealed where we'll be next, but keep checking the FanCon website for updates. We could be in your city soon…" I trail off as the hotel door *clicks* and Farrow waltzes inside. Carrying a Wendy's bag in one hand and a cardboard tray with two drinks in the other.

Yeah, he left to get us breakfast. My internal alarms blare in warning. I have rules. Safety measures. Protocols.

Don't look in love.

Don't act like I'm semi-obsessed with someone off-screen.

Don't appear fucking interested in the six-foot-three maverick who's about to bring me breakfast in bed.

You can't know about Farrow Redford Keene.

"So anyway," I say to the viewers and sit up more.

Farrow nears the bed and hands me a paper to-go cup. The exchange off-screen.

I sip the hot liquid. *Earl Grey.* "I have my tea—" He chucks the Wendy's bag onto my lap after he takes a bowl and spoon and his coffee. I soak in his assured gait, the way his hands shift. I could watch him move around a room in silence for hours. Is that weird?

That's weird, right?

Jesus, I'm so fucking weird.

Farrow climbs on the bed beside me. Still out of frame and completely aware that he can't talk. He arches his brows at me and cocks his head.

Dammit. I'm literally ogling him.

I glance at the comments.

Who are you looking at???

Omg someone brought him food!

Watcha eating?

I can't catch the rest. Too many comments. I'm up to 99.1k viewers. "Plan is to eat some breakfast," I tell them, "take a shower, and I'll be meeting some of you soon. Stay safe, everyone." I end the Instagram Live at that and dig into the Wendy's bag.

He smiles into his coffee.

"What?" I ask, unwrapping a chicken biscuit. We unconsciously draw closer together, side-by-side, one of my legs hooking his.

"You had *fuck me* eyes," he says matter-of-factly.

I grimace and do my best to smother a smile. I want to be an asshat to him for once, but I'm struggling. "Thanks for stating the impossible."

"It's possible." He sets aside his coffee and stirs his oatmeal. "I saw it."

No way. "I wasn't thinking about fucking you, so I couldn't have had *fuck me* eyes."

The corner of his mouth upturns. "I'm fucking with you, Maximoff."

I blink and blink. "It's like you want to be kicked out of the bed." I bite into my chicken biscuit. "You get a pass for bringing me breakfast. You're welcome."

"I didn't say *thank you*," he tells me.

I shake my head. "I swear you get off on pissing on my sarcasm."

He lifts his brows in a wave, but his smile slowly and surely morphs into a real frown. I realize he's been stirring his oatmeal. Not eating. Farrow pretty much always eats hurriedly in case SFO needs him.

I straighten even more. Then I take a larger sip of hot tea. "What's up?"

"We need to talk."

My stomach nosedives, and my brows cinch. "What about?" I jump to the worst conclusion. This is the end of my short-lived relationship. He woke up this morning and realized he couldn't bear to spend another day with me.

I think about last night. I think about sex. Did I hurt him? Was I somehow selfish? Is that it? No...*no*, that can't be it.

Even assured about that, something raw and cold impales my chest. Like an iron fist banging against my ribs. I solidify to stone.

Dear World, did he just bring me a "break up" breakfast? Is that even a thing? Worst regards, a broken-hearted human.

My guards skyrocket.

I mortar my face with nothingness. Pushing out the hurt. Preparing myself for anything and everything. Bones rigid, shoulders squared.

I can handle this.

Farrow scoots around to face me, his knees casually bent. He keeps a hand on my leg. I can't tell if it's in pity or comfort.

"Generally," I say in a flat voice, "when someone says they need to talk, they *talk.*"

"I'm getting there." He's not looking forward to this conversation. That's for sure.

Appetite lost, I wrap up the chicken biscuit and shove it into the Wendy's bag. I can't sit in tense silence. "If you want to break up, just do it—"

"Whoa." He raises a hand, eyes narrowed. "I never even considered breaking up with you. It's not what I want." Farrow sweeps my blank face. "...do *you* want that?"

"No, *no.* Not at all." I'm fucking confused. "We're still good together."

"Really good," he says, his confidence fortifying those words.

"Then what?"

Farrow stretches forward to put his oatmeal on an end table. "That Instagram account that I showed you back at the lake house." He seizes my gaze. "It turned out to be a real threat."

I shake my head. "No, there's no way."

"We traced the IP address to Philly. The entire security team is treating the user as a high risk to *your* safety."

I stare off, processing this fact with little to no emotion. "Who is it?" I open Instagram on my cellphone.

Farrow hangs his arm on his bent knee. "We're still trying to identify them." He's quiet. "I'm not supposed to share any of this with you, but I know you'd rather be aware."

I nod a few times. Even before we got together, he always kept me in the loop. Even at the cost of disobeying the security team. "Thanks," I say. "You know I won't share with anyone but Janie." I'm not about to scare my younger cousins.

I click into the @maximoffdeadhale account.

Farrow watches me, our silence more uneasy. I thought that tension would disappear.

"You don't need to worry," I tell him. "I'm not afraid of stalkers."

"I didn't think you were." He combs a hand through his white hair. "There's more."

I frown at him before looking at the account. 52 photos. Most recent one shows me lying bloodied on a neon Cleveland sign, their Photoshop skills top-notch.

My first and only thought: *I'm happy it's me and not Farrow, not Jane, not my siblings, not my family, not anyone I love.*

And I think about that. How I'm staring at dozens of pics where I'm dying or already dead and the only thing I feel is *gratitude*. Happy that the user didn't choose to mock-kill someone else.

Farrow adjusts his earpiece, gaze drifting like another bodyguard is speaking. When his attention returns to me, he says, "It's likely the account belongs to someone you personally know. Someone who hates you. Someone you've intentionally or unintentionally pissed off, and since I'm closest to you, I need to narrow down a list."

I think back. Who did I piss off? "Most of my fistfights with hecklers made the news, so those names are somewhere online. That should help." I stare faraway. "I can't think of anyone else who'd want me dead besides anonymous trolls."

Farrow slowly edges into the next question. "What about any of your hookups?"

Blood just drains out of my head. I'm not an idiot. I rapidly connect all the pieces and fully comprehend his reservations.

He needs to search my old NDAs for possible suspects.

And by *search*, I mean *discover the names and number of people I've fucked.*

I start shutting down. Brick upon brick upon brick. I climb off the bed and grab a pair of boxer-briefs.

He stands. "Maximoff—"

"I'll go through my NDAs," I say confidently, pulling my underwear to my waist. "I'll give you the names of anyone that I think could be capable of creating an account like that."

His jaw tics. "That's not how this works. *I'm* your bodyguard. I protect *you*, Maximoff. You can't do this yourself—"

"Why not?" I shake my head, my neck stiff and hot. "I've met these people. You haven't. I can filter out the ones who would never—"

"How the fuck do you know they'd never hurt you?" he snaps, not backing down. "You were only with these people for one night. How much do you even know about them?"

I cast a glare at the wall. *Not much.*

"Omega wants to research all of your NDAs, and I agree—"

"No," I say out of impulse and step back from him. Two feet. Three and four. Hands up. "You don't need to know the faces of every person I've ever slept with."

Farrow laughs out a pained smile. "Man, you think this is easy for me? I don't want to rifle in your past when I know it hurts you for me to be there."

"Then don't." I gesture to his chest. "Give the job to me or if not me, then Akara—"

"*I'm* your fucking bodyguard." His narrowed gaze drives deeper into me. "Not Akara. Not anyone else. And as your bodyguard and your *boyfriend*, I want to protect you. It's my job to take care of your NDAs, your safety, and if you don't let me help you, then I'm hurting you by being a worse bodyguard than what you need."

I set my hands on my head, almost out of breath. Like I just swam a 400-meter IM without coming up for air. I just stop. I breathe, and I try my best to understand him. Because I don't want to fuck with his job.

My mind reels, and I just say what hits me. "I want to not care about the fucking NDAs, the faces, the names," I tell him. "I get it. If our positions were reversed, I'd hope you'd value your life over something trivial. And that you'd let me sift through papers about your one-night stands and let me help…" I cringe at the thought of anyone stepping into a sex life that I kept private from the world.

From you.

How do I open a door that I padlocked, chained, and bolted shut? "Fuck," I breathe, glaring at the ceiling.

"It's not trivial," Farrow says, swiveling the knob to his radio.

"What do you mean?"

"What you feel, what's important to you—it's not trivial," he clarifies and sits half on the desk, casually stuffing his hands in his black pants pockets.

I can't unglue my feet from the middle of the room. "I'm not ashamed of my number, but if you learn about all of this—I don't want it to affect our relationship."

"It won't," he says strongly. "I promise you, Maximoff. I don't give a flying shit about your number or who you've fucked. I've never judged anyone for being promiscuous." He shrugs. "It's a personal choice, and that's your business, not mine."

"Exactly."

He rolls his eyes and stands off the desk. "Unless this psychotic dickhole is someone you enraged after fucking them, then it becomes my business."

"I'm not an asshole," I say, my chest tight. "I'd like to believe I treated all of my one-night stands with respect."

"I know." His voice is almost a whisper.

I crack my knuckles. "I always thought about how every hookup had to sign NDAs and jump through hoops to sleep with me. To protect *me*." I look up at Farrow. "And I always thought *who's protecting them?* And I knew, I fucking knew, that it was my job to protect the people I had sex with. I had to care or else it felt like my life meant more than theirs because I'm famous. And that's just bullshit."

Farrow stares deeply. "And now I just want to protect the fuck out of you ten times more."

I lick my lips, knowing that I need to let go of control. I need help, and I need him. If I create a roadblock, then I'll lose Farrow as my bodyguard. He'd probably quit his job before he failed me—and maybe he's been struggling with that idea.

Maybe he still will. But I have to make it easier on him.

So I say, "I'm okay with that."

Farrow closes the distance between us before I unfreeze. I hold the back of his neck, and he clasps my jaw, his hand affectionate and forceful. I hear our heavy breaths.

His brown eyes melt against my forest-green, and he says, "I'm really, *really* in love with you, and whatever happens, keeping you safe is my priority."

"Same here."

He begins to smile. "You're going to keep me safe?"

"Yeah." I nod heartily. "No one's fucking with you."

"They're not fucking with me because I'm not the famous one," he says. "And unfortunately for you, it's my job to jump in front a bullet that's aimed for your head."

I grimace. "Thanks for reminding me." We eye each other's lips, a half-second from kissing, and then my phone rings. I pull away. "Sorry."

"It's okay." Farrow leaves my side to pick up his oatmeal, finally eating.

I take the call. "Hey?"

"Moffy, can you come into the gift store downstairs?" Sulli whispers softly. "Please? Fuck, this is so hard."

I already start grabbing a clean pair of jeans and a crew-neck shirt. "I'll be right there."

15

Farrow Keene

I REST MY ASS partially on a table of folded Cavaliers shirts. "Why the phone call?" I ask Akara and Donnelly. We hang out at the gift shop's entrance.

Our clients talk towards the back. Near a rack of keychains and souvenir mugs. And in my peripheral, I clearly see Beckett eating Wendy's fries, Maximoff unwrapping his chicken biscuit, and Sulli speaking too quietly to hear.

Akara wears a backwards baseball cap and bounces a rubber ball. "She said she's having a hard time picking out a souvenir for her little sister."

My brows ratchet up. Because that's not a reason she'd call Maximoff. I eat a spoonful of oatmeal, and Donnelly listens while he tries on winter beanies.

"What's she actually doing?" I ask Akara.

"Looking for a birthday present for me and pretending like I don't know what's up." He observes them out of the corner of his eye. "She opened the curtains in the room this morning and saw someone outside carrying a *Sullivan the Sasquatch* sign. Probably heading to the convention."

I let out a long whistle. Dipshits thinking they're clever are the least clever.

"She's freaking," Donnelly pipes in, tugging a Mohawk beanie over his chestnut hair.

"She's not freaking." Akara catches the ball. "She's just feeling out the water, and she's used to having Maximoff beside her in new situations. Which is why she called him."

That sounds more accurate. He's the moral support for 99% of his family. Minus Charlie.

I'd say that Sulli did fine at the Camp-Away event, but the FanCon isn't that comparable. Only three-hundred fans attended the Camp-Away and she took breaks in her cabin for solitude.

The philanthropy sold a *thousand* tickets for the Cleveland FanCon, and that's just one tour stop of many. Here, all the famous ones are obligated to shake hands, hug strangers, and take pictures for hours with little to no rest.

Not my thing, but that's why no one's paying for my selfies.

Donnelly subtly eyes them while facing us too. "Those mugs are bugging Beckett." I can't detect Beckett's annoyance. But not a second later, he realigns the mugs in a neat row.

Maximoff gesticulates from his chest to Sulli, speaking extremely fucking empathetically to his cousin.

I skim him, a smile playing at my lips, and I take a swig of coffee. "He's about to hug her." On cue, Maximoff wraps his arms around his cousin, and she squeezes him back.

Akara bounces his ball. "She'll buy a Sagittarius something for me. Wait for it…" We watch Sulli scan the shelves and then veer to a display of zodiac jewelry. She plucks a silver Sagittarius keychain off a hook.

Spending 24/7 with a person has this effect.

"Bodyguard powers on point," Donnelly says and switches his beanie for a demon-horn headband.

Sulli checks over her shoulder to ensure Akara isn't looking. She can't tell that he notices everything she's doing. She tries to slyly head to the register.

I almost laugh.

Akara points at me with the bouncy ball. "She's not the only one who does that."

True. I stand off the table and really laugh at a thought. "I love when our clients think we're oblivious to what's happening."

Our job description: *watch them.*

Donnelly checks himself out in a full-length mirror. "They must think we're plannin' tea parties and brushing each other's hair." While I toss my empty bowl in a nearby trashcan, he adds to me, "Maximoff is looking over here for the third time."

"Fifth," I correct and fix my earring. "It's *like* he likes me, he really likes me." I turn and purposefully catch my boyfriend staring. I raise my brows at him.

He tries to hold a scowl.

I'm tempted to mime something dirty. Especially since the store is empty and the cashier isn't in sight. But instead, I call out, "Need anything, wolf scout?"

Maximoff watches me lift my coffee to my mouth, and he tells me, "I already got what I wanted last night." His forest-greens make a show of descending my build. "Thanks anyway."

Damn. Heat clenches my muscles.

Donnelly grins. "He likes that Farrow di—"

I cover his mouth. Teasing Maximoff is *my* job. I study my boyfriend as his eyes dart between me and Donnelly, then the cashier appears, and he turns his back to us.

Donnelly licks my palm, and I wipe my hand on the side of his face. "You motherfucker."

He grasps the hat rack. "True. I've fucked moms before." His blue eyes drift to Akara. "Boss didn't like that."

I notice Akara sending *me* a disapproving look.

Why he's upset: we're in public and made off-handed comments about Maximoff and me being together. "That was nothing," I assure him. "Don't be Thatcher and overreact here."

"Farrow." Akara adjusts the wire to his radio, abs showing in a red muscle shirt. "Not all of us chill in hurricanes." He's saying I never "overreact" when I should. "And keeping your relationship secret is serious."

I rest against the table again, arms loosely crossed. "Then trust me that I'll keep it secret. Because I'd rather all of Omega be more concerned about the Instagram threat than this shit." I continue, "I was the one who had to suggest and coordinate metal detectors and extra security at the entrances. If that were Sulli in a pic being butchered on a Cleveland sign, it would've been a priority."

Akara inhales a short breath and tries to temper his reaction. "Look…" He returns the bouncy ball to an aquarium bowl full of rubber balls. "I can't imagine what it's like seeing those pictures, but we don't have enough intel yet." He looks away, thinking.

"And if that were Sulli," I tell him, "the whole tour would be shut down by now."

Since it's Maximoff Hale—the one in charge, the leader of three families, a guy who can convince the Tri-Force that he's capable of anything—we're letting him put himself in more harm's way than we would *anyone* else.

Akara nods. "I'll ramp up the extra security when he exits the venue." He takes outs his phone.

"Thanks," I say but we all eagle-eye an incoming hoard of preteen girls. Giggling and shrieking at the celebrity sighting.

Donnelly flings his headband off. "See ya." He lowers his middle and ring finger into a hand-gesture that means *love*. And he beelines for Beckett at the cash register with Sulli and Maximoff.

Akara and I reach them before the girls are halfway into the gift shop. Sulli collects her receipt and bag, hesitant. "Are we leaving?" She glances at Akara.

See, Beckett and Sulli only greet fans in controlled, pre-secured environments. Not every day life.

"It's up to you," Akara says.

Beckett shoves a fry in his mouth. "I'm not staying, Sul." He waits for his cousin to make a decision.

Maximoff is definitely staying. It's what he always chooses, and it's more dangerous with the Instagram threat. But that's why I'm here.

He already waves to the twelve girls, and they scream in unison. Snapping selfies with Maximoff towering in the background. "DO YOU SEE HIM!?!?"

I smile.

I see him.

Maximoff gives me a look like *would you scream like that for me?*

I shake my head. *No.* At the very least, he'd have to work for it.

Sulli turns to Maximoff and whispers, "How pissed will they be if I leave?"

"It's not a reason to stay," he says quietly. "Some people will hate you no matter what. It's just what happens when you're more public."

She nods. "Right. Fuck, okay. I'm going. Beckett?" He clasps her hand, and they move out of the store. Akara and Donnelly create a barrier between their clients and the fans. No one able to approach them.

I stand right next to Maximoff.

He gestures the girls forward. "Want a photo?"

More screaming. "THIS IS THE BEST DAY OF MY LIFE!"

I increase my radio volume to drown them out, and I eye their pockets and purses and hands. Staying alert. Eh, I don't typically do this for preteens.

The chance is low.

The risk is low.

But I realize I'm more vigilant than I've ever been. Most bodyguards would add precautions. And I don't mean extra security. They'd tell Maximoff to change his lifestyle. Sacrifice these interactions. Be less public.

He'd feel choked, and I still want to provide him that safe middle-ground. Shit, I *love* giving him what other people can't.

I'm not forcing him into a cushioned room with no windows unless it's dire.

I just can't do that to him.

16

Farrow Keene

WE'VE REACHED THE ONE-HOUR mark of the Cleveland
FanCon. The crowds are massive. Crew and assistants buzz around the
conference room like invisible insects, and temporary security manages
the long, weaving lines of excited fans.

My sole focus: *Maximoff Hale*.

Five velvet-roped aisles lead to plain-white backdrops. Jane,
Maximoff, Sullivan, Beckett, and Charlie stand in separate aisles.

Different lines.

Less chaos.

Fans cue up and wait for their turn to meet their favorite celebrity.
A line coordinator motions for a twenty-something brunette girl to
approach Maximoff. She wears a FanCon shirt and eagerly sprints
towards him, throwing an arm around his neck like they're long-lost
friends.

He hugs back, smiling genuinely.

I stand only a few feet away, hands cupped in front of me. I'm out
of the photos, but close enough in case there's trouble.

"I'm *such* a big fan. I love you so much!" She speaks hurriedly. "Are
you okay? How's your nose? Who brought you breakfast? Did you
have a nice shower? Oh my God, I can't believe this is real. I'm meeting
you right now." She pets his arm.

I chew my gum a little harder. This is the sixty-seventh time I wish I could say *he's mine*. I know what I like and what I don't like, and I've never been into people "caressing" a boyfriend.

But I've also never dated a celebrity.

"I'm good, I promise." He squeezes her shoulders in a side-hug. "What's your name?"

"Penny. Oh my God, please say my name."

"Penny," he says with a bigger smile.

She squeals.

"Want a picture or autograph?" he asks. "Q&A will be later. Hopefully we'll be able to answer some of your questions then."

"Yes, yes! Can you sign my shirt?"

"Yeah, definitely."

An assistant is ready and passes Maximoff a Sharpie.

Penny clutches his bicep while he uncaps the pen. I hone in on her hand that veers to his chest, dives down his waist, and even reaches his belt. I wait, wait, and her hand moves south—I step in, my mere presence an electric shock.

She jolts backwards, wide-eyed at me and my tattoos.

"Try to keep your hands above his waist." I've repeated this phrase too many times today.

Before she pales, Maximoff smiles again like nothing is awry. Distracting her from being called out. "Where do you want the signature?"

"The back of my shirt. Thank you *so, so* much."

When she leaves, his eyes briefly flit to me in thanks.

I nod. Dick-grabbing crisis averted. The only person touching his cock will be me.

Oscar's voice floods comms. "Now confirmed, this is taking forever."

We've barely made a dent in the lines.

"It's Sulli," Quinn says through mics. "Someone tell her to stop having twenty-minute conversations with fans."

Oscar returns. "Look at you, little bro, trying to take charge and keep an eye on a Meadows girl."

I click my mic. "Shit, it's like he's Akara."

"He wants to be," Oscar says, his tone half-joking.

"Fuck you, bro." That was a real *fuck you.*

"Hey," I cut in. "He's fucking with you, man." I've seen some Oliveira fighting flare-ups on the bus, and to be honest, I don't like it. I prefer all of us ribbing Quinn and him smiling at the end. Not this pile of shit.

"He's a fucking asshole," Quinn growls.

I can't believe I've gone from mentor to mediator. I speak into my mic. "Akara, this is all yours."

"Chill on comms," Akara says, "and leave Sulli alone. She's new to this. I'm getting her line coordinator to usher people out faster."

"Smart thinking, boss," Donnelly adds.

Thatcher has been absent from comms, and I quickly scrutinize Jane's line next to me. Three feet from her, he stands like a brick wall, hands cupped in front. Zeroed in on fans who excitedly bob up and down.

"Maximoff, this is for you!" A boy hands Maximoff a scrapbook he made. I watch the friendly exchange.

"Redford," Oscar says in my ear. "Look at Charlie's line."

I reroute my attention for only a second and crane my neck to the very end of the set-up. Charlie is the furthest from Maximoff, and his line is almost empty.

One blonde girl snaps a picture, and I read Charlie's lips that move with one word: *bye.*

The girl grins from ear-to-ear. Taking no offense to his curtness. And she slips into Beckett's winding line.

I click my mic before he rubs in the success. "You mean the guy who has a reputation of being elusive can blow off his fans and none of them bat an eye? If others copied him, we'd have *Celebrity Crush* calling them rude bitches and assholes."

Oscar laughs. "Look who became a publicist."

"Sucking Maximoff's dick must give superpowers," Donnelly says without thinking.

"Cut it out," Thatcher snaps.

I'm not easily offended, and Thatcher's all up-in-arms because Donnelly is speaking about a client's dick. Not necessarily because that's my boyfriend's dick. But I'm of the mindset that if you dish it, you better be able to take it, and I dish a fucking ton.

Not listening to the bane of my career and my sanity, I speak into my mic. "And no one knows what sucking Donnelly's dick does because no one wants near it."

Donnelly lets his laughter filter through the comms.

"Farrow," Thatcher warns.

I roll my eyes. I let go of my mic. Still observing Maximoff and the overzealous fans. I have faith in our entrance security, so I'm not paranoid about concealed weapons.

Maximoff accepts a basket of cookies from a girl, and he's about to pass the present to an assistant. But I tell her that I'll get it.

Maximoff hands me the basket, and I ask, "How are you doing?"

"Good." He nods and flashes a smile at his line. The fans erupt in cheers, and then he turns to me and whispers, "How are Sulli and Beckett doing?"

"Sulli's just mismanaging time, and Beckett is getting asked to lift girls for pics."

"Like ballet lifts?"

"Yeah."

"His arms are going to be sore." Maximoff scrutinizes his cousins in a quick sweep.

"That's what Donnelly keeps telling him, but he's having trouble telling the girls *no* since they paid to be here."

Maximoff nods and asks me, "How much longer do you think?" He cranes his neck, searching.

"Four hours—"

"You've got to be shitting me." He zeroes in on Charlie's empty space. True to Charlie Cobalt form, he's left the building. Oscar is gone too.

"You're glaring," I warn Maximoff.

Before the line coordinator ushers someone forward, Maximoff says to the crew member, "Give me a second."

He grabs his water off the floor and then fully faces me. Back turned to the fans. His caustic glare could drill holes into the wall.

Charlie touches a raw place inside of Maximoff that I've never seen anyone else reach. Not even a heckler. It's another level of hurt and frustration and spite.

"He'd better be in the bathroom," Maximoff says.

I want to wrap my arm around his shoulders. But I pull against that natural impulse. I may as well yank against a taut bungee cord. It just makes me want to snap forward that much more.

I chew my gum and do what I can to help. Clicking my mic, I ask Oscar where he's at. I share the answer with Maximoff. "They'll be at the other hotel until the Q&A starts."

"He said he'd stay and help Sulli if he finished early."

I frown. "You two talked? To each other?"

"Texted." He hands me his phone, and I skim their short back-and-forth that goes something like this:

If you're done early with pics, can you stick around and distract some of the fans in Sulli's line? It'll make her less stressed. — Maximoff

Okay. — Charlie

I look up at Maximoff.

His eyes flash hot. "Tell me he got sick. Food poisoning or some flesh-eating bacteria? Maybe an emergency phone call? Or no, wait, Charlie doesn't ever have an excuse. He's just bored, and he bolted, right?"

I sense something deeper and more painful. He told me in more detail about the yacht fight with Charlie. And how Charlie bailed on him a week before his freshman year at Harvard.

With no explanation why.

I put a hand on his broad shoulder—and a six-foot-seven devil nearly blows out my eardrum. Fucking hell. I let go, my nose flaring.

Maximoff rubs his face. Trying to shelter his anger from the fans.

"Take a five-minute break," I say.

"No. No, I'm fine." He rakes a hand through his hair. "I'm fine." He puts his fist to his mouth, and the toughened look he wears also begs, *closer.*

I can't. My muscles burn. We're both pulling against a force that wants us to draw near.

Do your motherfucking job, Farrow.

I need to step back, but I say, "You look like you want to punch someone."

"I do," he says. "I want to punch my cousin."

"How about you take that down to an I-want-to-have-a-civil-talk-with-my-cousin?"

"Never heard of that one," he says, sarcastic.

"Clearly."

Maximoff almost smiles. He nods to himself, taking a deeper breath. This is where we'd hug or kiss or do something other than what I'm about to do.

Avert my eyes.

Step back.

Let air fill the gap between my body and his.

Doing my motherfucking job.

A short olive-skinned guy is next. He approaches Maximoff with an armful of Superheroes & Scones paraphernalia. Maximoff pops the cap to a Sharpie—the lights go out.

Darkness cloaks the conference room. Power cutting, voices blaring in my ear. Fans shouting, "What happened?!"

I block out every distraction, every possible threat or *what if* in the pitch-black, and I move urgently.

"Maximoff." I seize his waist and direct him towards an exit. SFO marked Ballroom E as a "safe area" in case these situations occur.

We can't see two feet in front of us, but I whip out my cellphone like a few other people and point my camera light.

"Jane." Maximoff tries to turn back around.

My hand cuffs his forearm tightly. "She has two bodyguards. Don't stop in the crowds."

There are five jaw-droppingly famous celebrities to one thousand adoring and semi-crazed fans. The lights could switch on or he could get stabbed in the dark. We're not sticking around to find out which.

A tour organizer uses a microphone to speak. "We'll have this all figured out soon. Please, stay calm and stay where you are."

"They're leaving!" a fan shouts, riling some people to chase after the celebrities and catch them before they go. Maximoff and I move assuredly in the dark, step-for-step, and I touch my earpiece as Akara speaks.

"Technicians are looking at the power. The entire first floor of the hotel is dark," Akara informs us. "Lights won't return for at least another five minutes."

"Still go to Ballroom E," Thatcher orders.

We push through a double-door exit, and sure enough, it's dark everywhere. Phone lights swing back and forth. I'd say that I guide Maximoff, but I'm sure he'd tell everyone that he's guiding me.

"MAXIMOFF!"

That's a fan.

I can't see the person, but it sounded like a "wait up" wail.

"Take one picture with me, please?! I didn't get one!" Hands are about to grab onto his shirt. I slip behind him and cut people off.

"Move," I tell Maximoff.

He's stopped to speak to them, and he's hesitating. Because he would genuinely place *giving a fan a picture* above his safety. Knowing it'd make their day, their month, year, or eternal existence.

Lucky for him, I don't give a shit.

I only care about his life.

"*Maximoff*," I say through my teeth. "*Move*. Or I'll drag you—" There we go.

He faces forward, our strides lengthy and hurried. "I could've taken one picture."

"No, you couldn't." I fixate on two guys ahead of us. They beam their phone lights on Maximoff. He shields the brightness with his hand.

"Hey, that's Maximoff!"

I step in front of him while we walk. "You can see him later," I tell the guys casually, but their lights have already created a giant spotlight on Maximoff.

"Maximoff!!" too many people scream and they're running towards him.

We're still far from Ballroom E. "Three-o'clock, there's a bathroom," I say to Maximoff and lead him by the shoulder—someone grips his shirt.

I shove the person back, and the fabric rips.

And that's when the sheer amount of people dawn on me. We may as well be at a concert venue, and he may as well be a singer stuck in the pit. Almost a hundred bodies swarm us.

All wanting close. All wanting to say they "touched" Maximoff Hale. All happening at one time.

In the dark.

I physically pry hands off his shirt, his biceps, and he pushes forward. When I tear off one more set of hands, he breaks through and sprints to the bathroom.

I'm right behind him.

I shut and lock the door. They bang and shout. No lights, still.

"Maximoff." I redirect my phone light on his body for a split-second. He's clutching the sink edge. Slightly hunched forward, abnormal for him.

I can't focus on him yet. It's killing me not to.

I click my mic and swing the light to the entire bathroom. I kick open stall doors. Empty, empty. "Farrow to Omega, we're not making it to Ballroom E." Empty, empty, empty, empty. This is a girl's bathroom, about twelve stalls.

Empty, empty.

Outside, fans start chanting, "Maximoff! Maximoff! Maximoff Hale! Maximoff! Maximoff! Maximoff Hale!"

Empty, empty, empty. I click my mic. "We're in a secured bathroom." I run to Maximoff in two strides, and I shine my light on him. "What's wrong?"

His eyes are tightened close, jaw clenched. And he swallows hard. *He's in pain.*

My stomach backflips. "Maximoff—"

"Where's Jane, Sulli, Beckett—are they okay?" He opens his eyes, only severe worry in them.

I click my mic. "Farrow to Omega, where's everyone?" I listen to their replies and examine his build, easily noticing the bone popped out of his shoulder socket.

"Farrow," he prods for the answer.

"Sulli and Beckett are in Ballroom E, safe. Crowds cut off Jane, but Thatcher and Quinn took her outside. She's safe in a cab." I gesture him to turn towards me. "Let me see your shoulder."

He says, "I'm fine." He wants to be.

"You're not fine."

People must've grabbed his shoulder and held on, pulling back while he moved forward. I should've shoved them off faster.

He tries to move his left arm, and he bites down, pain cinching his brows. "Fuck," he curses.

From behind him, I clutch his waist and slide my arm around him in affection. He almost leans into me, remembering who I am. Being honest here, he's still a marble statue.

"Let me help you." I shine a light on his shoulder.

"It's just sore."

"Your shoulder is dislocated."

Maximoff breathes through his nose and then grasps the sink ledge again. "Is that your professional medical opinion?" he asks. "Just by looking?"

"MAXIMOFF! MAXIMOFF!" they grow louder outside.

"Yeah." I stay behind him. "Also, you're a stubborn smartass. Point this at your shoulder." I pass him my phone.

He uses his good hand and directs the light. He watches me through the mirror.

"You can pop it in?"

"I can." I gently place a hand on the back of his shoulder, another on his elbow. Bracing his forearm with mine. His pulse is racing.

My stomach overturns. Wanting him to just calm. Relax. But he's hurt, and I know I'm at fault.

"MAXIMOFF! MAXIMOFF HALE!"

"I have to tell you something," I say seriously.

"If you're trying to distract me, it's not going to work—"

"I kissed a crew member."

"What—"

I click his shoulder back into place, and he lets out a long groan. "*Fuuuck*," he curses, and one breath later, he's glaring at me.

My brows lift. "I was kidding."

He breathes stronger but shakes his head. "You couldn't joke about literally anything else?"

"Nothing else would've worked."

He exhales. "And you're a fucking asshole." His arm curves around my shoulders.

"That too." I clutch the back of his neck, the light dancing around us as we shift. "I'm sorry—"

"Not your damn fault," he says, voice firm, and he subtly eyes me for any injuries. Seeing that I'm okay. "My old bodyguard would've done worse."

Yet, I should've done better. "You'll need to ice the shoulder, and you should call my father to look at it if the pain gets worse."

His brows furrow. "You just looked at it."

"Ligaments protect the shoulder joint, and four tendons are connected to your rotator cuff. If you tore any of those, you may need surgery. My father is more experienced. He'll know."

It surprises me when I think, *I wish I knew more than Edward Nathaniel Keene.*

My father has been wishing that too.

17

Maximoff Hale

CLEVELAND FANCON IS CANCELLED from hotel power outage.

Even on route to the next tour stop—Chicago, here we come—the news headline gnaws at me. The hotel confirmed that the power blew, and technicians couldn't fix the issue for at least 24-hours.

Security called the FanCon a wash. Ending the event early—it's an irremovable knife in my chest.

No promised Q&A. Majority of fans never met us. Some spent a lot of money just traveling to Cleveland.

And we fucked them over.

I tried to resolve the problem. I made calls, talked to the crew, and I could've shifted the event to another conference room in a nearby hotel.

Akara and Thatcher refused. *We haven't done prep for a different hotel,* they said. *It's not possible.*

I'm supposed to move on and forget Cleveland's mishap. *Think of this like trial-and-error,* Akara told me. *The Chicago FanCon will be better.*

I can't just forget. These *errors* I make hurt people—and I'm not okay with that.

"You need to brainstorm," Farrow tells me while he crunches his abs in a sit-up.

We're in the second lounge with Janie, a U-shaped couch back here. Pretty quiet since half the bus is asleep in their bunks.

Farrow isn't working out on the ground. He's lengthwise on the gray couch. I sit so damn close that his bent knees steeple my legs. My hand has been sliding down his thigh, and my other forearm rests on his kneecap while I cup my phone.

My childhood crush doing sit-ups right up against me—that should without a doubt be the *best* damn distraction from bad press. Sweat glistens his inked skin, pirate tattoos peek from his black Adidas V-neck, and a piece of white hair keeps falling to his brown lashes. Causing his fingers to constantly push the strands back.

Jesus, it's unnatural how hot he is. And how fucking attracted I am to him. *And still*, my mind derails and circumnavigates to Cleveland. To a colossal fuck-up.

He lifts his body in a crunch. His face a centimeter from my face, and he eyes my phone. The screen is popped up on a news article that I've read a billion times.

> The H.M.C. FanCon tour in Cleveland was a massive technical disaster with no backup plan. Maximoff Hale was unprepared to handle an event of this magnitude. If this is any indication of how he runs H.M.C. Philanthropies, it's clear he's too young, unprofessional, and inexperienced to be the CEO of a corporate company.

Farrow skims the words in point-two seconds and then chucks my phone behind his head. It hits a pillow and thuds on the floor.

"Thanks," I say dryly.

"Fuck them," he tells me with raised brows. "Calling you young and unprofessional is a cheap shot, and those journalists will take it every time." He lowers his back and rises in another sit-up. "That's the truth. I'm not blowing smoke because I'm dating and fucking you."

He lowers again, casual and cool. Acting like he reported a simple weather forecast.

Fuck me. I feel my smile try to take shape.

"Je suis d'accord avec lui, Moffy," Janie says, sitting on the couch's other long side. Mirror propped on her thighs. She applies an avocado mask, her hair twisted in a pink towel.

I agree with him, Moffy.

My mouth inches upward a bit more. I'm trying my best to let go, but some things are clinging to me like fucking tar.

I adjust my ice pack on my sore shoulder and remember what Farrow said about *brainstorming*.

So I lower my voice, ensuring Beckett, Charlie, and Sulli won't hear me. "I've thought about people who'd want to create a murder account," I tell him, "and I came up with absolutely nothing."

Farrow increases his sit-up pace. "Not one name?"

He already said he's taking care of the one-night stand NDAs, and he's been waiting for lawyers to send him those contracts. I only need to help brainstorm other people. Like a high school rival, a pissed off neighbor, or a scorned college student.

I picture…no one. Not really.

I did deal with my fair share of harassment in high school. Like the snide comments about my mom, the dick drawings, and accusing me of being a bastard.

Some guys hated me because they needed someone to hate. But I can't see them, years later, wanting me dead.

"If they exist," I tell Farrow, "I don't know about them."

His muscles flex on his way up.

"Janie?" I ask.

She cleans her hands on a towel and shuts her mirror. Blue eyes on me, she offers her complete attention. "You were always sweet to people and well-liked. And very famous. Many people had a crush on you in high school. Even the neighbors."

Farrow rolls his eyes.

I give him a look. "Come on, if I'd been around your age growing up, you would've had a crush on me too."

"And there goes your humility." On his way up, he twists to the right, near enough to kiss me.

Kiss me.

His mouth quirks before he leans back down. Such a tease.

I lick my lips. "Just stating the truth."

Amusement rests behind his eyes. "The truth is that you would've 'wanted' me to have a crush on you." He rises. "And you always, *always* would've been infatuated with me."

"That's already bullshit since I've never been infatuated with you."

He lets out a short, dry laugh before his smile expands. "Weren't you the one who dreamed of me taking your virginity in a shower?"

I blink.

Yeah.

I feel like he flipped over whatever metaphorical board game we were playing. Chess? Backgammon? Candy Land?

I feign confusion. "Was that you and me? Could've been another guy who looks like you."

"No one else looks like me," he says in that matter-of-fact voice that grips my body. He rises to his knees and twists…away from my face. He's smiling wide, still teasing the hell out of me.

It's working.

I swelter inside out, and I keep a hand on my ice pack to cool off.

Jane points her phone at us and snaps a candid photo of me and Farrow.

I tell Janie, "That better be evidence that *he* looks more infatuated than me."

"Memories." She examines the photo. "And from what I can see, you share equal infatuation."

I gesture to Farrow. "There it is."

He pushes back his hair, and our eyes caress in a powerful moment.

I inhale—and I break eye contact. My phone vibrating on the floor. Jane just texted me the picture. Perks of extra phone security, I now have photos of my boyfriend without fear of hacks.

But I leave my phone where it is and reroute back to the topic. "If Janie can't even think of someone who'd make a murder account, then we're doomed."

Farrow crunches up. "You're telling me no one was jealous of you? You're a wealthy, attractive celebrity who swam competitively."

I stare off, thinking.

"Moffy." Jane perks up in a sudden thought. "Jason, Ray, and Clark."

"Who?" Farrow asks, noticing my darkened frown. He stays upright, his arm on the back of the couch.

"Guys on the swim team with me," I answer. Remembering the yacht, the summer bash, from years ago. My cheekbones sharpen. "The last time I talked to them, we beat the shit out of each other."

Farrow sweeps my features. "I need more than that."

"Before I fought with Charlie on the yacht," I say, "I overheard them talking about my mom in the master cabin. And I went off." I shake my head a few times. "I was almost in a blackout rage, okay? I'm not proud."

Farrow stares deeper.

"What?" I ask.

"I was on that boat." Farrow pauses, his jaw tensed. "It's just hitting me that while I was laughing and drinking, you were below the deck getting beat to shit."

I let out a sharp breath. "I did worse to them—"

"You're not a trained fighter, and it was three-on-one. You were probably on the ground."

He's not wrong. "I held my own." I study his protective gaze, and I realize he wishes he could've been there for me. "You want a time machine?"

Farrow almost cracks a smile, but the gravity of the situation keeps him more serious. "What are their last names?"

Jane picks at her avocado mask. "Ray and Clark were both awarded scholarships to swim out of state. They wouldn't have a Philadelphia IP address."

"Jason Motlic would," I say. "He stayed in Philly." I look to Farrow. "You can put his name on the list."

"Okay." He doesn't reach for a notebook or his phone or *anything*.

"So it's an imaginary list."

Farrow arches his brows. "My memory is better than yours. I don't need to type out and print eighty-four lists."

I make a face. "How do I like you, man?"

"I think you mean *love*," he teases.

Don't fucking smile. I lick my lips again and again, and before I reply, I notice Janie lying down on the other side of the couch. She kind of tucks her knees to her chest. Something she only does when she has cramps.

"Ça va?" I ask. *Are you okay?*

"Oui." She splays the back of her hand on her forehead.

"Si tu ne te sens pas bien, je peux te trouver quelque chose." *If you don't feel well, I can find you something.*

"I weather this storm every month. I can manage on a bus." She blows out a measured breath. "Peaches McEntire."

My brows scrunch. "No way."

Farrow starts another rep of sit-ups. "Peaches is a fruit or a…?"

"Girl," I explain. "She's our age, and we were all counselors at Camp Calloway together. She was even a troop captain in Wolf Scouts." I look at Jane, her cat pajamas wrinkled. "And she's *nice*."

"She was hopelessly, madly in love with you, and she was a passionate person. She could've felt scorned when you told her you just wanted to be summer camp friends. Don't you remember, she stopped speaking to you after that?"

I sigh heavily, frustrated that I may've hurt someone unknowingly. "Maybe." I glance at Farrow as he crunches upward. "You can add Peaches to your brain."

He'd probably reply, but Thatcher breaches the second lounge.

We all go quiet.

The security team has no clue that Jane and I know all about the @maximoffdeadhale account. Farrow has "gone rogue" in the team *many* times before, so it's not exactly a new dilemma.

Farrow looks more annoyed by Thatcher than anything.

The Omega co-lead pretty much ignores me and Farrow, and he takes a seat near Jane's feet. She scratches her neck and props herself on her arm. "Thatcher," she greets.

"Jane," he greets too, like they haven't seen each other all day. When *clearly* they have.

I give Janie a weird look, but she's tuning me out. I turn to Farrow, but he's zeroed in on the interaction.

"Thought you might need this," Thatcher says as he hands her a hot water bottle.

Jane gawks in surprise, fingers to her avocado-masked cheek. She clears her throat slightly. "Merci." She nods to him.

He nods back and leaves without another word.

"What the fuck was that?" I whisper.

Farrow glares at Jane. "You can't like him."

"She doesn't like him," I say to Farrow. "She would've told me."

Jane is still staring at the spot where he left. Blue eyes enlarging like a god granted immortality to her cats. "He must've seen my Instagram story. I said that I had cramps and forgot to bring a heating pad on the bus." She glances at the hot water bottle that'll help her cramps.

"She likes him," Farrow says in pissed disbelief. "*Jane.*"

"Who? What?" She finally turns to us and our words seem to register. "No, *no.*" She shakes her head a few times. "I just find him beautiful to look at. Like an Italian painting. He's exquisite, don't you think?"

"No," we say together.

Jane smiles coyly. "Liars. You both know he's handsome."

I don't say anything and remove my ice pack. Is Thatcher fucking hot? Scruffy, muscular, six-foot-seven and domineering. Yeah.

He's hot.

He could probably star in movies if he wanted to. But Farrow hates him, and Thatcher is dropping off my *favorites* list.

Farrow narrows his gaze on me. "I'm waiting for you to say *he's ugly.*"

"I'm waiting for you to say the same fucking thing." I pull my Batman shirt over my head.

"He's ugly," Farrow says distantly, skimming the cut of my biceps and six-pack. Mostly, he hones in on my shoulder blade.

"Agreed," I lie and motion to Jane. "And?"

"He's handsome and sweet, and that's all that's happening." She sends us a look that says, *do not badger me on senseless things,* and she curls back up and tucks her hot water bottle to her stomach.

"Lean forward," Farrow says.

I do, my elbows on his knees that still steeple my legs. He has a better view of my shoulder. He presses on the muscle.

I bite down. *Christ,* that feels tender and sore.

"Raise your arm."

I stretch my arm upward. The muscle is pretty tight. I rotate my arm—*that's really tight.*

"You need to keep icing it," Farrow says.

I nod. Calling his father for advice opens a can of worms, and I'm not sure how much longer I should wait.

18

Maximoff Hale

I WAKE EARLY AND FORAGE for cereal in the first lounge. Yawning into my bicep a fucking ton.

I think Oscar is behind the wheel, but the privacy door is shut. So I can't see into the driver's quarters.

Near the bathroom door, a coffee pot sits on a granite counter. I bend down and open a cabinet, finding most of the dry foods.

I hear movement from the narrowed hall. Where the bunks are located.

Farrow climbs out of his. Feet hitting the cold floor. I watch him rub his eyes roughly with the heel of his palm. Hair messy, he's shirtless, and his drawstring pants hang low on his sculpted waist. Tattooed sparrows peeking out of the elastic band.

God, my chest rises in a shallow breath. My body, brain, and everything in between is *begging* me to abandon my cereal hunt and push him up against the wall.

I'm used to fucking Farrow morning and night—and that routine has been shot to hell with the bus set-up.

Don't think about jumping his bones. Don't think about his dick rubbing against your dick. Don't think about his arms wrapped around you or his hand sliding down your chest and up to your throat.

I'm obviously thinking about every position, every embrace—every nerve that wants pricked and lit. I stare off and imagine *all of it*.

I blink a couple times to tear out of a fantasy.

And his eyes are on mine, his know-it-all smile slowly rising. I kid you not, I have to look away like I'm in fifth fucking grade and worried I'll spring a boner in class.

Focus.

Cereal. Right.

I push aside a box of Cocoa Crispies, which belong to Sulli, and that's when I sense his presence like overwhelming lightning. Raw voltage strikes my body. Head-to-fucking-toe. It ripples down my arms, legs and chest.

Scorching me.

He leans on the damn counter, his feet right up against me. I have a fantastic view of his bare calves, an inked ship on the left.

I rub my jaw, my muscles blistering with a million desires. *Focus.* My gaze narrows to fired pinpoints, and I purposefully ignore him. Continuing my search.

"Someone looks like they're having fun," he says.

I'm afraid if I respond it'll be with *fuck me*. Right now, that needs to be more of a *fuck you* and not the sexual *fuck you*.

Like a real fuck you, fuck you.

"I'd help you," Farrow tells me, "but I kind of like this view."

I push around a box of Cheerios. "You do love to do that whole towering over me thing." I don't even know what the hell I'm trying to find anymore.

This just seems like the best distraction.

Fuck my high sex drive.

"You usually don't let me do it unless you're about to blow me," he says casually.

Yeah, I've been trying *not* to imagine taking him in my mouth.

"But you haven't even looked in my direction once," he continues. "Blow jobs are off the table then."

"Kitchen blow jobs in front of everyone are *definitely* not happening." My voice is more serious than I intended.

"It was a joke, wolf scout," he says coolly, calmly—like his entire world resides on a beach somewhere sipping Mai Tais with zero stress and zero irritations.

Finally, I swing my gaze up to him.

Sure enough, he's doing the whole towering over me thing. Elbow on the counter, lips curved, and head slightly tilted. It's sexier than what I pictured in my head. He seems taller.

Older.

Stronger.

His silver rings lightly drum the granite with a *click click click*.

And yeah, I'm in a perfect position to blow him. Every bone in my body screams at me to clutch his ass, suck him off, and watch him come.

I'd like to do a lot of damn things that can't happen on a crowded tour bus.

My muscles burn. "Your jokes aren't funny today."

Farrow lets out a low whistle. "I'd ask who pissed in your Cheerios, but you're still looking for them."

"Again," I say and then snag a box of Raisin Bran. Rising to my feet, we meet at eye level since he's slouching. "Not funny."

Our eyes catch and hold. *Fuck me hard, man.*

"Noted," he says, and he reaches out, about to touch my neck—I jerk away.

"Don't touch me." My voice is firm. For Christ's sake, I need to be a hundred feet from this guy. No eye contact. Definitely no skin contact. Not until we reach the next hotel.

Farrow straightens up almost instantly. Worry shades his face. "Okay, now I'm going to ask," he says. "What's wrong?"

"Nothing." I tear open the Raisin Bran and walk stiffly towards the couch. "Walk" is honestly an exaggeration. The counter and the couch are barely three feet apart—and I'm fixating on stupid shit on purpose.

"Maximoff."

I turn.

His barbell rises with his brows.

I breathe out an agitated breath. "Fuck, man. We haven't had sex in a while. I can't look at you." I recognize that I can go masturbate, but I'm dying for him.

Not for my hand.

He rests more against the counter and fixes his bed-head hair. Back to being cool, calm and collected. It's like a switch that I apparently don't possess.

"Because you want to jump my bones," he adds and eyes me up and down. "How are you unable to keep my company now, but you did fine when I was *just* your bodyguard? You weren't having sex then and that was two months."

I don't know.

I honestly don't know.

I start shaking my head. Maybe it's because I have access to him. Because my imagination satiated me back then. Now that I have him, *God*, I want him.

"I don't have the answers," I say seriously. "I just listen to my body."

"And what does it say?" His voice is a graveled whisper.

I rake a hand through my hair. "Need. Want…*You.*"

Farrow nods slowly, as though repeating those words over and over. His thumb skims his bottom lip, and he glances over to the bathroom door. "So there's a shower here—"

"That has thin walls," I cut him off.

"We'll be quiet."

"And when we walk out of the bathroom together, people will just think we were in there knitting sweaters," I say, sarcasm thick.

He steps away from the counter. "They'll think we were fucking, wolf scout." A smile plays at his lips. "And you have to be okay with that."

Privacy in my sex life is like a rope I'm hanging onto while suspended over a bridge. But today is different. Today, I'm far willing to loosen my grip on that damn rope.

19

Farrow Keene

MAXIMOFF RAMS MY BACK to the tiled wall, a breath and grunt ejecting from my throat. Hot water pelts our flesh, shower glass fogged. *Good fucking God.*

Our locked gazes dig deeper, and I hold his face, gaining control as our mouths crash together with force and fire.

He kisses like he's been depraved of my tongue and body. I reciprocate like my greatest want is to satiate this gorgeous-as-fuck guy. And it is.

I'm extremely attracted to turning him on and watching him get off. Fuck, I'm going to make him come hard.

I catch his lip between my teeth, and his hips thrust forward for closer contact. My mouth curves, seeing clearly that he wants to plow me. He fists my wet hair, and a husky noise rumbles inside of my lungs. *Fuck.*

The small confines of the shower fall to the wayside with our heat. Our touch. Both of us lean but muscular and cut, both nearly the same height, both at equal strength—we play for an advantage and his *needs* fuel mine.

Still clutching his jaw, my other hand trails down his wet chest to his abs and then I grip him and stroke his rock-hard length.

He buries his mouth against my neck and tries to stifle a low, pleasured growl that rouses my cock.

"*Fuck*, Maximoff," I breathe, water still raining down on us.

He fists my wet hair, and he watches my fingers that wrap around him and pump. Driving him to a cliff.

Maximoff grinds aggressively into me, and then he starts rubbing me with a mind-numbing speed—*fucking hell.*

I go to rotate us—so his back will slam against the tiles—but he pins me harder.

Breath knocks out of me, my lips almost lifting. *So it's like that then.* He wants me here, and I reach a place where I can't flip him.

We jerk each other off faster, hands up and down. In a melodic, heady pace. Our foreheads nearly touch. His forest-green eyes devour me whole, and beads of water roll sensually down his sharpened jaw.

Steam rises.

I grit down as the pressure builds. My head tries to loll back, but it touches shower tile. He takes both of our erections in one hand and pumps us in a closed fist. Back and forth. Our pre-cum coating his palm.

Pressure and friction fuses in an explosive combination. Hardened like brick, my pulse hammers in my cock.

I grip his face tighter, and he breathes lowly, "I want to fuck your mouth."

I eye his pink lips. "We have a problem then. Because I want to fuck your mouth." I tilt my head. "Who's first, wolf scout?"

Maximoff answers by letting go of us, and he places a strong hand on my shoulder. It's cute that he tries to push me to my knees, but I already willingly kneel.

I clutch his round ass with one hand and grip his shaft with the other. He soaks in every minuscule movement I make with rapt attention. I almost come just watching him watch me.

Before I take him, I suck his balls, teasing, and he lets out a harsh, breathy curse, "*Fuck me.*" He pounds a glare in me. "*Farrow.*"

"You're impatient," I tell him.

"Old news." He combs my wet hair back. "I need you—*goddamn.*" He swears when I abruptly suck his cock.

Maximoff tries to "fuck my mouth" and thrust forward, but I tighten my grip on his ass and shaft. Maintaining control, my head moves back and forth. I lick the length of him at one point, and he shudders before I take all of him to the back of my throat.

He swallows a groan and rests his forearm on the tile, hand in a fist. His muscles flexed. Nearing the edge. I'm on the same exact one.

We latch eyes—and I taste him. He comes hard, his legs contracted and eyes pierced in a glare at the ceiling before they roll back. Jaw like carved marble and noise trapped in his lungs. He breathes heavily through his nose.

Fuck.

His cum-face is by far my favorite thing. I engrain every second in my mind.

I swallow and milk his climax with my hand. My mouth trails up his waist, sucking his chiseled abs to his chest, and by the time I reach his neck, his mouth descends. Sucking my neck, then his tongue toys with my nipple barbell piercing.

My nose flares, *fuck.* I flex and watch him suck my nipple.

I brace my shoulder blades on the tile and wipe water out of my face. Keeping a hand on the back of his head as he lowers to his knees.

He drinks in my entire build, my pelvis arched casually towards him. When our gazes hit, I raise my brows. "Need to take a picture?"

Maximoff gives me a middle finger. And then he pushes that finger in my hole—*good God.* He massages my prostate while his mouth wraps around me. *Damn.* Nerves ablaze, I start reaching a new height.

I grit down so hard, my jaw aches. Not allowing any noise to escape.

My hand stable on the back of his head, I move him back and forth. Maximoff makes a ragged noise, not excited about me taking charge. His broad shoulders bind, and before I shift, he slides a second finger inside me—*fuckfuck.* The pressure and nerves well, amplifying.

I breathe hot breath through my nose. On another plane of pleasure. Of intensity. To the point where my hand drops from his head to his neck.

He gains full control of my orgasm.

Consuming me. His hot forest-green eyes fuck me as powerfully as his mouth. My body tightens, and in one surging moment, I release. Hitting a peak. My head on the wall tile, my pulse thumps like heavy bass, and a groan strangles in my chest.

When my mouth does part, I breathe out, *"Fuck."*

Maximoff swallows and then rubs me a few times, eking out the tension. My chest rises and falls as I catch my breath. More steam blanketing us in heat.

I remember what Jane said about most people "crushing" on Maximoff. I can believe it. He's such a man's man. People either admire him, want to be him, or want to fuck him.

And I never forget that out of everyone, he fell in love with me.

"GAME PLAN," MAXIMOFF TELLS ME. "I'LL GO OUT

first, and then you'll wait five minutes to leave the bathroom."

I rub a towel through my damp hair. My smile is fucking killing me. "As adorable as you are sneaking around, you can't control this. They all know we're both in here together."

We can clearly hear chatter in the first lounge. Which is right outside the bathroom. Most of his cousins and the other bodyguards are awake. Oscar even knocked on the door and said, *"I need to piss."* That means Akara is now driving. Sulli most likely woke up because she's notorious for not wanting to miss anything.

And others followed suit.

Maximoff knows all of this.

Yet, he says, "We don't know that." He zips up his jeans.

Good luck steering that ship, the security team told me. I almost smile because Maximoff being headstrong is as expected as finding a tree in a forest.

And there's no reason to ask why he suddenly cares. I'm assuming reality is catching up to him, and he really, *really* dislikes when people know the details of his sex life.

He can easily talk about sex in generalizations, but when it includes "when" and "where" and "how often" he's used to shutting down.

I wrap my towel low around my waist. I didn't bring extra clothes in the bathroom. Leaning on the sink, I say, "How about I leave and you wait five minutes in here?"

Maximoff pulls a gray shirt over his head. Water drips off his wet hair and runs down his temples. He's thinking.

"Or," I say, "we can walk out together." I pass him in the cramped space, our chests brushing, and I place a hand on the doorknob. "Your choice, wolf scout."

"Alright." He takes a confident breath. "I'll leave with you."

I open the door and step into the first lounge with ease. Besides Akara and Sulli in the driver and passenger seat, every person is packed in here.

All three Cobalts are squished on a couch, busy on their phones, and Omega bodyguards cram in the booth and the adjacent couch, eating cereal.

Their heads whip to us, and the chatter dies when Maximoff emerges. His jaw is tensed like he's ready to enter a fight.

SFO eagle-eyes him ten times more than they scrutinize me, their curiosity apparent. Before I came along, security used to talk about Maximoff's one-night stands like a myth and legend, and no one has ever seen him "after" before.

My jaw tics, face all hard territorial lines. *Back the fuck off* written numerous times. They divert their gazes. I comb a hand through my hair and watch Maximoff reach the small counter. He makes hot tea, his body rigid.

"Didn't you have to piss?" I ask Oscar.

He stands and whispers to me as he passes, "You lucky bastard." The bathroom door shuts behind him.

As normal chatter returns, I enter the narrowed hall. Sliding the curtains to my bunk aside, I grab my small duffel and pick out clothes. I change in the empty second lounge, cracking the door.

Black pants on, I slip my leather belt into the loops and clasp the buckle—suddenly, all noise fades again.

Something's wrong.

I gently kick the door open wider. Able to see down the hallway and into the first lounge.

Shit.

Charlie leans forward on the couch and stares Maximoff down like he's trying to hook a fish for dinner.

I ditch my shirt and reroute back to everyone just as Maximoff sets his mug aside and says to Charlie, "If you have something to say, just say it."

I fill the doorway and hang casually onto a pull-up bar above me, one that Sulli and Beckett put together. Oscar is already out of the bathroom, and Jane is inside brushing her teeth. I sense Oscar silently telling me to "stand down" and not intervene in a Cobalt-Hale feud.

As bodyguards, we're not allowed, but that's *my* boyfriend on the end of someone's glare. And I've never sat idly by and let a man I love fight a battle alone.

Charlie flips his phone from hand-to-hand, and his twin brother whispers in his ear. I can't hear what Beckett says, but no one expects Charlie to hold his tongue.

"You pride yourself on being respectful," Charlie begins, "and in your mind, I guess fucking in a shower that nine other people use lands in that category."

Fuck him. My hand drops off the pull-up bar, and swiftly, Oscar, Donnelly, Quinn, and even Thatcher stand and block my path.

Maximoff glowers at Charlie. "You haven't spoken to me *once* since we started this tour, and that's the first thing you tell me?"

Thatcher whispers to me, "Calm down."

"Don't talk to me," I say in a calm voice. I'm not thrashing around or about to pop off, but they're very aware that I can slip into a fight and cold-cock Charlie.

"You're the one who just asked me to say something," Charlie says and then laughs bitterly. "I'm sorry it's not what you wanted to hear, but maybe you shouldn't surround yourself with people who kiss your ass all day, all long."

Maximoff inhales a sharp, agitated breath. His jaw severely sharpened, and he turns and looks briefly around. He's trying to find someone. A guy who believes he can do everything on his own is searching for one other person.

For me.

His gaze lands on *me*.

I step forward—Oscar puts a hand on my chest.

"Oscar—"

"Leave my client alone," Oscar says, his voice non-threatening. We're both familiar with Charlie and Maximoff going head-to-head.

I lower my voice. "Tell your client to back off mine."

Oscar shakes his head. "Charlie only listens to Charlie…and *sometimes* Beckett."

Charlie still zeroes in on Maximoff. "Here's the cold-hearted truth. You actually *like* boasting. You get off on being better than all of us, so you come out here, practically bragging about fucking your boyfriend, whenever you want, whenever you like."

Coarse hands splay over my mouth, restraining the string of attacks that I could've and probably would've spewed. Because I know just how deep and cold those words go.

I'm not surprised when Maximoff charges Charlie, but Beckett shoots up, standing in front of his brother.

"Stop," Beckett says calmly, but Maximoff already rocks back, his fists at his side.

"Charlie," Jane warns from the bathroom, toothbrush in her mouth.

I try to tear Donnelly's hand off my lips, but he shakes his head at me a few times. Quinn whispers to me, "Let them be."

Okay, I'm not taking advice from the youngest, greenest bodyguard. I rip Donnelly's hand off, freeing my mouth, but I stay silent.

Thatcher motions for me to sequester myself in the second lounge. I ignore him.

Sulli shouts from the passenger seat, "Can we please have a non-hyped and non-fucked-up conversation?"

"No," Charlie and Maximoff say.

Charlie is the only one still sitting, besides Akara and Sulli up front.

"You're so fucking far from the truth," Maximoff says, "that you don't even realize—"

"That you're arrogant and conceited and a bigger asshole than you'll ever admit? I realize I'm a lot of things, but why can't you? Oh." Charlie cocks his head. "Because you're a coward and a hypocrite."

"Jesus fucking Christ," Maximoff growls. "I don't pride myself on anything, let alone being respectful. You want me to admit I'm an arrogant fucking asshole? Then I am one. I'm shit on the bottom of your shoe, and that's what I'll always be to you, Charlie. At this point, you're just trying to piss me off."

Charlie leans back and rubs his lips. "Think what you want," he says more quietly. "I'm not going to argue with you. You'll only listen to yourself."

Maximoff takes a short breath, and his phone rings shrilly in his pocket. Charlie and him stare each other down for one beat longer, and then Maximoff retrieves his phone and pushes towards the hallway.

Towards me and the wall of bodyguards.

As he nears, they all part to let him through. I don't move, and so he faces me.

His chest collapses and rises heavily, but his defenses start imprisoning his expression. Blank and cold.

Everyone is watching us.

I have to step back and let him through, but I catch his wrist and whisper against his ear, "You're not alone, Maximoff."

He inhales stronger, and his expression almost breaks through. But he says, "I have to take this." I watch his lengthy stride down the hallway, and then he disappears into the second lounge. Shutting the door.

Oscar brings me to the aisle of bunks. "You don't want to get in the middle of that," he whispers. "They've been at each other's throats for years."

I comb both hands through my hair. "I can't watch Charlie beat him down," I say just as softly, but all the Cobalts start talking in French on the couch. In deep conversation.

"They're both beating each other down," Oscar whispers. "The fact that you're not seeing that is the problem. You're too close to this shit. Back away for the sake of not starting a war on the bus."

"The war is going to start with or without me," I tell him.

"Without you then." Oscar places a hand on my shoulder "Promise me, Redford. Because if he goes at you and you jump in, I'll lose my job defending your impulsive ass."

"Don't defend me," I say easily.

Oscar pushes back the curlier strands of his hair. "You can pretend like you have no close friends, but you and me are encroaching a decade here. You're stuck with us like we're unfortunately stuck with you."

I grab onto a bunk, my arms loosening. "Okay—"

"Farrow!" Maximoff calls me, door ajar.

"Saved by the boyfriend," Oscar says, and I roll my eyes, quickly reaching the second lounge.

By the time I'm alone with Maximoff, I study his furrowed brows and the phone tight in his hand. His upright posture screams "damage control".

"What's going on?" I ask.

"That was your father."

I frown. Maximoff called my father about his shoulder yesterday. The last time he lifted his arm at ninety-degrees, he said he felt like the muscle was pinching. I told him that, at the very least, he should just make the call. When my father didn't answer, he left him a message.

"He was calling me back," Maximoff says and opens the mini-fridge, a game console stacked on top.

"And?"

He pops a can of Fizz Life. "It looks like I need to find a new doctor."

I'm hearing him wrong. "My father is still your physician."

"No. Dr. Keene said *it's a conflict of interest* since you're my boyfriend and you're his son." Maximoff swigs his Fizz Life, handling the bad news like he's delivering morning stocks. Outlook: *shitty*.

"Call him back or I will—"

"No," Maximoff says firmly. "No, it's not worth the trouble. I'm moving forward from this." He's pivoting, swimming at break-neck speed above a current trying to yank him under. But this isn't the same as paparazzi ruining his morning commute.

This is a big change in his structured life. Fuck, he's *always* had my father. It's a constant, a safety, and this is a rug ripping out from under him.

I thought he'd be more rattled. "What aren't you telling me?" I ask.

He looks away, then back to me. "It's nothing."

That's bullshit. "You want to protect your cousins and your siblings and your parents, go ahead. But the last thing you need to do is coddle me. Give me the fucking courtesy that I'd give you and tell me the entire thing."

He stares at me like he's weighing the outcomes.

There's only one outcome. "Maximoff—"

"He told me to tell you something." He stops there.

"Getting better. Keep going." I wave him on.

Maximoff now looks thoroughly irritated, and I'd smile if the subject matter weren't skewed towards serious.

"He said," Maximoff continues, "that if you complete your year residency, I'd be able to have one of the best physicians. Someone that I could trust. Someone that's even better than him."

I roll my eyes in a dramatic circle. *Seriously.* I almost can't believe that my father took it there. He's consciously fucking with my boyfriend's life just so I'll return to medicine.

It's low.

And desperate.

Maximoff adds, "But I told your father that you're not going back. That's not what you want. I think he just wants me to convince you."

I let out a short laugh. "I can't believe him." My face contorts through a series of emotions that I can't name. If he really wanted me to be a practicing doctor, he should've tried repairing our torn relationship first, not destroying the last shreds.

I look up at Maximoff. "And he thinks me being your doctor is somehow *less* of a conflict of interest?"

"Strangely, yeah. I don't want you to do it, but in an alternate universe where you did, I still wouldn't have a concierge doctor for a full year while you did your residency. He's leaving me with little options, and he knows it." Maximoff gestures to me with his soda. "I even asked him if he could recommend a new physician, and the only name he could give me was yours."

"That's fucked up." I run a hand along my jaw. Calling my father back won't change his mind. He only wants one thing, and it's not words.

Maximoff nears and hooks a couple fingers in my waistband. We draw closer, and his stoic gaze thunders against me, the heady beat saying we're dealing with this shit together. Not apart.

I grip the hem of his shirt, but he takes over and lifts the gray fabric off his head. Knowing I'm examining his muscle again. He has swimmer's shoulders, really used to being stretched and rotated. Especially with the butterfly stroke.

There's no bruising and the swelling is gone. *Better.* "How does it feel?" I ask.

"Just sore," he says. "I haven't been swimming as much while on tour, and I think maybe I'm just tight. I need to stretch more."

I nod. "I'll keep an eye on it."

He tucks his shirt in his back pocket. "I know I'm making it worse—the friction between you and your dad."

"It was never going to get better."

Maximoff offers his Fizz Life, and my mouth rises as I accept the can. Taking a sip.

"That's kind of how I feel about Charlie and me," he says, his large hand on my waist, pulling me closer. Our legs knock, and neither of us shifts back.

I hold the curve between his neck and good shoulder. "Have you ever talked to him about Harvard?"

He shakes his head. "Even if I wanted to, I can never get that far. He makes it impossible." Maximoff frowns at a thought. "I know I don't make it any easier, either. It's just…" His brows scrunch. "…some people aren't meant to be friends. Maybe that's just us."

20

Maximoff Hale

CHICAGO, THANK GOD we're here.

We're alive and breathing and no one's been punched, in case you were concerned.

So at 3:00 a.m. in our hotel room, Farrow got a call. Spoiler Alert: it's not a bad one this time. Akara invited him to the hotel bar for drinks. All the bodyguards are there, *off-duty*, while my cousins are safe asleep.

As soon as Farrow hung up, he turned to me and said, "You're coming along, wolf scout."

I was already wide-awake. Sending out work emails and trying not to think about tomorrow's meet-and-greet. And I wasn't about to reject a rare offer to hang out with Security Force Omega.

Farrow and I—we're still in the early stages of our relationship. I'm pretty damn sure. Like 70%. If we're basing the "stages" on time, then I'm confidently 99%. Because we haven't reached a six-month mark yet and that seems like a solid relationship number.

I think. Because if we calculate hours spent together, our number is ridiculously high—*stop thinking*.

Obviously I don't know how any of this works. There's no playbook for dating your bodyguard. If there was, I'd own about a million goddamn copies. But I still want all of his friends to treat me like a regular guy and not just Maximoff Hale the Celebrity Client.

I'm not even positive that's an achievable goal. Maybe it's something completely out-of-this-world impossible and I'm shooting beyond the stars.

But I gotta try.

I zip up my green jacket. "So which one is your best friend?" I ask Farrow as we ditch the elevator and jog down a flight of hotel stairs. Anything to move around a bit. The cavernous cement stairwell is also empty, no strangers lurking.

Farrow is step-for-step in line with me. Descending the stairs swiftly, he fixes his earpiece and says, "None of them."

"Bullshit," I retort, "they're definitely your best friends."

Farrow tosses his head from side-to-side, considering. "No."

I make a face.

He puts a piece of gum in his mouth. "They're all aggravating on any given day."

"What are you, allergic to friendship?"

He rolls his eyes into a smile. "Allergic to friendship," he repeats, chewing his gum. "I don't enjoy owing people anything, and having 'best friends' is a commitment that I'm not actively signing up for."

"I get it," I say. "You don't like anyone tying you down—"

"One person can tie me down," he cuts me off and then glances at me. "You're smiling."

"I'm not." I sort of was. I unhinge my jaw, ridding whatever expression is causing him to overflow with satisfaction.

His grin has landed in James Franco territory. "I didn't say that person was you."

I blink. "You ever hear of that annoying six-foot-three guy with bleach-white hair who died in a Chicago stairwell?"

He laughs. "You mean the guy you have a hard-on for."

"No, the other one," I say dryly, and when I jump a couple stairs, he easily keeps pace. "So which one do you hate the least then?"

"Like I said, they're all aggravating."

I sigh heavily and stretch my arms while we descend the stairs. "Give me some slack here, man. It's not like you needed cliff notes when you met Jane. You practically already had the Jane Cobalt Encyclopedia."

His expression softens. "Okay. Cliff notes. I grew up in the same neighborhood as Akara, but we never talked, not even in high school. Different social circles. That shit." We pass the fifth floor doors, and he adds, "I met Oscar at Yale. Donnelly, I met him a little before I went to college. Then he followed me, and he'd crash in my dorm, my apartment—he's like an infection you can't rid."

"An infection that did some of your tattoos," I say.

Farrow glances at me, more serious. "No, he did most of my tattoos. I met him when he was an apprentice, but he can draw and I liked his style. He became really good."

Huh. "What's most?"

"I'd say about eighty-five percent is Paul Donnelly."

I stop on the third floor, and he follows suit, leaning casually on the railing. My eyes graze the crossed swords on his throat, wings on his neck. I'm not an expert on tattoos, but I always considered Farrow's ink nothing short of *breathtaking* and fucking gorgeous.

"So let me try to understand," I say. "You've known Donnelly for almost ten years, you let him tattoo you, crash at your place, you probably introduced him to security work, and you still don't consider him your best friend. In fact, you refer to him as an *infection*."

His lips rise. "If you knew him better, you'd realize he'd take that as a compliment."

"I'm being serious."

Farrow shrugs. "It's not like you and Jane. You two are *best* friends. See, what I have is a group of guys that I sometimes get along with. Sometimes I don't. Sometimes we hang out. Sometimes we don't." He smiles off my confusion. "It's not that complicated, wolf scout. That's how I like it."

A BULBED *CHICAGO* SIGN BACKLIGHTS THE SMALL hotel bar and array of liquor bottles. But no bartender mans the counter. Blue and red Chicago Cubs posters decorate wooden walls, and all the rustic high-top tables are vacant except one.

The five bodyguards instantly spot us—and their talk pretty much vanishes. I'm aware that Thatcher, Akara, Oscar, Quinn and Donnelly are eyeing me, not Farrow.

Jesus.

I'm starting to think I've been cursed with a superpower that causes verbal paralysis.

"Hey," I say confidently, and most of them reply, "Hey, man."

Akara slides another wooden stool next to the only unoccupied one. I figured they had no clue I'd be joining Farrow. So I'm not as shocked as they are.

"Look who showed up," Oscar says to Farrow.

"Not for you, Oliveira."

Oscar cracks a smile, and Farrow and I take a seat on the two open stools. He rubs my thigh, almost to say, *don't overthink.*

Good idea. I hadn't thought of that one before.

My palm brushes his hand, and I end up resting an elbow on the circular table. My attempt at *not* sitting like I'm about to run an Ironman Triathlon.

Battery candles, dice, nuts, liquor bottles and whiskey glasses scatter the wooden surface.

Donnelly doles out three dice to everyone, a cigarette burning between his fingers. "Maximoff would know…" he trails off at a no-nonsense look from Akara.

Oscar mimes slicing his neck. I'm guessing he's saying, *don't go there.* But I can't be sure.

"Talk about something else," Thatcher says, voice stern.

I'm guessing they're censoring themselves around me. I've been with bodyguards off-duty plenty of times before—like the Hallow Friends Eve and even just on the tour bus—but they try not to dig for secrets and they dodge certain topics about my family.

Farrow splays his earpiece wire over his shoulder. "Which one of you fuckers scared the bartender off?"

"Bar and kitchen closed five minutes ago," Akara says while texting and then he pockets his phone.

Quinn swishes a bottle of Jack Daniels. "Bought it before the bartender left."

I'm still super-glued to the *Maximoff would know* comment. "Donnelly," I say, all eyes on me. "You can ask me. It's alright if it's about my family." I already know how the world perceives the Hales, Meadows and Cobalts, and security can't view us worse than strangers who are fed tabloid lies.

Donnelly blows smoke into the air, and the bodyguards exchange cagey glances that I can't fucking read. They must come to a verdict because he speaks and no one stops him. "Heard about Eliot and been discussing whether it's real or rumor. Figured you'd know."

I know about that incident thanks to a hundred texts at midnight, and Luna, Eliot, and Tom FaceTimed me together. "What'd you guys hear?"

Oscar cracks a peanut and pops it in his mouth. "I heard he got a week suspension."

"For messing with some guy's Porsche," Quinn chimes in and pours whiskey in an empty glass.

Donnelly sticks his cigarette in his mouth and mumbles, "If someone fucked with my Porsche, I'd have him by the nuts."

Farrow chews his gum with a growing smile. "You know we've left reality when Donnelly thinks he has a Porsche."

Everyone laughs, including me, and the mood lightens, Omega starting to relax around me.

Donnelly nods to me. "Real or rumor?"

"Real," I say. "You hear what he did to the Porsche?" *Farrow knows.* I already told him.

"Nah, no one's said yet."

I think about how this won't ever reach the public. You'll never hear about Eliot's suspension thanks to the Cobalt's lawyers, but I'm betting security will find out tomorrow morning.

And SFO is about to find out by me tonight.

"In red paint," I tell them, "he wrote *'the most unkindest cut of all'* on the windshield." I shake my head a few times, conflicted. I wish I could defend my eighteen-year-old cousin, but he vandalized another guy's car. Eliot is a Cobalt, innately passionate. I swear he can never do anything half-heartedly.

"What the hell does that even mean?" Quinn asks. "The most unkindest...what?"

"Should've gone to college, little bro." Oscar throws back a whiskey shot.

Quinn scowls. "Maximoff didn't go to college—"

"He's a billionaire. He didn't need to go to college." Oscar outstretches his arm. "If you quit boxing, you should've gotten a degree, not followed me into securi—"

"Guys, be cool," Akara interjects. This isn't the first time the Oliveira brothers have argued on tour. At least they never get physical like Charlie and me.

Quinn clenches his jaw and screws the cap on the whiskey bottle.

"It's a quote from *Julius Caesar*," I explain. "You know Tom was with Eliot?"

Donnelly smirks. "My Cobalt children, slayin' together."

Thatcher shakes his head. "Let's not advocate vandalism, especially among the teenagers."

"Advocado-what?" Donnelly pretends to be dumb.

I laugh with some of them, and Farrow eyes me a bit, his smile stretching.

"How'd Tom get out of trouble?" Akara asks me.

"Eliot just took all the blame for them." I pause, their heads turning to the entrance. Vigilant as a middle-aged woman peeks in the bar and pops out. I hear her tell a friend that it looks empty in there, and their footsteps fade away.

Not spotted. For once.

Their attention fixing on me again, I finish, "The whole thing was Eliot's idea anyway."

Oscar digs through the peanut shells. "Why'd they do it?"

I decide to be vague, the whole truth too personal. "The guy was messing with my sister."

Luna clued Tom and Eliot in on the pregnancy scare, and they said the guy she slept with was spending his holiday break telling his friends that Luna Hale is a slut.

I wish I could've teleported to Philly.

So I could do something. Be there for her. I don't know if she told our mom and dad yet. And I honestly can't tell you what I would've done if I were the same age as Luna, in school at the same time— would I've reacted similar or worse than Eliot? *I don't know.*

The bodyguards nod. Not pressing for more details. I bet they can sense when I'm being reserved.

Quinn slides a newly filled glass to Farrow, but Thatcher steals the drink midway across the table.

Farrow rolls his eyes. "I wasn't going to drink it, *Mom.*" He slides off the stool and walks backwards to the empty bar. "What do you want, wolf scout?"

I think about how that's stealing—fuck, he can totally tell I'm considering all the rules. His smile widens, and I swear "so pure" is on the edge of his tongue.

I lick my lips. "I'm good."

He chews slowly. "Even if I leave cash behind?"

"I can get it—"

"I'm already here." He's behind the bar and opens the fridge below the counter. "Water?" he asks me.

I take out my wallet. "Yeah."

"Don't worry about it." He's buying me a drink. A bottled water since I don't drink alcohol, but still, my boyfriend is buying me a drink. I thought I'd make that move first and buy him one.

I'm kind of shocked, and I wonder if the bodyguards can tell this is new for me or a first or the fact that it means something. Because it does. These little things mean more to me than I ever thought possible.

I never even dreamed about falling in love until I fell in love with him.

As I face the table, Quinn asks Akara, "Why can't Farrow drink? I thought we're off-duty…oh, damn, right." He glances at me.

I get it. Since I'm not *safely* tucked into bed, Farrow is at work. On-duty. But if he wanted to drink, he wouldn't have invited me here.

I unzip my jacket, getting hot.

Oscar leans back on the stool and calls out, "I'll take a Corona, Redford."

"Nice choice, get it yourself."

Donnelly joins in, "Make me a bloody one."

Oscar says, "Changed my mind, I'll take a Blue Moon with an orange slice."

"Still don't care." Farrow shuts the fridge and raises his brows at me like *what'd I tell you about them?* Truthfully, it seems like they're his closest friends.

He returns with a bottled water and Lightning Bolt! energy drink. "What are we playing?" Farrow positions his stool nearer to mine before he sits down. His thigh right up against my thigh.

My hand slides on his knee, and I grab my water with the other.

Our eyes lock for a second. I wish I could sling my arm around his shoulders. But I can't.

We can't.

We're in a public setting, and a stranger isn't catching us at 3-something-a.m. in Chicago.

"Liar's dice," Thatcher says and gently sips his whiskey.

"How do you play?" I ask.

Oscar explains the rules. It sounds simple. Every round 1 person loses a dice, and you're out of the game when you have no dice in your hand.

The crux of the game: when you lose a dice, you have to choose a truth or dare. They already wrote a bunch of truths and dares on shreds of napkins. All of which are randomly mixed together in Akara's baseball hat.

Stakes seem higher for me than for them, but I trust SFO. So I'm game.

"Hey, everyone." Akara drums his fingers on his whiskey glass. "Maximoff should be able to skip any dares or truths that he wants—"

"No," I cut in. I was afraid of being too domineering again, too stiff and stringent and they'd treat me more like their employer, but I can't be passive here. "I can play the game like you guys."

Akara shifts on his stool. "You sure? You can skip anything I wrote down. You should, really. I didn't think you'd be here."

Oscar hooks an arm around the co-Omega lead's shoulders. "Akara strongly suggests and recommends it."

Alright, they all have some sort of knowledge that I don't, and before I even ask Farrow, he pops his gum and says, "Kitsuwon plays dirty."

And by *dirty*, he means *sex questions*. Got it.

Akara holds my gaze. "I would've gone easier with the truths for you."

I can't expect these guys to treat me like I'm one of them if I need half the truths and dares removed. I said I wanted all-in on Farrow's world, and I'm going all-fucking-in.

So I say, "I'm glad you didn't know I'd be here then."

Akara smiles and raises his glass in cheers, and the first round of the game starts. Dice hits the table, we make bets, and Thatcher loses one dice first.

"Oohh," the table erupts.

Thatcher takes the hat, not saying a damn thing. Being around him on tour, I've noticed that if he's not discussing work, he's quiet. Brooding. He unfurls the shred of napkin.

"*Truth*," he reads. "*Strangest place you've ever had sex?*" One sip of whiskey, he answers, "Back of a Walmart outside." He crumples the napkin.

Oscar and Akara rib him for choosing Walmart, and he just nods.

Dice in hand, we roll again. More bets and swigs of whiskey, water and Lightning Bolt! and Quinn loses the round.

"Get it, Quinnie," Donnelly jokes as Akara jostles the baseball hat to the youngest bodyguard. Quinn digs his hand in the napkin shreds.

"*Dare, lick the floor.*" Quinn shakes his head at Donnelly and slides off the stool. "You're sick, bro."

Donnelly smirks.

"Need a puke bucket?" Farrow banters.

Quinn humphs and kneels down. Licking the floor in point-two seconds. Then he's back on the stool. We roll. Cosmic justice at play, Donnelly loses a dice next.

"*Truth*," he reads a napkin, "*how much longer do you see yourself working in security?*' 'Til I'm dead or fired, whichever one comes first." He sucks his cigarette and slides the pack to Akara. Filmy haze of smoke clouds the air. It doesn't bother me, but I'm not much of a smoker.

Donnelly loses another dice. "*Truth, who has the best ass here?*' He drums the table and then points to Oscar. "For the self-esteem boost."

"Aw, fuck you." He messes Donnelly's chestnut hair.

We all laugh, but in the back of my mind, I think about how he's chosen two easy truths. Leaving behind more difficult ones.

And after I make a bad bet, I lose the round. One dice gone, and as I pick a truth or dare, no one speaks. Air strains.

I flatten the napkin, black pen scrawled across, and I read, "*Truth, worst sex you've ever had?*' Fuck.

Farrow curves his arm protectively around my waist but leisurely swigs his drink. I can handle this, and I'd be pissed if he spoke on my behalf. So he's not trying.

"Please tell me it's Farrow," Oscar says. "The guy needs knocked down a couple pegs after landing you."

Farrow's amused smile gradually expands. "Feeling threatened? You really did need that self-esteem boost, Oliveira."

Oscar claps.

"Worst sex I've ever had…" I draw their attention. "Is easily a girl I hooked up with a couple years back." I rest my forearms on the table, sort of leaned forward. "She started crying about five minutes in, not upset. Just overwhelmed. She kept saying how she loved me—and I get it, that's not that big of a problem, but we agreed to a one-time, one-night thing. And I don't really like fucking people while they're crying."

Quinn winces. "Damn, bro, that'd kill me too."

Akara pats my back.

Oscar nods, not even marginally surprised. "I bet people lie to you about their virginity all the time too. Just so you'll still fuck them."

"*Lied*," Farrow corrects his misuse of present tense.

Oscar throws a peanut at Farrow, who catches it and throws it back.

"Probably," I tell Oscar, and I think that the truths or dares can't be more sexual than that. But I'm also not that damn lucky.

Next rounds fly by, and Quinn is out of the game, losing his last two dice. He accidentally keeps choosing Donnelly's dares. He sniffs Donnelly's armpit and then tries to chug whiskey while doing a handstand.

"*Truth*," Oscar reads after he finally loses a dice, "*tell us your most recent lay.*" He ties a blue bandana across his forehead. "Cleveland—"

"No way," Quinn says.

"Learn, my little bro, you take the short windows of time, and you make it happen. Your dick will appreciate you. Just like my dick appreciated the tour's hairstylist."

"Olana?" Akara asks.

"Ol-ana," Oscar says like *fuck yeah*.

Akara inhales. "She's a babe."

"Top-shelf," Donnelly agrees.

I hired her, so I'm starting to feel protective. But I realize that Olana could easily be talking to the female FanCon crew about the bodyguards. In the same exact way.

Farrow loses his first dice the same time he lights a cigarette. He's smoked around me a few times before. "*Truth*." He blows smoke upwards. "*Who's the sexiest person here?*" He catches me staring at him, and his brows lift. "It's not you."

He's about to name himself. I couldn't care less about being the "sexiest" guy in any damn room, but I crave to beat him at something.

My brows furrow at him. "I didn't fucking realize you were on the Sexiest Men Alive list. Unless your name is Maximoff Hale."

They laugh, and Farrow can't detach his gaze from mine. I lassoed him somehow, and the more intensely he stares, the more blood pumps south.

Fuck me.

I skim his mouth.

His Adam's apple bobs hard, and he reluctantly tears his gaze. Putting his cigarette back in his mouth, he says, "You're something else." He picks up his dice and announces to the table, "I'm the sexiest bastard here. Clearly." His hand on my waist subtly slips beneath my T-shirt, on my skin. Warming me—God, that feels more than good.

Next round.

Akara loses. "Fuck." He picks out of the hat. *"Truth, describe losing your virginity."*

"That one time at band camp…" Farrow banters.

"Hilarious," Akara says with a warm smile, and he even explains to me, "all Farrow remembers about me from high school is that I was on the drumline. And I remember nothing about him."

His lips quirk, and he taps ash on a tray.

"I was sixteen," Akara tells everyone. "First girlfriend. Both of us were virgins, and my parent's place has a pool house. We decided we were ready, and first time, I made her come."

I swig my water. "That was beautiful," I say, sarcasm thick.

"Pay up." Donnelly holds out a palm to Oscar.

"Fuck you, Akara," Oscar curses. "I bet fifty that Quinn would get the Hale sarcasm first."

I screw my cap on my water bottle. "I did it to Farrow first."

Donnelly opens a new pack of cigarettes. "We eliminated Farrow from the bet since you always rib him."

Farrow steals the cigarettes out of Donnelly's hands. "Go bet on your Cobalts and leave the Hales alone. Or go for the Meadows—"

"No, off-limits," Akara says, defending his client. There are some moments, some small, others big, that I see and *feel* how much love and pride they carry for the people they protect.

For three famous families.

For us, and it means more to me than I can ever articulate. I end up smiling, one that courses through my whole body and brightens every fucking piece of me.

We play the next round.

Oscar loses and reads a truth, *"Oldest person you've fucked?* Maybe a forty-year-old a couple years ago." He shrugs. "I was twenty-eight."

Another hand, and I'm down a second dice. *Here we go.* I reach into the hat. Unfurl the napkin.

I read the words silently. "I can't drink," I say with the shake of my head. A dare to *take three shots of whiskey* is a hardline that I won't let anyone peer-pressure me to cross.

Cigarette between his lips, Farrow tosses the napkin shred back in the hat. "Pick again." *Fuck me and his movements.* My blood heats at his sheer confidence that matches and wrestle-fucks mine.

I choose again. *"Truth,"* I read the neat scrawl that I think belongs to Thatcher. *"What's your greatest fear?"* I pause, not needing to contemplate long. "Watching someone I love die."

Farrow rubs my back beneath my shirt, and we all roll again. Making bets, Donnelly loses his last dice and picks the *three whiskey shots* dare.

My phone vibrates as the guys start pouring shots. A text message from my little sister Kinney at 3:24 a.m., a witching hour, means only one thing.

I asked the Ouija board if you suck and the ghost told me yes. – Kinney

She's still pissed that she's not allowed on tour. I text back: I love you more than the ghost hates me. I pocket my phone. At my choice of words, I instantly recall the past. Something my dad said to me once.

I can practically hear his voice.

"You can hate me for two days, Maximoff, but I'll love you for a thousand more." I was almost seven, and my parents grounded me for the first time. I screamed, "I hate you!" at my dad. Not thinking, not realizing how much that must've hurt him.

And that's what he told me.

The memory sticks with me for a while, but I try to retrain my attention on the game. Donnelly downs his third shot.

Farrow swigs his energy drink and studies my expression.

I'm alright. Our eyes meet, and I just move out of instinct more than anything. I wrap my arm around him, sort of clutching the base of his neck and shoulder. My thumb gently skims his skin—

"You shouldn't be touching," Thatcher tells us.

Fuck. I drop my arm. Feeling like shit. I don't value touching Farrow over the jobs of SFO. *I don't.*

I'm just juggling a relationship with these major consequences—and I never claimed to be good at any of this.

Farrow snuffs his cigarette on the ashtray. "I was wondering when our chaperone would show up."

"I never left," Thatcher retorts. "Remember that."

"I'm choosing not to," Farrow says easily.

Thatcher opens his mouth, and Akara says, "Moving on." Thatcher nods and the game continues with another hand.

Farrow loses. "*Dare, let the person you least like write something on your chest.*" He already tosses a pen at Thatcher, and then he grips the hem of his shirt. He looks at me with a rising smile that says, *try not to get hard, wolf scout.*

I glower, my tongue running over my molars. *Don't fucking smile, Maximoff.*

He pulls his black shirt over his head, his tattoos and cut muscles in full view, but it's his unabashed, casual confidence that almost strokes my cock.

Almost.

I can contain a hard-on.

Farrow climbs off the stool and stands in front of Thatcher. "Wherever you can find space to write *fuck you, Farrow,* go ahead."

Thatcher uncaps the pen. Without a word, he writes *I promise to follow the rules* near his collarbone.

Farrow just rolls his eyes, and then he tucks his shirt in his back pocket. Returning to the stool beside me.

Another roll, and Thatcher is fucked on the bet. He loses his second dice. "*Truth,*" he reads, "*how hot do you find your client*—no, this is inappropriate, Oscar."

"I can explain," Oscar says in a professional tone. "I meant for Akara to pick that."

Akara shakes his head repeatedly. "No."

Donnelly lights another cigarette. "On a scale of one to ten, Thatch, how hot is Jane Cobalt?"

"It's Thatcher," he corrects Donnelly.

This isn't that bad. Janie would be beyond fucking curious just to hear the answer. And I'd tell her in a heartbeat.

"I'm not answering this," Thatcher says adamantly.

"To the surprise of no one," Farrow declares and then motions for another round to start. When Akara loses next, his *dare* says to call the 5th contact in his phone and propose to them.

His fifth contact is Banks Moretti, and he has Thatcher's twin brother on the line in less than a minute. "Banks?" Akara says, phone cupped to his mouth.

"Yeah?" His voice sounds identical to Thatcher's.

"Hey, you know I love you, man."

"Uh, yeah?"

Thatcher starts smiling, maybe for the first time all night. I know that look. I've worn it before. That's his family, his home, and it shows.

Akara sips his whiskey. "And you're my number five, my ride-or-die guy—"

"Alright, now you're full of shit."

"Will you marry me, Banks Moretti—"

"Goodnight, SFO." Banks figures out that Akara is on speakerphone. He hangs up, and Thatcher loses his third dice. Out of the game.

He picks his last truth or dare. "*Truth, when's the last time you jacked off?*" He finishes off his whiskey. "Three hours ago."

"Hotel pit stops are saving us all," Oscar says and refills his little brother's whiskey glass.

Farrow, Akara, Oscar, and I only have one dice apiece. Last one left with a dice wins and doesn't have to do a third truth or dare, and honestly, I want to win.

I play conservatively, but Farrow loses. He sticks his hand in the hat. "Hoping for a dare." He pulls one out. "Perfect. *Dare.*" His smile is out of this goddamn world as he reads, "*Fake an orgasm at the table.*"

Wait. What.

21

Maximoff Hale

FARROW TOSSES THE NAPKIN, not flinching or hesitating. Not for a fucking second. He stands and white-knuckles the edge of the table, and then inhales through his nose like he nears a peak. *Holy shit.*

Shirtless, his abs noticeably tighten. He bucks his hips into the table a fraction like he's caught mid-thrust.

I flex, my muscles scorching hot.

Farrow grits down, then mock groans, "*Fuuuuck.*" His head lolls back; his eyes flutter like he's experiencing mind-numbing, euphoric pleasure.

A brutal noise rumbles in his throat, struggling to break free. He narrows his gaze, eyes partially rolling back, and then suddenly, he sets them on me.

He starts smiling.

Like he caught *me* jacking off.

I glare. Trying not to show that I'm turned on like a damn broiler.

"You need a second?" he teases.

More than a fucking second. A solid, hard half hour. I play it cool. "To drink some water, hydrate, and maybe nap, read a book, plan my trip to the fucking moon, yeah. Give me a second."

They all laugh.

Farrow smiles. "Always a precious smartass."

I give him a middle finger, and he catches my hand as he returns to his seat and tells the table, "That's how it's done, boys."

Donnelly and Oscar throw napkins at him, and Donnelly says, "Here, wipe yourself up."

Farrow ignores them, still grinning at me.

Only two rounds left. One winner. We roll, and Akara makes a bad bet. He reads the napkin. "*Truth, who is your celebrity crush—*" His phone rings on the table.

Everyone goes quiet.

He gingerly picks up his phone and puts it to his ear, cigarette between his fingers. "What's up? You feel alright?"

I can't hear the other end, but Oscar mouths the word *Sulli* to the table.

"We did agree on that," he says, lips lifting. He stacks a tower of dice. "Tomorrow. Bright fucking early. That's what you said." He smiles more. "You forgot. I know you forgot...okay, yeah...I'll be there. Bye." He hangs up. "That was—"

"Your celebrity crush," Oscar says.

I go rigid. *Naturally*, I want to look out for Sulli. That's my cousin who I've known way longer than any of these guys.

Maybe Akara can tell because he puts a hand on my shoulder. "Don't listen to Oscar."

"He doesn't like buddy-guards," Farrow tells me.

"Too close for comfort," Oscar gives his reason.

Akara ignores him. "My celebrity crush is Alicia Vikander from *Tomb Raider.*"

"I'd bang her," Donnelly says.

"And she wouldn't let you," Farrow adds.

I laugh, and Thatcher hones in on Akara. All business. "What was that about?"

"She woke up and thought she forgot to tell me that she planned to hit the hotel gym at six." Akara searches the peanut bowl, but most are eaten. "Beckett's coming along."

"Cool," Donnelly says.

Sometimes I wonder when they all sleep, but I've seen them nap whenever they can. Used to bizarre sleep schedules.

A malfunctioning timer beeps on my watch. I turn it off and look up at Akara. "You know I told Sulli to text Jack Highland?" I suggested that she contact Jack for interview pointers. I thought it'd help calm her nerves since Jack has experience with fans and media as an executive producer on *We Are Calloway*.

Akara breaks apart a peanut shell into tiny pieces. "You did?"

"Yeah," I say, not able to read his expression. "What's your issue with him? Pretty much everyone likes Jack."

Akara brushes the shells off the table. "This is the first person that Sulli seems to trust enough to be friends with…and I don't want her to get hurt."

I nod, feeling the same. Maybe not about Jack specifically but just protecting Sulli from anyone new in her life. In my cousins' lives. Partly, it's why Beckett has his guards up with Farrow. We all feel the need to vet the people that come into our trust circle.

From experience, outsiders are the ones that fuck us over the most.

"We should've ordered food," Akara mutters.

"Oscar has food in his hotel room," Donnelly says.

Oscar swigs his whiskey. "If you're talking about the cookies, they're gone. I let the crew have the tin for two seconds, and they ate all of them."

Everyone groans.

"Audrey's cookies?" I'm guessing. I heard that my youngest cousin *mailed* homemade cookies to the hotel. Just for Oscar.

"Yeah…it's…you know, she's young." He finishes off his whiskey, almost wincing. She's twelve and putting him in a weird spot. I'm starting to think she's going a bit overboard since he works for our families.

And he's *thirty*. I have no fucking clue why she can't crush on a kid around her age.

"I'm sorry, man." I rub my jaw. "I can try talking to Audrey."

"Don't. I wouldn't want to break the girl's heart," he says. "It'll pass."

Farrow nods. "When she's prescribed glasses."

Oscar chucks the peanut bowl, but it sails towards me. I grab the bowl midair before Farrow reaches over, and he glares at Oscar, shaking his head.

"Just hitting you where it hurts," Oscar tells him. "Go for Redford's boyfriend, and you awake the—"

"Fuck you," Farrow says easily and hurls the bowl back like a Frisbee.

It knocks over Quinn's glass and shatters on the floor.

"Shit," Farrow curses.

"Party foul." Donnelly stands and tosses down some napkins on the glass.

Akara mentions taking care of the spill and broken glass later, and we're only one hand away from finishing the game.

Oscar and I face off with a dice-roll, and a bet—*fuck*.

Me.

Oscar grins and passes the baseball hat to me after my loss. "Last one, bro."

I dig in the hat and grab a truth or dare. "*Dare*," I say aloud, "*read the last dirty text you sent.*" A dying groan is strangled between my ribs. Before anyone else can react, two guys around my age slip into the bar and their eyes widen at me.

Spotted.

Donnelly whispers, "Under the table."

"I'm not hiding under the table." They already see me. It's a lost cause.

"Maximoff Hale!" one shouts, approaching our table. He wears a Chicago Cubs T-shirt, and his friend has on a Superheroes & Scones beanie.

All the bodyguards are quietly alert, and Farrow is sitting too close to me. He knows it, and in a sly second, he slides off the stool while unwrapping a piece of gum.

And he extends a hand to them, "Watch out for the glass." He motions to the napkins.

"Oh shit," one guy says and steps around the broken glass. Nearing me. I stand off the stool, but I rest my forearm on the table. It's hard to tell if he's a fan, a guy who likes comics, or a troll.

They ask if they can shake my hand, and you know what, the strangest thing happens. My gut reaction is *no*. I almost never say *no* to a fan.

I think about how Farrow Keene lingers a foot next to me. How if I shake their hands and they throw a drink, a punch or pull a knife, my bodyguard will block their path.

And he'll be the one doused with liquor. Hit in the face.

Or god-fucking-forbid, *stabbed*.

Telling Farrow to not do his job—that's not an option. But I'm realizing that if I want to protect him, I need to step back.

Whenever I can, I need to be more careful. He can't take a bullet for me if the gun is never loaded. And I'm not scared of what people can do to me. I've always been afraid of what they can do to the people I love.

And I fucking love him.

So in a resolute, unwavering moment, I tell the guys, "No, sorry. Not tonight."

Farrow's eyes flash to me, surprise in them.

"It'll be super fast," the geeky guy says.

"Sorry," I say, not budging.

Farrow adds, "The bar is closed."

The sportier guy points to the Jack Daniels. "Then how'd you get that?"

"We're special," Oscar says.

"Whiskey?" the geekier guy says with the shake of his head. He puts his hands on his S&S beanie and looks to me. "You shouldn't be drinking, dude."

It almost makes me smile, how much he speaks like we're best friends. I like that I'm something for someone out there, and maybe I was for him. When he needed the idea of me, I existed.

"I know," I tell him.

"You're supposed to be sober," he says, genuinely concerned.

"Still am. I promise."

The Chicago Cubs guy sways a little like he's been drinking, and he points at me. "Danny is right. Stay away from the booze."

Thatcher rotates on his stool. "Maybe you two should call it a night?" His tone is like an older brother to a little sibling.

"Can we get some selfies first?" Danny asks, pushing his beanie off and fixing his auburn hair.

"Not tonight," I tell them.

"Really?" His shoulders sag, bummed, and that's the worst part. But weighing the safety of my boyfriend over the two-minute happiness of a fan, there's no contest.

Farrow is going to win every damn time.

"Sorry," I say, wishing he could see that I'm standing five feet away on purpose. Wishing that he could, maybe or somewhat, take into account that it's pushing 4:00 a.m. and I might be tired. Or anxious or nervous or scared—because if I were Xander, I'd be all of those things.

And I don't like thinking about my brother or sisters or cousins in these situations without me there. Right now, most of them are miles and miles away from me.

Cubs guy squints in the dim light. "Is that dice? Can we join? You betting or what?"

If I say *no* for a third time, I'm the dick. They'll forever consider me a rude, standoffish celebrity. In an alternate universe where I'm single and not with Farrow, and I say *yes*, then my night is over. There's no such thing as just hanging out with strangers or fans or whatever.

I have to put on a public persona like a facemask. It's me, but not all of me. It's not completely real.

Right when I'm about to say *no*, Farrow cuts in and tells them, "We're actually done with the game."

Cubs guy wobbles and checks over his shoulder. "Is Jane Cobalt here?"

I solidify.

The entire bar goes quiet. I wait for him to mention the rumor, but maybe he's just asking because she's Jane Cobalt. Or maybe no one even cares about the tabloid garbage fire anymore.

I can't tell yet.

"Nope," I say. "Not here."

"But she'll be at the meet-and-greet tomorrow?"

"That's what you two are here for?" Farrow asks, chewing his gum.

"Hell yeah," Danny says. "I'm a huge fan of *The Fourth Degree*. Gotta get my merch signed by the son of Halway Comics. I missed you at Comic-Con last year."

I didn't attend that one, but when I do go, I usually stop by the Halway Comics booth. My dad built the comics publishing company from the ground up before I was born.

I nod a couple times. "Jane will be at the meet-and-greet."

"Cool, *cool*," Danny says and nudges his friend's arm.

Cubs guy takes one step forward. "Hey, do you think I could get like a private interview with her or something? I'm not shitting you when I say…that I think she might be my soul mate."

Thatcher stands off his stool. "Don't push your luck, kid. Security will be tight tomorrow. No private interviews or anything in quotes or asterisks."

"What about italics?" the Cubs guy snickers.

Quinn sticks up for his client too. "No, seriously, she's a real person. If you're just trying to fuck with her—"

"No, no," Danny butts in. "Sorry, my friend's kinda drunk. He just likes Jane Cobalt. He won't be weird, I promise." He smiles sympathetically at me. "And that totally sucks about the tabloids. Just so you know, no one I've talked to at the FanCon here believes it."

I nod, my chest rising. Not even realizing how badly I needed to hear that from a stranger. "Thanks. I appreciate it."

They spend about two more minutes telling me how they wish Loren Hale could be at the FanCon. They love my dad, and at that, they leave the bar.

Tension evaporates, and then Oscar reminds me and all of SFO, "Someone has a dare to fulfill."

Great.

Read the last dirty text you sent. I keep an elbow on the wet tabletop. Standing near Farrow. I scroll through our text message thread with one hand. "Hold on." It's not like we're apart a lot and *need* to text in the first place.

But have we before? Since the phone security update?

Yeah.

We have.

Farrow and the other bodyguards make small talk while I search. Quinn mops up a spill. "She's into you," he tells Akara. "I saw her watching you in Cleveland."

"Who?" Oscar asks.

"Macey," Akara says and puts his baseball hat on backwards. "Jane's line coordinator. She's cute."

"But…" Farrow waves him onward.

"She's tour crew, and I'm a lead in the security team."

"Yeah." Donnelly nods, smoke billowing out of his nose. "I've heard of that romance movie before. It's on Lifetime."

"Hallmark," Farrow quips.

Akara gathers all the dice. "Not into that drama."

I suddenly land on my recent dirty text—and my brain flat-lines, short circuits. Sputters and spins. Warning signs flash like *do not pass go. Stop while you fucking can.*

Mostly, I feel like I need Farrow's consent. This is a text *about* him. Us. Fuck. I rub my mouth and my eyes lift.

They're all staring right at me.

Farrow balances his knee on the peg of a stool. At ease. I was about to ask *do you care if I share this* but I can already tell he doesn't. Maybe he even remembers the text word-for-word.

Donnelly hunches forward. "High-key anticipating this."

I take a breath, confident. No reservations left.

Instead of reading the text to them, I turn slightly. More towards Farrow. And I tell him, "I'm going to fuck you deep and hard until your legs give out."

Farrow smiles so fucking wide, and he lifts his brows in a wave like *that just happened, wolf scout.*

Yeah.

That just happened. And I can't believe I'm smiling.

"Damn," Quinn says.

"Coulda used some emojis," Donnelly suggests.

"Fuck," Oscar says with a breathy whistle. "Was the promise kept, Redford?"

"Jealous?" Farrow asks, but his gaze never leaves me.

22

Maximoff Hale

"CAN YOU GUYS HUG and make up? Please," Sulli says with one hand on my shoulder, her other hand on Charlie's.

We're in a backroom at the Chicago FanCon. The photo and signing portion went off without a hitch. No power outage. No dislocated shoulder. And now we're minutes from going onstage for the very first Q&A.

Baskets of sweets, candy, stuffed animals, scrapbooks, and other homemade gifts tower unsteadily on a coffee table. All from fans. Reminding me that people are here for us. They're counting on us.

And I'm not going to let anyone down this time.

"We're okay," I tell Sulli.

Charlie nods, both of us avoiding each other's eye.

Sulli sighs and digs in a sweets basket. "They're gonna notice this fucking...fuck whatever you call it." She waves a hand between us, then dumps chocolate snowcaps in her palm.

"Tension," Beckett defines, squatting down and rising. He tries to stretch his arms, muscles shot from lifting girls for five hours.

"You okay?" I ask him. "You can take a break."

Charlie watches his brother keenly, concern evident.

Beckett cricks his neck. "I'm not ditching. I'll be fine." Sulli gives him a side-hug.

Jane has been scribbling math equations in a notebook. Something that helps clear her mind. But she shuts the notebook. And then scans our uneven huddle. "Look at us."

My eyes drift to each of my cousins. We look like we're five colossally different people who come from the same unconventional place.

Beckett is dressed in The Carraways merch, supporting Tom's band, and colorful tattoos sprawl down his arm.

Sulli wears cut-off jean shorts in the winter, a dolphin pendant roped around her neck, and her dark hair cascades down her chest.

I'm in jeans and a green Halway Comics shirt. Arms crossed, shoulders squared but thankfully not sore anymore.

Janie is decked out in pastels and sequins, pants snug on her waist. Wavy brunette hair uncombed.

And Charlie always looks like he just got fucked in a bathroom. Four buttons undone on his white, wrinkled dress shirt.

Beckett gives his sister a *what-the-fuck* face. "We look like a hot mess, sis. This isn't a revelation."

"We look like we're close. The five of us together. But somehow we've all come apart." Jane doesn't say the cause, and it's not the rumor.

If anything the rumor brought us together with this tour—but what pulled us apart was me. And Charlie.

"Moffy and I won't sit next to each other," Charlie suddenly says. "Easy enough."

We all nod.

"We shouldn't sit next to each other either," Jane tells *me*.

I spin on my best friend, my face sharpened and brows cinched. I get that this is the first time we've opened ourselves to questions since the secret affair rumor. But there's a hitch. "It's going to seem fucking weird if we don't sit next to each other, Janie."

She thinks for a moment, then nods. Pink bedazzled cat sunglasses shield her eyes, but her freckled cheeks pull in a smile that says *I'm ready for battle.*

The FanCon coordinator pops her head in and tells us it's time.

And I assure Beckett, "It won't be three hours."

Charlie grabs a water bottle. As he passes me, he whispers, "Don't make promises you can't keep."

FANS PACK THE BALLROOM, EVERY CHAIR FILLED.

An aisle splits down the middle and leads to a microphone where fans can ask questions.

A giant banner—*FanCon presented by H.M.C. Philanthropies*—backdrops a decent sized stage. Five chairs are already lined up in a row, and the tour's moderator touches the microphone at the podium.

As soon as the moderator introduces us, we step on stage. The crowd *roars*. Cheering and whistling. Cameras flash, and I smile, wave.

I grab a microphone off my chair and take the second seat. Because at the very last second, we decided to sit oldest to youngest: Jane, me, Charlie, Beckett, and Sullivan. It'll cause the least amount of gossip, but it also means I'm wedged beside Charlie.

Be nice, I try to tell myself.

Don't act like you'd rather sit next to a Death Eater.

Excited fans make it easier. My smile grows, and I raise my microphone to my mouth. "Hey, Chicago," I greet to another bout of cheers. I grin. "You're all great. How are you enjoying the FanCon so far?"

They woot and holler.

Janie speaks in her mic. "We've loved meeting you, and we're very appreciative that you've bought tickets for a good cause."

Clapping, and someone screams, "I LOVE YOU, CHARLIE!"

The corner of his mouth inches upwards, but he doesn't say a damn thing.

Sulli taps her mic. "Is this on?" Her voice booms. "Oh, fuck whoa." The crowd laughs.

Sulli reddens. "Uh, hi? It's rad that there are so many people here, and yeah, I'm really fucking excited. What about you, Beckett?"

Microphone to his lips, he says, "Absolutely."

More cheers.

Charlie slouches, ankles crossed, and he grips his microphone by the head, uncaring. Typical Charlie.

The moderator makes a brief introduction, and then a line coordinator ushers the first fan to the audience's microphone.

She must be no older than fifteen or sixteen. "Um, hi…I have a question for Sullivan."

"Sweet," Sulli says.

"First, um…" The girl reddens. "Can you say the f-word?"

"Fuck?" Sulli says uncertainly, but people still cheer. It's not a weird question since Sulli says *fuck* a lot, and her dad is known for his constant f-bombs.

The girl rocks on the balls of her feet. "And what's it like being the daughter of Ryke Meadows?"

"He's the greatest fucking dad…" She loses track of her thought, and she looks to us for help.

Jane raises her mic. "The Meadows family is the sweetest. One time Sulli broke a rope swing, the kind attached to a tree limb, and she bloodied her knees—how old were you, Sulli?"

"Maybe, fuck like eleven?"

"She was eleven *glorious* years," Jane says triumphantly, smile brightening, and her breezy voice captivates the crowd. "But Sulli being Sulli, picked herself up, not a tear in sight, and she started climbing the maple tree to fix the rope. Her dad saw, and Uncle Ryke hoisted his daughter on his shoulders. He helped her reach a sturdier branch to tie the knot. Adventure and love for all, that's the Meadows way."

The audience practically swoons.

"Last question, I promise," the girl says quickly before the line coordinator shoos her away. "Sullivan, is there anyone that you look up to like a brother since you only have a sister?"

"Yeah," Sulli says easily and cranes her neck and waves at me. "Hey, Moffy."

"Hey, Sul," I say in the mic. I think it's easier for her to speak to me than the crowds.

She keeps eye contact with me. "I know you didn't talk much about me on *We Are Calloway* because I asked you not to. I kind of wanted to be…anonymous, or as anonymous as I could be, but…" She shrugs. "You're my big brother. We went to hundreds of swim meets together, and fuck, we got busted shins and elbows from skateboarding…and you were always there. You still are."

"Awww," people coo.

I raise my mic. "Sulli was nervous to speak live, but she's doing better than all of us, huh?" The crowd applauds for Sulli, and she takes a huge breath.

The line coordinator leads the girl away, and a new fan in a Halway Comics baseball cap approaches the microphone. "My question is for Maximoff. Who do you like better: Ryke Meadows or Loren Hale?"

Jane sends me a quick glance like *I'll take over if you need me.*

In the past year, that question would've put my thoughts in a grinder. But I'm not pummeled backwards anymore.

"I love them both," I say, my tone easygoing. "At the risk of sounding *cliché*, I wouldn't be who I am without my dad *and* my uncle."

I'm aware that there are hundreds of phone-cameras filming me, and I can almost feel my dad back in Philly smiling. Happy that I'm finally embracing the truth publicly.

"My dad is amazing, loving, funny and protective," I tell the audience, "and I got to love a dad who was sober because he has a brother who's kind, compassionate, strong and unfaltering. I honestly can't imagine not having either of them."

I hear people sniffling, and I catch several brushing their watery eyes.

"I LOVE LOREN HALE!" someone shouts.

Jane speaks in her mic. "We love him terribly too." Her blue eyes smile at me like *well done, old chap.*

The next few questions are tame. Sulli talks briefly about the Olympics, we all banter back-and-forth about late-night sleepovers at the Meadows tree house, and Beckett tells the audience his favorite ballet: *Giselle*.

A twenty-something slender guy grips the microphone. "Charlie," he says. "Are you dating anyone?"

Charlie lazily lifts his mic. "No." He drops his arm. That's it.

I bite my tongue, wanting to tell him he could at least try harder to care.

After about ten more innocent questions about our childhood, Jane is asked about her career. "I'm happy to be the CFO of H.M.C. Philanthropies."

I wait for her to add *for now*. But she never does.

She has a whole semester of online courses before she graduates Princeton. One semester to figure out her future, but I'm not going to let her give up.

I'm still thinking about Janie when I miss the next question. Unfortunately, a college-aged girl directed it at *me*. Hundreds of eyes land in my direction.

I sense the awkward dead air.

Greaaaat.

Charlie puts the microphone to his mouth. "Daydreaming runs in his family."

I turn on him, eyes hot. He didn't just say that to the *public*. "What is that supposed to mean?" I ask.

My mom discussed all the times she got lost in her head on *We Are Calloway*. Fantasizing about sex. He knows this.

And if Charlie is implying—

"Luna has a vivid imagination. She's been daydreaming about aliens and other planets since she was little," Charlie says innocently, as though he never intended anything else. "Why? What did you think I meant?"

More phones are elevated. Recording. Pointed like pistols, but nothing can hurt me. Not online. Not in the tabloids. After what I went through with Jane, I'm fucking bulletproof.

Charlie stares flatly, but behind his eyes all I see is *come at me*.

So I do.

"At least being an egotistical asshole doesn't run in my family," I say, and as soon as the hot-tempered words leave my lips, I regret them.

Low whispers escalate like a rumbling storm.

"I think that one skipped over me and landed on you, actually." Charlie flings back.

Jesus Christ. I scan the ballroom quickly, and I find Farrow in the back. Leaning against the closed conference room double-doors. Arms loosely crossed. Aviators on inside.

He makes a hand motion that I think is supposed to mean *calm down*.

And he also blows an actual bubblegum bubble.

His nonchalance helps me, somehow. I breathe. No one needs to tell me that my short fuse is fucking horrible. I know. When I'm around Charlie, I feel like he strikes the match. But I light the bomb and always detonate myself.

"Boys, behave," Jane says lightly, garnering a few audience chuckles. "Next question?"

The college-aged girl must divert her original question because she asks me, "Do you and Charlie hate each other?"

The moderator smiles sheepishly, and the line coordinator taps the girl's shoulder. She never detaches from the microphone.

They're losing control of this Q&A. Much like we just have.

Charlie swivels to face me. "What do you say, Moffy? Do you hate me?"

"No," I say flatly.

Charlie turns to the audience. "There you go."

I'm not here to play 5D chess with Charlie, but he keeps roping me in. I try my best to reroute the conversation off us. "How about we talk about your relationship with Beckett. What's it like being a twin?"

Charlie hates that question.

He glares at me. "What's it like being the most beloved human on the planet?"

"I'm not—"

"Don't be so humble, *Maximoff*," Charlie says. "They love you." He faces the crowd. "Isn't that right?" He raises his mic out, and they all cheer, scream, yell.

I catch the moderator's gaze, and he balks and fumbles with notecards. "Settle down," he says. "Okay, let's get back on track here."

Everything is out of control, and I'm not sure how to right the train on the track since I'm mostly to blame for shoving it off.

Ignoring Charlie, I say into the mic. "We'll take a few more questions from the audience."

Instead of being disappointed, they all raise their hands in the air.

Don't punch your cousin.

At this point, that's my low-bar level of success. And I'm just barely reaching it.

23

Farrow Keene

I CONSIDER MYSELF abnormally fearless, not a lot has ever rattled me, but a nightmare just kicked my ass awake. I'm caked in sweat, drawstring pants and black shirt suctioned to my body, and I open a cupboard on the dead-quiet tour bus.

Ripped Fuel is what I need, and the jug lies sideways on the shelf. A sticky note is attached. In guess-whose handwriting: *do not take more than 3 a day*.

I'd roll my eyes at Thatcher's unnecessary instructions, but that takes energy on him that I don't even want to use.

I twist off the cap while simultaneously plugging a cord in my phone. I fit earbuds in my ears, and then shake two pills in my palm. The fat-burning supplement contains ephedrine and caffeine, an easy trick to stay awake.

Because I'm not going back to sleep after that mind-fuck.

It's 2:42 a.m. and the bus is parked at a Kentucky campground for approximately three-point-two more hours. We all agreed on a pit stop to let the drivers recharge for the next leg of the tour.

I'm a driver, and I can see the irony as I leave my bunk behind and unlock the bus doors. Clearly not sleeping.

My boots hit the dirt, a fire pit charred and extinguished.

A full moon illuminates the mossy campground, only one other RV in sight. Trees rustle in a gust of wind, and the winter breeze cools me off.

I scuff a stone and shuffle through my phone's music. Nine Inch Nails. *Play*. Bass blasts in my eardrums, and the first song doesn't end before the bus doors creak open.

I overturn a large rock with my boot. Watching Maximoff step onto the earth like he's mentally and physically prepared for any hell.

Lips lifting, I pop an earbud out. "Miss me already?"

He glares at the night sky. "God, spare me."

I almost laugh. "Dramatic and *infatuated* with me." My smile grows but then slowly fades as seriousness hardens his forest-greens.

He stretches his arms over his chest. "You woke up in a cold sweat."

See, I tried not to jostle him, but we slept in the same bunk. A confined single-bed. Our legs were intertwined. My jaw was on his chest. I was more surprised that he didn't bolt upright instantly when I left.

"Bad dream," I tell him and then study his shoulder as he rotates his arms. He's not flinching or wincing. It's healed better than I initially thought. *Good.*

I'm hoping he never needs a doctor again. Because he no longer has my father. *That fucking asshole…*

"What was the dream?" Maximoff crosses the campground, opening and closing his switchblade absentmindedly.

I comb a hand through my hair. "You were drowning." *And I couldn't save you.* I breathe hot breath through my nose and rest my boot on a log bench.

Maximoff clicks his switchblade closed. Standing stoically, he reminds me of an unshakable marble statue again. A man who refuses to let anyone or anything topple him. At least not without putting up a hell of a fight.

And I'm not surprised when he tells me, "That would never fucking happen."

I toss my head from side-to-side, considering that. Something never happening is a spearfish becoming a horse. Of course people can drown. Shit, even Olympic swimmers can drown. But I can't wade inside these fears or let them leech onto Maximoff.

It was a nightmare.

Not reality.

Our gazes catch in a forceful grasp. Not letting go. "You're right," I tell him. "You're not drowning. Because you have me."

He pauses in thought. "I'd survive either way." He gestures from my chest to his chest. "Between the two of us, I'm the trained swimmer."

I smile. "I meant *metaphorically* drowning."

He glowers. 2% amused, 98% irritated. I'm a 100% satisfied, and we unconsciously near. Our boots scuff the dirt and moss.

"I'm not losing at anything," he says, still trying to assure me.

I won't say this out loud, but fuck, I agree—he's capable of surviving 8 out of 10 scenarios. But I'm here for those 2 that he needs someone else. And he will.

He does.

He knows it too, but like me, those words rarely meet the air. I'd rather tease him for as long as I can, and he'd rather combat me.

"You're not losing at anything," I repeat his words and then say, "you'd lose to me in an MMA match in less than a minute."

"Or I'd win," he refutes.

I laugh hard.

"I'm fucking serious." He pockets his switchblade, standing about an arm's length away. "Let's see who's better."

I'll have him on his back in less than two seconds. "Someone teach you? Because I know I didn't."

"I did some research."

My smile is hurting my face. "You mean you Googled *MMA moves*?"

He glares. "Are we doing this or not?"

I suck in a breath. "Wow, you must really want me to be on top of you."

He licks his lips to hide a smile. "Maybe *I'll* end up on top of *you*." He gestures me forward.

Wind whistles. No paparazzi here. The only cameramen tailing us lost our tracks around Chicago. The rest stayed in Philly for money-shots of his parents.

This informal match is just for us, but my fist isn't hitting his face. We quickly agree to no jabs, hooks, uppercuts or kicks. Leaving mostly wrestling and grappling.

We circle one another, and then he approaches like a bullet. He tries a clinch takedown, pushing my chest while sweeping my right foot out from under me. I maneuver out of the inside trip, and then step forward, drop to a knee. And swiftly shoot my hands behind his legs and pull.

Balance gone, his back thuds to the dirt. "Fuck." His breath ejects.

I smile. "Double-leg takedown," I tell him the basic move.

"Let me try again." He picks himself up, and I stand. The second time I try to shoot for a takedown, he crouches out of range and drives his weight into my upper-body.

Damn. His muscles carve as he taps into his strength. I grit down and dig out of the hold. Slipping behind him, then we circle one another again.

"I learned that from YouTube," he tells me.

I smile. "Okay, smartass." I remember how his siblings said he's better than average at everything he tries. Maximoff trying to keep up with me and actually succeeding—it's extremely fucking attractive.

But I'm not going easy on him. Next time, I trip him from the inside, and his body plummets. Back to dirt.

We grapple on the ground. Tangled up, our legs and arms hooking. Muscles blazing, sweat building. Flipping over in mud and moss, skin and clothes dirtied. I smile each time he attempts to hit a more advanced move. He even tries a rear-naked chokehold, but fails.

He's gassed, exerting twice the energy as me. After a guard pass from me, I gain the advantage and end up on top of him. My knees bear on either side of his waist, basically mounted on Maximoff. I rest a palm by his face.

And the world seems to still.

His chest collapses, breathing heavily beneath me, and I pant a little bit too. In the calm, the quiet, our eyes never detach. Dirt streaks his cheekbones and jaw, and I'm sure mine are similar.

I look deep into this guy and remember why I'm awake, why he's here. I could've told him to go back to bed, but I didn't. We spend an insane amount of time together, but whenever I'm around Maximoff, I only want him to draw closer, and I think, *another minute, another hour.*

And then those minutes turn to days and hours to weeks, and before I even blink, I'm consumed. Hook, line, and sinker. He has me.

Maximoff clutches the back of my neck. If his eyes could speak, they'd be whispering, *kiss me, fucking kiss me.*

Before he tries to bring my head down, I cup his jaw and lean forward. Our breaths are ragged, but not from wrestling.

My mouth slowly skims his, teasingly close, and his chest expands in a wanting breath. *Fuck.* I hold his face with two hands, and we both close the short distance.

Our lips meet with hot power, and everything bursts inside of me. His skilled tongue parts my mouth, and I bear more weight on him as he drives the kiss deeper. Like he's reaching for the center of my soul.

And then a five-note *jingle bell* chime interrupts the most cinematic moment of my entire life.

"Shit," I curse and sit up but I'm still straddling him.

"What was that?" he breathes hard and props himself on his elbows.

I take my phone out of my pocket. "I set that noise for notifications." Specifically for the @maximoffdeadhale account.

Maximoff rubs his lips like he still feels me on them, and he watches me unlock my phone and pop open Instagram.

I frown at the two new pictures. Mentally, I push past the photoshopped gore, and I fixate on the locations. The first pic is clearly set in Nashville, a sign in the back, and the second city landscape is recognizable to me.

Boston.

A rock lodges in my throat, and my muscles tighten. Nashville and Boston are the next two tour stops. And both haven't been publicly announced yet.

It can't be a coincidence anymore, and if I woke up Omega, I'm certain they'd all say the same.

"What is it?" Maximoff asks.

My jaw tics. "You have a stalker."

He's not afraid. "Officially?"

"Officially. Whoever's running this account knows about the tour before the public." It's someone close to the families, to security or crew, and if they have this kind of inside information, I wonder what else they have access to.

24

Farrow Keene

"I'M GOING TO ASK you this once." Thatcher confronts me on Christmas Eve. All of SFO—except for Oscar who drives us to Atlanta—are secluded in the second lounge. Not for a meeting.

Not for a lecture or a pointless fight.

We're all undressing.

For a Hot Santa Underwear Contest. Our clients are the judges, waiting for us in the first lounge. We randomly picked underwear styles out of a hat. From tame to nearly-naked. Akara dubbed tonight "chill" and "fun", but everyone forgot Thatcher has no concept of either.

As I pull my black shirt off my head, I try to suppress an eye-roll. "Okay, ask me," I say. Multi-colored bulbs flash to the beat of a holiday jingle, and more lights are strung throughout the bus.

Thatcher unbuttons his charcoal shirt. "Did you tell Jane and Maximoff about the stalker?"

I unbuckle my belt, a bitter taste in my mouth. I can name a hundred other topics that deserve *anger*, and keeping my client and his client in the loop isn't one of them.

Akara, Quinn, and Donnelly undress around us, listening and watching a shit storm brew. I can already tell Akara is pissed. His eyes pierce me as he wads up his muscle-shirt in a fist.

"Yeah, I told them," I say easily. "I assume you overheard them talking about it."

"I did." His voice is strict. "There are *rules*, Farrow. Rules that protect the mental well-being of Maximoff—"

"He's desensitized to this shit," I cut him off. "It's more helpful keeping him informed—"

"No it's not," Thatcher retorts. "We can gather intel without him. We know everything about his relationships, his life. There's nothing he can give us that we can't learn ourselves."

That truth bothers the hell out of me. I can consume his past without even speaking to him or asking for permission, and that's not what I ever want to do. I prefer a less invasive route.

I extend my arms. "I told him the truth. I don't regret it. I wouldn't change it, and if you're looking for something different, I can't help you." I understand the rule about keeping demented shit secret.

I followed that rule when Lily was my client. It applies to her and kids like Xander. Anyone who may get anxiety.

But Maximoff hates being kept in the dark, and I don't tell him every tweet, every bullshit internet post. This was a real threat, and he's the last person who needs water wings.

Thatcher steps forward. "I don't care how you feel about the rules. They exist for a reason, and like I told you in Cleveland, for every single one you break, there'd be consequences."

I glance at Akara as he tells me, "We're deducting your pay. You'll be fined a grand for every infraction." He shoots me a no-nonsense look. "Starting with the one you just broke."

Meaning, I just lost a grand.

I tense.

If I calculate all the times I slip between the rules, I may be fined to the point where I'm working for free. Or worse, I could owe them more money than I make.

I grew up fortunate. My father paid for my undergrad and medical school at Yale, but I don't have a trust fund. His money is his money, and I haven't accepted a dime since I changed careers. My salary is entirely from security work.

I can live on less than I have right now. The Hales, Cobalts, and Meadows pay for security's housing. I don't own a car, and I already paid off my motorcycle. I just need to be careful about spending. Because I'm not changing how I do this job.

"Fine," I say. *Merry Christmas to me.*

"That's not it," Thatcher says as he removes his button-down.

Quinn and Donnelly undress to their underwear and mutter under their breaths to one another. Looking grateful that they're not under this spotlight.

"You'll be asked to do a series of physical activities as punishment." Thatcher nods to me. "Right now, drop and give me fifty push-ups." He's serious.

I don't blink. "No."

Thatcher is now two feet from my face. Towering, glaring. "This isn't negotiable."

This is bullshit. "I'm not a green bodyguard. I've paid my dues, and I'm not dropping to my knees every time you're pissed at me. *No thanks.*" I take a seat on the couch just to put distance between us, and I untie my boots.

He's fuming.

Akara is more at ease since I agreed to a pay cut. He's down to his boxer-briefs, and he digs in the shopping bag for the contest's underwear.

Thatcher scratches his unshaven jaw, his gaze narrowing on me. "When doctors told you to do something, is that what you said to them, *no?*"

I yank hard at my laces. See, I listen to authority. I respect authority like Akara, but I've lost some respect for Thatcher the more he comes at me. This personal vendetta is getting old.

"Did they even let you see patients," he asks, "or were you a liability for them too?"

I glare. I'm not wasting my breath boasting about doing rotations. When the hospital was short-staffed, some attending physicians treated me more like an intern. Like an asset. Because I wasn't afraid to listen to my gut. I knew my shit.

I thought quickly, and I didn't treat textbooks like the know-all, end-all. And that's exactly how I am now.

Here.

I kick off one boot. "If you think I'm a liability, then fire me."

"I should've," Thatcher says coldly. "And I still can—"

"No," Akara interjects. "We need Farrow."

Quinn nods strongly. It almost makes me smile.

Donnelly opens his mouth, but he catches my gaze that says, *don't*. He's not a lead of a Force, and they'll just yell at him for interjecting. Donnelly doesn't give a shit. "You fire Farrow, I'll walk out."

I cringe. "Man, be smarter than that."

"You die, I die—"

"Oh my God," I mutter and pinch my eyes.

"Stay out of this," Akara says to Donnelly in his harshest voice, then to Thatcher, he repeats, "We need Farrow."

Thatcher shakes his head once, but he knows I've never made a mistake that's truly jeopardized the safety of a client. I've just done things differently than the status quo. And it unnerves him.

"What the fuck do you want from me?" I ask him and kick off my last boot.

"Be committed to this profession."

I clock two hours a sleep a day trying to track a stalker. I spent the last four tour stops, including Nashville and Boston, securing the convention space just on the chance that they would appear and attack Maximoff.

And what's worse: I've added my own father to the short suspect list. Because he has access to the families. To security. Knowledge of the next meet-and-greet stops.

And it makes me physically sick to think he could be harassing my boyfriend.

To hear Thatcher say that I'm not committed is a slap in the face, but I want to know why he thinks that I don't care. Especially when my actions say I do.

I stand up with a deep frown. "Tell me why I'm not committed."

"Since the start," Thatcher says sternly, "you've had one foot in, one foot out. At any minute, you can leave for a hospital. So *leave* if this isn't what you want to do. Go."

"Hey," Akara snaps. "He's staying."

My nose flares again. I've been in a cold war with my father over choosing this career. I'm fighting against a generational legacy just standing here. But if he can't see that, then there's only one way to prove that I'm serious about security. The team, this job, this lifestyle, my client.

It matters to me.

As much as I can't stand Thatcher, I drop to a push-up position, and I say, "I'm not going anywhere."

25

Maximoff Hale

"WHAT ARE THE JUDGING parameters?" Sulli mutters to herself and uncaps a pen with her teeth, blank paper on her lap.

I zip up the back of Jane's reindeer onesie.

"Merci," she smiles and drops on the floor in front of Beckett. She could sit on one of the two gray couches in the first lounge, but Beckett pops open a sewing kit. Planning to attach antlers to Jane's hood.

He already sewed Sulli's, who wears an identical onesie. Now she sits cross-legged on the opposite couch. In deep contemplation.

My lips start rising.

This is our first Christmas Eve away from our families. It's weird, but not bad. Beckett and I sport ugly holiday sweatshirts, winter beanies, and camping socks. We decorated the bus with Christmas lights, candy canes, and plastic ornaments. Bought gingerbread cookies and made eggnog, Janie's favorite, and now the air is light-hearted.

No tension.

Maybe because Charlie refused to participate tonight. He's holed up in his bunk.

I was about to ask if he wanted to join, but Beckett stopped me. He said that Charlie wouldn't see the invite as an olive branch. I just learned that in Charlie's mind, me *being nice* is the equivalent of being pompous, overly heroic, goddamn flashy and ostentatious—like I'm fucking Gaston in *Beauty and the Beast*.

Beckett said, "Let him do his own thing."

Fine with me.

I hand out mugs of eggnog to everyone, and I tap Sulli's shoulder so she pries her face out of the paper.

"Oh, fuck." She cups the mug. "Thanks."

I sit beside her. "Vote for whoever looks the best." *Farrow*, my mind blurts out in response. I swear my brain is one terrifying step from making shrines of the guy. Which is not cool.

Not cool.

And my mouth wants to upturn, but *that* I can control. I'm not smiling. I do steal a glance down the hall. The door to the second lounge is still closed.

The front of the bus is quiet without SFO. But Oscar is in earshot and in view from behind the wheel. Eating pizzelles that Thatcher's brother sent.

"What is considered *the best* though?" Sulli bites the end of her pen.

Beckett threads a needle. "It's called *hot* Santa."

Jane nods. "The hottest Santa should win."

"Alright." Sulli jots a note in a margin, and she goes to sip her eggnog. Pausing, she looks to me. "Alcohol is in mine, right?"

"Yeah." I can't be a moral authority on whether she should be sober or not. She hated her first beer, but she wants to try spiked eggnog. So I made her a glass. Oscar's and mine are the only non-alcoholic drinks.

"Are there categories?" Sulli asks after a tiny sip of eggnog. "Do we rate from one-to-ten? Are there deductions?"

"Valid questions," Jane says. "Let's make two categories: runway and how they respond to a short Q&A."

Oscar cranes his neck to peek at us. "If I don't win, there's a conspiracy at play and you've all given preferential treatment to your bodyguards."

"He's right," Jane says, "we should try to be unbiased."

Everyone is looking at *me*. I make a face. "If I rate Farrow high, it has nothing to do with the fact that we're together."

Jane smiles into a sip of eggnog. "I suppose we'll just have to take your word for it."

Beckett finishes attaching her antlers and lifts her hood. She kisses his cheeks with a *merci*, and then she sits beside him, ankles crossed.

"We should tell them about the scoring," Sulli says and then shouts, "Kits!"

The door down the hall cracks open. "Yeah?!" Akara calls, and she explains the scoring system.

Donnelly sticks his head out, a smirk cresting his mouth. "You should just rate us one-to-ten on who's the most bangable."

He's yanked back into the second lounge. "*Paul*," Thatcher chides.

"Damn," Quinn says out of sight, "he got a *Paul*."

The door shuts.

Jane gasps, and I focus on my best friend. She cups her phone in one hand. "Eliot sent me a video of all the cats." She presses play and angles the screen for us to watch too.

Kittens and cats race around the townhouse. Darting beneath the Victorian loveseat and hopping on the rocking chair. The camera zooms in on a gray cat that prances around the fireplace.

Eliot's voice booms through the speaker. "*Licorice*, now do the cat walk. Do the cat walk!" He layered on techno music.

We all laugh, and Jane wipes the corners of her eyes. We watch the camera flip and face Eliot.

Squared jaw, a pretty-boy haircut, and the second tallest Cobalt, he could play Superman in a summer blockbuster, but a devilish grin always inches up his lips. Mischief glimmering behind blue eyes.

You know Eliot Alice Cobalt as the *king of drama*. Literally, he's starred in local plays from William Shakespeare to Arthur Miller and Tennessee Williams, and he's already signed to a theatre company for the next two years. He often films himself and posts humorous soliloquies about a lamp or toothbrush, and he's not afraid to be uninhabited and wild.

I know him as my passionate eighteen-year-old cousin who thrives in chaos. Who, 9 times out of 10, will light a napkin on fire if I'm at dinner with him. Who loves stories but struggles with reading. Can't make sense of street signs or restaurant menus. Can barely pick apart a single sentence. Who used to ask Jane, his brothers, and me to read books out loud. Hardbacks pile high in his bedroom, and for fun, he writes plays using a voice-app. He's dyslexic, and a fucking brilliant, soulful actor who can make an audience cry with a few words.

Fair Warning: even with all the mayhem he brings, I love this guy, and I'll drive a sword straight in your gut if you fuck with him.

"By the time you receive this," Eliot says in the video, "I'm at the lake house. It's Christmas Eve, and you've all left me, which means I'm terrifyingly the oldest here. Moffy, if you're watching, I don't like this responsibility. Come back, *save me*," he says dramatically. "I hate you all, but I love you all. Oh the tragedy." He grins and lifts a calico kitten to the camera and waves the paw in *goodbye*. "Don't do anything I wouldn't do." The video goes black.

Quiet lingers, all of us missing family. Sulli stares off, more downcast and homesick, and Jane and I exchange a *damage control* look.

Janie tucks her phone away and stands. "No more videos of home. Let's enjoy tonight."

I hug Sulli around her broad shoulders. "Remember, we're on an adventure."

Beckett raises his mug to his lips. "That includes half-naked bodyguards. What you've always wanted to see, Sulli."

She chucks a pillow at him. "Very fucking funny."

He laughs.

But she's smiling. "I know I really fucking miss my parents and sister and everyone else, but I like that we're all together with our bodyguards...this is cool."

Jane unzips a baggie. "And there are chocolate cookies." She passes out three cookies, and everyone accepts them but Beckett.

He picks a holiday playlist for the underwear contest. "Christmas" by Darlene Love booms.

Cocoa in the cookie is fucking overpowering. I cough in my fist and swig eggnog. Jesus.

"We're ready!" Akara calls from the ajar door.

Jane pretends a candy cane is a microphone, angling towards Beckett's phone as he films, the footage just for us. "I'm your host and one of four judges *Jane Kitten*." She bats her lashes. "The Hot, Hot, *Hot* Santa Underwear Contest features the bodyguards of Security Force Omega. Who will win the ultimate prize this Christmas Eve? Let's see. Starting in alphabetical order, we have...Akara Kitsuwon."

Akara slips out of the second lounge. Shirtless, muscles cut, and fire-engine red boxer-briefs hug his thighs. He walks the length of the hall towards us, and Sulli whistles in a cat-call.

He mock beauty pageant waves.

I smile as Jane narrates a bio on the fly, "A Muay Thai pro, this strapping bodyguard just turned twenty-six this December and owns the *extraordinary* Studio 9 gym. He's a bossy boss and a friendly friend."

Akara puts a hand to his heart. He halts at the coffee pot counter, and Beckett tosses him a candy cane.

"Akara," Jane says, "what do you want most this Christmas?"

Candy cane to his mouth, he says, "World peace."

We applaud, and Sulli already marks 10 in the *runway* and *question* categories. And they said *I'd* be fucking biased. Akara takes over driving so Oscar can go change.

"Next up," Jane narrates as Donnelly emerges, same red color underwear. Different style.

This time, he has on trunks, similar to boxer-briefs, but higher cut on the thigh. A tattoo I've never seen peeks out of the elastic band, a scorpion with fire out of its tail.

He blows kisses to us and the invisible audience.

"Donnelly, Paul Donnelly," Jane says, "a twenty-six-year-old Leo and former tattooist. He hails from an Irish household and knows how to kick serious ass in mixed martial arts."

Donnelly twirls at the end and then bows.

I'm subconsciously eating these shitty cookies. I finish my third one, and I'm surprised Sulli likes them enough to grab the bag for more.

Jane straightens. "Donnelly, what word best describes you?"

"Thirsty."

Beckett cracks up laughing, and Donnelly blows a kiss to the camera. Then he plops down in the booth, waiting for the next bodyguard.

My bodyguard.

"Farrow Redford Keene," Jane says his full name, and Farrow saunters out with casual confidence. Only wearing red *briefs*. The cut shows off his thigh muscles and sculpted waist—Christ, his package… the underwear barely holds him in.

And his *many* tattoos are on full display. Blood-red swallows fly through the mast of two pirate ships, symmetrical near his collarbones. Between them, half of a skull is inked on his sternum. A candle burns at his wrist, smoke billowing up his forearm and bicep to swarm another skull and crossbones on his shoulder.

Plus more. All black and gray except for the colorful birds. All striking.

His body is an art piece, and he knows it.

Look up.

I need to look up, and the moment my eyes hit his eyes, he's full-on smiling that know-it-all smile. His barbell lifts with his brows. He definitely caught me checking him out.

I scribble a giant *zero* on my piece of paper and flash it to him.

He rolls his eyes, his smile out of this fucking world.

Jane narrates, "At twenty-seven, he's the second oldest bodyguard in Omega. A maverick and an Aries, Farrow can make a delicious egg and bacon sandwich."

Beckett gives Jane a *what-the-fuck* face.

Jane shoos her brother. "He's the most medically savvy and also professionally MMA-trained. Farrow," she says as he stops and takes a candy cane from Donnelly, "who is your favorite celebrity?"

He speaks into the candy cane. "Everyone but Maximoff Hale."

God, I'm smile-grimacing. There's something seriously wrong with me.

"Boo," Sulli says.

"That's two zeroes," I tell Farrow.

His lips quirk. "I think you mean two *perfect tens*." He sits at the booth, and his tattooed fingers push his white hair out of his eyelashes, too sensually. *Fuck me.*

"No." I lick my lips. "I meant *zero* plus *zero*. Which equals a load of nothing."

"And look at that," he smiles wide, "your honesty merit badge is gone."

I'd react somewhat differently than cringing, but my head and stomach feel weird. Like dizzy? I don't know yet. I tear my gaze off his, but I sense him studying my features.

"Oscar Oliveira," Jane announces.

He emerges in red silk boxers, and he baby-oiled his golden-brown skin, his abs shiny and more defined.

"Cheater," Donnelly boos.

Oscar struts down the hall. "You were never going to win, Donnelly."

I sip my eggnog. I can't tell if the taste is off or not. Did I give Sulli the right mug? I did…I'm not drinking alcohol. *I'm not.*

Right?

"…a thirty-year-old Taurus," Jane narrates, "and Yale graduate, this former pro-boxer likes snack breaks and not very much surprises him. Nothing catches this man off-guard."

Oscar halts and flexes a bicep.

"Oscar," Jane says, "if you were a candy bar, what candy bar would you be?"

"Snickers. You're not yourself without me."

Laughter, and Donnelly drums the table. I stare at my mug, fixed on the creamy liquid. *I drank alcohol* blares in my head on high alert.

A lump lodges in my dry throat.

"Maximoff."

"What?" My head swerves—Farrow is *right* next to me. On the couch. Jesus Christ. I didn't even see him walk over here. It's not like he had far to go but…I'm fixating on stupid things. Avoiding my reality. *I drank alcohol.*

I go rigid.

"What's wrong?" he whispers.

"Quinn Oliveira," Jane announces, drawing my attention for a second.

Holy shit. My eyes widen. Quinn is only wearing a red *bow.* The plastic kind used for gift-wrapping, but it's large enough to cover his package. He holds the bow so it won't fall.

He must've drawn the worst style.

Sulli's jaw unhinges. "Fuuuck."

Quinn laughs and walks more stiffly than the other guys. Farrow and I take our eyes off him at the same time. My head is spinning.

I hand Farrow my mug. "Sip this."

"The youngest bodyguard is a lovely Gemini and vegetarian," Jane narrates. "He's Brazilian-American, a former pro-boxer and the little brother to Oscar. You'll want to bring this stud home to your parents."

Oscar and Donnelly clap, and Akara drums the steering wheel.

Farrow takes a large swig of eggnog. "It tastes fine."

"What?" *It can't.* I motion for him to sip again.

He frowns, confused. *I'm* fucking confused, and I need Farrow to solve this riddle, mystery, whatever-the-fuck I'm dealing with because I can't see the answer.

"Quinn," Jane says, "which bodyguard in Omega inspires you the most?"

He hoists the candy cane. "Akara Kitsuwon."

Akara waves in thanks from the driver's seat.

Oscar claps. "My little bro, a kiss ass."

Quinn lets out an aggravated sigh, and he ends up sitting next to Jane.

Farrow swigs the eggnog and says, "He's joking with you, Oliveira."

"I'm over it," Quinn mumbles.

Jane clears her throat. "And lastly, we have Thatcher Moretti."

Farrow takes a third sip. "It's not spiked."

I lean back. Trying to relax at that news, but I still feel weird. I take off my beanie and pull my sweatshirt off, boiling hot.

Oscar whistles.

I turn my head. Thatcher walks like a six-foot-seven brick wall in a red *jockstrap*. The fabric cups his dick. Nothing left to the imagination.

"Um," Jane loses thought, "Thatcher…Moretti is a twenty-seven-year-old…and he's quite tall."

"The end," Farrow says.

"No," Jane rebuts, but Thatcher has already stopped at the counter. "Merde," she mutters. "Thatcher, if you were stranded on an island, what would you bring?"

"A knife."

Farrow rolls his eyes.

"Spin around, Moretti," Oscar says.

Thatcher hesitates, but then he spins, elastic bands framing his bare ass. Sulli and Jane cheer, and the guys golf-clap. Except for Farrow, who couldn't care less.

My cousins start marking their scores, and Thatcher takes the driver's seat, letting Akara return to the lounge.

I rest my elbows on my knees, hunched.

"What are you feeling?" Farrow asks me.

"Lightly spinning," I tell Farrow. "It's not that bad right now…" I lose track of my thought as Charlie appears. He drops down from his bunk and determinedly beelines for the driver.

I can overhear him through the music and chatter. "Stop the bus at the next exit," he tells Thatcher. "You need to park at the Dairy Queen."

What? I call out to Charlie, "It's Christmas Eve. Dairy Queen isn't open."

Charlie ignores me.

I bottle whatever weird feeling sits in my stomach and head. My shoulders more squared. Alert.

Thatcher turns the wheel, the bus coasting along the exit ramp. "Is there a reason?" he asks Charlie.

"You'll see in a second," Charlie says, more concerned than usual. His arms crossed over his chest. He even stays at the front of the bus.

Beckett shuts off the music and stops video-recording. Everyone is quiet.

Oscar pushes to the front and speaks hushed to Charlie, who barely responds. Chatter escalates again, and I give Janie a look. "I wish he'd share something with us."

"We don't know what it is yet," she whispers.

Farrow wraps an arm around my waist. I want to lean my weight into him, but my joints feel unoiled and immovable.

I'm on guard.

Maybe Charlie can feel my glare drilling into him. Because he swings his head over his shoulder and says, "Patience isn't a strong suit of yours."

"Then tell me why we're going to Dairy Queen," I retort.

Charlie messes his already messy hair. "You always have to be in everyone's business. Just relax. Take a back seat for once in your life." Spite drips off those words.

"I don't want to drive your fucking car, Charlie. I just want to know where the destination is."

"I thought we were going to Dairy Queen," Donnelly says to break the tension.

It doesn't work.

Nothing *ever* works when it comes to Charlie and me. The bus rolls to a stop, and an unlit Dairy Queen appears outside the window. Parking lot empty except for a green beat-up Jetta that I don't recognize.

As soon as the bus idles, a knock pounds the door.

I stiffen.

Who the hell did Charlie invite on the bus?

Thatcher unbuckles, and he's the first to head down the stairs and unlock the door. I hear him apologize about his underwear, and he warns the person about the contest.

It's a girl.

I just know it's a girl.

I stand. Farrow stands.

My pulse thumps a mile-a-minute. Footsteps sound on the steps, and then…my little sister pops into view. Light brown hair tied in a loose top bun.

Luna hooks her fingers in the straps of a neon green backpack. Looking between all of us, cheeks rosy from the cold, she says, "Hey. Hi. Heidi. Ho. Howdy." And waves like this is nothing.

Dear World, how did she get here? Why is she here? How did Charlie know? Did she call him? Why didn't she call me? Do our parents have any idea where she is? Sincerely, a concerned brother.

Farrow beats everyone. "Where the fuck is J.P.?" Her 24/7 bodyguard.

Akara already has a phone to his ear.

I kneel on the couch and careen my head to try and peer out the window. No one else is in the parking lot.

"Oh…" Luna glances at Charlie. "You didn't tell them yet?"

"I thought you should," he says, hands in his black slacks.

"What the hell is going on?" I almost growl.

"So yeah." Luna rocks on the balls of her feet, but keeps eye contact with me. "I kind of ditched J.P."

I see red. Tunnel-vision on Charlie. The one person who fucking *knew.* I storm ahead and grab Charlie by the sleeve of his sweater. "Outside. Now."

26

Maximoff Hale

ICE ON THE ASPHALT crunches underneath our soles. We near the curb of the Dairy Queen entrance, and wind whips around us as furiously as I feel.

Farrow and Oscar hover close. The only other two people outside with us. Probably to ensure Charlie and I don't kill each other.

"She called *me*!" Charlie yells. "You're mad at the wrong person!"

"I don't think I am!" I scream, cold stinging my throat. "You're the one who could've told me. Told *us*. Told a fucking bodyguard—anyone on Omega should've known she'd be here *without* her own bodyguard." I shake my head, rage throttling my bones. Screaming at me to drive closer. To shake him.

To make him see.

See how my sister could've been hurt. Could've been kidnapped, raped or murdered on her journey across the fucking country. Alone.

"You knew she was driving here, and you didn't tell anyone!" I yell. "What the fuck is wrong with you?!"

"What the fuck is wrong with you?!" he shouts back, edging closer. Closer, only five feet apart. "I'm the one who kept tabs on her!" He points a finger at his chest. "I'm the one who gave her directions here! I'm the one who made sure she didn't get lost or drive off the side of the fucking road!"

"Great," I sneer. "*Fucking fantastic*, Charlie. If your brothers reached out to me, I would've *never* let them travel without a bodyguard. So thanks for helping out my sister, thanks a lot."

Charlie looks like he wants to rip off my head.

I want to poke out his eyes with a goddamn serrated knife. I am out for blood. I feel like he *knowingly* hurt my sister. He's smarter than anyone I've ever known, so why the hell would he risk her life like this? "You have beef with me, fine, but don't drag my sister into this—"

"I didn't," Charlie snaps, and I back off for a single second. Because he looks twenty, his actual age, and his eyes flit in hurt.

That accusation hurt him.

"She called me," he repeats. "There isn't an ulterior motive. I'm *not* sorry that you can't stand the fact that she didn't call you. That for the first time in forever, you weren't the chosen one. Get the fuck over it."

"Fuck you," I snap. "This isn't a pissing contest. It's about my sister's safety—"

"She told me not to tell you. How about that?" Charlie retorts.

I'm already shaking my head.

"Of course you don't believe me." Wind tosses his golden-brown hair. "She didn't want you to worry, Moffy. Because that's what you do."

I bite down. "But you could've still told me."

"Like you would've told me if that had been my siblings. If that had been Eliot or Tom or Ben or Audrey—like you would've *shared* anything with me?"

I gape. "I've fucking *tried*. For years, Charlie, I've *tried*. You never answer, you never reply. You hang up on me, so I stopped. You want me to start filling you in when they call me? I will, I fucking will."

Charlie grinds his teeth, pain leeching his face.

What is it?

What did I do? I feel like I'm close to an answer that I've never seen. Never held. "Charlie—"

"I'm not your wingman or your *sidekick*. I don't need you."

I breathe heavily like we're running for our lives in the same endless circle. "Then you don't need me, but being a good brother, a good cousin, even, means protecting the people we love. And what you did could've killed her."

He nods slowly. "Just say it, you coward."

"You're a *shit* cousin."

Charlie charges me. I let him tackle me to the asphalt. I even let his fist bang into my jaw. Then I return the blow. We're all anger and fists and unspoken pasts and pain.

I don't see clear until hands wedge underneath my armpits and thrust me backwards. I spit a wad of blood onto the ice.

Charlie's cheekbone swells, and Oscar seizes him around the waist. Restraining my cousin.

Regret gnaws at me. From behind me, Farrow wraps his bicep around my collarbone, the embrace protective and calming.

Oscar looks between Charlie and me. "You two get that out of your systems? The moment we step onto that bus, it's a no-fighting zone."

We're quiet.

"Maximoff," Farrow says, his even-keeled heartbeat thumps against my back. Soothing me, and I take these deep breaths that ache with regret.

"We're good," I mutter, but a *for now* hangs in the air. Because even with fists and fleeting hugs and half-hearted apologies—our discord never seems to end.

WE RETURN TO THE BUS, AND CHARLIE DARTS FOR

the bathroom. Beckett springs up from the couch and follows. Door slams, and an ornament attached to the ceiling thuds to the floor.

Jane, Sulli, and Luna are on one couch beneath a giant fleece blanket. Watching *Babes in Toyland* on the screen. I meet Janie's big blue eyes that say *calm down. Be nice.*

I'll try not to be a hardass.

Akara's voice escalates from the privacy of the second lounge. "No, you can't talk your way out of this! There's no defending it!" Donnelly, Quinn, and Thatcher must be in there, and I'm guessing they're on the phone with J.P., Luna's bodyguard who fucked up.

Farrow and Oscar glance at each other.

"I'm not going back there. I've had enough drama." Oscar camps out on the driver's seat and slides the door shut, blocking out the first lounge. Bus is still parked.

"You need ice?" Farrow asks me.

"No." I crack a reddened knuckle, and we both sit on the available couch. So close together, my thigh presses against his thigh.

Luna gawks at my bloody lip. "I didn't think you'd fight with him."

"It's fine." I rake a hand through my thick hair. "What's not cool is that you ditched your bodyguard. You know how unsafe that is? Paparazzi could've run you off the road, you could've been hurt—"

"I was safe," she says quickly. "No paparazzi tailed me, and I traded my Kia for that used Jetta. I had a plan. A *solid* A-plus plan. And J.P. would've snitched on me to Mom and Dad. They both would've said *no,* and I wanted to be…here with all of you."

She sniffs, eyes watering.

"Did you call Mom and Dad?" I ask and stand up.

She nods. "Dad wants you to call him."

Alright.

I near and bend down to hug my sister. I squeeze tight, and she squeezes back tighter. "I'm glad you're safe, Luna. I love you."

Her tears wet my shoulder.

I kiss the top of her head, and when I back up, Jane gives Luna a side-hug. "We're lucky to have you here. This bus was missing some Luna love."

"Totally," Sulli agrees and passes the cookie bag to Luna.

"Watch out," I say, "those are disgusting."

At that, Luna basically shoves the whole cookie in her mouth and mumbles, "Cool, pot cookies."

"Wait, what?" My mouth falls.

Farrow rises.

Color drains in Jane's cheeks. "Merde."

Sulli's green eyes grow to saucers. "Huh?"

Luna chews, crumbs fall out of her lips. "You guys don't taste the weed?"

Farrow snatches the cookie bag as she goes to grab a second one. *Thank you.* He sniffs the cookie and then yells, "Donnelly!"

Back door cracks open, and Donnelly slips out, shutting it behind him. "What? Beckett?" He walks past the bunks.

"He's fine," Farrow snaps. "Did you bring pot cookies on the bus?"

Donnelly relaxes. "Yeah, some girl was selling them at that last rest stop. They're good, right?"

Mystery solved. I'm high.

Fucking A.

Jane leans forward to look at Donnelly. "Why didn't you tell us?"

"You didn't know?" Donnelly frowns. "They're not mild. They taste like—"

"Okay, these *three*," Farrow says and points to me, Jane, and Sulli, "have never smoked weed. Let alone eaten edibles. They don't know what that shit tastes like."

Sulli can't pick up her dropped jaw. "I thought it was organic."

Donnelly looks around for his client. "Beckett would've tasted the weed."

Wow. So I just learned my younger cousin has smoked pot before. And so has my little sister.

Awesome…facts. I rub my dry, scratchy eyes. But sarcasm aside, I'm glad I know.

"He didn't eat any," Jane tells Donnelly.

Sulli has her fingers to her lips. Her deep contemplation face at play. "When will we feel…the effects?" she asks.

"I dunno." Donnelly shrugs and leaves for the back like nothing happened.

"Probably soon," Farrow answers, and he's staring right at me. Assessing. Kind of smiling. He's always smiling, come on. Am I going to be paranoid? Will I just fall asleep? My stomach keeps tossing. Maybe I'll puke and be done with this—or I won't feel anything. I'm immune to pot.

The pot killer.

That didn't sound right. I laugh. Oh Christ…why am I laughing? I hone in on Farrow, and he has a hand to his mouth.

"What?" I lower his hand that hides full-blown amusement.

"You're so pure."

I let out a dry laugh. "You're so funny."

He runs his tongue over his lip piercing. "I wasn't that funny."

I blink and blink. "Thank you for reminding me that you're a kill-joy."

"I only kill *your* joy, wolf scout. I leave everyone else's alone."

"Thank you twice over, then," I say, sarcastic, and I nod a few times. He nods as well, his smile growing and I'm trying damn hard not to smile back—my phone rings. Interrupting whatever that was. Flirting? Head-nod flirting isn't a thing.

I'm not trying to make it one either. It's weird.

I'm weird.

Caller ID: *DAD*.

Alright, I'm high for the first time. And I can without a doubt say that I'm not prepared for anything right now. I haven't had a long conversation with my dad since the lake house. I can't even tell you how we left things.

It was like we placed a semi-colon or an ellipsis on the end of a sentence. *To be continued.* Without an idea of when or where.

Answer the call, a voice whispers somewhere.

I know I'm really high because I listen to that fucking weird-ass voice. And I accept the call.

27

Farrow Keene

MAXIMOFF IS SO OUT of it, he lets me clasp his hand and *lead him* to the second lounge. I'd smile, but I still can't believe he answered that call.

He holds his phone to his ear, listening to his dad talk. Not saying anything yet in reply.

I swing open the door. Finding Akara and Thatcher in a heated discussion about J.P., and I say, "Get the fuck out. Maximoff has to take a call, and both your clients are high in the first lounge."

They all bolt into the hall.

Alone, I shut the door, and Maximoff sinks down on a couch, clothes littered everywhere from when the rest of Omega and I undressed. I lower the volume of the musical Christmas lights, and he presses *speakerphone*.

"…she's having a hard time here, and I've thought about flying out to you a million goddamn times," his dad says, "but if your mom and I drag Luna home, she could just leave again. Next time, it could be somewhere worse…and at least she ran to you."

I sit calmly next to Maximoff, but hearing his dad talk reminds me of the years I spent beside Lo and Lily. And each time he turned to me, talked to me.

Trusted me.

At a café breakfast while we waited for Lily in the bathroom, Lo told me, "I woke up this morning, and I went, *goddamn, I'm an adult.* It still blows my mind that I lived this long, and Lil and I somehow managed to gift the world those four dorks." He stared lovingly at his teenage children, a few tables away.

Kinney, Xander, Luna, and Maximoff loudly discussed who was better: Batman or Iron Man.

"Parenting never gets easier," he said to me. "Not when you love them, and you need to be hard on them, but you're afraid to break them. And you think you're doing everything right as a parent because you know what's wrong, but still, it's inevitable. We'll fail. We always do, but if I learned anything in my fucked-up life, it's that picking ourselves up is what matters. And Lily and I—her and me—we can survive anything. And if we can, they can." He nodded, then looked to me. "Words of wisdom from an unwise man. Take it or leave it."

I told him, "It's better than anything my old man has ever said."

He put a hand on my shoulder. "No offense, I'd believe you more if you weren't fighting with him."

I smiled. "True." But I tried to find a memory where my father looked at me the way that Loren Hale looked at his kids.

Medicine was supposed to bring me closer to family, but I'd never felt the strength of one until I joined security. Shit, I could *feel* how deep and connected Lily and Lo were to their kids. It doesn't surprise me how empathetic Maximoff is when he has parents like that.

On the tour bus, Maximoff digests his dad's words slowly. "So…" he says. "You want Luna to stay?"

"Do I *want* her to stay? Hell no," Lo tells him. "But when she talked to me and your mom, she said she felt internally 'trapped'—like she couldn't breathe, and she just needed to get out."

Fame is a motherfucker. Stifling. And Luna is flighty, restless. With that combination, I'm not that shocked she'd try to leave Philly if the opportunity appeared. And it did with this tour.

I unwrap a piece of gum, and Maximoff lies back on the couch, his legs outstretched over my lap. Phone on his chest. He fixates on the blinking lights.

I wave a hand in front of his face. *Come on, wolf scout.*

"Huh?" He rubs his eyes.

"Can we FaceTime?" Lo asks, concern in his voice.

"I'm alright." He licks his lips. "So let me get this straight. Luna is staying here?" He tries to sit up, but he just falls back down.

I restrain a laugh and pop gum in my mouth.

He flips me off.

"We're hoping a *short* experience away from home will make her feel better," Lo explains. "One month on the bus, then we're flying her back to finish homeschooling. And she's agreed to see a therapist again." He pauses. "You can say *no*, Moffy. It's a lot to handle, and if you're too stressed—"

"No," he says quickly. "I mean…*no* I'm not too stressed, and *yes*, I want her here. I can take care of Luna, I promise." Maximoff pinches his eyes. His head is spinning.

"I know you will, bud," he says strongly. "Hold on." He hangs up too fast for Maximoff to protest, and then calls back for *FaceTime*.

"Fuck," Maximoff groans.

I grab his forearm and pull him to a sitting position. His shoulder against my shoulder, and the phone falls to my lap.

"Do I look like I'm high, honestly?" Maximoff asks me.

I chew my gum, studying his reddened eyes, his ashen cheeks. He's *Maximoff* Hale, the chance that anyone—his family or security—would think he's high would be slim to none.

But truly, he looks 5% high and 95% close to puking.

"You look sick," I tell him.

"I can go with that." He angles the phone towards his face. Keeping me out of the frame, and then he answers FaceTime.

Lo pops up on screen. A ten-foot Christmas tree decorated in garland and gold bows twinkle, and a towering cardboard cutout of a twenty-something Connor Cobalt stands behind him, a Santa hat on and scarf around its neck.

In December, that cutout is shifted through the lake house every morning. A tradition for their families. People have Elf on the Shelf. Maximoff has a six-foot-four replica of his uncle.

Lo's brows cinch. "What happened?" He's talking about Maximoff's busted lip.

His eyes widen. Paranoid.

My mouth stretches. *Maximoff.* I squeeze his knee. *Speak, man.*

He blinks rapidly a few times. "I'm high."

Shit.

"What?" Lo laughs. "You're kidding."

Maximoff cringes. "I'm not. I ate an edible and it tasted like shit." He rubs his face. "I can take care of Luna. This isn't a reflection of the tour…she's not around drugs or anything. I promise."

"I trust you," he says confidently. "Your lip?"

"Fight with Charlie. It's nothing."

He winces. "I wish you two would just—"

"So does everyone," Maximoff cuts him off, and he stares at one spot on the floor. Breathing through his nose, pale. We're encroaching 98% close to puking here.

I put a hand on his back. Guiding him up. When he stands, he's more in control. "I'll be back," he says, dropping the phone. He leaves for the bathroom.

Just as I reach for the phone, Lo says, "Farrow?"

Either he knows I've been here or it's a shot in the dark. Whatever the case, I decide to answer. Let's see what he has to say.

I flip the camera towards my face, and I take a seat, elbows to my knees. Hunched forward. Casual. I fix my earring that keeps loosening.

His amber eyes dagger me, but I didn't expect anything softer. "Maximoff isn't in earshot?"

"Right," I say.

"I need to know something." He's walking around, chatter and voices echoing throughout the lake house, and then he slips into a bathroom. Quiet, more private, and he asks me, "How long have you wanted to be with him?"

I take out my earring to adjust the backing. "Since I realized he wanted to be with me and not just sleep with me."

He takes a seat on the edge of a tub. "When was that? Before or after you were hired to security?"

"Way after, Lo." I fit my earring back in. "Around the time I became his bodyguard."

His brows cinch. "But you knew he liked you before that?"

I pop my gum. "Back on Lily's detail, sometimes I could tell he was attracted to me, but I knew he wouldn't act on it."

"You weren't attracted to him then?" he asks, voice edged.

I look away and comb a hand through my hair. "You're asking hard shit."

"How is that hard?" he snaps.

"Because he's…" I roll my eyes and say clearly, "He's your son."

Lo drills an iced glare. "He was my son before you slept with him, too. But that didn't stop you from talking to me then."

I rub my bottom lip. "Okay, but I don't want you to revisit all the conversations we've ever had in the past and think that I was standing there *pining* after your son. I wasn't."

Lo clenches his jaw. "I want to believe you, but I'm finding it difficult trusting you for some strange reason. Oh wait, I remember why." He flashes a dry half-smile.

"How about we start over?" I ask.

Lo is petty, and I'm not surprised when he says, "Maybe, maybe not." He waves me to continue. "You never answered me." About being attracted to Maximoff…

I chew my gum slowly. "I wasn't always single, Lo. Did I care about Maximoff? Yeah. Was I attracted to Maximoff, three, four years ago? *Yeah*, but I can be attracted to men and never date them or fuck them. Shit, I wouldn't even call us friends. We were barely acquaintances back then." I shake my head in thought. "He was young, and I was doing my own thing."

Lo contemplates my words with a paternal glare that's never been directed at me. I glance at the door. I want to check on my boyfriend, but I can't hang up on his dad.

"You broke Lily's heart," he says, which means that I broke his too.

I swallow a rock. "I know." She made me promise to keep Maximoff safe, and I know she's blaming herself, believing that I slept with him instead of protecting him, and she trusted me. "I'm sorry." I eye the door again, and I stand and grab a water from the mini-fridge.

I wait.

Lo watches me.

"Anything else?"

"No." He hangs up at that, and I roll my eyes again. Out of this room fast. All the girls are in a giggling fit on the floor. Pointing at the ceiling.

Oscar nods to me, then the bathroom. "Boyfriend is—"

"I know." I enter the small bathroom and find Maximoff sitting against the wall, near the toilet. His forearms on his bent knees. Skin more flushed. Looking better.

"Hey," he says. "Sorry about that."

"No problem." I hand him the water bottle, then I take a seat in front of him, my knees bent just like his.

In the quiet, our gazes unearth each other. Air strengthens to where breath feels like iron and fire, and I slide my arm over his arm.

His chest rises. "What was it like the first time you got high?"

"First time I got high," I say, starting to smile, "I bought a joint, watched *Wizard of Oz* alone and passed out."

His lips lift like he bested me. "I have you beat on the better story."

Fuck, I can't stop looking at him. "It's a better story because we're both in it."

He laughs once. "Pretty sure my face in a toilet put it over the top." He chugs water and then his arm clasps my arm in a tighter grip.

As though to say, *don't fucking leave yet*.

I'm not going anywhere.

28

Farrow Keene

I CAN'T SLEEP.

Lawyers finally sent me some of the old NDAs. *Find the stalker* sits at the forefront of my mind. I just want an identity. That way if this fucker ever nears Maximoff, I can restrain them. And possibly knock their teeth out.

I pour a coffee, turn on an iPad, and sprawl out length-wise in the booth. Half the bus sleeps off a pot high, the other half are passed out from the drama.

And besides Oscar who's driving, I only find two other people awake.

Donnelly draws in a notebook on the other side of the booth. Reading glasses perched on his nose. Next to him, Luna flips through *Foundation* by Isaac Asimov.

Luna lowers the orange book, her charm bracelet clinking. "You know something funny?" she says to me.

"What?" I rest my iPad against a bent knee and open my email.

"I kept thinking my brother would end up with someone boring, annoying, or high-maintenance. Someone I'd hate. Kinney, Xander, and I talked about it all the time, but Moffy actually fell for someone cool."

In seconds, I'll be prying into his sex life. To be honest, I like the distraction she's tossing my way.

Donnelly smirks. "He's not cool." He never looks up from his notebook. "You know he was in *honor society* at Yale."

"That 'society' was actually a program." I use air-quotes.

"Same thing."

"No," I say matter-of-factly. "One you show up and participate in events. The other, you just take classes with an *H* beside the number." I snatch his notebook, and his blue eyes narrow. "And stop shitting on people who try in school."

He yanks the notebook back. "I tried. Still didn't do well."

"Ditto," Luna says and uses one of his Sharpies to draw on her kneecap.

"Didn't graduate either," Donnelly adds and erases some of his sketch.

Luna smudges the black ink on her kneecap. "From high school?"

"Yeah."

Luna glances at him, then me. "I think I'd be okay without high school."

She has a trust fund. She would be fine, but something needs to motivate her to finish this goal. Most people don't have the luxury of quitting.

I gesture for the Sharpie that she caps. "Give me." She tosses it, and I bite off the cap and outstretch her arm on the table. I write the first three lyrics to "Dreams" by The Cranberries across the inside of her arm.

I glance up at Luna. "Being a high school drop-out with no GED is sad."

Donnelly grins. "You tell her, Farrow."

"I could secretly be a sad alien," she tells us with a goofy smile. "My weapon is my tear ducts."

Hales. I start smiling.

Donnelly returns to his sketch. "Sad Alien would be a cool band name."

"Uh-huh, think of the Sad Alien merch. Plushies, toothbrushes, condoms, dildos—slogan: *I want a sad alien in me.*"

237 LOVERS LIKE US // 237

I laugh.

"Girl, take my money," Donnelly says, accent thick.

Luna admires the lyrics on her arm after I finish, then she randomly asks, "Were you two friends with J.P.?"

I cap the pen. "No. I didn't like the guy."

"Me either," Donnelly says.

"He never believed half of what I ever told him. He would always chuckle with an *okay, huh-huh* like I was stupid." Luna bites her thumbnail. "But I feel guilty that he got fired." In a unanimous vote, the Tri-Force terminated J.P. tonight.

I'm not complaining.

"Shit happens," I say. "Your brother, your parents, and the whole security team would rather you had someone you trusted."

Donnelly nods.

Quinn is now Luna's 24/7 bodyguard. When Akara made the announcement tonight, Oscar grabbed his brother by the cheeks and said, "You're ready for this, little bro. I taught you all I know."

"I think you mean *I* taught him everything," I said. I wasn't that excited about the shift. Not just because Quinn is easy to be around, but because Thatcher is still temporarily Jane's bodyguard. I thought he'd be gone by now. Back to Epsilon.

He even made the effort to remind me, "Nothing has changed. I'm still watching you and Maximoff."

I still have a fucking chaperone.

Donnelly lowers his notebook to erase the pencil, and I notice the flying saucer sketches. That's not something he would draw.

"He's giving me a tattoo on the bus," Luna suddenly fills me in. She couldn't have told Maximoff because he'd be awake right now if she did. I can't picture him talking her out of a tattoo. He's mentioned that he's surprised she didn't already have one, but he'd be here for moral support. A hand to hold.

I swig my coffee. "You don't want to wake your brother up?"

She shrugs. "He looked tired."

I nod. "He is."

"I'll show him in the morning."

I eye the flying saucer drawings. "What are you charging her?" He usually only does tattoos for money or favors. Never free. I'm glad because he could easily waste his talent on freebies for friends.

"She's writing me a fic," Donnelly says and climbs over Luna to go grab his tattoo kit. "She said she could do an original. A shifter story." He returns and sifts through his ink.

"With hints of extraterrestrial-ness," Luna adds.

Donnelly opens a brand new needle. "Where do you want it?"

She pulls off her *Thrasher* sweatshirt, only a bra underneath. Okay, at least she's not naked. Her brother would flip-the-fuck-out if Donnelly saw her topless.

"I'm thinking, right here." She motions to her ribs, the spot beneath her green bra.

"I'm no longer here," I tell them. "If you need me, I'm ignoring you both." I fit earbuds in my ears and drown them out with Nirvana.

For the first time, I focus on the lawyer's email, a zip file attached. The number of documents blinks into view. There are a lot.

I skim a few paragraphs. *This is the first batch. We'll send the rest along when we can.*

I meant what I said about his number not mattering to me. But I can't lie, I thought it'd be high—but I didn't think it'd be *this* high. More than anything, it means I have a hell of a lot of work to do.

I click into the first attachment.

Name: *Caitlyn Rice.* Date is about four years ago, and his previous bodyguard included a note with a location. *New York City.*

I search on the internet for any info. Two minutes later, I conclude that she's in a sorority, currently dating the president of Alpha Sigma Phi, and she's in Lake Tahoe for the holidays.

Social media makes it that easy.

Not a threat. I chart the findings in an Excel spreadsheet. Tri-Force wants all the intel documented. I'm in charge of searching his one-night stands, and Oscar and Akara have been looking into Maximoff's old philanthropy employees. Donnelly even found out that Peaches

McEntire is married. Since she has no real motive, she's less of a suspect.

Not a threat. Not a threat. Not a threat. I yawn after an hour of non-threats. Standing, I search the cupboards for the Ripped Fuel.

"Over here, Redford." Oscar points to the passenger seat where the jug lies. I sink down and slouch on the seat, iPad under my armpit. I open the jar, kicking my feet on the glove compartment.

I pop three pills in my mouth.

Oscar glances at me, then the road. "Did you just take three at one time?"

"I did." I tune him out with my earbud.

He rips the cord out.

"I'm working," I say with raised brows.

"I'm not even clocking your hours, and I can tell you need sleep." His eyes flit to me again. "Bro, you're not driving the next shift. I'm waking Akara."

I don't care. I put my earbud in, and go back to work.

Thirty minutes pass and I flag an NDA from a celebrity-obsessed girl who's prolific on Instagram. Another one sticks out to me, a guy whose SnapChat stories include running through traffic.

Then I land on *Vincent Webber*.

Heir to an oil tycoon. His recent tweet:

@CelebrityCrush Maximoff and Jane are weirdly close. You don't need to apologize. Shit is true. Seen it firsthand.

Celebrity Crush replied on their real account:
@WebTown333 would you DM us? We'd like to get in contact and ask you some questions.

@CelebrityCrush sure. I could bury that bastard.

My nose flares, and I stare, unblinking, at his Twitter account. Maximoff slept with this fucking dickhole.

"I know that look," Oscar says.

"What look?" I type *Vincent Webber* into the Excel sheet.

"The territorial pit bull look you get when someone is fucking with your guy." He switches lanes.

I type in more info. "I don't like knowing he fooled around with guys who couldn't give a shit about him." I shake my head. "Especially given the fact that Maximoff *cares* about people." Even his one-night stands.

"That's why he's not researching any of this," Oscar tells me.

"I know."

Maximoff doesn't need to know that a hookup is talking shit about him. It's my job. Not his. I finish inputting more data.

Vincent Webber just rose on my list. Right beside Jason Motlic, the ex-swimmer.

Find the stalker. My fastest has to be fast enough.

29

Maximoff Hale

A FEW HOURS AGO, Janie tried to prepare me for New Year's Eve at a Dallas nightclub. Hands on my shoulders, she said, "Repeat after me, *I, Maximoff Hale…*"

"I, Maximoff Hale," I said with crossed arms. Ready for an apocalyptic ending tonight. It's what Donnelly said: the Hale Curse. What goes wrong will go wrong to the Hales. Now there are *two* Hales on this trip, and I was alright with catastrophes happening to me. To my sister?

No fucking way.

"*…will trust Jane Eleanor Cobalt,*" she continued.

That was easy to say. "…will trust my best friend."

She smiled. "*To be the best wing-woman to Luna Hale, which includes copious amounts of fun, a midnight kiss from a stranger, and safety of the highest caliber.*"

I scowled. "Janie—"

"It's a girls' night out, old chap." She lifted her chin. "I'm partying with Sullivan and Luna, and you're not allowed to hover or protect. They're my responsibility, and that's that."

I trust Janie with all my fucking heart. So I nodded and gave in.

Spoiler Alert: I lost sight of the girls within twenty minutes. The nightclub is gigantic. Three-stories of balconies overlook a packed

dance pit. Colorful strobe lights stroke the swaying and gyrating bodies.
A DJ spins on a table, amps blasting my favorite electronic music.

This could've been a disaster zone for security and our bodyguards,
but the public has no clue we're in Dallas. Plus, the strobe lights
obstruct our features. Becoming nameless, faceless humans. None of
us have been spotted.

Not once.

I'm not even rigid or alert. I'm in the pit, dancing as much as anyone
can with jam-packed bodies. Bright pinks, oranges, then purples bathe
the club. Light sweeping the crowds.

Like I'm in a fantasy world. Music pumps and magnifies my pulse.

I let go.

A hand slides across my neck. Farrow is in front of me. Pressed
up against me as we move to a hypnotic beat. *In public.* We're in public.

The fact elevates this euphoric, light-as-air feeling that dizzies me.
Heady, intoxicating—and I pull him even closer. My strong hand on
his abs, rising up his back.

His gaze drips in a scorching trail down my body. Sweat blisters on
my skin, and even with people all around us—someone at my back, my
sides—I only see him.

Right here. Now.

NYE sunglasses with the year rest on his hair, pushing back the
white strands. He's fucking beautiful. Blue lights cast over his face.
Then red, then fuchsia.

I devour him and this moment. Our eyes dance along our bodies,
and when they meet, they caress over and over again. *Kiss me, man.*

His hand warms my skin and clutches tighter. Foreheads almost
touching, we move with carnal force. And my mouth parts in a shallow
breath, a raspy noise stuck in my throat. Farrow hones in on my lips,
his hand shifting to my jaw.

Am I dreaming?

Christ, this feels like an exhilarating, out-of-body dream. Emotion
overwhelms me to a point of no damn return. My eyes sting. My pulse
speeds. Never in my life did I think I could experience *this*.

A man to call a boyfriend. A man to dance with in a crowd. To wake up to. To go to bed with.

To love.

And be loved.

But here he is.

"Farrow!" I yell over the music.

He reads my heady gaze, and a taut, earth-turning beat passes. Words lose meaning. He fists my shirt, leaning even more into me.

His lips brush my ear, and he breathes, "Me too."

Goddamn.

Cannons of glitter and confetti explode from the vaulted ceiling. Showering the dance pit and his hair, my shoulders. Paper streamers thwart our view. My body thrums with untapped energy that dancing won't release.

Our hands seem to clasp at the same time.

Both of us on the same page, we push out of the masses.

I CAN'T TOUCH FARROW. NOT WHILE WE STAND AT the check-in counter of a five-star hotel.

Marble flooring, gold chandeliers twinkling up above, guests in swanky cocktail dresses and suits congregate at a nearby speakeasy-style bar.

Bet you think I go to these ritzy places a ton. I don't.

Not really.

We're not dressed for an uppity establishment. Me, in dark jeans, a white long-sleeve shirt, and a small travel-duffel is slung on my shoulder. Farrow, black pants and a black *Ramones* V-neck. He leans on the counter and texts Omega that we left the nightclub.

From behind the counter, the concierge—a well-groomed, tuxedo-clad man—scrutinizes my features. He knows who I am, but he's not positive. Maybe I'm a Maximoff Hale lookalike.

I take out my wallet. "One night, your best suite." I don't want to hear the cost. Trust me when I say, I almost never spend money this flippantly. But I slide a black Amex and my ID to the concierge.

Farrow catches sight and surprise lifts his brows.

The concierge perks up at the cards. "Right away, Mr. Hale. I believe our very best suite is available. Let me check with management. It'll only be a second." He glides away to alert staff that a celebrity is here.

Farrow pockets his phone, his surprise still there. "You have a black Amex?"

Since he's been my bodyguard, I haven't taken it out before now. "For the travel benefits," I explain. "I don't use it a lot. Definitely not for strangers or…" *one-night stands.* I check the time on my canvas watch. "It's not a big deal."

He smiles and scans the chandeliers, the marble statues that flank the revolving entrance, the bellhops, and then me. *Knowingly.*

I have the means to treat my boyfriend to something other than a crammed bunk bed or a bland room, and so I'm fucking treating him.

Abruptly, the concierge returns, and while he talks, he hands me keycards in an envelope, smiles pleasantly, and describes the hotel's many amenities. But I'm thinking only one damn thing.

Don't look in love with the guy next to you.

I force myself not to turn. Not to meet Farrow's strong gaze. I could be swept up in him. Fucking easily.

Once my exchange with the concierge ends, Farrow and I enter the nearest elevator. He stands right beside me, a fucking breath away. *Don't look at him.* I press the highest number and take stock of the security cameras.

Don't look in love.

The doors slide shut. Ascending.

My muscles flex; I can feel him shifting, his breath deepening. The elevator a sauna, his casual confidence radiates like molten sex. *Don't look at him.*

Jesus Christ.

The numbers tic upward too unhurriedly, and alone, in this elevator, my willpower just plummets. And I look to my left. Right at Farrow.

His head slowly turns to me, and his eyes burrow into mine, our chests rising in a taut breath. Burning. Up. Tension winding to an unbearable, unsound degree.

I ball my hands into white-knuckled fists. *Don't move. Don't touch him.* Blood pools, pulse hammering in my cock. God, I want him.

I eye Farrow again.

He hooks his NYE sunglasses on his V-neck and then combs his fingers through bleach-white hair. "You're fucking killing me." He tries to look away, but after a millisecond, he looks back at me. "*Fuck,* Maximoff."

I have no clue what kind of eyes I have. *Kiss me, fuck me, love me—* something greater than all three.

My biceps flex as I rest my palms on my head. I imagine Farrow coming up behind me. His hands raking down every damn inch of flesh: my arms, my abs and chest, lower…gripping me—and my head tilts back.

Fuck me. I blink out of a brief fantasy. I'm holding the back of my neck, and I'm actually, for real, staring up at the elevator's ceiling. Glaring.

I glance at Farrow.

He smiles and gives me a slow-burning once-over. "Never thought I'd be jealous of the imaginary version of myself, but I'm getting there."

Elevator dings.

The hallway is a blur. I tap into a one-track mind that says, *door, unlock, fuck him, my cock, his cock, come.*

So by the time we're inside the luxury suite, Farrow kicks the door closed, and I instantly push him up against the wood.

"Fuck," he curses huskily. *Closer. More.* Our fevered hands work like we're dying and welding together is the only way to survive.

Body against body, our mouths collide like a car crash. He bites my lip, and a wolfish noise rumbles inside my ribcage. *Fuck yes.*

He clasps my jaw as I part his mouth with my tongue. Heat exploding inside and outside and everywhere between. Farrow fists the fabric of my shirt.

I touch his neck, his arms, his chest, his waist, his ass. My palms don't know where the fuck they want to land anymore.

They just want all of him.

Farrow hooks his arms underneath mine. Spinning me in one movement, my back hits the door. A grunt expels from my throat, nerves lighting up like the flick of a switch.

He stretches my arm high. Over my head, pinned to the door, and my fist unbinds to lace his tattooed fingers with mine. Farrow sucks on my neck, my jaw, and my head tilts. *Fuckyes.*

My free hand dives down his back, beneath his waistband and boxer-briefs. I grip his ass hard. He mumbles my name and a curse against my shoulder.

Gathering strength, I draw our arms downward and then walk him backwards. Slowing us, and we stay attached. My hand still on his ass. He clasps my neck, his mouth hovering close to mine. But his gaze drifts around the suite.

No bed near.

We're in the spacious, glitzy living room of the humongous suite. Oleanders perk in slender gold vases. A crystal chandelier hangs above two emerald chairs and a midnight-blue, velveteen couch. And a tinted window spans the entire wall, Dallas skyline glittering in the dark.

A sort of New Year's Eve magic crackles the air.

"Wow," he murmurs, then his eyes touch mine, and his smile takes shape. His tattooed fingers unbutton my jeans while I walk him backwards to the midnight-blue couch.

Our tounges wrestle, and I slide mine sensually, slowly along his, and I hear his choked groan before I ask, "I'm the better view, huh?"

"You're definitely the cockier view," he whispers against my mouth. His piercing brushes my lip.

We pass the mini-fridge, and I break our mouths just to ask, "Need a drink?"

Farrow smiles. "No. Do you?"

I skim him, fucking gorgeous sparrow tattoos on his waist. Drawing my attention downward. I lick my lips. "Replace *drink* with *your cock.*"

He unzips my jeans. "You need my cock?" Christ, his husky voice is practically stroking my erection. "Looks like we want the same thing, wolf scout. Because I need yours."

Fuck. I yank his Ramones shirt off his head. Our movements stronger, faster. Starved. My hand descends the ink along his chiseled abs, then I unbuckle his belt. Hurried.

His back hits the full-length window. He pulls off my shirt, collar tearing. We're limbs and skin and breath slamming together as we both fight to make the other bare.

He kicks denim down my thighs, and I'm going to lose this struggle because he has on high-laced boots that'll take me a goddamn century to undo.

I slide my hand down his waistband. Finding him aroused beneath boxer-briefs, and I fist him with perfect pressure.

His muscles contract, and he grits down, hot breath through his nose.

"*Fuck,*" he curses, his hand holding my face, then my throat. Careful, he's always careful about that.

Farrow palms my cock over my boxer-briefs, then squeezes—*fuck me.* I growl out a deep noise, my hand in a fist on the window by his jaw.

He whispers against my ear, "You liked that." He rubs me.

Fucking Christ. My waist moves. Thrusts. Wanting more. And more. And *more.*

"Fuck, Maximoff," he grunts.

I clutch the back of his head. "Just fuck me, man," I groan. Dying. His cock stirs beneath my hand. "You want to try? Tonight?"

I nod, assured. "Yeah."

A smile edges across his mouth.

I've been impatient at the other hotel stops, and we've needed sleep. Though, I'm aware that I usually wake up to him working. But we haven't progressed *me* warming up to bottoming in a while. Not since back in Cleveland.

Tonight, that changes.

30

Farrow Keene

MAXIMOFF'S HUMILITY ENDS in bed, but damn, his ego is warranted. Just kissing him is like a divine awakening.

But I'm here for more than the mind-blowing experience. He's never trusted anyone how he's about to trust me, and I take that seriously.

Lying naked on the midnight-blue couch, I bear my weight on Maximoff beneath me. Our mouths crush together, and to keep him relaxed, I don't rush. Breaths heavy, our hands and mouths explore one another in prolonged, boiling minutes.

Even under me, even more vulnerable, his headstrong confidence doesn't wane. His entire body bucks up into mine, hand fisting my hair. A hot rock lodges in my throat.

We kiss rougher, and chest-to-chest, pelvises grinding against pelvis, I grip our erections and stroke us together—his calloused hand moves mine away. Taking over, he rubs us. Adding intense friction—*fucking hell.*

This can't end before it begins.

I shift my knee and spread his legs apart. Tendons in his neck and thighs pull taut.

"Fuck, man," he mutters, eyeing my movements more fixatedly. He inches his broad shoulders up the armrest, slightly angled and raised.

I cup his jaw and kiss his cheekbone. "Relax," I breathe.

He exhales a ragged breath. "Thank you, I didn't think of that," he says, all sarcasm.

I roll my eyes into a smile and then I guide his hand off our cocks. "Don't jack us off, smartass."

He flexes at my voice. "*Fuck*," he growls, head almost lolling back. *Damn.* He places his palm on my ass, and I drop my foot off the couch. To the floor.

I lean over and unzip the duffel. Lube, check. Dildo, check. Not as long or wide as my dick, but this is the exact brand and size he's used to. We have to start somewhere, and if he's done this alone, then he should be able to do it with me.

My mouth returns to his while I coat the length of the dildo. He deepens the kiss, and I hook my arm beneath his knee and then grip the velvet armrest. Elevating his leg.

He breaks our lip-lock, his chest rising and falling like he's running up a steep hill.

I slowly suck his jawline, his ear, and I whisper, "I'm not going to hurt you, wolf scout." *Trust me.*

Maximoff looks straight into me. As though he's remembering who I am. He sweeps my features: my carved biceps that protectively encase him, and my eyes that caress his forest-greens.

He eases, muscles unwinding. *There we go.*

He bends his other knee towards his ribs, giving me access, and seizing my neck, he brings my head down to his—our mouths meet. I start smiling, his rough, aggressive kiss fuels my own need. My red hot-veins throb.

Sweat builds on his tanned skin, and I graze his hole with the lubed dildo. He breaks apart from my mouth, and I shake my head. "Relax, relax," I whisper into a tender kiss.

My voice soothes him. I can clearly tell. His chest collapses in a deeper breath, and his muscles start to loosen.

I study his reactions and push deeper. Arousal parts his mouth. *He really liked that.*

His grip tightens on my bicep and my ass. Our faces inches away. I keep one hand on the armrest to ensure his leg stays hoisted. But my knuckles whiten, muscles burning.

Fuck, I want to pound my cock into him. I grit my teeth, but my hips arch into Maximoff on instinct.

He bites down, turned on, and his eyes narrow in a glare. Drilling hot into me. "Fuck me, man," he almost growls out in pleasured agony, his gnarled groan fisting me.

Fuckfuck. My ass flexes, and I drive the dildo deeper.

His neck is strained in desire. "God." His eyes almost roll. "Harder. *Harder.*"

I'll take him being bossy over him being afraid every day, every night. I catch his lip between my teeth, then I move rougher. I grind against him.

And I fill him. I can tell he's used to this because he tries to reach for it, but he remembers that I'm controlling the speed.

He just lets go. His hand returning to my bicep. Trusting.

I kiss him strongly, and I pump the toy.

His head tries to hang back. "*Fuck,*" he groans.

I tuck a pillow beneath his ass. Lifting him up, and when I drive into him again, his legs vibrate, overwhelmed, hitting the most sensitive spot.

Fuck, Maximoff.

Our erections stand at attention against our hard chests, and each time I thrust forward, we rub together. I time my movements with the toy, and his face reddens, caging breath.

My nose flares, sweat blistering my skin. I'm walking the same edge he's on.

"Farrow," he chokes, his eyes try to roll again.

Fuck, I can't stop *looking* at him, his arousal primal and raw; it's sending me to a new height. Our pre-cum wets his chest, my chest.

Our mouths brush as I rock forward, close. Fucking close—he makes a noise he's never made before, almost a wolfish whimper.

"Oh, fuck," Maximoff moans. "*Come on me.*"

I am roped into his fucking existence. I pump my hips faster, the friction like a hand, and he lets go of my bicep just to stroke me. That pressure—I jerk forward. *Fuckfuckfuck*. I come, dripping, and his chest glistens.

I groan, my waist rocking. I push the dildo deeper, and his mouth breaks, head tilted. Contracting around the toy in a prostate orgasm. I wish that were my cock.

His eyes puncture the ceiling in a glare and then roll back. *There's my favorite cum-face.*

I grip him just like he gripped me. His muscles spasm, and he comes on our chests. I could easily harden again.

But I focus more on him as he comes down. He looks satiated, content. I start smiling. *Good.*

I ease the dildo out of Maximoff and set it aside, then wipe my hands and chest with a towel. He sits up a little more and stretches out his legs, interlacing with mine.

Still on top, I clutch the velvet armrests next to his shoulders. Watching him eye me, more intense. He's staring at me like I'm more than a fantasy.

"I'm real," I breathe, causing his breath to shallow, "and older, stronger, wiser—"

"Thank you," he says dryly, "for those additional lies."

My lips quirk more. "Anytime, wolf scout."

New Year's Eve fireworks blast in the city night. Loud *bangs* strike the air, and the sparkling light flickers through the window and illuminates the five-star suite.

More than the nice shit, I'm enrapt in the fact that he made this view happen for me. When he doesn't do this for anyone. The gesture thunders in my core.

Maximoff hones in on my mouth, and I read *kiss me, man* in his forest-greens.

I don't give in that easily. I lean close, and huskily, I tell him, "My cum is on your chest."

His jaw tenses, his cock almost rousing. He glances down at his abs, then up at me. "I don't know what the fuck you're talking about."

I whistle. "Now he's really lying."

Maximoff looks straight into me, his defenses lowered but an iron-willed strength toughens his eyes. "I couldn't have done that with anyone but you."

That gets to me. I inhale. "I'd say…" I kiss him, tender and brief, and he returns it, just as soft and quiet, our pulses slowing together. "…'imagine what it feels like when you have the real thing' but I'm sure you've already imagined it a thousand-and-two times."

He grimaces. "I like how you just picked a randomly specific number out of your ass." His sarcasm is clear.

"Good, I'll do it more." I rake my hand through his thick, disheveled hair. "That was easily in my top five."

"The sex?" he asks.

"Yeah."

His mind is reeling, and it's hard to guess where his thoughts just spiraled. He's partially sitting up against the armrest, and his arm hooks around my shoulders.

His focus returns to me, and he asks, "You prefer to top?"

Maximoff. "I like both, equally." To make it clear, I tell him, "But I could be fine with just doing one or the other."

He thinks hard.

I give him a confused look. "If you don't want to bottom ever, tell me now."

"I want to," he says, voice firm. "Obviously." His jaw sharpens, his abs tight. "I'm thinking about which one you prefer more and if I've ever been selfish—"

"Let me stop you there," I say, and I quickly figure out a way to explain this. "You're bisexual—"

"I am?" he jokes.

Such a smartass. I roll my eyes, but I continue on, "You commit to me. You don't *need* a girl. But you're attracted to girls. Same thing. I like both, but I'm fine with one forever. Make sense?"

"Yeah." But he stares off. Thinking again. Fuck.

I retrace my words. Okay, I said "forever" and I'm not sure he ever thinks that far ahead. He's young, and I'm his first boyfriend. I'm not trying to scare him off. At all.

"I didn't just propose to you," I say casually, "calm down, wolf scout."

Maximoff growls, "I'm calm." He hears his edged voice, then sighs out his frustration. He almost smiles when he catches sight of mine.

He nods once, eyes on me. A look that lights me on fire. We sit up fully at the same time, and he seizes the back of my head. Our mouths crush together again.

Fireworks explode in rapid succession for a finale, but neither of us are ready for this night to end.

31

Farrow Keene

AFTER A QUICK SHOWER in the suite, we hurry out. I throw a towel at him, both of us dripping water. Our phones started buzzing at the same time.

I check mine.

Turn on your radio — Akara

u need ur radio, boss is getting mad — Donnelly

Radio. — Thatcher

bro, get your radio. — Oscar

Everyone told me to text you to get your radio — Quinn

Could be serious or unimportant. I'm not panicked. I glance at Maximoff who reads his own texts before I leave for the living room. Finding my radio beneath a tufted chair. I crouch and grab the thing.

Maximoff appears, phone in hand. His shoulders are squared like he could join a rescue team. I almost smile. Because this is his posture when he's just brushing his teeth.

"And?" I ask while I untangle the cord to my earpiece.

"The girls left the club." He uses his arm to rub water off his temple. "They're at a 24/7 diner and asked if we wanted any food to-go."

"*Shit*," I curse, flicking a switch to my radio. "It's dead." I stand quickly and collect my pants, digging in the pockets. No batteries on me.

See, if SFO changed locations and they believe Maximoff will eventually meet-up with their clients, then they'll want to stay in touch with me via radio. Hence, the onslaught of text messages.

I step into a new pair of black boxer-briefs. "I have more batteries on the bus," I say, grabbing my pants and belt. We parked the tour bus at the nightclub's VIP parking. Only a ten-minute walk from this hotel.

I'm not going to be fined for pointless shit, and losing a grand for a dead radio is about as pointless as it gets.

Dressed fast, Maximoff and I breach the crisp night. He draws the hood of his Philadelphia Eagles sweatshirt, and I zip up my leather jacket.

Dallas still alive as the New Year rolls in, drunken people cheer on the sidewalks. Gold top hats on heads and feather boas on necks. More fireworks crack, but less frequently.

I love high-strung cities that never sleep.

Maximoff drinks in the frenzied atmosphere. No paparazzi or screaming fans interrupt the moment yet.

We walk step-for-step in sync, edging close to each other. He almost catches a yawn, but it escapes with a soft, "Fuck."

My mouth upturns. The suite was a secure room, so I say, "You could've slept back at the hotel. I'm capable of grabbing batteries alone."

His cheeks are flushed from the cold, and he stuffs his hands in his sweatshirt pockets. "You'd probably get lost," he says dryly. "Directional skills are the first thing to go after I make someone come."

I laugh once. "That's cute, but you don't need an excuse to hang out with me."

He growls into an aggravated groan, "Fuck off." The corners of his lips start lifting.

My smile is fucking killing me. It takes all my energy not to grab his hand. Instead, as we face straight ahead, I lean closer, and our shoulders touch.

His carriage rises.

"Is that Maximoff Hale?" I hear the female voice, about twenty feet ahead of us. Clusters of women smoke outside an upscale bar. Mid-to-late-thirties, all in sequined cocktail dresses, they wobble in heels and zero in on Maximoff.

I lower my voice. "Ignore them. Don't do anything." His gut-reaction will be to acknowledge fans, but for the sake of his cousins and their anonymity, he can't let this location leak.

Maximoff is more rigid. He shifts his head slightly. His hood partially conceals his features, but not that well. We have to walk towards the women and the bar, just to pass them.

A woman cups her hands to her mouth. "Maximoff Hale!"

"Can we get a picture?!" another woman shouts.

"I want more than a picture," one says suggestively and too loudly.

I'm not "gawking" at Maximoff or the women. Bodyguard 101 for this situation: stare straight ahead.

Walk.

Don't engage.

"Oh my God, he's hotter in person."

"Is that really him? Can he hear us?"

We step in direct line with the bar.

"Are you Maximoff Hale?" A blonde woman is about to cut us off, but I slyly move out of my path and step towards her. Causing her to stay put and blocking her from my client.

"He gets that a lot," I tell the woman as I walk backwards, towards Maximoff who never stops sauntering ahead.

She checks me out. "Who are you?" she asks, but I'm already spinning around. Lengthening my stride, I'm beside Maximoff in a quick second.

I try to read his expression. "What?"

He blows on his cold hands. "At first I felt bad about not stopping for them, then I saw you do *that*—"

"My job," I define.

"—and now I want to fuck you," he finishes strongly.

My blood heats. "Can't get enough of your bodyguard," I tease.

He raises a middle finger.

Okay, we need to reach this bus. Because all I want to do is wrap my arm around his shoulders. Warm his hands. Touch him.

Most of the trek, we stay quiet, and he people-watches more than people watch him. The sleek black bus sits in the back of the VIP parking.

I greet the nightclub employees with a head-nod and curt wave. And we reach the bus doors. I unlock them, and we both climb on.

We stop cold in the first lounge.

Hearing deep groans.

High-pitched moans. All originating from the back. Second lounge door is shut.

"What the fuck," Maximoff mutters.

"It might be Jane," I say, but she never said Nate would be joining us in Dallas.

"It can't be. She's with the girls." Maximoff is already charging for the back. *Shit.*

I follow close and grab his shoulder, stopping him before he clasps the doorknob. "You don't know who the fuck is behind that door," I say lowly. It could be SFO, one of his cousins, or a stranger, *his stalker*, someone we haven't vetted.

I pull him behind me.

Orgasmic wails pitch the air, loud as fuck. Most likely a girl. "Ahhhh!" she shrieks. Sounds like bad straight porn.

Not my thing.

"Exactly," Maximoff whispers, anger lancing his edged voice, "we don't know who it is. We need to—"

"*I* am. Back up."

"Farrow—"

"What if it's your sister?" I whisper. "You really want to walk in on Luna having sex? Let me save you from that." I put a hand on his chest.

He complies this time. Stepping back, arms crossed. *There we go.*

I bang on the door. Laughter and curses respond.

"Who is that?" a girl giggles. She's not one of ours. I instinctively reach for my radio mic, but it's dead. Maximoff actually starts searching my bunk for batteries.

I bang again. An indistinguishable voice says *hold on* and the door swings open.

Completely naked, Beckett Cobalt slips out, loosely cradling a decorative pillow near his crotch. He shuts the door behind him.

My brows spike.

Surprise = mid-tier

Threat = low

Me = bowing out

I let Maximoff take over, and I rest my shoulder on a nearby bunk. He hands me the batteries and approaches his cousin.

"Hey." Beckett nods to him.

"Who's back there?" Maximoff asks.

"Two girls from the club. A Kylie and a Laura." Beckett briefly glances my way. *Hi there.* I pop the new batteries in my radio, and he sizes me up for the eighty-fourth time.

"It's not a good idea to bring strangers on the bus to have sex," Maximoff says, drawing Beckett's attention. "It's fucking dangerous. They could steal everyone's stuff, take pictures, and they haven't been vetted."

"Donnelly vetted them." Beckett talks smoothly, quickly, *calmly.* "I'm not going to go through ten other people—half that I'm related to—in order to fuck someone. I haven't let the girls out of my sight, except for right now. And I'll clean the room when I'm done."

Maximoff rubs his jaw, not happy about this. "Please be fucking careful. Trash any used condoms." He rattles off a few more general rules to keep his cousin safe.

I couldn't care less, and Beckett notices.

He gives me a look.

Not the iconic *you're full of bullshit* face, but a brand new one that he reserves for me. I'd think I was special, but it's a you-aren't-good-enough-for-my-cousin face.

I consider myself extremely patient, but I'm nearing a line where I'd like to just snap *go fuck yourself.*

"You don't agree with Moffy?" Beckett asks.

"Right." I hook my radio on my belt. "I don't care what you do with your condoms." He's not my client, and those girls aren't a threat to anyone.

His brows knit together in that *bullshit* face. "He's your boyfriend."

"And I don't always have to agree with my boyfriend." I'm giving Beckett a pass because he's never been in a relationship, but he's trying to measure how much I value Maximoff off the wrong shit.

"If you two don't agree, then maybe you're not compatible," Beckett says like he's charting a pros and cons list for his cousin. With no pros and all cons.

I fit my earpiece in, done with this guy. I can take blunt honesty to my face—and Maximoff *likes* it, but I'm reaching a limit with his cousin.

Maximoff sends Beckett a warning glare. "Stay out of it."

"I'm just looking out for you," Beckett says calmly, kindly, even sincerely, and he switches his hands on his pillow.

I raise the volume on my radio. "Where's Donnelly?"

Beckett points to a bunk about chest-high. He's in a bunk? That doesn't make sense. Donnelly would've heard me and Maximoff walk in.

Something's not right.

I drift further into the narrowed hall, and I hear Maximoff ask Beckett if he needs anything. If he's okay. What he always asks family.

"Beckett!" the girls call. "Come back!"

Beckett smiles warmly. "With that. As my little brother would say, 'I bid you farewell'." He waves in salute with his unoccupied hand, and then turns around, his bare ass in view. He disappears into the second lounge.

Maximoff almost smiles, shoulders loosening, and he passes me, texting the girls back. "Food?"

"Omelet." I sling the bunk curtain.

Donnelly lies down with headphones on, just staring upward in a daze. He doesn't turn, but he can see me in his peripheral.

I frown and shake his arm. "Donnelly."

He pulls one pad off his ear and mumbles something, his South Philly lilt too thick. He only gets quiet like this when he hears from his family.

"Is it your mom?" I ask.

Donnelly tugs at his chestnut hair with a hot breath, then nods. He sits up but slumps. "She got caught with 8 grams. Been out of prison for one week."

My frown darkens. "Man, I'm sorry." I don't ask what drug. I know it's meth.

"I thought it'd be different this time." Donnelly scrolls through his music. "Fuck me, right." He hands me his cell. "Pick out somethin'." He lies back down and puts a T-shirt over his face, headphones on.

I shuffle through some artists and then play "Do You Realize?" by The Flaming Lips. I tuck the phone under his pillow, and close the curtain.

I rejoin Maximoff in the first lounge. He's about to pocket his cell. "Is Donnelly okay?"

"Not really." I catch his wrist. "Text Jane to order him a waffle."

He types out a message. "If he needs to go home, I'll pay for the flight—"

"He won't want to." I keep a hand on Maximoff's waist. "Whenever this shit happens, he stays away from home. It's played out before." I pause. "Mom problems."

Maximoff nods. He's aware of Donnelly's family.

"Not that I really know what those are," I add since I'm the only one on the bus without a mom.

Maximoff fits his cell in his back pocket. "You never had problems with your stepmom?"

"No. She's nice, but we're not close."

He knows the timeline. He attended the wedding. I was a senior in high school when my father dated Rachel, then a freshman in college when they married.

Maximoff holds the back of my neck, and we draw together, legs knocking—"Ahhhh!" a girl moans again.

I roll my eyes, and then a five-note *jingle bell* chime plays in my pocket.

"That's fucking creepy," Maximoff says, referring to the noise, not what's attached to the *jingle bell* notification. Because he couldn't be less afraid of the stalker if he tried.

I dig for my phone. "Don't worry," I say casually. "I'll keep you safe."

Maximoff glares. "I feel *zero* worry. Nothing." He cringes at the app. "Jesus, don't look at it. Forget it tonight. It's New Year's Eve."

"It's New Year's Day," I correct, opening the @maximoffdeadhale account, "and this is my job." My voice sinks with my stomach.

What the...fuck.

The stalker posted a close-up of the tour bus. *This* exact bus, and beneath the windows, the words *DIE MOFFY DIE* drip in blood-red paint.

It looks real.

My gut says someone just painted this bus. Outside. Right now.

Fucking hell.

32

Farrow Keene

I MOVE TOWARDS THE stairs, unclipping my gun from its holster. "Stay here," I tell Maximoff.

He's right behind me, of course.

"Maximoff."

His jaw sharpens. "I get that I can't follow you outside, but Donnelly can."

"No. He's distracted tonight. I'm not bringing him as back-up." I unlock the bus doors.

Maximoff tugs at the collar of his sweatshirt. He's more than frustrated. His nose flares, and he shakes his head repeatedly. He hates this. Waiting back. Feeling helpless when he's trying to keep *me* safe.

It hurts me knowing how much this is killing him. *But...* "I shouldn't be your bodyguard if you won't let me do my job."

He takes a tight breath. "Alright. Go."

"Lock the doors behind me." I toss him the keys and leave the bus.

My boots fall hard on pavement. I scan the VIP area. Valets aren't at their podium. No bodies wandering. I check the bus.

Clean.

The other side faces hedges, and I carefully circle the bus, passing the hood.

No one here.

The exterior is clean.

I only relax when I check the rear and the eight other vehicles parked here.

Safe.

But it looked real.

My gut is usually right. The worst part: I'm disappointed. If I knew who this son of a bitch was, it'd end the unknown. And I wanted to end it tonight.

I return to the bus. Maximoff stands with crossed arms on the first step, and as I approach, he unlocks the doors from the inside.

"What was it?" he asks.

I hand him my phone and then sit on the armrest of the passenger seat.

Maximoff studies the photo and drifts towards the driver's seat. He barely blinks, and when he looks up, I see clearly that his concern lies with me.

"This is really getting to you," he says. "Isn't it?"

"No." I holster my gun and take my phone back. "I'm fine."

He rubs his mouth and lowers on the edge of the driver's seat. He's looking everywhere but at me.

"Just say it."

His tough eyes hit mine. "You're not sleeping."

"I've always had weird hours. Anything else?" My tone is a lot more strict than usual.

We're both stubborn. I'm not going to quit my job unless I'm doing worse than the best, and right now, I'm still the best damned bodyguard. No one would be better for Maximoff than me.

He pulls off his sweatshirt, hot. "Are we fighting?" he asks seriously.

I ease a little bit. "You tell me, wolf scout."

He shakes his head. "Christ, I care about you, Farrow. And you're sitting there, denying that the stalker is affecting you. But I'm around you every goddamn day. I can tell."

I comb my hands through my hair, and I let out a deeper breath. "It'll be over once we identify the person." I'm confident about this.

But Maximoff stares at me with uneasiness. "There'll always be another stalker. Another anonymous troll. It doesn't fucking end. I've come to terms with that—"

"It's going to end," I say assuredly. "This is different, Maximoff. It's a real threat." The stalker is from Philly. They know where the tour stops are located before they're announced. It's serious.

His gaze turns to the windshield. Thinking.

"And I'm glad you've come to terms with it," I tell him. "Because it's my job to care about the threats. Not yours. So let me do my job—"

"I am," he combats. "Jesus Christ, I'm watching you down Ripped Fuel and stay up past 48-hours." He laughs a dry, pained laugh. "And you know what, I'm starting to think that makes me a terrible boyfriend."

My chest hurts. "It doesn't."

His Adam's apple bobs, and he holds my gaze. "Selfishly, I don't want to lose you as my bodyguard. It might be the most selfish thing I've ever fucking wanted in my life. But I need you to do something for me."

"What?" My eyes are burning.

"If being my bodyguard while being my boyfriend is hurting you, step back."

I run my thumb over my lip piercing. "You mean quit."

"Yeah. Can you do that?" He means, *in the future*. If it comes to that. I've never lied to him, and I'll never start.

"No," I say matter-of-factly. "I can't do that. Truth, I'd run my body in the ground to do my job well, but several hours of sleeplessness is nothing."

His face twists in deep, agonized thought. "I keep thinking that if I really cared about your health, I'd just fire you."

I shake my head.

He's searching for the *right* path, even if it costs his happiness, but fuck, he doesn't need to make that sacrifice for some arbitrary "moral" good.

"No," I say easily. "You don't need to fire me to protect me. Just set down the sandbags for these hypotheticals. Because I'm okay, and the shit sleep I'm getting is going to end. All you need is to believe that."

He lets this sink in for a long moment. "I think I can, but…stay honest with me. Tell me where you're at mentally, physically with this job. No lying or skirting around the truth. Can you do that?"

"Always," I promise.

Maximoff nods strongly. "Then I'll let go. No more building doomsday shelters for a *what if*, and you gotta stop throwing 'I'm doing my job' at me, man. I'm highly aware you're on-duty eighty-five percent of the time we're together."

I nod with a brief wince, kicking myself a little. "I will. Sorry." I push back strands of my hair, and when our eyes meet, we both almost start smiling. Back on track, side-by-side together. It feels like a perfect fit.

I stand.

He stands.

And we instinctively connect.

My arms slide around his arms, his arms curve around mine. Our gazes never separate.

His pink lips rise even more. "The other day, Luna asked me if you were my sidekick or if I was yours."

"What'd you say?" We kiss gently, moving closer. Legs threading. Unable to back away.

"That there's no Robin to a Batman, and I said we'd probably be two Batmans—she cut me off and said, *no*." Maximoff laughs, his eyes carrying more love than I can express. "She said I was moral to a fault and you can be impulsive, headstrong. We're fucking different but we're still two superheroes who'd die for each other. In any era, any alternate universe. Like Captain America and the Winter Soldier."

My chest rises against his, and I whisper, "I can believe that."

Our embrace strengthens. We hug tighter, tighter, his hand lost in my hair. I hold the back of his head. And his heart thuds in a calm rhythm against mine.

33

Maximoff Hale

JANUARY PASSES INTO FEBRUARY, and before I even think *all is well*, a figurative storm slams head-first at every damn one of us.

Evening sun shines through a tinted hotel window. It's encroaching 24-hours since my cousins, my little sister, and SFO have been trapped in one double-bed room.

I stand rigid at the window. And I stare out at the Los Angeles street below. No one can see me through the opaque glass, but I see them.

I see you.

Hundreds upon *hundreds* of bodies pack the road. Not a single piece of pavement or sidewalk in sight. Paparazzi mix with the masses, cameras flashing and flashing. Extra security on the ground has been trying to clear the street for hours, but the swelling crowds look like fans preparing for a music festival headliner.

We're not Red Hot Chili Peppers.

And this isn't normal.

I accounted for more paparazzi at the L.A. FanCon because it's L.A.—but this chaos isn't because of the FanCon.

People cram at the hotel exits and entrances. Hoping to catch sight of us when we leave, but we can't step foot into the hysteria. Fingers and cameras point up at this room, this fucking window.

I see the tweet.

@CherryCarrie: Tenth floor. Third window from the right. Just got confirmation from someone inside the hotel. #HotBodyguards #HMCBodyguards

I don't move.

I haven't slept in 24-hours. My phone rings nonstop, and I've tried to fix *this*. I can't stop trying, but now there's only one solution: *stay put, do nothing, wait for the street to clear.*

With a long glance behind me, I check on everyone.

Charlie slouches in the corner, forehead to his knees, hands on the back of his head, frustrated and irritated. I know my cousin.

He likes his space, and he already sacrificed that to join this tour. Now he's stuck in a small room with eleven people.

Beckett is asleep on the edge of a bed. Next to him, Jane, Sulli, and Luna squeeze close and peer at the only laptop, perched on Jane's thighs.

They're okay.

But Omega isn't.

I've never seen them this tense. Thatcher and Akara seclude themselves in the bathroom for privacy, speaking to the Alpha lead for over two hours.

Oscar has been hawk-eyeing the road near me. His gaze darkened, serious. On the second bed, Donnelly flips through news channels like an uneasy tic. Then there's Quinn, pacing the length of the room.

"Stop," Farrow tells him for the hundredth time. He's the most *at ease* here. His shoulder is propped casually on the wall beside me. With a quick glimpse, he checks on me like I check on him, then he eyes the street.

Donnelly switches channels, television on mute. "It's the Hale Curse."

Farrow chews his gum slower and gives Donnelly an annoyed look. "Shut the fuck up with the Hale Curse."

"I'm just sayin' out of all places this has to go down, it's in L.A. where hundreds of paparazzi live. That's a curse."

"The Hales didn't do anything," Farrow says. "It's not a curse."

It's a perfect shit storm.

Being trapped in a hotel room isn't why everyone's on edge. It's a billion times worse. In the masses, fans hoist posters that say *Hot Bodyguards* and *I love SFO!* and *hire me!!!*

Some even scrawled names: *Future Wife of Quinn. Akara is my babe!*

Everyone in Omega is on a goddamn cliff.

One push from being fired.

Including my boyfriend. Despite barely sleeping for the past fucking month, determined to find my stalker, I still *want* Farrow as my bodyguard.

Christ, I need him. Even selfishly.

Luna looks up from the laptop. "What's a Hale Curse?"

"A made up thing," I say and my phone vibrates in my clenched hand. I've spoken to lawyers, every uncle, every aunt, my parents, security, the board of H.M.C. Philanthropies, publicists, tabloids, journalists— exhaustion tries tooth-and-nail to tug at my limbs and sink me.

I barely blink.

I stare in a hard daze.

Thinking, thinking, and I feel three reactions rip at me in different directions.

One part of me says *keep everyone safe, be resolute, resilient.* I stand still.

One part pleads *swim, run, go outside and taste the fucking air.* I almost tilt my head back, shut my eyes and feel cold water with each forceful stroke, then tree branches slapping my arms and legs, running untiringly until my lungs fucking pop.

The last part of me screeches, *drop to your knees and scream.* Heavy pressure bears on my chest, but I'm not dropping.

I'm not screaming.

"Merde," Jane says. All three girls look wide-eyed at the laptop.

I head to the bed. "What is it?"

Jane rotates the screen.

GBA News, a primetime station on par with ABC, picked up the story. The headline:

Media and Fans Congest L.A. Streets to Spot Bodyguards of the Hale, Meadows, Cobalt Families.

I bend down and use the track-pad to read the article.

> A "Hot Santa Underwear Contest" video featuring the famous families' Security Force Omega has gone viral on Twitter and other social medias. The hashtag #HotBodyguards has been trending for over 24-hours, and Facebook shares are quickly growing over a million.
>
> The overnight fervor and fame has had a serious impact on L.A. traffic. Multiple roads are currently shut down including...

I straighten. We were all hoping it'd be fleeting. Like fifteen minutes of fame. But if GBA publicized the story, it'll air on the 7 o'clock news.

"Say something," Jane says to me, a pink sleeping eye-mask on her head. But like me, she hasn't slept. Guilt clouds her blue eyes.

"It's not your fault, Janie."

She narrated the Christmas Eve video. Beckett filmed it, but neither of them leaked it.

"But you talked to the security company," she says like she's filing all the details again and again. "It couldn't have been a hack."

I nod. "It wasn't a hack, but Beckett texted the video to family and security. Which was fine. We're all on a secure line, so it's not his fault either." He couldn't have known *someone* would share the video and break the circle of trust.

We just don't know who did.

Farrow pops his gum. "A famous one or security leaked it to the press, Cobalt."

"Our families *wouldn't*," Jane says passionately.

"Epsilon," Donnelly theorizes a culprit. "Someone narked."

Oscar turns. "Doesn't matter. The moment we leave this hotel, we're all fired." He gestures to the chaotic street. "Look at that. We can't protect anyone if more security needs to flank *us*."

Quinn paces again.

"Oh fuck, go back." Sulli is motioning for Donnelly to change channels.

He returns to the last one, entertainment news, and increases the volume.

"…Christmas has extended its stay and is bearing more gifts for us," the female reporter says on a sound stage. "Take a look at the viral video of the men who protect the Hales, Meadows, and Cobalts. And be warned, you may need an ice cold shower after this one. So ho, ho, ho, watch these hotties, and let us know if you ship it."

Strangely, her words lighten the tension. Donnelly and Farrow are smiling.

The video plays on the television. But this one is slightly different. The news station added bright text over each bodyguard as they saunter down the mock runway.

Akara is first with the words: *The Boss*.

"Truth," Donnelly says.

Jane and I exchange a wary look. They're labeling SFO from the bios Jane created on-the-fly, and it's not an original concept or a coincidence.

It's a homage. Our parents were once labeled just like this, and over twenty-two years later, media and fans still call Uncle Ryke "the jackass".

"Please let them all be positive attributes," Jane says in a soft breath.

On-screen, Donnelly appears in red trunks. *The Ass-Kicker*.

"Sweet." Donnelly smirks.

Farrow is next: *The Maverick*.

I glance at him, and his lips almost rise. But he doesn't really smile anymore. Come tomorrow, he may not be my bodyguard and some other guy probably will be.

But we did dodge one bullet. The video never showed us embracing, and the audio didn't catch us flirting.

So the world thinks he's just my bodyguard.

And I'm just his client.

Knowing we weren't the ones who ruined Omega—that our relationship didn't catapult their fame—it doesn't really help. No matter the cause, their jobs are still on the chopping block.

Oscar pops on-screen, muscles oiled. *The Pro*.

In the hotel room, he hardly bats an eye. Not surprised.

The entertainment TV station presents the entire video package like a wet dream. Confident, unabashed men in red underwear, sculpted builds and six-pack abs—I'm shocked they didn't go ahead and call them Sexy Fuckers Org.

Back on-screen, Quinn walks out in only a bow. *The Young Stud.*

Jane starts relaxing, the titles not as bad as she thought. Akara and Thatcher exit the bathroom the same way they entered. Stringent and grave. But their attention routes to the television. Watching with us.

A phone pings rapidly.

"That's me." Donnelly ditches the remote for his cell. "…fans found my Twitter. I just gained 10k followers…another thousand… holy shit. They keep askin' if anyone on SFO is single."

"Don't respond," Thatcher orders.

"It won't matter," Oscar chimes in. "GBA news already profiled our relationship statuses. Single as a Pringle. All of us."

Multiple pairs of eyes dart from Farrow to me, but I bury a reaction. Inside, my brain blares on repeat, *he's taken, he's fucking taken.*

Our room quiets when the entertainment segment shows Thatcher. He towers on-screen in his underwear, leaving nothing to the imagination, and he spins around. His bare ass is in full view. To millions of viewers. Words flash across his back.

The Jockstrap.

Great. I almost cringe. Under any other circumstance, I could see Omega laughing—but the room tenses.

Thatcher's strict features never change shape.

Jane looks horrified. Like she committed manslaughter against her bodyguard. "Thatcher, I'm terribly, *terribly* sorry."

"It's fine." Thatcher lowers the volume using the TV button. "None of it bothers me."

Jane is still pale.

I reach out and squeeze her hand. She squeezes back.

"Jane." Thatcher catches her gaze, and very seriously, he says, "I'm relieved it wasn't you on the television. That's all."

She death-grips my hand, almost cutting off the circulation. But I let her hold longer, and Akara snaps his fingers to his palm.

"So this is it," he begins to deliver the news, good or bad—and my phone rings. Jane instantly releases her grip, and I check the Caller ID: *Kinney Hale.*

For FaceTime.

I can't ignore my sister. Our mom and dad are in New York City tonight at a charity event for children. Sponsored by Halway Comics. Which means she's home alone with Xander.

"Sorry," I tell everyone. "You can talk without me..." I gesture amongst the group while I return to the window and grasp at the illusion of privacy. But I like that I'm closer to Farrow.

I answer the call.

She swings the camera. What the fuck is she doing?

Her features are blurred, brown hair whipping every damn way, black eye makeup streaming down her round cheeks. Gangly limbs shifting in and out of view.

"MoffyIcantIcant." Her voice is a jumbled out-of-breath, tearful mess.

"It's okay. Take a breath, Kinney. Tell me what's wrong." I block out the pit that wedges in my ribcage.

She cries and pounds her fists at wood.

"*Kinney.* Focus on me."

Farrow ditches his spot and stands next to me, peering at the fuzzy FaceTime screen.

"I can't...I can't get a hold..." She rattles the knob. "OPEN THE DOOR!" she screams helplessly, and I make out an Elfish sign on the wood. Xander's room. And I know.

My brother broke a rule and locked his door.

I go rigid and abandon my emotion. "Kinney, listen to me." I glance over my shoulder to alert my cousins. So they can call family, so security can call bodyguards—but everyone already rises.

Beckett is awake. Charlie is on his feet. Phones are being drawn, numbers called.

"Eliot, are you down the street?" Charlie says.

"Mom?" Luna says.

"Dad, are you near the Hale's?" Sulli asks.

"Tom?" Beckett calls.

Jane speaks in hurried French.

"Get Banks," Akara says to Thatcher, then he lists off other names, and the rest of SFO starts dialing. Phones to their ears. All but Farrow.

He puts a hand on my shoulder, zeroed in on Kinney with me, and I tune out the rest of the room.

"Kinney, Kinney," I say in a calm but forceful voice. I watch my thirteen-year-old bony sister—barely ninety-pounds—run at the door. Arm slamming into the wood. Tugging at the knob. Pounding her fists. Trying to break it down.

I'm painfully aware that she's going to fail.

"Slow down, look at me," I tell her. "*Look at me.*"

Kinney breathes, steadies the camera; her smudged eyes look broken but murderous.

"Go wait at the front door," I say.

"I'm not leaving him!" she screams at me like I'm not helping Xander. But right now, I can only help her.

And I'm not letting Kinney find our brother...

I go cold.

Farrow's thumb strokes the back of my neck, and he tells Kinney, "You need to unlock the door for Banks."

That works. Kinney runs downstairs, rubbing at her cheeks. "If he did something...I'll never forgive that turd—" She cuts herself off in a sob. "I didn't mean it. I don't want him to."

"It's okay," I say, a knot in my chest. "Don't think about it. Just unlock the door. Stay downstairs."

Flying through the foyer, she lands on the welcome mat and flicks the locks. Then she *sprints* to the kitchen.

"Kinney!" I yell.

She opens a drawer and grabs a carving knife.

"You can't *cut* a door down—*stop.*" She's going to hurt herself trying to unlock his room. Kinney races back upstairs.

Farrow looks at Akara. "She has a knife."

"Kinney, *look at me*," I growl. The camera is on the floor. She chips at the wood.

I hear footsteps and a faraway voice. "Kinney, I'm coming! Back away!" That's Banks Moretti.

"*Kinney*," I force.

She angles the phone to her face. "Moffy, I can't just…" she cries, the knife still in hand.

"*Please*," I say with everything in my fucking soul, "go to your room. Wait there."

More footsteps.

Kinney sobs and drops to her knees in a heap.

I want to be in Philly. Where I can pick my sister up and carry her far, far away from this. "Shh, it's okay," I say, chained and shackled here. Watching her pain and heartbreak through a phone screen.

Goddammit.

My eyes burn.

I'm numb. Ignoring a weight that descends on my body.

Kinney flips the camera, not wanting me to see her cry. But now I see the hall, his bedroom door and flaked wood.

Heels clap, and Aunt Rose rounds the corner fast. Urgent.

Banks Moretti runs past, and behind Rose comes Uncle Ryke and Aunt Daisy, her blonde hair blowing as she runs towards my sister.

Rose notices Kinney too and squats. "Kinney, give me." She tears the knife out of Kinney's fingers, strokes her head, and stands at the ready.

Daisy does what my mom would want to do. She wraps her arms around Kinney and hugs her tight. Kinney bawls in our aunt's shoulder.

"We're here, we're here," Daisy whispers in the sweetest voice.

Banks and Ryke kick the door twice, and they disappear inside the room with Rose. Agonizing seconds pass. More security floods the hall, then about four of my younger cousins rush in behind. Bodyguards restrain them from reaching Xander's room.

Kinney must drop her phone. Screen is black, and voices jumble, too hard to piece apart the chatter.

I turn my head to check Luna. Christ, she was supposed to be on a plane back to Philly *today*. But she missed her flight five hours ago. Thanks to the crowd outside.

Luna is on the hotel bed, burying her head beneath her *Moody Blues* shirt, but Jane holds my sister against her chest comfortingly.

I look at Farrow. Instinctive. His hand is off my shoulder while he clutches his phone.

His eyes bore into my eyes. I inhale, but my defenses shut down any emotion that fights to surface. *Numb.*

I'm numb, and he knows not to touch me or hug me. Because I'll flinch. I don't want to be cut open and bare. Not here, not with an audience.

He nods, and I don't just see an *I love you* written in his softening gaze. I feel it growing like a light inside of me.

"What was that?" Akara is on the phone, the only line of communication now. "Okay…" He eyes all of us. "Xander's okay."

I'm caging breath. Air still strained.

"He…" Akara stares off as he listens to the other person. "He was in his bathtub with headphones on…okay, thanks. Hey, yeah, okay…" He lowers his cell and tells us, "He didn't hurt himself. He's on the phone with his mom and dad right now. Lo wants Alpha to remove the hinges on his door."

Now everyone collectively breathes together.

He's okay.

My brother is okay.

"Thank God," Oscar mutters.

Donnelly plops on the bed. Quinn blows out the biggest breath and crouches in a squat.

Charlie returns to his spot on the floor.

My brother is okay.

I crack my stiff neck. My eyes are dry and sear like I took a branding iron to each one.

And as I look around the hotel room, I start thinking about Omega. How these six people just shared in a private, raw moment that the world won't ever see. Or feel. Or know.

AFTER AN HOUR OF FAMILY CALLS, PHONES ARE

pocketed. Heavy silence descends. We're all scattered around the hotel room. I cross my arms, standing rigid beside Farrow who leans his shoulder blades on the window. Relaxed, at ease. Cool.

His demeanor is like a fucking drug. Almost entering my bloodstream and helping me breathe.

Akara faces everyone again. Tension builds towards the conversation that my phone abruptly spliced. I've been thinking about Omega's fate.

Imagine replacing them with six other guys—it seems inconceivable, wrong. Like shuttling a family to the moon without a spacesuit.

The next bodyguards in line for hire may not care as much. May not love our families as much. May not want to be here for reasons greater than money and fame. And I don't just feel lucky that these six guys exist in our lives. Here today.

I feel like they're necessary. Integral pieces of our world that not many others can really fill.

So I break the quiet. "We're not firing any of you," I tell them. "If you want to fucking quit, you'll have to quit voluntarily."

Quinn raises a hand. "I'm not quitting."

"It's not up to you, little bro." Oscar nods to Akara and then Thatcher. "The Tri-Force makes the call."

Dear World, want to gift me that mind-reading superpower? Stat. Sincerely, a tense human.

I rotate my tight shoulder.

Akara fits his baseball hat on backwards. "We've decided that there has to be some changes. It's inevitable, guys. If we act like nothing's different, we're jeopardizing the safety of our clients, of all of you…" He looks at my family. "None of us want that."

Thatcher scans the bodyguards. "We've discussed ways to minimize the impact of our popularity, and to remain a part of Omega, with the same client, there are new *nonnegotiable* rules." His warning glare lands on Farrow.

I quickly process the news.

Oscar beats me to the question. "We're not being fired?"

Akara begins to smile. "Everyone's staying."

Shoulders start loosening. We all start *really* breathing for the first time in 24-hours. Oscar takes a seat, collapsing on the bed next to Donnelly.

I rub my mouth, something powerful surging through me. I'm about to look at Farrow, but Thatcher speaks.

"Think of it as a test-run," he says.

Farrow pops his gum, and I can almost feel his eye-roll at Thatcher.

But Akara nods in agreement. "We'll finish out the tour and prove that we can still do this job. If there aren't any major security mistakes, we'll stay bodyguards, guys. If we fuck up, there'll be six termination papers. Easy as that. But like I said, there are changes."

The nonnegotiable rules.

Thatcher crosses his arms. "First, delete all personal social media accounts. No Instagram, no Facebook, no SnapChat, no Twitter, no *anything* that fans can find you on and follow you."

Oscar ties a bandana around his forehead. "Goodbye to Donnelly's drunken SnapChat dick pics."

Donnelly leans against the headboard. "Those were sober, man."

Farrow chews his gum into a smile.

Beckett laughs.

Thatcher shakes his head, but he stopped saying things like *your client is in the room* and *that's inappropriate* the third week on tour. The fact that they're even having a security meeting in front of me and my cousins and not privately in a bathroom—that means something.

"You're not here to promote yourself," Akara reminds them, "or Donnelly's dick."

Donnelly nods heartily. "What about Twitter? I need to keep up with fandoms."

"Need or want?" Thatcher asks.

"Both." He digs in his pocket and pulls out a pack of cigarettes. "I need it and I want it."

"You *need* to delete it," Thatcher says. "You're here to protect your client. If you need Twitter for security reasons, we'll have anonymous security accounts made. But if we see you searching for television shows or porn, you'll lose password access."

Beckett tosses Donnelly a lighter. "You can use my Twitter."

"Thanks, man." Donnelly puts the cigarette between his lips.

"Second," Thatcher says, "don't reach out to tabloids. Don't accept any interviews, not even to defend yourself."

That'll be easy for Farrow. I can't see him volunteering for a Q&A with *Celebrity Crush*.

"And lastly," Akara tells SFO, "don't sleep with fans. Let's maintain a level of professionalism. While we're under this spotlight, we're representing the Hales, Meadows, and Cobalts. Do them proud."

To me, they already have.

The official meeting ends, and bodies move around. Trying to stretch, go to the bathroom. We're not just lacking sleep. We have no extra clothes, no luggage or toiletries. Things that'd make my cousins and little sister feel better and more comfortable after 24-hours holed up here.

I could be completely fine with little to nothing for a lot longer. But I'm aware not everyone is me.

Janie searches her sequined purse where she had a sleep mask.

"De quoi as-tu besoin?" I ask. *What do you need?*

"I wish I wore pajamas." She unbuttons her pastel pants and sighs in relief. "Tellement mieux." *Much better.*

Oscar stacks mini-bottles of liquor on the desk, and Thatcher talks to Akara about being in contact with ground security.

I turn to Farrow. "Four hours longer here?"

"Looks like six more." He chews his gum and observes the street with me. It's more congested than five minutes ago.

Security wanted us all in one room together just in case a doomsday happened and paparazzi or fans found their way inside the hotel.

I crack my knuckles. "There has to be vending down the hall. I can get some drinks…" I trail off at a loud knock.

We all quiet.

Thatcher is closest. He peers in the peephole, then unlocks and opens the door to a dazzling smile, jock-build, a duffel strapped across a broad chest, and a pastry box in hand.

"Beautiful people," Jack Highland greets as he enters. "Twenty-minute shopping spree and a five-mile walk later, I've made it."

Finally.

I near and clasp his hand. We draw in and pat each other's shoulders. "Thanks for coming."

Jack smiles brighter. "Looking forward to it."

He means the FanCon. I invited him on tour with us. The last Q&A derailed after a fight between Charlie and me. We needed a better moderator. Someone we could trust.

Jack was the only name on the list.

Throughout *years* of time—while he's been an exec producer on *We Are Calloway*—I've talked about painful memories, spilled secrets to him, and at last minute, I told Jack, *don't air it*.

None have ever leaked.

Since he plans to sleep on the tour bus, I decided to share the secret about me and Farrow. The first thing he said after I told him I'm in a real relationship was *you deserve it*. I don't know. It fucking got to me.

Jack slings the duffel on a bed. "I thought you'd need some toothbrushes, deodorant, some extra clothes, and food."

Oscar stands up. "You're now my favorite person, Highland." He unzips the duffel and finds a bag of Doritos. Janie helps unearth the clothes and toiletries for everyone.

Jack swerves, searching. "Where's Sulli?"

"Here." Sulli is doing push-ups between the two beds. She rises to her feet and twists her dark hair in a high bun. "What's up?"

His smile radiates. "Come here for a sec."

Akara casts a narrowed look at Jack. The *you hurt her, you're dead* threat unmistakable.

Sulli approaches Jack, our attention super-glued to them, and he lowers the pastry box.

She smiles. "God, if you bought donuts, I could seriously fucking kiss you."

Akara makes a face at Sulli. "Your first kiss for donuts?"

"Uh, yeah," she says like he's being weird. "Not for payment, but donuts are happiness. Now dry cereal on a donut, that's heaven."

Jack grins. "It's better than donuts."

Sulli snorts. "No fucking way." She pauses. "Is it a waffle? Because that's a close second, then pancakes."

"You're off," Akara says.

Sulli swings her head to her bodyguard. "You know what it is?"

He shrugs.

She breaks into a smile. "Okay, now I have to see." She flips open the pastry box, her eyes lit. When she tilts the box a bit more, I catch sight of two-dozen turquoise cupcakes, iced together to form a wave.

"Happy 20th Birthday," Jack tells her.

It's February 4th. Our indoor waterpark plan to celebrate Sulli's birthday pretty much died hours ago. To salvage the day, Jane has been trying to get a cake delivered.

But Jack Highland beat us to it.

Sulli is lost for words, but then she starts with, "You didn't have to—"

"I didn't," Jack says and then nods to Akara. "When he found out I was coming by, he told me to pick up the order."

Correction, Akara Kitsuwon beat us to it.

Sulli looks overwhelmed. "Thanks, Kits."

He shrugs again, his lips inching up. Then he glances at Jack. "Her mom has a theory that cake fixes everything."

Sulli lingers on Akara for a long moment, then plucks a cupcake out of the box. "Right on fucking time."

Jane has already unloaded all the supplies, but I don't see any drinks. Charlie has walked the hall a few times, so it shouldn't be a problem for me. As long as I'm fast.

34

Maximoff Hale

AN ICE MACHINE RUMBLES in the vending enclave. I crave to run, to swim, to feel *something* other than confined, hollowed out or empty.

I smack the side of a black-and-gold Fizzle machine that won't spit out a Fizz Life.

"Move, wolf scout."

My pulse skips. Reminding me I'm alive. Breathing. Human. I look over my shoulder.

A six-foot-three, tattooed know-it-all comes up behind me. His brows raise and lower in a wave.

I feign confusion. "Who are you again?"

Farrow kicks the machine. A can drops. "Your boyfriend." He collects the soda from the dispenser and tosses the silver aluminum can to me. "Want to talk about it?"

Yes, a million fucking times yes. The can is cold in my grip. I want to express how I feel, but I'm not used to articulating any of this out loud. My guards scream *no*, my heart pleads *yes*.

And I end up saying, "You want a drink?"

He chews his gum slowly, our eyes not detaching. "Yeah."

I go to take out my wallet.

"I'm buying my own," he says casually, fishing out a couple bills from his leather wallet. "I can tell you something I've never shared with anyone."

"I don't want to force you—"

"I want to, Maximoff," he says with the tilt of his head. Trying to assess my reaction.

My muscles start to unbind. "What about?"

He smiles and then talks while he feeds money into the machine. "My second week of rotations in the ER. It was a bad night, understaffed, and the only attending available was an ass. At one point, there was just him, a first-year intern, two nurses, and me. And a teenage girl comes in with a stab wound to the heart." Farrow presses the regular *Fizz* button. "There was no time to rush her to the OR, and the doctor decides on an emergency thoracotomy."

The machine dispenses a gold can.

He grabs the soda and then faces me. "I knew the girl had a two-percent chance of living, and so I hung onto the excitement of seeing a thoracotomy. It made it easier when the attending cracked her chest open…" Farrow shifts his weight, his nose flaring. But he keeps eye contact with me.

I listen closely. He's never talked about any hard days during rotations before. Not like this.

He pops the tab of his soda. "The doctor sliced open the pericardial sac. It's a thin sac around the heart. A lot of congealed blood poured out, and the first-year bailed."

My brows knot. "He just left?"

"To puke," Farrow says. "The rest of us tried to remove the blood out of the sac while the attending sewed the cut." He pauses. "She died, and it wasn't the first time I watched someone die in the hospital. But it was the first time an attending turned to me, said *close her, speak to the parents* and walked away." Farrow winces at the memory. "That son of a bitch. I hadn't even taken the retractors out of her chest when her mom…"

His chest collapses, shaking his head.

My stomach overturns. "That would've gutted me."

His brows lift slowly. "It crushed me." His Adam's apple bobs. "The curse of having a photographic memory, I can't get rid of her face or her wail."

"Jesus," I breathe. And I draw towards him.

He leans back on the Fizzle machine, but his lips inch up at me coming closer. He takes a swig of soda. "That's the story that no one ever got but you."

I appreciate it more than he'll probably ever know. "Why me?"

"You're a good listener," Farrow says matter-of-factly. "And I have a thing for you."

I lick my lips and feel my fucking smile.

"Just so you know," he says huskily, "the thing *you* have for *me* is ten times bigger."

I try to glare, but it's difficult. "I have a tiny, fragmented thing for you. Thanks for asking."

"You're welcome, wolf scout." He smiles into another swig.

I think I can speak. Find the words. Grab them. Say them. I breathe. "I'm afraid for my brother. I'm afraid this'll happen again with a worse outcome, and I just want him to be okay." I swallow. "What's also getting to me is that today—it'll stay with Kinney for the rest of her fucking life." I crack my neck from side-to-side, my bones stiff.

"What about you?" Farrow asks, and off my confusion, he says, "It'll stay with you too."

"I can handle it." I laugh at a thought. Of where we are. "I'm standing in a hotel vending area."

Farrow frowns. "I'm not following."

I take a rough breath. "So when I was twelve, I went to Disneyland, and back at the hotel, I left for a vending area." I gesture to the machines. "Just like this. I slid down and just cried. My dad found me, hugged me, and that's when I asked him if my mom was a sex addict. I'd heard rumors…and that's where he said *yes*." I look up at Farrow. "The memory is with me, but it's not eating at me. The ones that hurt my family—those almost get to me."

"Almost," he repeats, studying my features.

I open and close one hand in a fist. My body tensing. I rotate my neck again. "I swear it's like I have two switches: *rage* or *off*. Sometimes I'm programmed for automatic shutdown."

"It's a survival instinct," he says.

I give him a look. "I thought you said I was desensitized to my own death."

His barbell ratchets up with his brows. "Trust me, you are, but when other people are in danger, you have to survive to help them." He adds, "Corpses don't save people."

"You're right, they eat people."

He rolls his eyes into a laugh. "You would take it to zombies." His gaze practically brushes my cheekbones.

I step closer, my knee hits the machine, our legs threaded. I'm alright to be touched, and he sees. Swiftly, he holds my jaw and I clutch the back of his neck, our mouths a centimeter away. Hard chests pressing together.

Warmth spreads through my body. I breathe and breathe and fucking breathe. *Kiss me.*

"Hey—"

I instantly break apart from Farrow at Quinn's voice.

He holds the empty duffel. "I thought you could use this to carry the drinks back." He nods to the Fizzle machine behind Farrow. "I can help."

"We have it," Farrow says, his hand casually planted on my waist.

Quinn rubs the back of his neck. "Okay, so I actually wanted to ask you something alone." He's looking at me.

"Alright." I swig my soda.

"I've been wondering if there's anything else about Luna I should know."

Once Luna flies back to Philly, her bodyguard has to fly back too. It'll be the first time Quinn is away from *Farrow* while on-duty, for longer than a week.

And a couple days ago all the bodyguards bought Quinn a six-pack of beer, toasted to him, and said their goodbyes.

Quinn sets the duffel down. "The team said Luna's normal day is reading and writing fan-fics, but you're close to her. I figured you'd know more."

I stare off for a second. Thinking about my sister. I saw the flying saucer tattooed on her ribs. Donnelly also permanently inked the lyrics Farrow scrawled on her forearm. She called that tattoo *spontaneous*.

I get that I'm a hardass, but I'm not a prude or her dad.

I'm her big brother. And I'm *glad* she did something that made her happy. If she could stay on tour longer, I'd let her in a fucking heartbeat.

I almost smile before I refocus my attention on Quinn. "Once she finishes homeschool, I think she'll want to get out more."

"Where?" Quinn asks.

"Concerts, coffee shops, bars, amusement parks, I don't know," I say honestly. "She's just ready to experience life like a regular person." *Which is impossible.* My gaze hardens at another thought. "She trusts people ten times more than Jane does, than I do. Just watch out for her."

Quinn rubs his knuckles. "She's eighteen. I have to listen to her if she wants to hang out with people that…"

"Shit on her," I say.

"Yeah," Quinn mutters.

"Be her friend, Oliveira," Farrow chimes in. "Then she'll listen to you."

I give him a look. "Was that your plan with me?"

He rolls his eyes again. "Wolf scout, I didn't need a plan with you. I wasn't a green bodyguard."

Quinn laughs. "Thanks." He edges back. "I'll leave you two to it." He also leaves the duffel on his way back to the room.

My mind reels. About fame and the bodyguards, the video leak. "Who do you think from my family or security shared the video?" I ask him since I'm all out of guesses. Any name that crops up seems like a colossal betrayal.

Farrow straightens, more serious.

I read his gaze pretty well. "Do you know who?"

"I have a good guess." His jaw tics. "My father."

I blink a few times, processing. Dr. Keene's number was a part of the text thread. He's grouped in the circle of trust. And he's been acting desperate to get Farrow to quit security.

"So he gets you famous," I say, "and you get fired." I'm rigid, my joints needing oiled. I stretch my arm over my chest. "I'll tell security to look into it."

"I already did. My father is denying, and there's no proof." Farrow combs a hand through his hair. "And his leak didn't work. Now I'm famous and still a bodyguard. I wonder what else he has up his sleeve." His eyes hit mine, and the insinuation is obvious.

"Your father isn't stalking me," I almost growl. Christ, even saying that sounds soap-opera-level fucked-up.

"He could be. It makes the most sense." His voice fades as chatter, laughter, and footsteps echo down the hall. Probably from hotel guests, but we drop the topic and start buying drinks for everyone. Shelving theories about the leaker and the stalker for now.

35

Farrow Keene

"FARROW, WHAT'S YOUR OPINION on kale?!" The obnoxious, over-enthused paparazzi point Canons in my face, fighting for a money-shot and bobbing up and down like Chihuahuas needing to piss.

A cameraman to my right screams, "Farrow, what's your workout routine like?!"

"Back up!" I yell like a threat. Maximoff stands directly in front of me, and I shove bodies back, not allowing anyone to edge too close.

He walks closely behind Jane. She dips her head, cat-eye sunglasses block the flashes, and she reaches back and clasps Maximoff's hand.

It's a big deal.

Jane hasn't really held his hand in front of cameramen since before the Camp-Away. Paparazzi don't adjust their cameras and fixate on their friendship.

Good. The media dropped the rumor, paparazzi followed suit since it's not profitable, and slowly, the public is getting there.

I don't give a shit what any "fans" think or what tabloids print. What's most important to me: Maximoff and Jane salvaging their friendship.

In the masses, Thatcher shields Jane from lenses and hands. We create a small but effective barrier.

Paparazzi have congested the path from our parked tour bus to the venue. We considered dropping the famous ones at the entrance, but fans would just rock the car. And paparazzi shouldn't even be here.

See, we're in Salt Lake City, miles and miles away from the disaster zone that was L.A.—but as soon as we left, paparazzi rode our asses down the highway. Basically eating our exhaust.

"Thatcher, have you ever considered modeling?!"

"How tall are you, Thatcher?!"

He towers above the frenzied crowd, but I'm staring at the back of his head. Still, I know he ignores them. That's what we're supposed to do. Like hell he'd break protocol.

"Farrow—" A hand grabs my arm and tries to tug, but my reflexes kick in. I seize his wrist and twist. He jerks back, and another cameraman attempts to rush forward in the space.

I shove him. So forceful he trips backwards into another body. Like an unstable cluster of bowling pins, I watch a thirty-something guy go down. His Canon crushes underneath his ass.

"I'm going to sue!"

Sure. Try me.

At the commotion, Maximoff glances back at me. Jane pushes forward, trying to tug him along. Their hands break, and an un-intentional gap forms between them.

"Walk, Maximoff," I say in a deep voice, my hand on his broad shoulder. I'm not standing out here and mediating this shit. And we're not holding a press conference in a parking lot.

A camera lens almost whacks against my jaw. I dodge the blow, but Maximoff looks murderous.

"Give him space," he growls.

"*Walk*," I say sternly, more concerned about Maximoff reaching the venue safely.

The empty space between him and Jane is already too wide. People start creeping in, and if he doesn't reconnect with Jane fast, then I need to walk in front of him and clear a path. Thatcher keeps his position ahead of Jane, barreling through the masses.

Before I make a move, Maximoff finally surrenders, and he charges forward.

His hand clasps Jane's again.

Random fingers tug at the hem of my black V-neck. Trying to hook into the waistband of my black pants. Not my favorite thing. Not even close. And yet, I know Maximoff goes through this every single fucking day.

We reach the venue, and once inside the building, we walk quickly down empty hallways and towards the dressing rooms. At our last security meeting, we made a call to switch FanCon locations from hotels to concert venues.

Securing the area is easier, and with a backstage, we can easily bring the famous ones on-and-off stage without hassle.

Photos of 70s rock bands hang on red concrete walls. My boots slightly grip the sticky floor.

Maximoff slows his pace to walk beside me. "I guess we'll find out who's better at dealing with paparazzi," he says. "Spoiler Alert: it's—"

"Me," I finish.

He blinks. "In an alternate universe."

"In our reality," I correct. "Walking through crowds of paparazzi is my thing. They grab. I shove. They yell. I ignore."

Jane looks back to ensure we're following. Maximoff nods, and her freckled cheeks pull in a smile at him, then me.

We turn a corner, and everyone comes to a stop. Dressing room is in sight, but at the other end of the hall, Beckett, Charlie, and their bodyguards approach. And the additional guest: Jack Highland.

They all took the east side entrance while we took the rear.

We were the diversion.

"How'd it go?" Thatcher asks Akara.

I open the dressing room door, and we all spill inside.

"Only a few fans and one paparazzi," Akara says. "You?" His head swings to me, and I give Akara a look like *we got fucked*. On purpose. Being the diversion, Thatcher and I volunteered to be fucked in this instance.

Yet, I was hoping that the paparazzi would've given up their quest around Nevada, but the majority made it to Utah and subsequently to our faces.

"More than a few," Thatcher answers while he surveys the dressing room: black leather couches, silver sofa chairs, a plastic foldout table, and two wooden vanities. We've assessed the room already, and no one is in here but us.

Tour crew hangs out in Dressing Room B, but assistants left individually wrapped sandwiches, drinks, chips, and baskets of cookies on our table. Most of us must be hungry because we go for the food.

"Are you guys alright?" Sullivan asks and unscrews a bottle of Ziff. Her green eyes ping from Thatcher to me. Not her cousins.

I unwrap a sandwich. "I'm fine. It was nothing." I peer beneath the sub bun: turkey, ham, lettuce, tomato, Monterey Jack. Eh, it'll do.

Maximoff tosses me a mustard packet.

My lips start to rise, but then the bane of my career speaks.

"It was manageable," Thatcher agrees, but it won't last long. He chugs his water and then turns to me. I take a seat on the couch's armrest, biting into my sandwich.

Maximoff stays standing near me, but he's in a conversation with Jack. Discussing the upcoming Q&A. The producer takes notes on a spiral pad.

Thatcher motions at me with his water bottle. "I heard someone mention *suing*."

I lick mustard off my thumb. "You heard that, really?" I ask seriously. "I'm shocked you could hear anything over all the questions about whether you've modeled."

"What happened?" Thatcher layers on a stern, 'I am your superior' voice.

"Someone got in my way." I take a large bite of sub sandwich and watch Thatcher wait for me to add more. I roll my eyes, chew, and swallow. "I gently pushed a guy aside, and he fell. Shit happens."

"Farrow—"

"I haven't even been sued yet," I argue. "And even if he did sue me, we've all been there." I gesture to Akara, Donnelly, and Oscar, all eating their lunch.

Quinn is too new to have been slapped with a lawsuit.

Thatcher is glaring, as though I'm not digesting the severity. And he'd be right; I don't see the importance. Because there is none. Being sued has always been on the bottom of the security shit list. It's not even considered a mistake.

Everyone knows this.

I pick a tomato out of my sub and eat it. My nonchalance is pissing him off. To the point where he snaps, "Could you stop and look at me?"

"I am looking at you," I say easily while still eating.

Our exchange steals Maximoff's attention. He quiets, watching with furrowed brows.

Thatcher tightens the cap to his water bottle. "It's not good timing for any of us to be in a lawsuit."

I'm in a no-win situation. It's clear he's just singling me out because I'm *me*.

The push-ups after I broke a rule only built one rung of a bridge between us. If he wants me to change who I am to prove that I care, he can go fuck himself.

Akara sinks on a chair and peels an orange. "Thatcher, he has to do his job. We can't be afraid to get sued."

"Agreed," Oscar says, hand halfway stuffed in a Fritos bag.

I raise my brows at Thatcher. Waiting for his response.

He stares me down.

I don't blink. "Yes, Mom?" I ask him.

Thatcher expels a deep breath. "This is new territory for all of us... we're trying to figure it out." His tone is softer than normal.

I overturn his words in my head. Some of us are used to swimming with the rough current rather than fighting for life jackets and rafts. Thatcher likes his rules, and we've all been thrown in rapids where it's better to use our judgment than set boundaries that could cost us.

I'm not the problem. I'm on his side. I'll be there when all the rafts sink and no life jackets are found. His personal hate towards me is just fucking with his best judgment.

I stare at him a second longer. "That sounded like an apology," I tell Thatcher.

"It wasn't."

I eat the rest of my sandwich and lick my thumb. "We'll agree to disagree."

A head pops in the room. The crew manager. "Thirty minutes until pictures."

We may've survived the paparazzi, but we still need to deal with hundreds of emotional and adoring fans at the meet-and-greet. And this time, we're not sure who they'll be screaming for.

I'M CALLING IT.

Out of the thirty-plus FanCons so far, the Salt Lake City one has to be at the bottom. It's not even a bad event: no power outages, no successful groping hands, minor heckling, and a sold-out concert venue. All in all, Maximoff Hale would definitely call this FanCon a victory.

I'm calling it weird as fuck.

Half the attendees in the concert theater aren't focused on the famous people. Maximoff and his cousins sit on stage for the Q&A panel, and the audience is distracted.

Phone cameras aim at the five of us. We're on the ground. Guarding either side of the stage near the stairs.

I put on aviators at the next camera flash.

Fans should be more obsessed with Maximoff and his cousins than security. They've been famous since birth. We've been news for a week.

One is not like the other.

I remember Akara's "suggestions" before we started the event.

Don't engage if they ask for photos.

Don't engage if they ask for an autograph.

Do not answer any of their questions.

Basically, shut up and do your job.

Easy.

I rest my boot on the second stair. Oscar leans into my ear. "That girl keeps staring at you."

I don't look. My eyes are on my boyfriend who waves to the audience as Jack Highland introduces him.

The audience cheers and whistles.

"Is she wearing an Adidas crop top?" I ask Oscar.

"Yep."

"She's been following me all day," I say.

"I'd say you have a fan," Oscar tells me, "but really it's just Maximoff's fan being confused and following you."

I pop my gum in my mouth and flip him off. A few cameras flash at me.

Fuck, I'm not used to that yet. With paparazzi, I can pretend cameras exist purely for Maximoff. In the venue, surrounded by fans, it's more obvious where their attention is trained.

I catch Maximoff staring at me, and my mouth slowly stretches.

He cracks his knuckle, licks his lips, and diverts his gaze. I want to tell him he can stare at me all day. Every day.

Jack mans a podium on stage and angles the mic to his mouth. "First question."

In the audience, an assistant passes a mic to a girl in the aisle. A line is already cued up for questions.

"Ummm...this is for Jane." The preteen pushes her glasses. "If you could date any of the bodyguards, who would it be and why?" She mumbles a *thank you* and darts to her seat.

Jane's eyes go utterly wide.

"Fuck," Oscar curses beneath his breath.

Jack Highland is fast. "Good question." He smiles sincerely. "But we're not answering any that involve bodyguards today. Next up?"

Maximoff noticeably eases. I'm just glad he had the bright idea of bringing Jack on tour to moderate.

I hook my aviators on my V-neck.

The assistant hands the mic to the next fan in line.

A short boy clears his throat. "Before I ask my question, I'd just like to say that I totally agree with the Jane-Farrow ship. Jarrow forever!" He pumps his fist in the air to moderate applause.

I roll my eyes, and photos snap my reaction. Probability that I'm a gif tomorrow = high. Someone even shouts, "Oh my God, he doesn't like Jarrow!"

Jane lifts her mic to her pink lips. "Farrow is a lovely person."

Maximoff raises his mic. "But he's taken."

Gasps flood the room, and my smile is killing me.

Oscar whispers in my ear, "Boyfriend's territorial."

I'm enjoying this.

"Taken by who?" the boy asks.

"That's for Farrow to know," Jack Highland says, his charisma softening the words. "Remember, we're all here for Maximoff, Jane, Charlie, Beckett, and Sulli." He waves his mic, and the crowd cheers for them. Many shout *I love you* to the famous ones.

The boy puts his lips too close to the mic. "Jane, who would you ship yourself with?"

"Happiness," Jane answers.

"Is that the name of a bodyguard?!" someone shouts.

"It's a noun," Beckett says with a *what-the-fuck* face.

Jack speaks to the boy. "There are no ships with bodyguards. Next non-bodyguard related question." He motions for the assistant to pass the mic to the next in line.

"But-but." The boy white-knuckle grips the microphone. "What about Sullivan and Quinn? Quinnivan is a real thing, right? Or Maximoff and Donnelly? Maxelly?"

I choke on my gum.

Oscar pats my back, and I cough hoarsely into a fist. That one isn't funny. I'm not shipping him with anyone but me.

Maximoff is laughing hard, and he lifts his mic. "Cute," he tells the boy.

The boy looks infatuated. "Thanks...I love you." In his daze, the assistant pries the mic out of his hands, and a line coordinator ushers him to his seat.

Maximoff steals a glance at me, his lips upturned.

I smile more.

No one calls out Maximoff and me as a potential pairing, but we haven't discussed what would happen if they did. SFO is already on unsteady grounds, and if we make a major mistake on tour, we'll all lose our jobs. There's no need to rock that boat.

36

Maximoff Hale

WE'RE IN THE MIDDLE of nowhere Kansas, and Farrow refuses to come to bed. Lawyers sent him another zip file of NDAs, and he's still searching. Still not getting any sleep. *It will end*, I remind myself.

I'm not going to hound him. So I let him work, and I crawl into my bunk and shut the privacy curtain.

There's only one person I want to talk to at midnight on a Saturday. And yeah, I know it's late in Philly. But I'm pretty sure he'll be awake. I'm just hoping he answers.

He does on the third ring.

FaceTime connects, and my fifteen-year-old brother fills the screen. His straight brown hair is longer, hiding his ears, and pieces fall over his forehead. Bulky red headphones around his neck, he rests his head on a pillow. He's in bed but still awake.

"You'd probably get better sleep if you didn't nap all day," I tell him.

Xander adjusts a pillow against the headboard, sitting up, more comfortable. "Are you learning medical shit from your boyfriend now?"

"That's just big brother advice," I say easily.

Xander tucks some of his hair behind his ear. "I'm glad you called." He flips the camera, his door gone. "Please tell Kinney's girl squad to stop putting crap in my room." He zooms in on a BMX bike and rock climbing gear. "Vada thinks I'll go dirt biking with her. I won't. Winona thinks I'll actually climb a goddamn mountain. She's crazy."

Everyone's been worried about him. "I'll pass the word," I say. "How've you been?" Our parents made him add an extra day of therapy to his schedule.

Xander flips the camera, relaxed against a mound of pillows. "Alright." He shrugs. "Not as…I don't know." He chews his bottom lip, then shrugs again. "Anxious, I guess. I'm not about to do anything, you know." He rolls his eyes at himself, then sighs. He's been suicidal before, more so when he was younger.

"That's good, Summers. I'm proud of you."

He drops his gaze. "For what?"

"Waking up this morning," I say seriously.

"Yay me." His sarcasm clear. "I'm full of accomplishments."

"Hey, that's fucking big." I watch his chest rise in a deeper breath, and then the camera careens a bit.

He leans over to a nightstand and grabs a Sprite.

My brows scrunch. "What the fuck are you drinking?"

He takes a sip. "Can you not read?" He angles the green and blue can at the camera. The label in sight.

"I see a Sprite. A Coca-Cola product," I remind him, "our family's competitor."

Xander chugs, then burps. "I've got a whole case under my bed. I keep telling Uncle Stokes to make a clear-colored Fizz drink. But he's not having it…so…" Xander hoists his can to the camera.

All four Calloway sisters have shares and stock in Fizzle. The soda empire ties the Cobalts, Hales, Meadows, and Stokes together. But after my grandpa stepped down as CEO, he handed the reigns to Sam Stokes.

You know nothing about the Stokes family. Poppy Calloway, the oldest sister, and her husband Sam Stokes managed to steer clear of the media. Their only daughter is an actress, filming a movie in Canada right now, and I keep in touch through text. But we're all in different stages of our lives.

Xander pops open a second Sprite can.

"Traitor," I say into a smile.

His lips almost lift, but honestly, I'm not sure the last time my little brother had a full-blown smile on his face. Maybe when we went LARPing a few years back.

He pries the tab off his can, his mouth down-turning, and his amber eyes drop again. "You deserve being called a traitor more than me right now."

What? I see myself in a tiny box on the FaceTime screen. My brows pull together, face sharpened. I shift uncomfortably on my bunk. The space suddenly feels cramped and small.

"Why is that?" I ask, my voice tight.

"You're not attending Mom and Dad's vow renewal," he says with a shrug, like it doesn't really matter, but he looks sad. "Just like you missed my birthday."

My muscles bind. I try to sit up a bit more.

I should've fucking known he'd surface this. Our parents just announced a second wedding in April to renew their vows. The media published the story like American royalty just declared the biggest ceremony of the year.

It made so many headlines that paparazzi raced back to Philly. Like ants returning to their mud hill. And about five hours ago, we lost the last van that'd been trailing our tour bus.

My mom and dad—they did that for Security Force Omega. Knowing a wedding announcement would reroute the media's attention. And seeing the look on the bodyguards' faces when the roads cleared…it made me immeasurably *proud* to call them my parents.

Maybe in Xander's eyes, if I really loved Mom and Dad, I'd be at their vow renewal. But it's not that easy.

The FanCon ends the same day as the wedding. It ensures that paparazzi will stay in Philly during the rest of the tour and not bombard us. Our parents chose that wedding date, knowing I wouldn't be able to attend.

"I made a commitment to this tour," I tell my brother. "If I could be there, I would. You know I miss you a fucking ton."

He squeezes the soda can, the aluminum crushing a bit. "Yeah, me too, and I get it. I guess." He sighs heavily, his hair hanging in his face as he slumps. "Hey, so I've been meaning to ask you…" He glances to his right, checking for any eavesdroppers where his door used to be.

"Yeah?"

He chugs his soda and wipes his mouth on his arm. "I know Mom was addicted to masturbating or whatever. That means we could be addicted to that kind of stuff, too. So what's like *too* much?"

"Too much jerking off?" I ask.

"Yeah. Is there…like a number or something?" He tucks his hair behind his ear again. I see myself at fifteen, questioning every damn thing.

"Are you having sex?" I ask, realizing we haven't talked about this stuff in a while.

"With my hand," he replies.

"That doesn't count."

"Then no." He tosses his crushed can somewhere. It sounds like it lands on hardwood. "If you don't give me a number, I'll just ask Luna, and she gives shitty advice, so I know you don't want that. Take pity on me." He belches.

I smile, about to tell him there's not a number, but the bus comes to a rocky, abrupt halt. A mechanical screech pitches the air.

Great.

Xander reads my face. "What happened?"

"I don't know," I say quickly. "Something with the bus. Can I call you back?"

"Bro, just give me a number first. It's killing me."

"One million," I say.

He flips me off, and I reaffirm I'll call him back and then I hang up. I swing my legs off the bunk and jump down. Entering the crowded lounge.

From the driver's seat, Thatcher cranes his neck over his shoulder. "Everyone okay?"

"What's going on?" I ask.

The next words are ones I didn't ever want to hear.

"The bus broke down."

PROGNOSIS: NO ONE KNOWS WHAT THE FUCK HAPPENED.

The bus just kind of died, and now we're waiting for a mechanic to drive out into the middle of absolutely nowhere.

All of my cousins and Donnelly, Oscar, and Jack sit on the pavement across from a wheat field. A plume of gray smoke sputters from the rear of the bus. I've helped my uncle fix up an old Jeep several times. So I understand cars, but this is a *bus*. There isn't even a hood.

Farrow laces his boot, and I check my phone for reception again. No signal.

I remember how Quinn and Luna flew back to Philly after crowds cleared in L.A., and right about now, I'm fucking glad she's missing this.

After talking in private, the co-Omega leads return to our spot, and Thatcher tells us, "You all should get back on the bus."

I give him a look. "You want my family and SFO to get on the thing that's smoking and may catch on fire? That's a hard no."

Akara fits his baseball cap on. "It's late. No one is coming until morning."

Fog rolls in from the distance. No street lamps. Only the bus headlights illuminate our eerie setting. Pitch black. Endless empty wheat fields. It's already the start to a bad horror movie.

But I feel safer keeping everyone out here than on an exploding bus.

Thatcher reads my resolute expression, then nods. "Okay. We'll stay outside."

Frogs croak and crickets chirp in the unnerving silence.

While on the ground, Beckett stretches out his legs and nods to me. "Virgins die first, right?" He doesn't watch horror movies, but he knows I do with Kinney.

I'm about to answer, but Donnelly muses, "Protect the virgins at all costs."

"Virgins raise their hands," Oscar says.

Only Sulli raises her hand and scrunches her nose. "What? Really? I'm the only fucking one?"

Jane squeezes her in a side-hug. "We love you most. But not because you're a virgin. That's just a coincidence."

We laugh.

Beckett smiles. "We'll all protect you, Sulli, just try not to outrun us."

"Virgins don't die in horror movies," I say and cross my arms as a breeze whips through. "You have it backwards."

"Sluts die first," Charlie says on the ground. He unbuttons another button on his white shirt. Even with the cold.

"Well, most of us will die then," Oscar says, tying a bandana around his forehead.

I catch Charlie's gaze. "Yeah, you're right." I nod, and everyone quiets as Charlie and I agree on something. A rarity on this damn trip. "*Death by sex*," I explain. "It's a trope, especially in older horror movies."

Farrow ties his other boot. "Moral takeaway: *sex is bad, kids. Protect your virginity.*"

Charlie leans back on his elbows. "But if the virgin does die, it's usually a girl and she's always the final kill." He smiles at Sulli. "Congratulations, you'll outlive us all."

"Fuck that." She stands and wipes the gravel off her legs. "We're all surviving."

"Goals." Donnelly blows smoke in the air. He tosses the cigarette pack to Beckett.

Farrow rises and stuffs his hands in a green Philadelphia Eagles hoodie. *My* hoodie.

I rub my mouth, trying to tell myself to *look away*. Stop staring like I'm fucking obsessed with him.

But my childhood crush is wearing *my* clothes. It's the first time he's dressed in something of mine. Maybe being in the middle of nowhere without paparazzi is the cause.

I skim him. Head to fucking toe. He took out his brow piercing, but he still has an earring, hoop in his nose and lip—and he has on my hoodie. Jesus.

Christ.

Fuck me and my short-circuiting brain. *It's just a fucking hoodie.* He's not wearing the meaning of life.

Farrow suddenly catches me staring. His lips quirk.

My neck heats, and I look away.

More smoke guzzles out of the bus. We all watch.

"Maybe we should put some distance between ourselves and the bus," Jane suggests. She hops to her feet and takes off down the deserted, dark road.

I quickly follow suit. Jogging to catch up. "So I gotta tell you, this is the part of the horror movie where we both die. We're the first to leave the group."

She smiles softly. "On the contrary, old chap. We're *leading* the group."

I glance over my shoulder. Sure enough, my cousins, their bodyguards, and Jack are following our trail.

Bodyguards click their flashlights, and I notice Farrow keeping pace with Oscar. He nods to me, but he doesn't run ahead. Maybe to give me some alone time with Janie.

The further we are from the bus, the darker. My best friend powers on her phone light, and I unclip my carabineer on my jeans, an emergency flashlight attached.

I look at Janie. "What's the chances we're leading them to their deaths?"

Jane ponders this. "With your survival skills and my wit, we'd put up a good match against any adversary ahead, but we're hopelessly unlucky, you and me."

I put an arm around her shoulders, and she leans into my build. Almost like old times.

Shining my flashlight on the street, I ask, "Did you talk to your mom today?" Aunt Rose has been calling Janie every single day since the tour began, and every single day, Janie has ignored the call and replied with a text: *not yet.*

"No," she says. "I thought about it. I did." She ties her wavy hair in a low pony. "But so much time has passed, now I don't even know what to say. They wrote those essays for me, and they both apologized. Now I feel like the brat that's icing them out."

"They fucked up," I remind her. "You can take however long you need. That's not being a brat."

Her long lashes lift up to me. "You forgave your parents in a couple days, Moffy."

"That's different."

"Is it?"

"My parents are…" I lick my dry lips, trying to step on the right word. I think about how people see the Hales. Fragile, breakable, humans—a row of dominos that topple with one blow. But that row of dominos always uprights again.

And again.

Again.

Strong.

My parents are strong, I remember, but it's a kind of strength that appears after raw vulnerability. Like a scar after a wound.

I don't like hurting them before they're healed. "They don't need me adding to their stress," I end up saying. "Your parents eat and breathe loyalty. It's okay to feel betrayed."

"I don't anymore though," she says and kicks a loose piece of gravel with her ballet flat. "I understand why they did what they did. They love me. We received the royal interrogation treatment that they'd give each other. It's actually quite flattering in this odd way."

I frown. "Then why aren't you talking to your mom?"

The wind whistles and wheat sways beside us. A cold chill snakes down my neck, and I zip up my gray jacket. Since we're ahead of everyone, the landscape is fucking creepier.

Jane presses closer and hooks her arm with mine. "Like I said, I don't know what to say."

"You could start with *hi*," I suggest. "Your mom will probably fill in the rest."

"Next time she calls, I'll pick up," Jane says with a determined nod. "I will." She smiles up at me. "Can you believe we got through a horrendous rumor unscathed?"

"Are we though?" I ask.

"Lightly scratched," she amends.

"Gently used."

"We're in the bargain bin now," she agrees. And we both smile.

"This tour—it helped, right?"

"Most surely," she says. "I don't think I could've stayed in Philly, and the money you raised, Moffy…it's incredible."

"*We* raised," I correct Jane.

Her big blue eyes say that I'm wrong and I'm the one who deserves the credit, but I've had too much help from too many fucking people to accept it.

Loose pavement crunches beneath my Timberland boots. "What's been the worst part?" I ask.

Jane doesn't even hesitate. "The sexual frustration. It's strong, and I can't even commiserate with you."

I actually feel bad about that. "Why don't you call your AWB? He can tag along for the last part of the tour."

Shock arches her brows "*You* want Nate on the bus?"

I grimace. "Not really, but I also don't want you to be sexually frustrated."

"And I don't want nine guys grilling him," she says into a sigh. "My options include me, myself, and my vibrator." She brightens her phone light. "Nate and I have sexted some, so I've had that."

I kick some gravel. "You could always ask your new bodyguard to help you out." I start smiling. "I'm sure he wouldn't mind."

Jane snorts. "Oh yes, in your life, bodyguard duties include giving head." She narrows her eyes at the dark road. "God, could you even imagine? What would I say? *Hello Mr. Moretti, I'm in need of some oral assistance. Would you be so kind to spread my knees?*"

Someone clears their throat behind us. "Maximoff."

That's not Farrow.

Fuuuck.

Jane and I suddenly freeze, her eyes about to explode out of her head. She flushes, fumbles with her cell, and the light blinks on and off. She curses in French before we both turn and face Thatcher Moretti.

"Yeah?" I answer him and glance over his shoulder. The others are further back. Not matching our pace.

Thatcher doesn't acknowledge Jane. Just speaking to me. "There's a small town a mile up. We're all heading that way."

"Alright, sounds good."

Jane is radiating embarrassed heat. But where other people tend to shy from it, she steps further into the light. Like that will be better.

"Thatcher," Jane greets. "I'm just going to come out and ask. Did you hear what we were talking about?"

His brooding, stern face is exactly the same. But he finally looks at Jane. "I did."

Jane crosses her arms, not breaking eye contact with him.

I'd like to make some posters, hoist them high, and they'd have an arrow to Janie and they'd say: *that's my best fucking friend.*

"And?" she asks him.

A gust blows through.

Thatcher unrolls the sleeves to his red flannel shirt. "And if you need any kind of oral assistance," he says, using her words which just entrances her more. "Then I can call someone for you. Nate or—"

"I can make my own phone calls, thank you," she says breezily. "That's all." She rotates on the tips of her toes, facing forward, and only I'm able to see her wide eyes that pretty much shout *what just happened?*

Thatcher looks to me. "You good?"

"Yeah." I nod.

He stays an awkward beat longer before leaving.

When I turn back to Jane, she says, "He offered to find a guy to go down on me." She pauses. "It's actually sweet. Why do I think that's sweet?" She touches her forehead like she's running a fever. "Merde."

I think a lot. How Farrow can't stand Thatcher. How Thatcher can't stand Farrow. How I'm *always* going to take Farrow's side in that rivalry.

But if Jane is into Thatcher, it'd complicate everything. So I just need to know… "Jane, do you have feelings for—"

"No," she denies quickly. "No." She shakes her head. "We're on a smooth trajectory, Moffy." She clasps my hand. "Don't you feel it?"

There's a leaker and a stalker out there, and I'm still on a bus with Charlie. "If by *smooth*, you mean *an asteroid is headed our way*, then yeah. We're on the smoothest trajectory there ever could be."

Jane laughs, but the noise fades fast and she points at the wheat field. Orange speckled light in the distance. "That must be the town up ahead."

37

Farrow Keene

WE CUT THROUGH A dirt path in the wheat field, leading us towards a small Kansas town.

Notifications ping and buzz on multiple phones. Cell signal must've returned. As we walk, I check my texts since I sent one to my father this morning. The first time I've texted him in years.

I said: if you're harassing Maximoff in the belief I'll return to medicine, tell me now. We can talk about it. It took me an hour just constructing that text. Because my first draft said *fuck you*.

He hasn't replied yet.

I pocket my phone, and Maximoff slows next to me.

Wheat brushes our arms on either side of us. I hold his gaze for a long beat. Like me, he's not afraid of the fog or the dark. I wouldn't care if he were. But there's something extremely fucking sexy about this shared fearlessness.

I begin to smile, and I increase my pace. Seeing if he'll keep up. His lengthy stride instantly matches mine, and soon, we've added plenty of distance between the others and us.

His forest-greens flit to the Philadelphia Eagles hoodie I'm wearing. Shit, I love being his first. Even for the simple, little things. He's been basically eye-fucking me for the past hour, but more sensual than a rough, quick fuck.

If eyes could make love, his eyes would be making love to me.

Maximoff catches sight of my growing smile, and he rakes a hand through his thick hair. "I don't know why the fuck you're smiling."

"Sure you don't." I tilt my head at him, my gaze descending his build. "It smells like you."

Maximoff rubs his mouth, then jaw, trying to hide a smile. "Fantastic, I'm assuming."

"Settle down, wolf scout. There's not a merit badge for smelling good."

He almost laughs. "You're admitting I smell good?" He touches his heart. "It's almost like *you're* obsessed with *me*."

I nod a couple times. "Man, it's cute how badly you want the tables to turn."

"They have," he combats.

I swing my head from side-to-side, considering for a half second, about to answer but my phone buzzes. A new text.

I check.

Call me tomorrow. — Dad

Curt, to the point. And also vague as shit. I flash the message to Maximoff.

His face is stoic. "Calling him may not help. I feel like you shouldn't reach out unless it's about you and him, not the stalker."

I shake my head. "There is no me and him. There hasn't been for over three years." To protect Maximoff, I'd call my father, but I also don't want to give him the advantage.

I message him: *you can talk to me over text*.

Just as I send it, the wheat field ends, and we kick up dirt as we walk forward. I change my mind: this isn't a town. It's three shingled buildings, two of which look closed. Light flickers in the windows of one.

All people vacated for the night.

I whistle, and the wind carries the sound.

Maximoff gives me a look to follow him. He's on a mission, and I'm not leaving his side. I sense where he's headed in an instant.

Signs swing on each building: Lucille's Drugstore, Antiques & Brass, and Savory Eatery with an additional sign that reads, *fortuneteller inside!*

Guess which is the only one open.

Maximoff climbs the wooden slatted stairs to the restaurant. Blue paint peels off the old door. I catch his bicep as he reaches for the copper knob.

"You're not going in first." I'm not trying to one-up him. He can lead the pack, but I'm still on-duty. And this is still an unsecured location.

"We're in the middle of nowhere," he retorts. "Whoever's inside this restaurant has probably never heard of Loren Hale, let alone his son."

"Sure, but they could also jump you, and then what?" I'm not backing down.

"They could also jump you." He's not backing down either.

"I'm a trained fighter."

"And I fight a lot," he combats.

My brows spike. "I have a gun."

"I have a switchblade."

I roll my eyes and let out a laugh. "You're so stubborn."

He hones in on my lips and piercings. "Same to you, man." His sudden *fuck me* eyes are killing me. My muscles burn, and veins pulse in my dick.

I watch him eye-fuck me, his forest-greens traveling lower, lower…I smile. "You'll see my cock later, don't worry."

"I wasn't, thanks," he says dryly, but his breath shallows. His body tenses. *Fuck me fuck me* is the predominant plea, request and sentiment.

And damn, I want to fulfill that. But we both acknowledge place, time: Kansas past midnight with nine other people.

Speaking of those people, they walk towards us, and our heads turn.

"Fortuneteller," Donnelly reads the sign. "Dope."

Maximoff ends up holding the door open, and we watch each person file inside one-by-one. I hang back with him. Omega goes first, canvassing the restaurant, then their clients.

When my boyfriend and I enter together, I scan the eclectic decorations. Lava lamps sit on the scratched bar, orbs inside fishnets dangle from wooden rafters, and an old jukebox plays Johnny Cash. There are only six wooden tables, the place small.

And empty.

Akara taps a bell on the bar.

"Anyone here?!" Sulli calls, noticing a kitchen door, and it whips open.

A withered, gray-haired waitress glides out, tying an apron around her waist. "Hey there. We usually only get truckers around this hour. Take a seat wherever you like." She gestures to the tables. "My name's Patricia. I'll be serving you."

Maximoff was right. She doesn't recognize the famous ones, and I doubt she'd care if we introduced them as A-list celebrities.

We all push a couple tables together. I upright a ketchup bottle that knocks over.

Chairs creak as people begin to sit. I choose a spot at the end, and Maximoff takes a seat beside me. Oscar and Jane in front of us. Seating arrangement isn't that random. We're the furthest away from Thatcher and Charlie.

Patricia plants her hands on the table. Bent towards Jack. "We only have three things on the menu, boys." She notices Jane and Sulli. "And ladies. Barbecue chicken, our nightly stew, and sour cream and raisin pie. Only one beer on draft, and we have some cold Fizz drinks."

"I'll try the pie," Sulli says first.

Everyone else orders the barbecue chicken, sodas and water. We begin talking about music as "Folsom Prison Blues" starts booming. Then beads smack an entryway, a figure slinking dramatically through like she's auditioning to play Madonna.

I balance back on two chair legs, thoroughly entertained.

"What the..." Beckett trails off, his brows cinched.

Smoky purple makeup shadows her eyes, and she aims for our table.

Patricia motions to the woman. "This is Fontina the Fortunate, my sister-in-law. All readings complimentary with your meals. Good luck, and I'll be back with your drink and food."

Oscar mutters to me, "Yeah, I'm not feeling this place."

"Good luck?" Jane repeats and exchanges a wary look with Maximoff.
The other end of the table is quiet and curious. Mine is about to
self-eject. Minus me. This shit is harmless.

But I understand how protective Jane and Maximoff are towards
their cousins and siblings. I'm sure they don't want a stranger telling
them that they're about to die. Or that their future is bleak and miserable.

Fontina slinks around us, her manicured nails skating across the
backs of our chairs. "I feel a strong energy in the room."

Sitting backwards on his chair, Donnelly smokes another cigarette.
"It's me, right? I know I've got some strong ass energy."

"That's just your breath," Oscar quips.

Donnelly blows him a middle-finger kiss.

"No, no, it's not you." Fontina circles the table. Eyelids hovering
closed, she sucks in a breath through her nostrils. "It's here." She waves
a hand towards my end. "No, wait…" She wavers.

I can't help but fucking smile.

Patricia carries out our drinks, setting them down, and once she
leaves, Fontina reanimates and places a hand on Sulli's head.

Maximoff goes rigid.

Sulli tries not to laugh.

"You, dear," Fontina muses.

"Yeah?" Sulli says.

"I sense…strong feelings around you. A destiny that you cannot
control."

Vague.

Beckett makes a *that's utter bullshit* face.

Sulli contemplates this hard. "In what fucking way? Like swimming
or…?"

"Love," Fontina says.

"But I've never been in love," Sulli mentions.

"I know, dear."

"Because she just told you," Beckett says pointedly, and Charlie
smiles, halfway slouched in his chair.

Fontina ignores him and puts another hand on Sulli's head. "You're a determined spirit, a go-getter, and many admire that…but there's a man who protects you most strongly…" Her hands drift to Sulli's cheeks, and Sulli stiffens, about 70% uncomfortable. "And you will fall—"

"No one's fucking falling," Maximoff interjects, forearms on the table to have a better view of his cousin.

Fontina lets go of her and circles the table, and Sulli mouths, *thanks* to Maximoff. Grateful for redirecting the spotlight.

I still teeter on my chair legs and fold a straw paper.

"You two…" Fontina muses, her hand hovering above my head and Maximoff's. "Powerful forces…connect you two in this life…and your past lives…"

A smile edges across my mouth, and I ask, "How much did he love me in our past lives?"

She sucks in a breath, channeling.

Maximoff blinks at me like I've asked a question that just sent him to hell. Also, he's struggling not to look at my lips.

"…great, great love," she muses. "It was…always you."

Maximoff is almost flushed, his body unmoving. Rigid. He tunes out the audience of his family and security, and he stares at the table.

Wolf scout.

Normally he has a comeback, but I can tell he's lost for a retort. I drop my chair legs and discreetly put a hand on his knee.

He's still a marble statue.

"That's beautiful," Jane says, "and you can read them without tarot cards?"

"Mmmhhhmm," Fontina answers. "I have an intuitive soul."

Maximoff takes a swig of water and says genuinely, "That's interesting."

Fontina smiles, but then she frowns deeply and seizes my gaze. "You're looking for someone, aren't you?"

The air deadens. I'm not even sure if I believe this shit.

"Weird," Donnelly says.

I'm still actively looking for multiple people. The stalker, the leaker— and my phone suddenly vibrates in my pocket. I reach for my cell.

"You'll find them soon, very soon…" Fontina trails off as the waitress waltzes to our table with a large tray of food. The fortuneteller says silkily, "Enjoy your meal." Then she leaves through the beaded entryway.

Jane asks the waitress, "How accurate is your sister-in-law with her readings?"

"I'd say about half is complete bull." Patricia wipes her hands on her apron. "But she slides some truth in there every now and then. Need anything else?"

I tune out everyone and unlock my phone to a new text.

Harassment is a strong word. — Dad

My jaw muscle twitches. I text: What word would you use then? I send the message.

Maximoff hasn't touched his food yet. "Bad news?"

"No news," I say under my breath. "He's being a vague asshole." My attention drifts as Oscar pops a metal tin. "You seriously brought Audrey's cookies here?" I didn't even notice him carrying them.

"Yeah," Oscar says. "We didn't know if anything would be open, Redford. I was thinking ahead."

My phone rattles on the table.

I would call it being proactive, productive, and professional. I shouldn't be the primary care physician to your boyfriend. It's a better role for you. Your talent shouldn't be wasted. Do what you're meant to do. — Dad

My nose flares. I grind my teeth, irritation crawling down my spine. I can't discern whether he's behind the Instagram account or the leak. He's only referencing how he's no longer Maximoff's doctor. That incident alone sets me on an aggravated edge I rarely near.

I'm not replying back anytime soon. I pass my phone to Maximoff. Wanting to keep him in the loop. And I look across at Oscar, who eats a heart-shaped cookie whole.

"How's the cookie, Oliveira?"

"Perfection." He picks another one, and his eyes narrow at the icing. He goes very still, serious. More methodical.

Something's not right.

I reach for the tin and sift through the cookies. Pink icing decorates half of them with two words: *I'm sorry.*

"I don't understand it," Oscar tells me. Neither do I.

"Did she get glasses?" I ask him. "Maybe she finally realized you're not hot enough for special deliveries—"

He aggressively chucks a cookie at *Maximoff*, who catches it easily.

My brows arch at Oscar. "Fuck you," I say and add a middle finger.

Oscar cracks a short-lived smile. He watches Maximoff inspect the *I'm sorry* cookie, then Jane sees them.

"I'll call my sister." Jane starts dialing a number, and Maximoff stares off in thought. The other end of the table is discussing the best barbecue they've ever had. I throw a wadded napkin at Akara.

He dodges. "Hey—"

"Catch." I toss him a cookie.

"Fuck, are they moldy?" Sulli wonders, noticing us. "That's the worst."

"No, they're not moldy," Jane replies, phone to her ear.

Akara flashes the cookie to everyone.

Thatcher sets down a steak knife and zeroes in on Oscar. "Did you do something where she'd need to apologize?"

"No," Oscar says seriously. "I don't really talk to her. She sends me cookies, I eat them. That's about it."

Charlie scrapes his chair back, capturing everyone's attention. "My little sister is fascinated with boys. But she crushes on ones she knows she can't and will never have. Because she doesn't actually want to see it through." He stands and saunters over to Jane. "Audrey just likes the idea of love more than the reality."

"Oui," Jane agrees. "She borrowed all my Outlander novels a year ago, and I haven't seen them since. She loves a good romance."

"*Fictional* romance," Beckett emphasizes, rising to join his brother and sister, and Jane stands too. I take note of those three, the Cobalts, on their feet together.

Admittedly, I may not be that partial to the Cobalts, but I can tell when they sense something's "afoot" in their family. Standing upright, their unity carries a profound strength that clenches the air. They may as well have buckled their armor and sheathed their weapons.

If I sense this, then so does Maximoff. He stares at his cousins, then at the phone. Weight strains the restaurant.

"Everyone quiet," Jane says as the line connects. She presses *speakerphone*. "Audrey, I know it's late, but Oscar just opened your cookie tin. He's next to me, and you're on speaker. We just wanted to know if everything's okay."

I hear sniffling. On the verge of tears.

Maximoff edges closer to the table. "Are you home?"

"Yes, hi Moffy," Audrey says softly. "I'm in my bedroom. I've grounded myself for eternity." Her whimsical voice sounds like she's starring in *Little Women* or *Tuck Everlasting*. "It's what I deserve most of all. Who else is with you?"

"Everyone," Jane says. "I can hand the phone over to Oscar if you'd like."

"No, this is better." She sighs morosely, then she sighs again, her voice quivering.

Donnelly winces, hating when the young kids cry. It's not my favorite thing either. I spin a saltshaker and listen to the Cobalts.

"Audrey," Charlie says. "What are you apologizing for?"

Her voice cracks. "I'm so sorry. I am." More tears, this time a sob.

Beckett whispers to Jane, "Take it off speaker."

Before Jane moves, Audrey blubbers, "I did it."

My breath gives, and I must be too fixated on the stalker because my mind immediately goes *there*. It's fucking irrational. Maximoff's thirteen-year-old cousin isn't creating death and murder images of him.

"Did what?" Jane asks, wide-eyed.

"I'm the one who shared the video," she says in a tearful confession. The Hot Santa video.

Beckett shakes his head repeatedly, arms outstretched. Like that's not right. It can't be his little sister, but she just admitted to it. Charlie softens his gaze on Beckett.

And then Jane motions for everyone to remain quiet, but Thatcher and Akara stand and pull out their phones. Texting the security team.

Donnelly barrels forward, face in hands. Yeah, his precious Cobalts fucked up. Guess what, they're all human.

"I don't understand, Audrey," Jane says. "Why would you do that? You knew it was private."

"I didn't intend for the press to have it," she cries softly. "All I ever wanted was for Emma Rodwin to believe that Oscar existed. She said I was lying, and I'm not a liar." She cries harder but still speaks clearly. "When Beckett sent the video in the group text, I only thought of what it'd feel like for Emma to know the truth. And I copied the video to a flash drive to share with her."

Charlie says, "And Emma sent the video to the press."

Beckett relaxes. "You didn't actually leak the video, Audrey. It was your friend."

She sniffs. "I'm an adjacent party to this treachery, you have to realize."

This is exactly why I'm fortunate to never be on a Cobalt family getaway. She just turned thirteen in January, and she speaks like she's fifty. And this is just *one* Cobalt. When all seven are together, it's an instant migraine. Stick me with the weirdo Hales any day. Fuck, I actually miss Luna right now.

"You didn't," Beckett says. "We can't trust anyone but family and security. Lesson learned, and now you move on."

"I can't," she cries. "What if I feel like I've done the worst thing a person could ever do?"

"You haven't murdered anyone," Oscar notes, cutting into his chicken.

Audrey blubbers more apologies to Oscar, and most of us start to relax. It's better that it's Audrey and not someone from security. As much as I dislike Epsilon, I wouldn't want them to hurt the families. But I wish the leaker and the stalker had been the same person.

Then I could've closed the book to the other one, too.

"I'm deeply, deeply sorry," Audrey says with a hiccup. "To everyone, I've failed the family. I should be banished."

Beckett and Charlie smile.

"We won't banish you until sunup," Charlie teases.

"I'll make all my amends before then." She sniffs, sounding better.

"Have you told Mom and Dad?" Beckett asks.

Audrey sighs. "No…Mother and Father will be so disappointed. I couldn't call anyone. I thought the cookies would do…but I should've called. I'm weak, so weak." I imagine her throwing herself on her bed in a dramatic heap.

Half of us try not to laugh.

"You're not weak," Maximoff says, eyeing the phone. "You're a Cobalt."

"Toujours," Charlie says, and I can translate that French word: *always*.

Audrey sniffs one last time.

"You have to tell Mom and Dad," Jane urges. "Tonight. Wake them."

"Will you throw flowers at my funeral?" Audrey asks.

Jane begins to smile. "Only roses. And you, mine."

"Of course, sister." She exhales, the conversation between the Cobalt girls weird as shit and slightly fascinating.

"Bye, Audrey."

"Bye, Jane."

They hang up.

Donnelly has unburied his face. "I love Cobalts." He smirks.

"That's called blind, stupid loyalty," I say. "One of them may've just fucked up our jobs."

38

Maximoff Hale

ALMOST A HUNDRED FANCONS under our belt, we speed through March in seamless fashion.

I booked interviews in *Forbes* and *Vanity Fair* to publicize the tour, and most media outlets pulled this quote from a business magazine:

> H.M.C. Philanthropies' FanCon Tour moves onto its last leg stronger than ever. With an estimated $150 million earned in just three months, Maximoff Hale has capitalized on his fame for non-profit. He's revolutionizing philanthropy by bringing in a new younger wave. It's not just about blue-blooded Wall Street investors anymore. He's found a group of twenty-somethings willing to spend money on him rather than a ticket to that new Taylor Swift concert. And the benefit: all proceeds go to charity. This twenty-two year-old is bulldozing his way through the philanthropy world. His last name is one of the most recognizable— but make no mistake—he's carving out his own piece of history.

I wish they would've mentioned my cousins and the work of the crew and security. I couldn't do this without them, but my spirits are

44

still high throughout the Seattle FanCon. I didn't need the accolades. I'm just happy with the number.

$150 million will help a lot of fucking people.

A line coordinator guides a lanky boy out after I hug him. Farrow stands several feet off to the side, and a few fans gift him portraits they drew. Bodyguard Fame is alive and thriving.

But weirdly, it's not bad. So far, they've all been able to ignore the attention. Mostly thanks to my mom and dad. It's easier for Omega without a giant, all-consuming paparazzi presence.

Our *FanCon* banners are erected on the Seattle concert stage, and velvet ropes section all five lines. In between greeting fans, I look around at the excited crowd, the overwhelmed smiles, and I think about the first meet-and-greets. How we smoothed out a lot of kinks.

How no one bailed.

I'm fucking proud of this tour. Of my cousins. Of security and crew. I'm already planning an end-of-tour party for everyone.

A line coordinator ushers the next fan forward. Up a set of stairs. On the stage. Towards me. The girl has chopped, dyed pink hair, and a black Superheroes & Scones T-shirt swallows her thin frame. She can't be older than fifteen.

Before my eyes even hit the girl, she's crying.

And by *crying*, I mean *bawling her fucking eyes out*. I've met a billion tears from fans on this tour, happy and sad and pained, but something about this girl slams at me and tries to rock me back.

Maybe because she has the same wiry build as my sisters. Maybe because she looks around Xander's age. Maybe because she stumbles over her feet, and when I catch her, she crumples in my arms.

"Hey, hey, I'm right here," I say strongly, and I mortar brick and steel inside of me. I don't rock back or sway.

She sobs and rubs at her cheeks. I support all her weight, holding her up so she's on two feet. If I let go, she'll sink to the floor.

I wipe her tears with the hem of my green shirt. "What's your name?"

She tries to stop crying, breaths ragged. "B-B-Britni."

My lips pull in a small smile. "That's a pretty name."

She cries harder.

Goddammit.

I look over my shoulder. At Farrow. He's fixated on this interaction, and I mouth, *parents*. We need to find her parents or whoever attended the FanCon with her. A family member, a friend, a goddamn adult.

Farrow waves over my assistant and speaks quickly.

I concentrate on Britni. "Want to sit with me for a second?" I ask.

She nods over and over.

So I slowly kneel on one knee and bring her down with me. I let go of her waist, and she sits on the stage, her legs splayed to the side. I rub her back and ask as gently as I can, "Want to tell me what's bothering you?"

She sobs into her Superheroes & Scones shirt.

Like *guttural* sobs. Each one tries to dagger my ribcage and lungs. My bones grind to a halt, locked, muscles tensing. My jaw sharpens, brows scrunched.

I'm not as soft as some fans think. I care wholeheartedly about these people, these fans I've never met, but *tough love* comes easier for me. And that's not what she needs.

I lick my lips and swallow a pit. I rub her back again. "Britni, everything's—"

"I'm s-s-s-sorry," she whimpers.

"I promise, it's okay." I nod to her, but she can't meet my gaze. "You're doing great."

"I-I just…I'm having a hard time in school and at home and my life is over. You're the only thing I need to make it better."

I go numb. Pressure tries to compound, but I fight off the heavy, heavier, and heaviest. I'm aware that I have such a short amount of time with this girl. Anything I say could make or break her, and I never take this responsibility lightly.

"Life can be hard sometimes," I say. "My mom and dad taught me that when you're not sure if you can keep going, you just need to take it one day at a time, one step at a time. Can you do that with me?"

She breathes heavily, and tears leak silently.

"You're here, today," I say, reaching for something in my soul to give to her, but it collapses my chest. "There are good things in this fucking world. It might not seem like it yesterday, maybe not even tomorrow, but it gets—"

"It'll all end," she cries and then clutches onto the collar of my crew-neck, grip frantic. Tugging.

Farrow nears, and I side-eye him, silently saying *not yet*. I even hold out a hand so he'll stay back for a fucking second. *Just hold on.*

Hold on.

You don't know that I used to cry myself to sleep at nine-years-old. Hearing bad shit about my family. About myself. Wondering what the fuck was real. I was a happy kid, but there were hours, days, weeks where I used to think every cruel, heartless bastard would break the people I loved.

I can't fathom the kind of lows my brother goes through. What this girl may be going through. Where they just want to quit. But I understand what it's like to wake up and want to scream.

And my parents would tell me, "One day at a time, one step at a time." Stand up.

Keep going.

Move forward.

"Britni," I start, but she twists the collar of my shirt.

I'm on both knees, holding her elbows and *trying* to get her to look at me. Her eyes are everywhere but on my face.

"You have to give me a chance," she sobs. "One date. Anything. You'll see." Her voice cracks. "You'll see I could be such a good girlfriend, and we'll be in love and everything will be perfect for once and happy."

Christ…I didn't think it was leading there. I grapple and claw for the right response. My joints rust, neck stiff. "I do want you to be happy—"

She chokes on her tears. "My parents got divorced. Everyone at school hates me…" She yanks at my collar. I wrap my arms around her shoulders. Hugging a fragile human being.

I'm not sure I can provide the right comfort. The right fucking words or the perfect strength. All I want is for her to be unequivocally, irrevocably happy, but I can't even give that to my own brother.

How do I fix this?

How can I fucking fix this?

"It's okay," I say, my voice more stilted. "Just breathe."

She sobs into the crook of my neck. Wet tears soaking my shirt. "Please, please, *please*. I don't want to die."

My pulse thumps like a hollowed drum. It's her and me, and I know I'm not enough. I need to put her in touch with health professionals—I've done this before. I can make sure she's okay. I can do that at least.

I turn my head. "Lydia," I call out to my tour assistant. "If her parents aren't here, get them on the phone." She hurries.

Farrow squats beside me.

"Britni," I say, "there are people who can help if you're feeling alone or—"

"You're the *only one*," she says through blistering tears. She clutches my collar again like I'm her literal lifeline.

Farrow gently peels her fingers off my shirt and neck.

"I'm not the only one," I assure her. "There are so many people out there who'll help you, who care about you—"

"Nonono," she slurs, shaking her head.

I could go into my fan line and ask a couple girls around her age if they'd want to come on stage. Sit with us for about five minutes. Keep Britni company with me. Cheer her up. Just talk and show her that people do care. Maybe she'd make a new friend.

I did that at the San Diego FanCon for an upset preteen, but here, with Britni, I don't know. She reminds me of Xander, and he'd flip the fuck out of if I brought strangers into his bubble.

Britni clings onto my shoulders, and Farrow has trouble tearing her off without being forceful.

"Jane cares about you," I say strongly. "My cousins care—"

"I only want you," she cries into my neck.

My muscles tighten, and Lydia lowers a phone into my hand. Britni's parents. While she's crying against my chest, I talk to them, ask them who attended the FanCon with their daughter.

They have no clue. They didn't even know she'd be here, and I'm not that surprised. I ask for consent to put her on the phone with healthcare professionals. They say *yes, of course*. Great, I go through the motions, but I'm cradling a human in my hands.

And I'm just twenty-two.

I'm not a superhero.

I don't have the answers or the meaning of life, but I'm fucking trying. All I can do is try.

When they want to quit, I'm not going to fucking quit on them.

It must be twenty or thirty minutes before Britni calms, speaks to her parents, and I have to leave her in the hands of our staff.

I'm on my feet, and the line coordinator, photographer, assistant, and my bodyguard all look at me for direction. I crack my neck, my muscles almost spasm they're that tight.

I lock eyes with Farrow. He chews a piece of gum, and he gestures his head towards the backstage exit. To take a break.

For just a minute.

I nod, and to Lydia, I say, "I won't be long." As I pass Farrow, we walk side-by-side, and he speaks into his mic, telling security that I'm on a short break.

I slip through the quiet backstage, and I enter a dressing room.

Gift boxes, scrapbooks, and sweets are stacked high on a table and couch. Makeup and hair products spread across a vanity.

I open and close my fist. Drifting stiffly to a rack of clothes, back to the vanity. Farrow locks the door, but I don't hold his gaze.

I put my hands on my head, restless but rigid. If I could, I'd be in the water somewhere. Some place. Then I'd climb out and run and run and fucking run.

I grip the edge of the vanity. Hunched forward, and in the mirror, I catch sight of my reddened, burning eyes and my soaked green shirt from her tears. Fuck. I wrench the shirt off my head. My jaw aches. I ball a hand in a fist.

I need to hit something.

Or swim.

Run.

Anger gnaws at my insides, the only emotion I can feel. I glare at the ceiling, my breath like knives.

"Need anything, wolf scout?"

Yeah.

It takes me a second. But I turn my head.

Farrow sits partially on the couch's armrest. His gaze sweeps me, assessing me, and when they lift to mine, they practically hold me, protect me, love me.

And I say, "You." My voice cracks.

Farrow moves.

I pinch my eyes that fucking burn and try to fill. I squat down, just as Farrow reaches me. His palm warms the back of my neck.

I cover my face with my hands, and I fucking scream. Pent-up rage, gnarled emotion coming out of me.

Not for long. I straighten up again. Pinching my eyes *again*. And I almost turn to grip the vanity again, but Farrow seizes my wrist.

And he draws me into his chest.

My boyfriend hugs me so damn tight. Our bodies welded, his heartbeat pounding against mine.

I fist the back of his shirt with one hand, my chest heaving against his chest. Hot tears wet my lashes. That girl got to me.

I can fucking admit that.

Farrow strengthens his clutch and tells me, "There's nothing more you could've done for her."

I hold the back of his head, my fingers lost in his white hair. I growl out a frustrated, pained noise.

Another beat passes, and I lean back.

Farrow holds my wet face. I don't even care to wipe the tears that run off my jaw.

His reddened eyes melt against me, easing my taut muscles and hot-blooded pulse.

I breathe heavily, my gaze bloodshot, throat raw, and I shake my head. "I don't know." I lick my lips. "I'll never fucking know if I made her life worse or better." At hot tear rolls down my cheek. I glare at the ground. Christ, what am I doing? "I'm not trying to unload this much weight on you—"

"Whoa, whoa." Farrow gives me a look like I've officially jumped off the planet. "I'm your boyfriend."

I can't even crack some sarcasm. I just swallow a rock.

Farrow lifts his brows. "You're supposed to unload on me. I've been unloading shit on you with my father and the stalker for months. It's a two-way street."

My chest rises in a bigger breath.

I pinch my eyes to dam the waterworks. I'll need to return to the FanCon and take pictures. Soon. Hopefully not with bloodshot eyes. "I must've missed *unloading shit* in the Boyfriend Manual."

He almost laughs, and his thumb wipes my cheek. "If there were a Boyfriend Manual—which there isn't one—right next to *that* would be giving 'unconditional emotional support'. And while you offer it to literally every person, I'm very selective."

I drop my hand off my eyes with another breath. "Who else do you give it to?"

His lips rise. "Just you."

My mouth curves upward, my body lightening, and I shake my head, surprised at what he makes me feel. I shouldn't be that shocked anymore, but I kind of like that I am. Everything always feels like the first damn time with him.

His hands fall to my shoulders. I'm shirtless, chest bare, and his touch heats me up. I stay still and hold his neck for a second.

My mind reels. I let out a rough noise in my throat. "I can't stop thinking about her."

"You can handle a lot, I'll give you that to start," Farrow says, nodding a few times. "But no one, not even me, can take on everything for everyone. Since you were, how young? Sixteen, fifteen? You've let thousands of people give you their emotional pain, and they want and plead for you to comfort them." He pauses. "At what point is it going to click for you that you're just one man. *One man.* That's one to millions. You can't. *You can't.*"

"I can try."

Farrow looks straight into my core. He pauses to consider my reply, and then he says, "But promise you'll listen to your body if it says you can't handle it anymore. You know, step back." His lips almost rise as he uses some of my words from a while ago.

I'm actually, really smiling. Once the FanCon ends, I'll have less close contact with so many fans at one time. It'll be easier than now.

But he's concerned.

For me.

"Step back," I say, feigning confusion. "Can't picture it, for either of us."

He nods. "We're both stubborn assholes."

"Tell me something that isn't new," I say.

"I love you," he says deeply. "And when you hurt, I hurt."

I inhale. We pull closer, foreheads pressed together, and I kiss him—but he'll tell you that he kisses me. Our mouths meet, and I urge his lips. In a sweet, yearning embrace that lights my lungs on fire.

And then a knock raps the door. Our mouths break, but his gaze says *don't detach; let them see, wolf scout.*

I can't. Going public as my boyfriend—maybe it wouldn't affect his job anymore because SFO is already dealing with notoriety—but it'd put Farrow through a ringer.

All the public scrutiny, media harassment, and extreme loss of privacy.

The kind of fame he's experiencing now is nothing compared to what he'd feel as "Maximoff Hale's boyfriend"—and I can't do that to him.

So I back up, our arms dropping off each other, and he nods, understanding. I think.

39

Farrow Keene

"WAIT, WAIT," MAXIMOFF BREATHES hard against my jaw. Every time I end up in the same tight bunk with him, it's a master class in restraint.

A flip-down movie screen plays *Everybody Wants Some!!* which we've abandoned several times to turn into each other. Legs interlocked, chest against chest. Hands gripping and squeezing and pulling.

Damn, I want deeper.

But our roaming hands pause at his *wait, wait*. I watch him catch his breath as he tries to suppress this carnal need.

A smile toys at my stinging lips. See, we're not about to fuck inches away from his cousins and my friends.

Restraint. It's harder than any class I took at Yale, but clearly I'm the one making better grades.

"Watch the movie, wolf scout." I eye his reddened lips.

"You watch it," he combats in a choked groan. "*Fuck*, just shut up for a second."

My voice turns him on.

Hot arousal tries to fist my cock, both of us only in drawstring pants. Thin fabric separates us, and the outline of his dick rubs against mine.

My goal isn't to sexually frustrate him or me. We're on route to Boulder for the next tour stop, but Colorado is still hours away. I could blow him in the bathroom again, but the only time we did that, a fight erupted with Charlie.

I feel his muscles flex against my firm body. "I can leave if you're struggl—"

"I'm not, thanks for asking."

I roll my eyes but they land on his gaze that's fucking me hard. *Damn, Maximoff.* I inhale a shallow breath.

Thing is, if I left this bunk, I'd just want to return.

There's not much more I can do about the stalker. I've hit a wall. Now that I've searched all the NDAs, the tech team is tracking everyone I flagged. They'll notify me if Jason Motlic, Vincent Webber, or the other top-listed suspects are in the same city as Maximoff.

What I can do: wait for the stalker to make a mistake.

My hand ascends to his deltoids, then neck, and my mouth skims his as I speak. "It's understandable."

Maximoff pulls closer. "What is?"

"You," I whisper, "finding me irresistible." I break into a wide smile as he growls out his aggravation.

He also bucks into my waist, grinding against my pelvis for friction—*fucking hell.* I clutch his ass, and our mouths collide. He tries to shift on top of me, *fuckfuck.* I use my strength and pin him to my chest. Keeping us on our sides.

Not here, wolf scout.

I bite his lip, and his muscles contract.

"Fuck," he breathes against my neck.

My veins pulse, and I'm breathing just as heavily. Shit, this is more difficult than I thought.

"Movie," he tells me.

I nod, but like our last six attempts, only our eyes move. On the flip-out TV, we watch college-aged guys play baseball, set in 1980. Not a lot of action, no superpowers or car chases.

"I'm surprised you like this movie," I tell him. Apparently he's seen it a "billion" times but he wanted to see it again with me.

Maximoff licks his lips a few times, like he still feels me on them. "One of the main actors was on *Teen Wolf*." There we go. "And he's fucking hot."

"Which one?" I wait for Maximoff to point him out, but he just groans, frustrated, his hands gripping tighter on my waist and neck.

"Stop, fucking stop," he almost growls. "You can't do that thing with your fingers."

My smile stretches. I'm gliding my hand in and out of his thick hair. Basically giving him a head massage. "What about now?" I clutch his jaw, his breath shallows. *No.* Then his neck, and he tries and *almost* shifts on top.

I hold his jaw again, my blood on fire. Muscles burning, my cock is dying to harden. "Maximoff," I breathe. His aggression is fucking killing me. It takes all my energy not to arch into him for that mind-numbing friction.

His eyes devour me whole. "Why am I so fucking attracted to you?" His ankle strokes my calf.

We pull each other closer.

I skim his cheekbones. "If you want me to list the reasons, wolf scout, we'll be here for hours—"

A *jingle bell* noise cuts me off and kills the mood. He doesn't tell me *don't answer*. Maximoff even finds my phone beneath the pillow and hands it to me.

The stalker is a good distraction for us right now. But I never look forward to dissecting these gory photos.

I click into the account.

Shit.

I stare intensely at the photo. No gore. No body. It's a headstone on a freshly dug grave. My jaw tics and eyes burn as I fixate unblinkingly on the etched words.

In Memory of Maximoff Hale, a bad person, a horrific friend.

Born July 13th I skim over the year of birth because the next part crashes into me. *Died April 4th.*

Tomorrow is April 4th.

Tomorrow is my twenty-eighth birthday.

Maximoff reads over my shoulder. He notices the dates. "It could be a coincidence."

I sit up some. "Or the stalker knows we're together."

"Your father is *not* stalking me," he says strongly. "He wouldn't write that part about me being a horrific friend."

Jason might, but there's a less than 1% chance that he knows Maximoff is in a relationship. Let alone with me. I comb a hand through my hair. Could be a kill date. A warning, a threat. That Maximoff Hale will die tomorrow.

"It's not real," he tries to assure me. But I have to act like it's real on the slim chance that it is.

"I'm going to call tech—" Our bunk curtain whips open.

Jane suddenly thrusts a phone at us, blue eyes pinging to me. "I'm sorry." Then she looks to Maximoff. "You need to get up. You have to call work, right now."

Before Maximoff tries to crawl over me, I climb out of the bunk. My feet hit the ground, then his.

"What's going on?" Maximoff asks.

She shakes her head frantically and places the phone in his hand. "They called me so you'd call them back."

His frown darkens.

I ask, "Who's *they*?"

Maximoff looks down at the call history. "The board."

40

Maximoff Hale

"THAT'S IMPOSSIBLE," I SAY, white-knuckling my phone, set to speaker. Jane pats the couch next to her in the second lounge, but I can't sit. I can't move.

Farrow closes the door, taking a seat on top of the couch. Feet on the cushion, elbows to his thighs, he's less nonchalant than what meets the eye. He keeps combing a hand through his hair, and his narrowed gaze keeps narrowing. Murderously.

Stalker on his mind.

I can't even think about the most recent post. Not now.

"You have to understand, Maximoff," Victoria Cordobi says in a stilted, manufactured voice like she's reciting ingredients off a shampoo bottle. "You've been gone for three and a half months."

"For an event that's helping the company," I say, almost too forceful. My tone is bordering hostile, anger pumping through me like gasoline and fire.

Victoria has been on the board of directors since H.M.C. Philanthropies was formed. She's the one who was tasked with delivering the news to me.

I've been fired.

Fired.

I don't understand how I go to bed as the CEO of a company I built from the ground up, and in *one* goddamn phone call, I learn that

I've been pushed out. What's eating at me, it's not just about a hurt ego because someone stole my baby.

It's more serious than that.

My family—the Hales, Meadows, and Cobalts—they all give a large portion of their amassed wealth to the philanthropy. Whoever is CEO has the greatest control.

Without me at the helm, I don't know who the fuck is handling *billions* of dollars.

"Regardless of why," Victoria says, "you've still been absent. And in your stead, Ernest has brought intelligent points to the philanthropy."

My blood boils. "Ernest Mangold?" I drill a glare into my phone. As if I can reach this conniving prick. Honestly…I'm fucking whiplashed. I can't make sense of this reality.

Ernest is pretty new. He came into the company only last year, and he's been relatively *quiet*.

So what the fuck changed?

"Yes," Victoria says, voice wooden. "The board feels as though Ernest Mangold is better suited to run H.M.C. Philanthropies."

This can't be real. "Victoria, if something's wrong, if the board is in trouble and people have been coerced or blackmailed, I can help—"

"No," she interjects. "We've been discussing this for months."

I blink, the shock like a hard slap. "You've been thinking about this for months? And no one thought it'd be a good idea to tell me?" A thought punches me cold.

I zero in on Jane. Her brother, Charlie—he's *on* this backstabbing board, and that means he's known for months that they planned to kick me out. While on tour.

And he said nothing.

Jane shakes her head vigorously. "Moffy," she whispers, "Charlie couldn't have known." But he's opposed me too often to be so assured.

I have no time to whisper back.

Victoria replies, "With the time differences and your spontaneous tour schedule, it was difficult keeping in touch. You've been gone."

If she says that again, I'm going to pop off like a 400-Fahrenheit firework. "I created this charity," I say firmly. "I have a good relationship with the board. Why would you even consider pushing me out?"

It makes no fucking sense.

Victoria clears her throat. Like she doesn't have a pre-written statement for that question. "I don't feel comfortable talking to you alone about this. We'll set up a meeting tomorrow and have the board talk over conference call."

"No," I say, not hesitating. "I'm flying in."

Farrow straightens up in surprise. But when our gazes lock, he nods confidently. He's with me, supporting me. If the board keeps harping on me being gone, then I need to be there. In person.

To fix this.

"That's unnecessary," she states.

"No," I retort. "What's unnecessary is the board voting me out behind my back. You will all show up, sit around the table, and look me in the fucking eye when you tell me you're taking this company from me." In one breath, I finish, "I'll be there tomorrow. You'll know when I arrive."

I hang up.

And I storm out. Only looking for one person. I fling open the curtain to his bunk. "Charlie."

He squints at the light and then glares at my scowl. "What?"

I open my mouth, about to say, *how long have you known the board would vote me out?* But I freeze, my vocal cords iced and immobile. My brain is telling me *no, don't go there. You're wrong, Maximoff.*

He's my cousin. He's family. He wouldn't hurt me. Then I remember my parents and the rumor—how badly that hurt. But I also remember what my dad said. To protect each other, we sometimes react out of fear and love.

For Charlie to not tell me, it'd just be out of cruelty.

So he couldn't have known about the board or the vote. I believe this.
I know this.

Because despite all the bad blood, I trust Charlie with H.M.C. Philanthropies and the wealth. It's why he's on the board. If an apocalypse happens, Charlie Keating Cobalt is the last safety net.

The one person who'd shut down any dissention.

And he's been absent from the office, with me, for four months. An ambitious prick could've taken advantage of that.

"*Moffy.*" Charlie props himself on his elbow. "What's going on?"

My muscles thaw. "The board just voted me out."

His face falls before his yellow-green eyes pierce the wall. Shock, then anger—his reaction isn't that far off from mine. "Who's the new CEO?"

"Ernest Mangold." I explain every damn thing that Victoria told me in less than a few minutes. "That's all I know."

"Son of a bitch." Charlie climbs out of the bed in boxer-briefs, his golden-brown hair messy. He follows me into the first lounge. Jane and Farrow hang back, letting us deal with this mess.

I find a laptop and open it by the coffee pot. Still standing.

Charlie hovers close. "Ernest must've manipulated the board—and those *fucking* idiots fell for it." He groans into his hands, then pushes his hair back. "People are so stupid."

"He could've blackmailed them." I'm still super-glued to this theory. I pop up flights out of the Denver airport. The tour bus will have to take a short detour, but my cousins will still make the Boulder FanCon in time.

Charlie watches me search for flights. "I should've left the tour weeks ago—"

"No." I risk a short glance at him. "I'm glad you stayed. You surprised me." I seriously thought he wouldn't last the whole tour. I thought he'd quit on everyone and just leave. He proved me wrong. "I shouldn't always think the fucking worst about you, Charlie. I'm sorry."

He flinches at the sudden apology.

I let out a pained laugh. "And now I'm the first one to bail." Sarcastic, I add, "Fifty points to Hufflepuff."

Charlie slides the computer towards himself. My hands slip off the keyboard, and he uses the track-pad and pops up a new window.

He logs onto a site where we book private jets. "Don't fly commercial. This'll be faster." Charlie angles the laptop towards me. He knows I prefer flying commercial, even though the paparazzi are like locusts at the airport. But private jets cost a lot, and they're bad on fuel and the environment.

Charlie waits for an argument.

But he's right. It's faster, and it'll help me reach Philly more inconspicuously. No media speculation or attention. So I fill out the flight box and I hesitate on the line: *how many passengers?*

My eyes flit to him. "You coming with me?"

He looks away in thought.

Even the idea of confronting the board without Charlie feels suffocating. He'll be the only person I trust there. He's the safety net.

I remember Harvard. How I felt the exact same back then. He was supposed to be the familiar face on campus, my one lifeline. Maybe I should've told him that. Maybe he has no clue what I felt.

Or maybe he still would've left me, no matter what.

But I can't just let him go this time.

"Charlie." I catch his gaze. "I need you to be there with me. I can't…" I shake my head as the words lodge in my throat, afraid of saying the wrong fucking thing. I lick my lips. "I can't do this alone."

He doesn't break eye contact. "Okay."

"Okay?"

Charlie nods, assured. "Count me in."

THE PRIVATE JET FLIES OFF THE TARMAC, AND FARROW and Oscar seclude themselves in the front of the plane. Giving Charlie and me space. Or maybe forcing us to talk. Something we rarely do.

Unlike the twelve-person sleeper bus, there's nowhere to hide. We can't retreat to a bunk and ignore each other. My beige leather seat even faces his.

We're on the same figurative side, fighting for the same purpose. But our past still wedges between us like a crater that we've never known how to fill.

Charlie drums his armrest and stares out the airplane window. I fold my paperback of Aristotle's *The Nicomachean Ethics*, barely able to read with the tense silence.

And as soon as his eyes drift to me, I take a chance and start talking.

"Do you remember junior year? When we had to do that video together on *The Iliad*?" I ask, trying to be casual.

Charlie nods once.

"You played Apollo," I say. "I was Achilles, and it was actually pretty damn good." I smile at the memory and then grimace. "That is until our dads had to get the lawyers involved."

They were afraid that students or teachers would publicly share the video and then the media would have a field day. Understandable since I was pretending to slay my classmates as Achilles. They thought that kind of negative press would hurt me.

Charlie doesn't say a thing.

So I continue, "You remember how Faye Jones had such a crush on you? She kept insisting that you play Paris—"

"You don't have to do this," Charlie says, and he messes his already messy hair.

My palms sweat on my paperback. "Do what?"

"Bring up high school. The good ol' times." Charlie holds my gaze. "I realize there was a time when we were friends."

"Yeah?" I tuck my paperback in the seat. "I remember us being close until that summer bash on the yacht. You know Harvard?" I inch towards the question. The one that I've never edged near. My tongue feels thick in my mouth. "You never really told me why you didn't want to go." I stop myself for a second.

I'm afraid.

And I don't know what worries me. The actual answer or the aftermath of knowing it. My heart practically bangs against my ribcage.

I find some fucking words. "What changed?"

"Me," he says without pause or extra thought.

My brows knit together and shock engulfs me. I'd always thought he'd blame me. "What do you mean?"

Charlie winces and sits up a bit more. Not slouching like usual. "You really want to talk about this? We're on our way to deal with a manipulative motherfucker, who could be a narcissist or a sociopath, and if things don't end well between you and me, we'll be walking in with welts and bloody noses."

I'd rather take the chance to do more damage than never try to repair what we broke. The hardest part was opening this door.

I'm not shutting it now.

"I don't plan on punching you," I tell him, "so that's not going to happen."

The corner of his mouth rises. "I never plan on hitting you either, but it still happens. You have a punchable face."

"Thank you," I say dryly.

His smile lifts more, but then morphs into a bitter cringe. "I wasn't lying that day on the dock. When I said I couldn't stand being around you, I meant it."

A knife slowly sinks into my gut, but I listen. I wait. I don't lash out. "Yeah?" I lick my lips, trying to form the right words. "So you bailed on Harvard because you didn't want to be around me. That's it?"

He lets out an exasperated breath. "You make it sound so simple. But it's not like that to me."

"Then explain it to me," I plead.

He leans forward in his chair and then back, and I think he's about to brush me off. But then he starts talking. Eyes on me. Not breaking. "I *hate* what I feel when I'm near you sometimes. I hate who I become." Charlie rubs his mouth, then sits forward again. "We're both living beneath the shadows of our fathers, but just imagine, for a second, what it's like to live beneath yours."

I go cold. It can't be easy for him. I get that, and I want to help make it better.

But I don't know how.

I inhale a sharp breath. "What is it like?"

Charlie shifts in his seat.

The topic is uncomfortable.

The air is tight, and we're passing a bomb back and forth. But for the first time, I feel like we have the tools to disable it.

He looks me right in the eye. "Fourth of July five years ago, my little sister burns her arm on a sparkler. She doesn't go to my parents. Doesn't even search for Jane. The first person she turns to is you."

I want to cut in, to tell him that I was probably just near her in proximity, but he's quickly spouting off to the next one.

"Halloween two years ago, Eliot crushes on the girl in that old local, corner bookstore. But I don't learn this from him. My little brother chose to ask you for advice about approaching her, even though you and I both have the same amount of experience with girls."

"Charlie—"

"Seven years ago," he says, still going. "Winona falls into the creek behind the lake house, and she starts sinking in that quicksand mud. I'm halfway to her. Already ankle-deep in water, but you come out of God-knows where with your shining white armor and ten foot rope."

His eyes are bloodshot, and he says, "It's all these little moments that have made you. You mean *everything* to my siblings. To the Meadows girls, to your sisters and brother, and that makes you a shadow I can't escape. Because I can't be *anything* to them when you're every fucking thing. So who am I?" Charlie points at his chest. "Who am I? And what the hell do I become if I go to Harvard with you? Lost and confused? I was already self-loathing and bitter, but I'd just be more resentful, *more* bitter—a guy who wakes up and hates himself for not being more like Maximoff Hale."

What...

"You're not self-loathing," I argue.

At least, that's what I've seen.

He tilts his head. "I don't always lash out at you because I hate you. I lash out because I hate how I feel when I'm around you. I hate that I want to become *you*."

I never knew this.

I never saw this or understood this. I think about everything all the goddamn time, but I never even fathomed that someone like

Charlie, a Cobalt, could be less than confident, less than colossally self-assured.

Charlie shakes his head. "I'm not a natural born leader. I don't want to be one, but sometimes it feels like that's my only path to be *someone* or *something* to the people I love. Then maybe they'd need me like they need you."

My eyes burn and stomach knots. "Charlie—"

"No," he cuts me off again. "I don't want to morph into someone else. I want to be *me*, whoever that person is, he's not like you or anyone else, and I'm fighting to find him. You make that impossible sometimes."

A rock lodges in my throat, an apology sitting on the edge of my tongue.

Charlie flips his phone in his hand. "And I'm not even blaming you. I needed to deal with these feelings, but I couldn't be your sidekick or live in your shadow."

Realization gradually sinks in. "Harvard…"

He takes a tight breath. "That night on the yacht, I decided right then that to escape your soul-sucking shadow, I'd have to escape you. No Harvard. No answering your calls or texts. You be you, and I…try to rediscover who I am." His voice cracks.

He almost always lets me see his emotion. You think he's brick-walled, but he's not like his dad. He doesn't contain a thing.

I thought ditching on Harvard was premeditated, but he said he decided to bail right then. In the moment.

I swallow, my heart beating fast. I want to reach out, but how do you extend a hand when you're the cause of someone's pain? "I can move out of the way for you," I say. "I'll try—"

"*No.* This is why I didn't tell you back then. You can't fix it, Moffy. Because I don't want my siblings to lose you, and I don't want to be you. There's nothing you can do, and look at your face. I know it hurts…"

My chest constricts like I'm stuck beneath salt water and I can't find the surface. My eyes try to well, and I tilt my head back against the chair. Bottling my emotion, face stoic. "Do you?" I ask since he's always lacked a certain amount of empathy for other people.

"I can see that it hurts you," he tells me. "You know, I used to believe that we were just meant to be opposites. That for all the compassion you had, I lacked. For all the responsibility *Maximoff Hale* acquired, I was left with none. And in everyone's eyes, you were the hero, and I'd become the villain." A tear rolls slowly down his cheek, dripping off his jaw.

It almost crushes my chest. "You're not the villain to anyone," I tell him strongly. "If anything, you're the anti-hero. And people usually love those more."

Charlie rubs another fallen tear. "I don't need anyone to love me. I can deal with hate."

I nod, just listening.

"But when everyone fawns over you and acts like you're indestructible, it's grating," Charlie says. "I can't bite my tongue, and my gut reaction is to go for your jugular."

"I'm not any better," I admit.

Charlie shrugs, and silence hangs but not as heavily as it could.

I want to stand. I want to do something more for him, but he keeps looking at me like, *this is it*. This is the end with no solution that I've asked to meet.

I drop my head, thinking. And thinking. "So are you saying I'll always make you feel like shit?" It kills me knowing that I've hurt him for so many years.

And that I'll just continue being a negative impact on his life.

"I can't see the future," Charlie says. "I'm not six-feet-three inches full of resentment anymore. I'm not sixteen. But it's still tough being around you. Where everyone praises you. Where I'm stuck in a shadowed place and I'm neither lost nor found. Doing my own thing makes me feel…"

"Free," I finish.

He nods. "Like my identity is mine. Not an extension of you or my dad."

I understand the shackles of our parent's past, but I had no idea I'd been shackling Charlie. "I'm so fucking sorry."

"I knew you'd care, but I also knew it wouldn't change anything."

"Right," I mutter. I'm just supposed to…deal. I'm not sure the hurt will disappear that easily, but the truth is better than the unknown. I can finally see the kind of terrain I'm standing on. In case you were wondering, the ground is littered with rocks.

I just wish they were the kind we could shave down or move together.

"I think about something a lot," I tell him. "How our dads are best friends. Our moms are sisters. In some cosmic way, I think you and I were fated to be rivals or friends." I lick my dry lips. "I guess *friends* isn't in the fucking cards for us, huh?" And I have to accept this.

"Non, il te suffit de m'attendre," Charlie says in a perfect French lilt. *No, you just need to wait for me.*

"De quelle manière?" I breathe. *In what way?*

"To be strong enough to be near you and not hate everything about you and me."

I'm fucking terrible at waiting around. Doing nothing. He knows this. You know this. But for Charlie, I'd try. If he needs me to be patient, I'll do that a million times over.

I nod strongly. "Okay."

We seem to breathe at the same time, and I try to relax and adjust the air conditioner.

Charlie reaches forward and steals my philosophy book. He slings his legs sideways across the seat and flips through the pages. When our gazes briefly meet, he says, "Merci pour le matériel de lecture." *Thanks for the reading material.*

41

Farrow Keene

AFTER MAXIMOFF LEFT the two-hour board meeting, he told me, "I'll explain at Lucky's Diner."

What I assume: it can't be outright bad news. Or else he would've popped a blood vessel in the car. He's been clinging to some fragment of hope.

And I'm clinging onto something else entirely.

I've spent the majority of the morning hawkeyed on hands and pockets. Making a mental account of every person we've crossed or encountered.

Shit, I see the headstone photo clearly in each passing second.

Died: April 4th.

Today.

"Is this peak Farrow Keene hyper-vigilance?" Maximoff asks across from me, both of us seated in a vinyl booth towards the back. He slides me a plastic menu and lowers his voice. "You haven't even checked me out today."

My lips want to rise, and I fix my earpiece, radio volume high. "Wolf scout, who said I ever check you out?"

"Pretty sure I didn't imagine you staring at my fucking ass yesterday."

I whistle. "Pretty sure you've fantasized about my ass before you even saw it."

Maximoff blinks slowly. "And now my brain has short-circuited, thank you." His sarcasm is thick, almost pulling my mouth upward. "And thanks for the *ass* digression."

"You're welcome." I pick up the menu, but I don't even skim the words yet.

I just canvas the bustling Philly diner: fifty paparazzi and twenty-something teens peer through the glass window, 3/5 of customers in booths and barstools crane their necks to watch the celebrity and his bodyguard, about 1/3 of those snap pictures and record videos.

Harmless.

"Order up!" a cook calls, and waitresses zip around tables, trays hoisted high. Bacon and maple syrup smells permeate. An atmosphere I typically love.

But today isn't a typical day. The stalker is a Philly resident.

Likelihood of them being close = too high for comfort.

I focus back on Maximoff.

He jots a note on a napkin, but he shields the words with his hand.

I eye him a little bit more. His dark brown hair is windblown, his cheekbones sharp, shoulders squared, and his gray Winter Solider T-shirt hugs the ridges of his muscles.

"Wanted me at the meeting with you?" I tease and motion to his shirt choice.

Maximoff frowns, then glances at the shirt. "Jesus Christ." He glares at the ceiling, then his forest-greens drop to mine. "It was un-intentional."

"I think you mean *subconscious*." I dump out the sugar packets and reorder them in the container.

Very quietly, he contemplates, "Subconsciously I'm in love with you?" He pauses. "Sounds about right."

"And consciously," I add.

"No. Just subconscious." His voice is firm.

I roll my eyes, and my small smile falls flat. Because our waitress approaches. Maximoff hasn't even ordered yet, but the tiny brunette carries a mug of hot tea.

"Glad to see you back in town," Ava says, usually the one who serves us when we're at Lucky's. She places the hot tea on a paper coaster.

"Thanks," Maximoff says sincerely. "Happy to be back."

I order a coffee, and we're still deciding on food when she leaves. Maximoff hones in on my tattooed fingers that fiddle with the sugar packets.

I shouldn't be smiling, not right now. But being in his company, all I want to do is grin ear-to-ear.

Damn.

It hits me again and again. How I could spend hours and hours upon hours doing absolutely nothing with Maximoff Hale. Just this.

Charlie and Oscar drove back to New York after the meeting, and for the first time in a while, there's no full tour bus, no extra SFO guys lingering, none of his cousins are here.

It's just us. And the paparazzi, the fans. But they've always been set decoration to his world. Now my world.

"Are you?" I ask him. "Happy to be back?"

Maximoff scans the retro diner. April rain starts trickling outside, and paparazzi and fans pull out umbrellas. Noises everywhere. Talking, dishes clattering, the door clings. An old man with a strong Philly lilt complains about the storm. And Maximoff smiles as two girls on bar stools wave excitedly.

He waves back and then focuses on me, but I already see the revere and fondness overtake his gorgeous features. "Yeah," he says. "I am. This is home."

Our attention drifts, Ava setting my coffee in front of me. "Ready to order?"

Maximoff and I exchange a look of confirmation.

Then he stacks our menus and hands them to Ava, along with the paper napkin note. *I saw that, wolf scout.* "I'll get the breakfast burrito, no jalapeño."

"Egg, bacon, cheddar bagel sandwich," I say, "and a side of potato latke."

Ava leaves again, and I tear open a creamer. I'm about to ask about the napkin note, but he suddenly spills the news.

"I have to cancel the tour." He pauses. "The board is shutting it down early."

I process this quickly. "They're not going to reinstate you as CEO then," I say with the tilt of my head. He's calmer than usual. I don't understand why.

Maximoff takes a swig of hot tea. "There was no reasoning with the board. Charlie and I came in hot, but their minds were made. No one was even pretending to care."

"You don't look that upset about it," I mention, coffee mug to my mouth.

Maximoff leans back. "Oh, I'm fucking pissed. But I'm not wasting my energy on them. I have to move forward, and besides…it may not be over."

I sip my coffee. "What does that mean?"

He cracks a knuckle and smiles briefly at a boy who calls his name. Forest-greens back on me, he says, "They were vague, but they said there might be a way for me to be reinstated as CEO. They didn't say what yet."

I tap my fingers against my mug, my rings *clink, clink*. See, I don't like that they conveniently left out what the hell he has to do. It could be anything, and they could tell him to *do* anything.

"They're in a position of power," I remind him. He has almost no leverage.

Maximoff nods. "I know, but it's all the hope I have. They said they'll tell me more in the second quarter."

At least he's not completely shut out yet. "That's good," I tell him.

He dunks his tea bag a few times. "I keep thinking about how tomorrow I'm going to wake up, and I have zero phone calls to make. No emails to send. No employees, no company, and I think about what else I can do. I can volunteer at the rehab center. I can help other charities, but this thing…" He gestures around, but I know he's referring to H.M.C. Philanthropies. "…I built this thing and it meant something to me. And now it's gone for I don't know how long. One day? Two months? Five years?" A beat passes. "Forever?"

I stop myself from stretching my arm across the table and grabbing his hand. *We're in public.* My grip tightens on the mug. "It's okay to feel lost when you've lost something."

Maximoff rakes a hand through his hair. "Have you ever felt like this?"

I recall my past. "When my life alters outside of my control, I usually feel a sense of nostalgia, but I also like change, so..." I raise my brows at him.

He has trouble containing a smile. "Sounds like a superpower."

I bring my coffee up. "That you don't have."

Maximoff growls out, but he blinks repeatedly to glare. And I'll be honest. He's not glaring. He's not even scowling. He's smiling, and I'm entrapped, unable to detach—*do your motherfucking job, Farrow.*

I abruptly break eye contact and survey the diner again. As soon as I look at the window, a few girls squeal, "Oh my God, it's Farrow!"

"Is Quinn with him?!" another shrieks.

"I will *die* if Quinn is in there!"

"Maybe he has Quinn's number?!"

Of course I do.

I keep scrutinizing the diner, the people, but I talk to Maximoff. "I wouldn't have even bet ten bucks on Quinn being the most famous bodyguard." But it happened.

Girls are obsessed with him.

"Where do you think you rank?" Maximoff asks.

I meet his serious gaze. "I'm the least famous," I say honestly. "Because I'm taken, remember?" He declared my relationship status to a FanCon panel, which reached the internet and the world. In result, Tumblr and Twitter lost interest in me. Not that I care.

I'm still the best damned bodyguard in the whole team.

Maximoff rubs his tensed shoulder. "Being the *least famous* bodyguard is like coming in first place. So you won."

I stare harder at him. "Okay…but I wouldn't mind being the most famous out of Omega."

Maximoff quiets, thinking, and staring off into space.

My pulse starts racing. I can't read him.

We haven't talked about going public with our relationship. Something that'd spike my level of fame. But it's a real, feasible option now. Especially since Omega lasted the tour without a major mistake. We proved we're too experienced to let notoriety ruin our careers.

And I need to know where Maximoff's head is at. "Maximoff—"

"It'll be worse than this. By ten billion times, and it'll bother you," he refutes, straightening up. "All the screaming in your ear, the articles on shit you wouldn't even expect, and the never-ending personal questions."

He's convinced himself that no one in their right mind would be fine with the invasiveness, but I've been around him and his family enough to understand what the hell I'd be sacrificing and signing up for.

I rest my arm on the table, my fingers close to his elbow. Can't touch him in public. Can't comfort him. Can't love him loudly or proudly.

"That shit won't bother me," I say, "and if it does, the tradeoff is worth it."

Maximoff knows the tradeoff is *him*. "I'm not worth it."

"Yeah you are." My eyes burn. I wake up every morning, and I'm more in love with him than the day before.

And I think, *can I do this for another year, two years, three?* The answer isn't just *yes*. I can picture us together for longer, stronger, and I've never seen that far ahead. Yet, I'm now in a position I've never been in before.

I'm sitting on the other side. Wondering what his answer is to the same question. Can he see us another year, two years, three? Longer, stronger? I'm a guy with almost no fears, but there is one change I'm terrified to face.

I'm terrified of losing him.

I just sit here and wait, my pulse drumming in my ears. I remember this is his first relationship, and I'm actually afraid to scare him off.

I want to go public, but I can't pressure him. He just needs to know where I stand.

I'm doing that now.

The rest is up to him.

Maximoff swishes his hot tea, thinking. "I can't do this to you, Farrow."

"I'm asking you to," I say.

He instinctively shakes his head. "I can't…once we cross that line, there's no going back. Your life is forever fucked—"

"Or it's better." My fingers almost brush his elbow.

He sets a hand on the back of his neck. "Or it's not."

My heart rate is at an all-time high.

Maximoff looks resolute. "I can't knowingly do this to you." He'll keep returning to this point. No matter what, and I understand. He was upfront with me at the jumpstart—about not ever wanting a public relationship, not wanting to subject his significant other to the media—and he's too stubborn to change his mind.

It's my fault for falling this hard for him.

"Okay." My stomach sinks. "It's okay."

Maximoff crumples a napkin and eyes me more intensely than I'm eyeing him. "By your expression, I feel like I fucked up somewhere."

My brows ratchet up. "What's my expression?"

"You're upset."

"I'm not upset," I say indifferently. I run my tongue over the inside of my lip piercing, and just nod slowly. Okay, I may be *nervous*. But I'm not upset.

What do I say: *Maximoff, you know how you were the one nervous about this being your first relationship? Yeah, well, now I'm the nervous one. Cheers.*

I don't say that.

I don't even say that I'm disappointed. He'd feel guilty, and I don't want to guilt him into going public. It has to be his choice.

Instead, I land on this, "I promise I'll be happy with how things are now. All I want is you, wolf scout, and in this scenario, I have you."

It's the truth.

Before he can reply, waitresses start singing loudly, *"Happy birthday to you! Happy birthday to you!"* And the whole diner joins.

I crane my neck over my shoulder. With five waitresses in tow, Ava carries my bagel sandwich, lit candles stuck in the bread.

My chest swells because I know…Maximoff did that.

With the napkin note.

I fucking love breakfast more than cake. And this gesture crashes into my body. Hard. Shit, I'm really, *really* in love.

I turn back to him.

Maximoff finishes singing the song with the diner, and his eyes just melt against mine. How no one else can see the affection, I don't know. It seems overpoweringly clear to me.

I'm choked up for a second. After all that we've been through on tour, coming back to Philly and having my boyfriend do this is priceless.

Ava sets the birthday candle bagel in front of me.

Maximoff leans forward. Almost like he could go in for a kiss. I smile, even though he stops. And my smile stretches as he tells me, "Make a wish."

At the moment, I only wish for two things: a public relationship and the stalker to be found.

Between the two, it's an easy choice which to pick. There's no real contest. No hesitation. I blow out the candles.

Hoping to catch this motherfucker. Once and for all.

"TEN, NINE, EIGHT…" MAXIMOFF COUNTS DOWN TO midnight on his watch. Back in his attic bedroom, I hover over his build on the mattress. Sweat built on our skin, our hair damp. We're down to pants and boxer-briefs. My hands are planted on either side of his broad shoulders.

Fuck, I've never been more ready for my birthday to end—and then I tense. A sharp noise rakes the window. I sit up off Maximoff.

"Farrow." He props himself on his elbows.

My gut says, *it's a tree branch, Farrow. Calm the fuck down.* I am calm as I climb off him and the bed to check his only windowpane.

I have to know for sure.

Maximoff glances at his watch. "Now it's April 5ᵗʰ. It's over, man."

"It's not over until the stalker is caught," I say and fling the curtain.

A twig scrapes the glass with another gust of wind. My shoulders slacken. Paparazzi are in sight of the old townhouse, lingering on the street curb below. I shut the curtain before they see me.

Exhaustion tries to draw me back to bed. But I rest on the edge of the windowsill. I cross my arms casually, but fuck, I wish that'd been the stalker. Then I could've chased and tackled that dipshit.

Before I even look up at Maximoff, my phone rings in my pocket. Caller ID: Acelighter (Tech)

Tech Team.

I put the phone to my ear. "Farrow," I answer and listen to them update me on the stalker. I frown. "Are you sure?"

Maximoff stands, coming closer. I mouth, *tech team* to him. He nods, and I thank the team and hang up.

"Your ex-swimmer friend, Jason Motlic," I explain. "Apparently, he left Philly. He's now in San Diego." If the stalker lives in Philly, it makes little sense why they'd leave once Maximoff just returned.

Maximoff digests this news. "He's probably not the stalker."

"Probably not," I agree. Crossing off Jason means that I only have two top suspects left. Vincent Webber, the asshole one-night stand who talked shit about Maximoff on social media.

And my father.

42

Farrow Keene

"GET THE FUCK outta Philly!"

That heckle originates from the south end of the smoky billiards and darts bar, too packed to distinguish faces. But from the gawking and middle fingers slung in our direction, I see clearly who's being heckled.

And it's not Maximoff or Jane or any of the famous ones.

Oscar racks up the pool balls and surveys the crowded bar and pissed off faces. "Donnelly is going to flip when he gets here."

He's definitely not the type who'd appreciate someone demanding that he vacate his own city. We all call Philly home, and the jeers began the moment Oscar and I stepped into The Independent. Our go-to spot whenever we're off-duty and not at the Studio 9 gym.

Becoming "somewhat" famous doesn't mean everyone loves you. I've spent plenty of hours with Lily Calloway and Maximoff, and I've seen how unwarranted hate festers out of notoriety.

I grab a cue stick and catch eyes with a bearded, tattooed dipshit. He flips me off with two hands and careens forward on his stool. His attempt to rope me into a confrontation.

I almost laugh and spin the cue stick. I'm not that easily snared. Sidling up to the pool table, I tell Oscar with the tilt of my head, "It's like they don't realize we're all trained fighters."

Oscar grins. "Idiots." He tries to align the pool balls perfectly, and his curly hair falls over a rolled bandana that's tied across his forehead.

My phone buzzes in my pant's pocket. I pull it out with a piece of gum. New text.

"When my little bro gets here, Redford, tell him you've only played pool once or twice." Oscar grabs a stick off the wall.

I chew my gum, not looking up from my phone. "You want me to hustle your brother," I say, partially interested. I read a recent message and lean some of my weight on my cue stick. My boot rests on the rung of a short stool.

I'd say this is heaven but it's missing someone… – Maximoff

He included a selfie that could be part of a Calvin Klein campaign. Fucking gorgeous. Halfway submerged in his family's pool, his wet hair is slicked back, and beads of water roll down his temples.

My mouth rises.

Luna photo-bombed him, her tongue touching her nose.

Our clients are spending the night at the gated neighborhood, visiting parents and siblings. Maximoff invited me to join him, but since the tour officially ended early yesterday, Omega wanted to go out.

And I need to be with security.

I start texting him back: I'd say you're missing a comma. Before I hit send, Akara plucks my phone right out of my hand. He wafts smoke out of his face, the bar clouding.

"When'd you get here?" I ask, noticing a beer bottle in his grip. I'm not sure how he managed to push through the hecklers at the bar without causing a fistfight.

Donnelly saunters towards Oscar, beer also in hand. Through the cigarette smoke, I make out his septum piercing, a new thing, and he cut holes in his Studio 9 shirt.

"Five minutes ago," Akara answers me, his sweaty muscle shirt suctioned to his chest.

I pop my gum. "You smell like a five hour workout."

Akara rubs my phone on his sweat stains, making a point. "We all agreed not to stalk the stalker tonight. You know Maximoff is safe with his family."

"I realize that." I don't need the reassurance. I'm confident whoever the fuck is behind the sick photos won't reach Maximoff at his parent's house. It's decked out in security alarms and cams.

I extend my hand for the phone.

Akara rubs it on his chest again. "You really want this thing back?"

"Man sweat really doesn't bother me." I motion to him. "Give me."

He slips my cell into his back pocket.

I roll my eyes. "Akara—"

"You can get it back later tonight." He squeezes my shoulder. "No client, no boyfriend. Just relax."

I chew my gum slowly. "I'm the definition of relaxed."

Akara swigs his beer. "You've been the definition of hyper-vigilant. I'll let you know when you're back to Farrow 'chilling in hurricanes' Keene."

I'm not dwelling on that. Mostly because a brawny fucker yells, "Go eat shit, posers!!"

Donnelly leans on the pool table. "Haters gonna hate."

"Get outta Philly!" a collective jeer comes at us.

Donnelly suddenly straightens up and outstretches his arms. "I'm from Philly! You get outta here, man!"

Oscar pulls Donnelly back by the shirt before he storms the bar, and then he steals Donnelly's beer.

"Hey," Akara says, "let it go. We don't need to make another headline. *Security Force Omega Gets in a Bar Fight* reflects badly on our employers."

Donnelly glowers at the bearded, tattooed guy who's been staring me down. "What about *Security Force Omega Wins a Bar Fight*, boss?"

"No," Akara says.

The hecklers shout some more bullshit, and we do a good job of ignoring. But a female bartender leaves the counter and nears us.

She ties her hair into a bun. "Hi, guys. Look, I can take your drink orders and serve you, but you shouldn't approach the bar. It's not safe, and the manager thinks this is a better deal for everyone, yeah?"

The bearded dipshit looks too pleased with himself. He thinks we're about to be kicked out, not given special treatment.

Amusement pulls my lips upward. I'm enjoying this.

"Sounds good," Akara says. "You guys want anything?"

"I'm buyin' a round of whiskey shots for everyone," Donnelly says, gesturing to all of us.

"Got it," the bartender says and departs.

I chalk my cue stick. "Who'd you tattoo?" I ask him since that's how he earns extra cash, and it's the only time he buys everyone drinks.

"Luna." Donnelly picks a cigarette out of a pack. "Thought about consulting with her dad first since he went ape-shit on me about the others, but then I thought, nah. He won't ever see this one."

My brows spike. "Man, if you tattooed her ass and her dad finds out, he'll—"

"Don't freak. It was a shooting star below her hipbone." He cups his hand over a flame and lights his cigarette. "And she's eighteen. If it's not me inking her, then another tattooist will, you know?"

I know.

But that's still Loren Hale's daughter and Maximoff's little sister. That's still the Hale family, and fuck, I'm not typically incessant on inserting myself in other people's shit, but I understand that family better than him. And I care about Luna.

Akara motions his beer bottle at Donnelly. "If she asked you to push her off a cliff, what would you do?"

"I'd say let's grab some parachutes first, babe." He smirks. "Then I'd clasp her hand and we'd go down…" He jumps forward and then slings an arm around Oscar.

"You playing?" Oscar asks him about pool.

"Later."

Akara shakes his head, his lips lifting. He does friendly disapproval well.

My smile widens at Donnelly. "Look who's never being put on Luna Hale's detail."

He blows cigarette rings at me.

"Hey, guys." Quinn approaches, his plain shirt torn at the hem, nail scratches on his neck.

Most everyone stiffens, but I'm still leaning on the cue stick.

"What the fuck happened?" Oscar instantly nears.

Quinn pushes his brother away. "You know how the crowds are." The ones in the street, outside The Independent.

"Nah, they aren't that bad," Donnelly says.

Akara frowns and assesses Quinn from afar, who tries to convince everyone with *I'm fine, I'm fine*, but it's clear that the fame has been harder on him than us.

"I just need a drink," Quinn mutters.

The bartender returns with a tray of whiskey shots, and the bar *boos* at her, more than at us.

"Sorry," I apologize to her, and she shrugs sheepishly.

Donnelly puts a wad of cash on her tray for a tip.

"Thanks. I'll leave this here." She sets the tray on a pub table and then tucks the cash in her back pocket.

I grab a drink. "Take a shot, Oliveira." I hand Quinn the glass.

He downs the whiskey shot, and then Thatcher, the last of Omega and my new roommate, joins us. I can't say we've been friendly. We've spoken one time since the tour ended. He asked if I saw Ophelia, Jane's white cat, who went missing for an hour in our townhouse.

I said *no.*

He said nothing in reply.

And that was the end of that shit.

"Who's playing?" Thatcher asks, the sleeves of his flannel shirt rolled to his elbows.

Oscar points his stick at me. "Redford is supposed to break."

I pop my gum. "No, I'm out." I pass my cue stick to Thatcher. "You go ahead." I'm not handing him an olive branch. This is me just not wanting to play pool.

Thatcher senses this, and he doesn't say *thanks*.

I down a shot, whiskey burning the back of my throat. And I sidle next to Oscar. About to place a bet on the pool game.

But the bearded dipshit with leathery skin and an eagle bicep tattoo stands off his stool. He must be in his early thirties, not much older than us, and four more men flank him. All look about three-hundred pounds.

Donnelly often says he's "a buck seventy-five" and the rest of us are lean and muscular like UFC fighters and boxers. Not heavyweight entertainment wrestlers. Shit, the only one who comes close is Thatcher. But even entering a fight underweight, we could easily knock all of them out.

We're not intimidated. To be honest, their bravado actually has the opposite effect.

"Go back to L.A., you dumbfucks, and get outta our city!" *That* though—that's getting annoying.

The six of us face them, and the "get outta our city" holler grates on more than just Donnelly. I'd like to punch one out. Collectively, we've spent more time in Philly than most people at that fucking bar.

For us, it's home.

For Donnelly and Thatcher and Quinn, it's all they've ever known. There was no college. No other place.

It's been Philly.

Always Philly.

Some people connect to a specific town like it's a person, a tangible part of them that they can't remove, and I've seen that in Donnelly's eyes.

"Say I'm from L.A. one more time!" Donnelly threatens. Since our fame originated in L.A., that's what some uninformed dipshits believe.

Thatcher starts yelling at the heavyset fucker on the end. He's that irritated, and being off-duty is making him chuck the rulebook out the window.

Oscar whispers to me, "South Philly guys are going to get us kicked out."

"No shit," I whisper. "You better add your little brother in that."

Quinn curses loudly, edging into an asshole's face, but Akara fists his shirt and draws him backwards.

We're all trained to deescalate situations, but it's easier doing our jobs when the insults aren't directed at us.

Oscar shakes his head and hunches over the table with his stick, lining up while this conflict is brewing. "SFO haters know the bare minimum. We're famous bodyguards. We're hot. That's about it. Everything else they invent to fuel their hate."

"True." I lean on the pool table, half-sitting.

He breaks and the balls scatter the green felt. Suddenly, he straightens up, more alert as the most vocal, bearded fucker approaches me.

I don't shift.

This guy nods to me, about my height. "You think you're hot shit?"

I chew my gum. "I know I'm hot shit." I can feel Oscar's harsh glare drilling into this guy from behind me, the rest of Omega minutes away from a real fight, too.

The bearded dipshit takes one step towards me.

My jaw hardens. "Don't get in my face," I warn.

"Farrow, Oscar!" Akara calls out. He's wrangled our two South Philly guys, plus Quinn, into a booth and the other hecklers loiter back at the bar. Impressive. And one reason why I'm not the Omega lead.

Before the dipshit can hook me into a fight, I back up and take the long route to the booth with Oscar. We slip in the cracked leather seat, and Akara stays standing at the end.

"I'm not gonna miss that about the tour," Donnelly says to Quinn. I catch them mid-conversation, and he picks through a bowl of half-eaten nuts.

"What?" I ask for the topic.

He pushes the bowl aside. "Laundry."

I chew my gum into a smile. "You can't miss something you never did."

Donnelly laughs.

"That was the worst," Oscar tells me. "If I never have to see another laundromat or hotel laundry bill again, I'll die a happy man."

The bartender squeezes through and leaves us six bottles of beer. "On the house for not starting anything with those guys over there," she says. "Manager thanks you."

As she leaves, I pick up a bottle, and in my peripheral, I notice the bearded guy trying to capture my gaze at the pool table. The more beer he chugs, the less likely he'll let this shit go.

"Okay, listen up." Akara steals everyone's attention, still standing. "I have three announcements to make."

I bet I know one of the three.

"First," he says, "if you haven't heard already, Luna is moving into Maximoff and Jane's townhouse. Which means Quinn is now back at security's place with you two." He gestures to Thatcher and me.

Knew that.

I raise my beer to Quinn. "Welcome back."

He clinks my bottle, plus the other guys who start to cheers. We all swig.

Akara sets his bottle down. "We decided that since Luna is staying with her brother, it makes more sense to have her bodyguard remain on Omega."

I figured that Quinn wouldn't be shifted to Epsilon. They're not equipped to train him, and Akara had been trying to keep Quinn in SFO even when Luna left the tour.

"Second…" Akara rotates towards Thatcher, who's been quiet at the booth, sipping his beer. "Thatcher signed a permanent contract to be Jane Cobalt's bodyguard this morning."

Shit.

We all thought he'd eventually return to Epsilon and Xander Hale's security detail. It's why he remained a lead and part of the Tri-Force during the tour.

"Because of that," Akara says, "he can't be a lead anymore. The lead has to come from Epsilon, and Banks is taking his spot." Thatcher's brother is now the third voice of the Tri-Force.

Thatcher gave up his power and his higher pay to stay in Omega and on Jane's detail.

But that fact isn't what makes me smile into my swig of beer. We now earn the same amount of money, on the same level in the body-guard hierarchy. We're now equals.

Fuck, that feels good.

Thatcher lets out a heavy breath at me. He hates that I love it.

"Third and last thing," Akara starts.

"Hey, pretty boy!" a drunk heckler yells at Donnelly. "Why don't you take that thing out of your nose and shove it up your ass?!"

That insult doesn't incite any of us.

Akara grabs his beer. "Tri-Force agreed that we can all keep our jobs and be famous, but it's coming with a cost."

"What?" almost all of us say.

Akara sighs. "We can't handle major security events. Sometimes even minor ones. Not without Alpha and Epsilon or temp bodyguards. They have to join us at concerts, galas, and any charity functions. Maybe even smaller locations. We need the extra bodies, guys. We can't do that stuff alone anymore. It's just the way it is."

We quiet.

I grit down and rub my jaw. I don't want to call in reinforcements for a job we're hired to do, but I'm not about to put my pride above Maximoff's safety.

After a minute, we all nod. Agreeing.

We're in the same restless ocean, a boat of six, and luckily, we're equipped to handle the roughest weather.

Even the bearded dipshit that comes at me with a cue stick. Right now. "If you're not gonna leave our bar, we're gonna make you."

Akara glares. "Really, man?"

He barrels forward in a drunken rage. There's no reasoning with that.

I stand, Omega stands, and we step out of the booth about the same time his friends swarm us.

"Get outta—"

Thatcher sucker-punches a hefty guy, and the bar erupts into a brawl. Fists fly, chairs clatter. Quinn jabs his knuckles at a guy's nose, and Donnelly left-hooks a three-hundred pound man who breaks a bottle.

The bearded dipshit swings the stick at my head—I duck. Then I slam my boot on his kneecap, a direct hit. He curses in pain and staggers, falling.

Next to me, Akara kicks another brawny heckler in the chest. He crashes into a pub table.

Oscar is chatting with the blonde bartender.

"Out!" the manager yells at us. "OUT!" Six or seven employees crawl out of the woodwork and start ushering us through the rear exit.

Quinn raises his hand. "I'm cool, bro."

"We're going, we're going," Akara tells them, and down a flight of stairs, we reach the road together.

Leaving the hecklers behind, we joke and meander down the Philly street like nothing is out of the ordinary. Laughing about the free beer.

But our short-lived time at The Independent isn't a regular night. That abrupt ending is usually meant for the people we protect.

Not for us.

Slowly, we each grow quiet, hands in pockets and trekking along. Our fame collectively sinks in, adjusting like we've been given a new uniform to wear.

43

Maximoff Hale

CATS DART UNDER the pink Victorian loveseat, rocking chair, and up the narrowed staircase of my old townhouse. I'm back home.

I missed the little things: the historic brick walls, all my family photos on the mantel, and how it always smells like coffee and hot tea. I could've stayed on the road longer. But I'm not racing to find a way back.

A year ago, the early tour cancellation would've just fucking devastated me. I know I hurt people. I've seen Twitter. Fans called me an asshole, a heartless human being, a stuck-up celebrity pretending to be humble. That I only wanted the praise. And I don't really care about you.

I'm done.

I'm done trying to prove anything to anyone. Even you. I am who I fucking am, and the truth will always be that I wish I could've done more. But I'm finally satisfied with the fact that I've given all that I can. Even if you can't see it or refuse to believe it.

Now I need to be home.

With all the people who love me unconditionally.

My family and security zip in and out of the townhouse, carrying cardboard boxes, plastic tubs and clothes on hangers. Alpha blocked paparazzi off the street. So it's been a pretty easy move-in day.

Dear World, don't jinx me. Sincerely, an unlucky human.

Jesus.

Christ.

I rush down the stairs. "Luna, watch out!"

Dear World, you suck.

Worst regards.

My skateboard rolls out from under the loveseat. Luna cradles *four* lava lamps and steps on the board. Tripping forward.

I sprint, and the skateboard bangs into the coffee table.

Luna starts tumbling, about to face-plant, and I snag her arm before she goes down. And I hold her upright. She hot-potatoes a lamp, and catches it by the cord.

That was fucking close. I take her lamps.

"Bad start, the usual," Luna breathes and crouches to pet Lady Macbeth. "I warned you I'd be a shitty roommate, right?"

I untangle the lamps. "And I reminded you that we used to be roommates for thirteen years."

Farrow isn't here to voice the technicality, but *technically*, we've never shared a room before. It's not like we'll be sharing a room now either. She's moving into the guest room, her own small space.

Luna rises as the black cat scampers away. "That's different. We were kids back then."

I smile. "Yeah, and now you're a high school graduate with a diploma and everything…" I trail off at her smile that she can't contain. Luna finished her last homeschool exam yesterday.

Luna shimmies her shoulders. "It's pretty cool, huh?"

"Really fucking cool." A few cousins pass us with boxes, and we edge near the fireplace. Staying out of the way.

I stare at my little sister and memories surface of us being just kids. I must've been five or six, and I'd constantly ask my mom if I could push Luna's stroller. Wanting to help out. I buckled her into a car seat and held her hand while we crossed the street. We'd play-fight with plastic lightsabers in Superheroes & Scones and swap comics.

Now she's eighteen.

I'm no longer holding her hand across the street. But she could've gone anywhere after graduating. And I'm highly aware that out of the entire world, she chose to be here with me.

I didn't even hesitate to say *yes*. "Don't worry about any of this stuff." I gesture to the frilly pillows, the skateboard, the coat rack with Jane's *many* bright-colored rain jackets. "This house is yours now, too. I want it to feel like your home."

She looks at the family photos on the mantel. "It kind of already does."

I smile, and as security trickles inside, I leave to the guest room and drop off her lava lamps. Kinney and Xander are unpacking her sci-fi books and stacking them on a shelf.

Trip number five, I descend the staircase again. This time, Farrow walks in from the adjoining door to security's townhouse.

Casually, he kicks back on the door, an open jar of peanut butter under his arm, and he unpeels a banana.

I hone in on his fingers that move precisely, assuredly. That shouldn't be that goddamn hot.

My blood heats, and his lips quirk—he's not even *looking* at me or even in my direction. How the fuck he can see me is superhuman. And strange.

But hot.

I almost groan at myself as I reach the bottom of the stairs. I could detour and go grab another box from the SUV, but my feet are already moving. Towards him.

Big shocker.

I pull out a folded paper from my back pocket.

"What's that?" Farrow asks, motioning to the paper. Coolly, he squats down to my ankles.

I watch him, my curiosity piquing. "A list." It's more than a list, but he is a walking, talking distraction that my brain subconsciously…and consciously loves.

"A list," Farrow repeats and lifts the leg of my jeans, revealing my bare shin and a sheathed knife.

I cross my arms, our eyes glued together while he unsheathes my knife. *Fuck me.*

Farrow smiles and rises, one inch taller. "He's still trying to turn me into a follower." Before I can respond, he says, "Let me guess what your list doesn't say. *Number one: I'm in love with Farrow Keene. Number two: he's always right.*"

"How'd you know?" I ask sarcastically.

Farrow dips *my* knife in peanut butter and then slices the banana. He eats the piece directly off the blade and licks the peanut butter off the tip.

Fuck.

Me.

I flex, my muscles blazing.

His smile stretches. "I have a PhD in Maximoff Hale Studies."

I compose myself and give him a look. "How'd you earn that degree? By following me around?"

"By beating you at everything."

My brows bunch in agitation.

He notices, and the corners of his lips lift more.

I need to hand him the paper, but I don't want this to end yet. "There is no such thing. So you actually earned a degree in Liars 101."

He whistles. "He can't even put me in a higher level than *basic* 101." He eyes the paper and sets the peanut butter jar aside. "Give me."

I hand him the paper.

He barely skims it and his brows rise. "This is called a wedding *itinerary.*"

"That's what I fucking said," I combat, and I rub my mouth. Christ, I feel my smile. "All the details are there." The upside to the tour ending early, I can attend my parent's vow renewal.

He's fixated on some portion of the itinerary.

"What?" I look at the paper upside-down, and the words *Maximoff Hale, no date, no plus one* stands out. "My assistant typed that."

Farrow puts the paper in his back pocket, still at ease. "Not a big deal, Maximoff." He eats another piece of banana off the blade. "I'm going to the wedding as your bodyguard. It's what I am."

LOVERS LIKE US // 365

I frown, thinking. He's more than a bodyguard to me, but he knows that. So then why does something feel off?

My eyes descend, and I just now notice *Thatcher* written in Sharpie on the banana peel. I'm less surprised that Farrow is eating Thatcher's food than I am by this, "Who writes on fruit?"

"Hall monitors," Farrow says as he slices the banana. He tosses the peel on my iron café table. "And I have to live with one."

"Sucks you don't have a boyfriend to crash with." I draw towards him, our legs knocking.

Farrow eats the last slice of banana, and his other hand clasps my neck.

I'm the first to grab him by the shirt, then wrap an arm around his shoulder—he spins us in a swift maneuver.

My back thuds into the closed door. God. Breath flames in my lungs.

Farrow sheaths the knife in his black leather belt. "You're not my boyfriend then?" He eyes my lips in a way that says, *I won't kiss you. I won't fuck you. Unless you tell me I'm yours and you're mine.*

It electrocutes every fucking part of me. His weight pins me to the door, and my cock begs for more hot friction.

"You must've lost your boyfriend," I say, my voice low.

Bleach-white hair hangs in his lashes. Our mouths edging close, he whispers, "You failed Liars 101, wolf scout. Because he's right in front of me."

Kiss me, man. I can't wait. I clutch the back of his head and kiss him deeply. Hungrily, our mouths crash together. I spin him around, his back to the door. When I think I have the lead, his hand slides down my back, and he grabs my ass.

Fuck. I groan against his lips, and he smiles against mine.

Someone clears their throat behind us.

Great.

I pull back, but I play as cool as I fucking can and stand straight. This is my townhouse. I live here. We kissed. He grabbed my ass. On the PDA scale, this is minor level.

Farrow rests his shoulders on the wood. A lot more naturally at ease than me. But that's normal.

Who saw us?

My dad.

He stands in the doorway, light rain pelting the street behind him. A box labeled *Luna from Thebula* is in his arms, biceps cut and features sharp-edged. His brows are cinched like he's slowly processing something. Maybe that Farrow and I are really a couple. Or maybe he's just stunned to see me with *anyone*.

He looks good though. Healthy, not edged or antsy.

He opens his mouth to speak, but voices escalate behind him. We all listen, but from where I stand, I can't see anyone.

"If I go in there it's going to be real," my mom says. "Maybe we should all have breakfast first. Anyone hungry? I could eat a waffle. Daisy?"

"Chocolate pancakes," my aunt says.

"She's not moving to fucking New York or across the country," Uncle Ryke retorts. "It's nothing to fucking agonize over."

"Easy for you to say," my mom replies. "Sulli wants to live at home for another year. My daughter is *leaving*. OhmyGod, I promised myself I wouldn't cry this fast. I'm already crying. Rose—"

"Chin up, shoulders back," Aunt Rose snaps icily. "What our gremlins don't know is that they're ours forever. No matter what geographical location they run off to and whether they like it or not."

My dad swings his head back and calls out to my aunt, "Take your talons off my kids, Cruella."

"Bite me, Loren."

"Weak," my dad retorts.

Farrow almost laughs, and I smile. God, I love my family

"They're all going to leave," Uncle Connor pipes in. "It's generally what children do when they get older."

"And now she's really crying. Good job, Richard," Aunt Rose says.

"No, no," my mom protests. "These are happy tears. Luna is grown up. That's a good thing."

My dad glances at me, then Farrow, and I stand more uncomfortably. I can't tell what my dad is thinking. At all.

When it reaches the point of maximum awkwardness, my dad rotates to the door again. "If you all keep lingering, we're never going to finish moving her in!"

One-by-one, my mom, two aunts, and two uncles file into the townhouse. Rain jackets on, and some shut their umbrellas.

This is the first time we've all really been together since Camp Calloway. In the same room, at least. But we've talked. All of us. I'm not going to pretend those conversations never happened just because they didn't take place altogether.

Anyway, kissing Farrow at the Camp-Away event feels like eons ago.

I feel different since then. Stronger in a different way. Maybe that's what happens when you meet quicksand and discover how to pull yourself out.

I break the silence before they do. "Can we not make this awkward?" I ask. "You all know Farrow. He's my boyfriend. That's not changing."

"I don't actually know him as your boyfriend," Connor says as he hooks his expensive umbrella on the coat rack. His all-knowing eyes meet Farrow's. "But I'd love to change that."

"Agreed." Ryke nods and then turns to my dad. "I'm sensing a fucking invitation here?"

And my dad—he's smiling. Genuine, and *happy*. It lifts the last bit of weight off my chest. "I think so, big brother." He looks to my boyfriend. "How about you start coming to our lunches with Moffy?"

My eyes widen. Seriously. That's what they want? To grill Farrow over tacos and salsa? "You can say no," I tell Farrow. "They're a lot to fucking handle."

"I can handle anything, wolf scout," Farrow says easily, and with a smile, he tells my dad, "Sounds like a plan."

My dad nods and adjusts his grip on the box.

"And," Connor adds to Farrow, "if we decide we don't like your company, your invitation is revoked."

"That's not happening," I say firmly.

Farrow hangs his head, his smile out of this fucking world right now, and he tries to downplay it a bit.

A calico cat rubs up on my dad's ankles. He tells me, "If Farrow is shitty company, it'll go to a vote."

I shake my head. "After my week, voting is *permanently* banned."

My dad winces. "You know I could—"

"No," I cut him off. "We talked about this." None of them are vouching on my behalf like I'm a kid. "It's my job. I'll take care of it."

My dad squints at me. "It's like you're an eighty-year-old man in a twenty-two-year-old body." He looks to my mom who bites her thumbnail, nervous about Luna leaving. "Love, you sure you birthed him?"

"I remember every second of it, Lo." She pauses. "Okay, not *every* second. But most of it."

My mouth curves upward. *This* right here. Us. It feels like we're back on some sort of track. Sure, there'll be blips and drama and some fights, but my family isn't going anywhere. Any world where they're missing is too lonely to conceive.

"Mom…" Jane's voice tugs our attention towards the staircase. She descends in a lilac tulle skirt, leopard-print sweater, and her brunette hair frizzes around her face.

Jane never ended up speaking to her mom. Not that day in Kansas. Not the night she returned home. This is the first real gesture.

We're all quiet, but Rose hastily unclasps her Chanel purse, her nails painted a matte black. Tabloids call my aunt an "ice queen" but her heart is fucking giant. I saw it as a kid when five-year-old Ben got poison ivy and she told her son she'd bear his pain for him if she could. She whispered in French, made him a hot bath, and sat with him the whole night.

And I definitely see her heart now. As she pulls out a pair of heels.

They look more like pink suede sandals with a chunky glittery heel attached. My aunt mostly wears simple black dresses and classic heels. These are eccentric.

These are Jane.

At the sight of them, Jane stops mid-stair. "What are those?"

Rose delicately holds the heeled sandals. "They're for you—but I'm *not* trying to buy your love," she snaps. "I saw them and they screamed *Jane Eleanor Cobalt*, my beautiful, brilliant firstborn daughter... If you don't want them, I'll return them to the store or I can throw them in a fire. Watch them burn..." She tries to raise her chin, fighting tears. She quickly brushes the corners of her eyes. "Whatever you want."

Jane smiles with a watery gaze. "I'd love them." She reaches the bottom of the stairs.

"Really?" Rose asks. "Because if you don't like the buckle or the sequins, I can have them altered."

"No," Jane says, holding the heels with her mom for an extra beat. "They're perfect."

I smile with practically everyone else.

My dad pipes in, "Good, she's been carrying those things around for *four* months."

"Lo!" my mom whisper-hisses and slugs his shoulder. "That's a secret."

"Oops," my dad says dryly, but he smiles at Jane who looks over-whelmed

"You did?" Jane almost bursts into tears.

Rose rubs her daughter's cheek. "I thought one day, you'd want to speak to me again. But I didn't know when."

Jane wraps her arms around her mom. Aunt Rose is notorious for hating hugs, but she reciprocates tenfold. I can't hear them whisper to one another, but I'm sure they're exchanging *I miss yous, I'm sorrys, and I love yous.*

I glance at my family. My mom and dad in a loving embrace: his arms around her waist, her body clung to him. And Ryke picks up Daisy and tosses his wife playfully over his shoulder. So she hangs upside-down, her smile as bright as the sun.

Everyone is okay.

For the moment. But it fills me up to the fucking brim.

When Rose and Jane break apart, her blue eyes land on her dad. Silently, Connor goes and hugs his daughter.

Jane caves instantly.

"Mon cœur," he whispers. *My heart.* "I emailed you an essay this morning."

She slightly pulls back. "I didn't ask for another one."

"It's a prelude to the first one," he says smoothly. "Three-thousand words on why you're an extraordinary daughter. The best we could ever have."

She puts her palms to her cheeks, overwhelmed. Tearful. *Happy.* And she just nods in thanks. Jane looks to me.

I smile more. *You did the hardest part, Janie.* And everything is better than what it was.

She smiles into a tearful laugh, wiping her cheeks.

My mom detaches from my dad and wanders towards me…no, not me. She faces *Farrow.* Those two haven't talked either. Not once.

Farrow straightens up off the door. "Lily—"

"No wait," my mom says and wipes her sweaty palms on her baggy Avengers Assemble shirt. "So I have something for you too…and just to be clear, I can't take back anything that I said or did at the Camp-Away. Because Maximoff is my son, and I want to be the kind of mother who's strong enough to stand up for him and protect him." She nods resolutely. "I didn't cower, and I'm proud of that."

You've always been that kind of mom, I want to say, but I inhale a tight breath, having no goddamn clue where this is going. But my dad sends me sharp looks to *let them talk.*

So I stay quiet.

Farrow nods just as confidently. "I'm glad you did."

My mom sniffs and reaches for a small hand-wrapped package she set on the coffee table. "So this is a welcome back to Philly…thingy."

"It's not a *thingy,*" Rose snaps.

"Yeah," Daisy agrees, still upside-down, "you said you wouldn't call it that."

"It's a gift," my mom says in a strong nod.

My pulse speeds. Is this normal? Mom's gifting their son's boyfriend a present. I think I'm overthinking. No, I *know* I'm over-fucking-thinking.

Farrow smiles, eyeing me a bit, and then he starts to tear at the tape. The package is wrapped in newspaper. Minimal effort—I'm thankful for that. Keeping it casual, Mom.

"You didn't have to give me anything," Farrow tells her. "This is enough." He means being on speaking terms and her acceptance.

"I wanted to," my mom says and she backs up into my dad's chest. He holds her and hunches to rest his chin on her bony shoulder.

Farrow slowly unwraps the square-shaped package. Glancing at me, he asks, "You didn't know about this?"

I shake my head. "No clue."

He tears off the last piece of paper, and his smile stretches from cheek-to-cheek—and I'm groaning.

"*Mom.*"

"What?" She balks. "You probably don't have any photos together of you two in public. I just thought it'd be nice—"

"I love it," Farrow says.

"You do?" My mouth parts, my pulse still beating in my ears.

Farrow rotates the wooden-framed photograph to me. The picture was taken from a celebrity news site, a little watermark in the corner. In the photo, I stand with crossed arms near the *love* sign at LOVE Park. Farrow is close as my bodyguard, earpiece wire hanging.

But our eyes are on each other. I'm laughing like he said something funny. His smile is full-on James Franco. If it weren't for the earpiece and the radio on his belt, he might look like a friend.

Maybe even a boyfriend.

But I hone in on the setting. Philadelphia. I remember that day. I was doing a photo-shoot for *The Hollywood Reporter*. It was *before* the tour. We'd just started dating.

My brows furrow. "Mom, this was before you knew we were a couple."

"Yeah." She clears her throat. "I had to scour some magazines for that one."

"She was stalking you," my dad says.

"Lo!" My mom slugs his arm.

He smiles affectionately. "Alright, love." He looks to me. "She wasn't stalking you."

Farrow only focuses on my mom as he says, "Thank you."

My mom practically beams. Her eyes dart from him, to me, back to him. Like she's fully feeling our relationship as reality. Her smile kind of looks giddy. Like she could root for us. Wave flags for us. Create banners and move mountains for us.

That means a fucking ton.

My dad is almost there. Maybe. Progress.

Farrow seems a little off as he wraps the photograph back up, his lips drawn into a thin line. I suddenly realize it was what my dad said.

Stalking.

He's thinking about the stalker.

My parents have no idea that someone is stalking me. I don't plan to tell them or worry them. The stalker hasn't been found yet, but now that we're back in Philly, the possibility is imminent.

44

Maximoff Hale

I WANT YOUR COCK inside of me. I sent my childhood crush that text tonight. In this reality, not a dream or some alternate universe or as a fucking joke.

Legit, I told him to fuck me.

I've been mostly into topping him, but this night, I'm mentally on a carnal loop. Where I can't break from imagining his cock pounding in my ass for the first time.

My muscles beg and plead with me to be beneath Farrow Keene, and after all the build-up to bottoming, I know I'm ready. Prepared.

My room. I'll fuck you hard. — Farrow

Goddamn.

My dick strains against my jeans. My body and my brain are desperate for him, but I take about ten minutes before I leave.

I enter security's townhouse through the adjoining door. Lucking out on not seeing Thatcher or Quinn. I climb the narrow staircase to the attic bedroom, the one that mirrors mine.

As the stairs end and I face his door, I just realize I've never slept in his room. Never fucked on his bed.

Not once.

I think about that first combining with the other first, and I may self-combust. My blood pools, body craving rough friction and strong pressure.

Fuck me. Muscles taut, I open the door and step inside. His small room is pretty bare: dresser, end table, bed, and a short bookcase with nothing shelved.

Farrow leans so damn casually on the brick wall, just watching a video on his phone, but as soon as I enter, he looks up.

I soak him in. His nonchalant and confident demeanor, the tattoos that crawl up his neck. His earring. The piercings on his nose and lip, his muscles outlined in a black V-neck. And his platinum hair, a few pieces brushing over thick brown brows that slowly rise. *Knowing* I'm turned on beyond human recognition.

His gaze rakes my body in an even hotter once-over.

I lick my lips, wanting him on them. On me.

In me.

Fuck me.

Tension wrings the air. His eyes meet my eyes and it snaps. We move closer, a fucking boiling urgency pulsating inside me. I pull my green shirt over my head.

He yanks off his black V-neck.

And somehow, some damn way, my gaze drifts. To his full-sized bed, the black sheets visible beneath a pulled-down black comforter. Heat brews in the attic, even in April, and whenever he's here, he probably doesn't sleep with more than a sheet.

That's his bed.

My brain fixates on that obvious fact. *This is his room.* I can imagine, way too well, Farrow driving his erection into me on that bed.

Fuck. I blink a few times. I've been staring faraway. I grimace and focus on a six-foot-three Yale graduate who rests an elbow on the dresser. Watching me.

His mouth curves upward. "Welcome back, space cadet."

I scowl and unbutton my jeans. "I barely spaced out."

His smile widens. "Let me ask you something. How many times have you fantasized about me fucking you on my bed?"

Christ. Am I that fucking obvious? "Zero," I say flatly.

He whistles. "You're a terrible liar."

"Maybe once," I correct and near.

Farrow unbuckles his belt. "Maybe once?" he repeats like I'm still lying. I'm just way underestimating here.

"More than once," I amend, my muscular legs knocking into his. I grip the dresser beside his bicep, and he unzips my jeans, our eyes not detaching.

We both step out of our pants, and my gaze drops to his black boxer-briefs, his cock long against the fabric like mine—*fuck me.*

I almost instinctively arch my hips forward to thrust. My grip tightens on the dresser, my breath already ragged. I palm him above the fabric, and he grows harder beneath my hand.

Farrow grits down in arousal, biceps flexed. And then he clutches the back of my head, the masculine force something I fucking crave.

He sucks the sensitive skin on my neck, his teeth biting— *fuckyesfuckyes.*

My muscles contract. "Fuck," I growl.

He pulls back and our eyes hit as he says, "Tell me what I did to you more than once."

I heat. "You want details?" *About my fantasy.*

Farrow eyes me with an edging smile. "Yeah. Give me the details, wolf scout." He lowers to a knee, rolling my elastic waistband down with him. I'm buck-naked, my rock-hard cock begging for force, but more than that, I want to see his.

"Take off your clothes and maybe I will," I say.

He rolls his eyes. "*Maybe* you will."

"I will," I say firmly. I rake a hand through my thick hair, dying for pressure. "Or I could go take a nap, find the meaning of life alone—"

Farrow stands, just to remove his boxer-briefs. *Fuck.* His erection seems larger than I last remember. I'm staring. Hard.

His knowing smile returns. "That's going to be in you."

My breath shallows, and we kiss twice before he breaks from my mouth and kneels again. I clutch the dresser while he grips me, the pressure on my shaft torching my nerves. A coarse noise scratches my throat.

Farrow almost pauses.

Tell him my fantasy. "You push me on your bed. Not angrily. Just in the moment…" My head tries to tilt back, his mouth wrapped around me. Moving back and forth, back and forth. "*Fuck me,*" I groan, my knuckles whiten on the dresser, sweat built on my skin.

My waist bucks forward.

His hand replaces his mouth before I choke him. "And then?"

"It ends," I lie.

He's about to stand up, but I clutch his shoulder. Keeping him on his knees. "Then we wrestle for the top, and when you beat me, you fuck me how you usually fuck all guys." Any other detail bursts in my brain.

Farrow rises to his feet, an inch taller, amusement behind his eyes. "Man, you don't know what I do when I usually top."

I stare at his mouth, my sarcastic retorts dying. "What do you usually do?"

His tattooed hand clutches my jaw, and his mouth brushes my ear, whispering, "You'll see."

I release my grip on the dresser and hold the back of his neck. He walks me backwards before I unglue my feet. Tonight, I don't fight to be the one to guide him.

I just steal a deep kiss, and my legs hit the mattress. His palm to my abs, he shoves me down hard. My spine meets his black sheets. Breath knocking out of me.

Farrow climbs on top, and we're all limbs and muscle, sweat and speeding heart beats. We wrestle for the lead, his strength all over me.

I'm burning up at a million degrees. Our mouths slam together, a fucking kiss that pushes my body against his. *Closer.* We tangle, then untangle, and Farrow pins me down. I'm lying on my chest, my knees digging into his soft sheets.

His pelvis is in line with my ass.

This position sends signals to my nerves to prepare for ultimate intensity. One last effort, I try to flip Farrow and hook his ankle.

Yeah, that doesn't work.

I just concede.

My forehead almost touches the mattress. Breathing heavily.

"Fuck," I mutter.

Farrow stands off the bed, and I fixate on his movements while he walks bare-assed to the end table. His tattooed build is carved with lean muscle, and his fingers gently open the drawer. Pulling out condoms, lube, and he tosses a couple towels on the bed.

When he looks back at me, he smiles. "You love this." His voice is a hundred percent gravel tied in silk.

Yeah.

I love how he moves. How he speaks, how he acts. Who he is. Just him. I love all of him.

"Maybe," I say confidently.

He checks me out like I just did to him. How I'm on my knees, my forearms, and I'm waiting for him. The bed undulates as he climbs back. Staying behind me.

I relax my muscles. It's easier for me since we've led up to this point. Especially after New Year's Eve in the hotel. My body trusts him. I trust him, and I'm not even partially afraid.

God, I just want him.

Craning my neck over my shoulder, I watch him rip open a condom and then sheath his erection. He places his knees on either side of my waist, his confidence like a hammer to my pulse.

He clutches my ass with that tattooed hand, and then teases me open with two fingers, the lube warm. *God.* My chest tightens, breath twisted in my lungs.

Farrow studies my body's reaction. That felt fucking *good.* Not bad. He sees, and slowly...slowly, he starts to push into me.

My head swings forward, the sensations gripping my nerves. Not able to watch, I bite down, nose flaring at the build-up—*oh fuck.* I growl into a groan as he goes deeper, *deeper.*

"Fuck," he mutters, letting out a shallow breath. "I didn't think you'd be this tight." He shifts his knee slightly, pushing even further into me. *Fuck me.*

Farrow rocks forward, thrusting in a perfect rhythm. I can't concentrate on words. My vocabulary dwindles to *fuck* and *Jesus Christ.*

While I'm underneath him and he's above me, he places his palms flat on the mattress. Only an inch above my hands that fist his black sheets. His inked arms stretch like pillars beside my biceps. He practically shields me with his body—as he rams in and out.

My twenty-eight-year-old bodyguard is fucking me.

His pace is rougher, faster—I choke out a groan, he's hitting a sensitive spot that tries to shake me limb-to-limb. My muscles flex, my eyes ache to roll back.

Jesus. Fuck.

I take a breath, stopping myself from coming. Christ, I'm not even touching my cock. He slows a fraction, giving me some time.

Glancing back, I catch sight of his clenched jaw, breathing hot breath through his nose. His arousal tenses his body, and damp pieces of bleached hair fall in his carnal gaze while he pounds into my ass.

Raw sex. This image beats every fucking-on-his-bed fantasy I've ever constructed.

I know how he prefers to top, too.

Rough and deep. Just like me. Not a fucking surprise. As his pace speeds, I can't look at him. I stare straight, my lips parted. I try to shut my mouth—I can't. I can't, *fuck.*

I cage all breath, my neck muscles strained. I can feel him in me. I white-knuckle the sheet, then I instinctively grab his arm beside me. Holding on. "Holy fuck," I moan roughly.

I've never done this with someone. Never let them in this far. I'm giving myself to a person in a way that I never thought possible. Warmth and safety bridges us together, and I wouldn't choose anyone but him.

"*Maximoff,*" he grits my name, the hot pleasure like another thrust inside me.

My body rocks with his force, and my brain short-circuits to single syllables.

Now.

Need.

More.

Want.

More.

Him.

Fuck.

He lowers his weight on me for deeper entry. More friction. His chest melded to my fucking back, and I fall flatter, his arm curving around my collarbone, his jaw skimming my cheekbone. We're that close. That connected together, and I'm riding a nerve-blistering edge.

I drill a glare into the wall where a headboard would be, my pulse thumping. "*Oh, fuck.*" A noise escapes that I've never made. I shudder, a peak rippling through my veins.

Water wells in the corner of my eyes—I'm not kidding. Farrow brings me to a level I've never reached, and I can't breathe, can't speak. I'm in a new universe that catapults me.

My eyes roll back, my fingers digging in his arm. *God.* I come, a sharp breath expelling out of my mouth. I rest my forehead on the bed, my energy draining fast.

"*Fuck,*" Farrow curses, milking his own climax. I think he hit his peak at the same time. If I was supposed to wait for him to come first, there's no fucking way I could've.

I rub my wet eyes on the sheet, then I turn my head. Our eyes on each other's lips. Our mouths meet in a slow, sensual kiss that mimics our come-down.

When we break apart, he pulls out, and he whispers with a peeking smile, "Better than your fantasy?"

I lick my stinging lips. "Beyond."

"SATURN BRIDGES HAS GOOD DESSERT AND COFFEE,"
Farrow tells me, buttoning his black pants, the elastic band of his
Calvin Klein underwear sticks out.

We just showered, and now we're back in his attic room.

I dry my wet hair with a towel and scroll through my phone, already
dressed in another pair of jeans and a black Batman shirt. "I've never
eaten there."

"But you've been there?" He buckles his belt.

"For their trivia nights." I pop open the website. We've been trying
to pick a place for late-night dessert. A semi-date.

I get that we're not publicly a couple, but we can still eat out together
since he's my bodyguard. PDA is just completely off the table, and no
eye-fucking. Obviously.

The restrictions don't bother me, but I sometimes imagine what a
full-date would be like. Twice as much paparazzi, no doubt.

"Fuck," Farrow mutters and opens a couple drawers. Overturning
pockets of some pants.

"What are you missing?" I ask.

"My wallet." Realization washes over his face. "I left it in your
bedroom."

"I can just pay for you, man," I offer, but I already know his response.

"No. We'll split." He attaches his radio to his waistband, not worry-
ing about putting on a shirt.

I get it. Occasionally, we both like paying for the other. It feels
good. Knowing we're dating. We're together. But I've stopped him
from buying my breakfast and dinner before.

Likewise, Farrow doesn't like being financially dependent on
anyone but himself.

"So Saturn Bridges?" I ask. "I can make a reservation."

Farrow smiles, his hand on the doorknob, and he lingers, our eyes
locked. *Don't fucking leave.* "Yeah," he says huskily.

Stay.

I almost edge near.

He rubs his mouth, his chest rising. "I'll be right back."

45

Farrow Keene

"WATCH IT, YOU LITTLE BASTARD." I snatch Walrus before the calico kitten darts into security's townhouse, and I kick the door shut. He meows and paws my cheek.

The corners of my mouth rise, but not because of this cat. I keep remembering Maximoff and me together only moments ago. Hell, I can't stop replaying each minuscule part: the wolfish noises he made, his daggered eyes, the purest vulnerability, the overpowering feelings. Fuck, I'm kicking myself for leaving shit in his room. Because I just want to be with him.

Let's make this fast.

I drop Walrus, and he leaps towards the kitchen. While I head to the old staircase, I spot Jane on the Victorian loveseat. Snuggled in a fuzzy pink blanket, she watches *10 Things I Hate About You* alone.

This wouldn't be unusual, but she invited Nate over tonight for a movie and sex. I saw the guy earlier in passing. He looks like a young, lightweight Scott Eastwood. Tall, preppy-styled brown hair, wide-jawed. A black blazer and gray button-down hugged his skinny build.

"Where's Nate?" I fix my earpiece, the cord cold on my bare shoulder and back, running to the radio on my waistband.

Jane scratches Licorice behind the ear. "He's using the bathroom."

I nod, not about to linger long. I ascend the creaking stairs.

Jane has a little bit more freedom with a friends-with-benefits than she would with a one-night stand.

See, Nate has been vetted multiple times and been in this townhouse even more. It'd be extreme overkill to keep putting a bodyguard "chaperone" on him.

And Thatcher is back at security's townhouse, safe from overhearing his client having sex. Not that I really care about what Thatcher hears and doesn't hear. We're not all meant to be "besties" and that's more than okay with me.

I don't want a thousand best friends, and fuck, I don't even want *one* best friend. I want my tireless, headstrong boyfriend and some reliable people I can hang with on occasion.

That's all I need.

Halfway up the narrow staircase, I reach the second-floor landing. And I pause. My gut says, *look.* I turn my head, the bathroom door in view.

No light streams beneath the crack.

Instinct overrides alarm, and I move quietly but urgently. I open the *unlocked* door and flick on the lights. No one is in this fucking bathroom.

There are only two other doors. Left goes to Jane's room. Right goes to Luna's room. I tune out motives, the *what ifs* and all the shit that'd cause me to stumble or falter. I concentrate on one task.

Find Nate.

I open the left door. Flick on the lights.

A quick scan of the room.

Empty.

I shut the door, turn to the right one. Luna's room. My jaw hardens as I grab the brass knob.

Don't be in here, you motherfucker.

The knob jams.

It's locked.

I listen for a half a second, no noise audible. I knock once, twice, and then feet patter. I lower my fist.

Don't be in here.

The door swings open, and Luna peeks out, a heart drawn on her cheek. Green marker stains her hands. "Hi, Farrow."

"Anyone with you?" I ask.

Luna glances behind her. "No…should there be?"

I have to look. "Can I see?"

"Yeah…"

I push the door wider. Glow-in-the-dark stars and planets are glued to the ceiling, lava lamps casting colors and odd shapes on her black chalkboard walls. Purple beads hang across her four-poster bed like curtains, but I can see through them.

And no one else is here.

Okay.

If he's not on the second-floor, then I know where Nate is now. And it's not good. My nose flares and eyes burn.

"What's this about?" Luna wonders. "Are you trying to find Moffy? I thought he's with you."

"He is. Stay in your room for me. Lock your door again." I wait for her to move. She hesitates, and my brows arch. "Luna." I check the staircase. No movement.

My body tells me not to overact. Don't jump the gun. Don't panic. Breathe and face this shit head-on.

"Should I call my brother?" Luna asks.

"No," I say. "I'm going to text him." I already take out my phone and type a quick text. Luna nods and then shuts the door. I hear the lock click.

Stay in my room. Lock the door. I send the message to Maximoff.

Pocketing my phone, I continue up the stairs to the third floor. Process of deduction: there's only one other place the stairs lead to.

Maximoff's attic bedroom.

Don't panic.

I inhale, not fixating on the reasons why Nate would want to be in Maximoff's bedroom. If I concentrate on that, I'll lose it.

My phone buzzes, but I don't bother checking his reply. I can't have a five-minute text conversation or a phone call with Maximoff. Not right now.

I climb the flight of stairs, quietly. Careful not to cause the old wood to squeak.

Each step is a razor blade held to my throat. Because I know exactly what I'm climbing towards.

A nightmare.

A kind of hatred that I've seen for months in sick photo after sick photo.

Last step, and I've reached the top. I face a door and listen for a short moment.

Hearing…I shake my head. I can barely distinguish the noise.

But someone is in there. I'm not painting a vivid picture of what's inside.

What I know: I need to end this tonight.

Turning the knob, I kick the door open.

And my heated gaze drills on a familiar face.

This fucker…

I grind my teeth.

Nate stands wide-eyed and eerily still next to the bed. At least two inches taller than me, could be more, his head almost touches the rafters and strung bulbs.

I hone in on his hands.

He clutches a stainless steel thermos, and in the other, he grips the hilt of a hunting knife. The mattress and orange comforter are already torn to shreds.

My muscles tighten; my jaw throbs from gritting, and I gently shut the door behind me.

As his shock wears off at being found, he narrows his gray-blue eyes on me. "You should understand," Nate says seriously.

I tilt my head. "*I* should understand," I repeat, acid dripping in the back of my throat. "What exactly should I understand, Nate?" *You son of a bitch.*

"You've seen Maximoff. You've seen him all over Jane."

"They're *friends*—"

"No," Nate cuts me off, shaking his head once. "Maximoff has *hated* me because he's jealous that I was sleeping with Jane. You know that? You know he wants her for himself?"

I let out a short laugh of cold disbelief. I'm unblinking. Staring at someone who created a twisted narrative off assumptions and fabrications, something more dangerous than the innocent truth. "You really believe that bullshit," I realize.

His glare grows hotter. "People can brush off the tabloids like they mean nothing, but there's truth there." Nate points the blade at me. "You know it, too."

My jaw tics. "I know you've been posting pics of Maximoff's death on social media." I'm 99% sure it's him and just waiting for confirmation.

He lifts his chin and hesitates for a second. Like he's unsure how to reply. But then his nose flares, and he says, "It's what he deserves."

"*Fuck you,*" I sneer, and a rampant fire ignites inside me. I charge, my stride lengthy and unrelenting.

Nate brandishes the knife at me less like a tool and more like a weapon. Ten feet away, his eyes warn me to *stay back.*

I don't slow.

Maximoff Hale deserves peace. And love. I'll always, *always* fight to give him the things that people rip away, and that's not changing now, a year from now, five years—forever.

Nate lunges at me, blade outstretched, but I slip left and catch his wrist. I elbow his temple, then I uppercut his jaw, the impact bangs my knuckles, and his teeth bash together.

He blinks, disoriented, and I twist his wrist. His fingers release the knife, and it clatters to the floorboards. But I strengthen my grip and pull his wrist further back.

I feel his bone crack.

Wincing, Nate spits, "Get off!" He thrashes to push me back, and I fist his button-down.

As he grapples and claws against me, the thermos overturns on us. Something red is in the steel canister, but I don't focus on that shit. I deck him in the jaw and dodge his blows as thick, warm crimson-liquid smears on our arms, my chest, our faces, his hair.

Blood.

It's blood.

I slam him to the ground, his back lands with a loud *thud*. He planned to dump *blood* on Maximoff's bed. Probably from an animal, pig or sheep, but I don't think long.

I pin Nate down, my knee digging into his ribs. Floorboards are so slick with blood that his legs slide beneath me—my legs slide. Both of us searching for better grip.

Fuck.

I sit up partially and throw my knuckles into his smeared-red cheek.

His head whips to the left, but he spits. And I stare at more sick hatred than pain. A sudden thought cuts into me.

Maximoff was supposed to be in this room tonight. Nate didn't know that Maximoff would be in security's townhouse with me.

My eyes sear as I seize his irate gaze, and I ask coldly, "Were you planning to hurt him tonight?"

Nate breathes hard through his nose, unblinking. Not affirming.

Not denying. Could be, he doesn't even know what he would've done.

He just leaves me to visualize that horrific scenario.

Fuck you. I can't unleash the words or spit them out. They calcify inside of me, and my actions come in swift succession.

I fist his shirt, lifting him in an iron grip, and then I slam him down forcefully. His head bashes into the wood. Eyes flutter. One more time. Up and down, his eyes flutter again.

I cold-cock him with a right hook. His head lolls...unconscious. His body slackens beneath me.

I sit up.

Breathing, breathing, my chest rising and falling. I find the cord to my mic and earpiece, hanging off and covered in animal blood. I click the mic, and instinctively, I say, "Farrow to Thatcher, come to Maximoff's room."

Not a second later, he replies, "Copy that."

With another heavy breath, I drop the mic.

I can't stand.

I can't move off him.

I spot the knife an arm's length away. *Grab the knife. End this.* I reach and clasp the hilt.

The door opens.

Maximoff enters like a quiet force of nature, coming forward, and his sturdy forest-greens make sense of this bloodied scene.

I'm drenched in red liquid.

Nate is unconscious beneath me.

What surprises me, more than anything, Maximoff ignores Nate. Doesn't look at him long or let his short-temper win. He's not storming forward to throttle an unconscious body.

His eyes lock on my eyes.

He notices the blood, probably smeared across my forehead, cheeks, caked in my hair.

"Not mine," I say quietly. "Animal." Most likely.

He's still coming forward.

He's still committed and unwavering.

I'm still unmoving, clutching the knife. Unable to let go.

We both know what Nate being the stalker actually means. Jane and Maximoff trust so few people, and Nate was granted access to their townhouse. To their family. To all of their personal things. He abused a power, invaded their safe space, which is violating on so many fucking levels.

And yet, Maximoff is only looking at me, his empathetic eyes redden. Not letting rage eat at him, not letting this fester, but I'd been carrying this demon. This draining, leeching motherfucking thing.

He sees.

Shit, he's known.

And it's still clung to me.

Maximoff comes behind me. His biceps and forearms slide around my chest and abs. He helps me rise.

His fingers skate along mine, the knife still firm in my grip. "Farrow."

I drop the knife. I blink.

And I breathe. But I don't touch him. My hands are stained red. Blood all fucking over me.

With his chest to my back, he pulls me away from Nate. We near the brick wall, and his heart thuds against my body. And very strongly, he says, "It's over, Farrow."

Four months of sleeplessness, of an agonizing unknown and obsession that clawed deep under my skin. Gone.

All of it.

Relief just crashes into me at his words, and I shut my eyes. Something wet and hot rolls down my jaw. I breathe out, and just as I turn to face Maximoff, the door squeaks open.

Thatcher slips inside, his features set sternly, and I expect him to acknowledge me as part of a crime scene.

But he just talks into his mic. "Thatcher to Tri-Force, we need you at Jane and Maximoff's townhouse."

I wipe my hands on my pants. That's not helping. Since Maximoff wrapped his arms around me, blood stains his bare chest and his hands too.

I'm not loitering here. Quickly, I tell Thatcher I'll return, but we're showering before security arrives. Before I need to rehash the events to everyone.

Maximoff and I exit, as quiet as possible but hurried, and we're in the small bathroom. I crank the shower on. Hot water rains on the tiles. I'm not looking in that mirror.

We keep our clothes on and slip into the glass shower stall. Water pelts us, and I comb my fingers through my hair. He tries to help scrub the blood out of the strands.

Pink water washes into the drain at our bare feet. His skin tanned from the sun, mine fair, but the tops of my feet are inked with two nautical wheels.

He passes me a bottle of shampoo.

One scrub later, and I'm sure it's not coming out. The white strands will stay tinted red. Maximoff knows too, his forest-greens set back on me.

"I'll dye it," I tell him.

"I can get it." He turns to leave.

I catch his broad shoulder. "Not yet."

Maximoff faces me again, and I can't stop staring at him, water dousing both of us. His chest rises in a heady breath.

My hand ascends to the back of his head, and he clutches my neck. Our foreheads nearly meet.

I can't lose this guy, and he's alive. *He's alive.* Not hurt, not injured, he's breathing right in front of me.

Maximoff licks his lips. "I didn't listen to your fucking text."

"No shit," I murmur, and he lets out a short laugh—but his eyes melt over me. We're drawing closer, *closer.* And more serious, I whisper powerfully, "*I'm glad.*"

He holds me stronger; my grip is tighter, and we pull towards each other abruptly, chest slamming against chest. As though we're trying to connect as deeply physically as we are emotionally, the intensity rattling me, and I cup his face. His fingers claw at my shoulders. We spin, wrestling for more, and my back hits the tiled wall.

We haven't kissed, but he's already devoured me.

"Maximoff," I breathe against his mouth.

His eyes scream *I fucking love you.* "Don't let go," he orders.

"I'm not." *I'm not.*

"Neither am I," he assures me

"Good."

And I realize and feel something. I would've self-destructed without him. He's been the prince in knight's armor.

Protecting me.

46

Farrow Keene

"MAYBE I SHOULD GO into the nunnery," Jane says softly while lying on the Victorian loveseat. She rests her head on Maximoff's lap and digs a spoon into a pint of chocolate chip ice cream. "That way I won't make any more dreadfully bad choices."

"Yeah," I say, "don't do that." While I sit across from them on the coffee table, I balance a mirror on my knees. A piece of jet-black dyed hair falls to my lashes as I fix my hooped lip piercing. Nate's fist must've caught my mouth. My bottom lip is a little bit swollen.

It's only been three hours since I knocked Nate unconscious.

Jane is still processing tonight's events. Maximoff runs a hand through her wavy hair, and he shares a cautious look with me like *it hasn't hit her yet.*

I know.

"I *can* do that," Jane says like she's preparing to debate me. "I'm an independent, strong-willed woman."

"You're not Catholic," I say, finished loosening my piercing. I stretch forward and steal her spoon. Scooping into the ice cream, I take a bite.

Jane narrows a look at me, searching for a rebuttal. She can't find one for once. I'm going to be painfully honest here: I don't like it.

I hold out the spoon for her to take it back.

She doesn't.

Jane.

Maximoff gives her a tough look. "Just let Farrow and me vet the next fucking guy. We'll grill him twice as much as security."

My mouth almost rises. "I am security, wolf scout."

He flips me off, but he drops his hand when Jane says, "No." Her calico cat springs up on her stomach, and she strokes Carpenter. "I'm serious, Moffy. I'm taking a break from all men with any sort of sexual benefits attached."

His brows pull together in concern. "Jane—"

"He *believed* that rumor." She sits up to better meet his eyes. Carpenter springs off the loveseat. "I'd been texting Nate throughout the tour, and he only knew about the locations to our FanCon stops, before publicized, because I told him. I trusted him. I didn't even consider that he could've…"

"*No one* did," Maximoff emphasizes.

"It's not your fault," I tell Jane.

If anything, this is on security. Me and the entire team. But at the end of the day, we caught the guy. Say we caught Nate months earlier, Jane would still be upset. There'd still be the *same* breach of trust.

The same ending.

But Thatcher doesn't see it like that. His anger isn't even directed at me. Jane Cobalt is his client. His responsibility.

In his mind, he should've seen Nate as a threat. Thatcher couldn't even speak when I asked him about charges against Nate. He's beating himself up over this shit.

Banks is spending the night at our townhouse. Hopefully his twin brother can help him realize that he couldn't have done more.

"I should've known," Jane says, setting down the pint on the rug. "*I* should've seen this—"

"*No,*" Maximoff forces.

"You weren't the one with his dick in you," she combats. "I literally let a psychopath into my body." She tries to stay witty and lighthearted, but the severity of this line sinks in fast.

Her hands fly to her face, and a sob breaks through. Her body heaves forward.

Maximoff holds his best friend against his chest and speaks in French, his tone harsh and somewhat loving. He's not that soft, but he kisses the top of her head. I hear the words *ma moitié*.

She rubs her face with the sleeve of her coffee-print pajamas.

I'm not sure what to say in this situation. "I'm sorry, Jane," I breathe.

She sniffs and wipes more tears, hiccupping. Five cats start to swarm the ice cream, a good distraction. "I'll be okay," she murmurs and leans down. "Come here, my loves."

Jane cradles Toodles and picks up the pint before standing. With a tearful gaze, she says, "I'll get you all little bowls. Follow me."

We watch Jane leave for the kitchen, five cats in tow, and then our eyes meet again.

I tell him, "That could've been worse."

"That was bad," he says with a nod. "A real fucking apocalypse." Jane being upset in any capacity always gets to him.

"Looks like we survived the 'apocalypse' then," I say, using air-quotes. "Since we're all breathing."

Maximoff cracks a knuckle, growing more serious, and he has trouble leaning back. His shoulders squared and posture upright. "What criminal charges do you think will stick?"

For Nate, he means.

I edge forward on the coffee table, my knees touching his knees. "Anything that happened in the attic, it's my word against his."

"So none of that," he realizes, staring off for a beat.

"Yeah." I sweep his sharpened cheekbones. I wonder if he wanted to charge Nate for raising a knife at my face. I study his features, and I'm certain that he did. Damn. It's cute that he cares about me, but I care more about him. "There's a stalking and harassment law in Pennsylvania," I tell Maximoff. "It's a first degree misdemeanor."

Maximoff contemplates this. "What is that, a year jail time maximum?"

"Or even less. He could just be fined a grand." I place the mirror aside. "But either way, he'll be slapped with a restraining order."

Security can now legally detain this fucker if he comes within distance of Maximoff. Even if Nate isn't behind bars for long or at all, we still obtained the ability to protect Maximoff in a greater way.

This is a victory, any way I turn it.

Maximoff must sense this because his shoulders lower. I put a hand on his knee, and he leans forward a fraction. He licks his lips, something biting at him, and he just lets it out, "What does this mean about your father?"

I was wrong about him, but I can't budge off one point. "He's still the same pretentious asshole that quit on you," I tell him. "Nothing's changed."

Maximoff thinks for a second and then shakes his head. "He's not the one who harassed me. So something's changed."

His words catapult me back to a memory, the one with his dad at a café. Where he watched his children and spoke honestly.

"Parenting never gets easier. Not when you love them, and you need to be hard on them, but you're afraid to break them. And you think you're doing everything right as a parent because you know what's wrong, but still, it's inevitable. We'll fail. We always do."

Back then, Lo had no reason to share that with me. He hadn't made any mistakes with his children yet, as far as I was aware. But my father had made one with me.

And Lo knew I was fighting with him. I wonder if all that time he was speaking to me about my father. Reminding me that he loves me. He's never been abusive or malicious. He's just doing what he feels is right, even if it's wrong.

I shouldn't villainize him or think he's willing to fuck me over. Hell, I believed he was capable of murdering Maximoff.

I shake my head repeatedly, and I almost laugh.

"What?" Maximoff asks.

"Words of wisdom from an unwise man," I tell him. "Your dad."

Maximoff smiles. "He's pretty wise for all the hell he's been through."

I smile just seeing his. "You're not too bad yourself, Harvard Dropout."

He gives me a look. "Christ, call the fucking Coast Guard. Farrow Keene just complimented my intelligence."

I suck in a breath. "Well now I'm questioning everything because there's no reason to call the Coast Guard, wolf scout. We're on land."

Maximoff feigns confusion. "You sure I haven't drowned you yet?"

I laugh, and our eyes dance over each other as I whisper, "Trust me, I'm very much alive with you."

47

Maximoff Hale

THE SILVER LINING TO losing my job and cancelling the tour early comes in lavender floral bouquets, tuxes, a hundred closest friends, family, and a garden gazebo today.

Spring flowers bloom, and I sit in the front row next to my siblings. Beneath the gazebo, my mom looks effervescent in a lilac dress, beaming at my dad, who wears a black-on-red tux. Both radiate with pure, blissful happiness.

I was at their wedding. Just a little kid, and unlike Farrow, my memories have faded and fogged over time. But this, right here, I immortalize.

My mom and dad renew their vows in front of all of us, and sure, press and cameramen are here too. But the world seems to still.

I swear to everything in this fucking universe—you can actually *feel* their love. It's in the air and the silence between their words.

The first thing I think is…*I love them.*

The second thing pauses me cold.

I want that.

It aches in me. To be able to stand up and declare my love in front of millions of people.

Proudly.

I turn my head and spot the line of security. All dressed in well-fitted, expensive suits. No ties. I find Farrow no problem.

Standing between Akara and Oscar, he cups his hands in front of him, his black hair swept-back. His winged neck tattoo and inked swords on his throat visible from his button-down. His earpiece fit in, the cord runs to the mic on his collar.

And in a split-fucking-second, he catches me staring. I have trouble looking away. I glance at my parents, then back to him, to my parents, then him.

His lips gradually stretch into a smile. So slow it looks like an epic shot in a movie.

I'm gone.

Completely fucking in love with him.

AFTER THE SHORT CEREMONY ENDS, THE GARDEN is transformed into a sparkling after-party. Light bulbs are strung across oak posts, and wooden circular tables landscape the greenest grass. A taco bar and five different kinds of cake line the overflowing food table, but I'm not near the tacos or even sitting.

I'm on the makeshift dance floor, facing a DJ stand, and every single one of my cousins and siblings surrounds me.

Press isn't invited, but a few drones have flown across the starry night sky.

We jump to house music, the bass pumping, and Jane clutches her little sister's hand. Audrey's red hair flies as they bounce together. And I spot my little brother.

Xander stands still in the pit. I jump to him, and he cringes like *this sucks*. I'm not fucking deterred. I clutch his shoulders and shake them to the rhythm.

All my sisters and my brother can dance goddamn well. Jesus, I've seen him break-dance in our living room a thousand times before.

His smile wants to peek. I lift his arms and clap his hands, then I let go and clap mine.

Xander continues with the beat, more heartily.

I mess his brown hair and shout so he can hear, "Looking good, Summers!"

Xander laughs and nods to the song.

Eliot Cobalt jumps past me in a black masquerade mask, and he sticks out his tongue. I smile, and not long after, the song switches to a Fleetwood Mac playlist.

"Meadows!" everyone howls since my family listens more to house music.

Sulli and I do the sprinkler dance. Jane sidles up and joins the easy motion, and then Sulli shouts, "Shopping cart!" We all change movements, and our siblings one-by-one begin the shopping cart dance with us.

Now onto the lawnmower, then the running man.

Luna is the best. By far.

When the song shifts to a slower ballad, everyone belts out the words. Beckett twirls a not-very-rhythmic Sulli, and Charlie flings an arm over Jane's shoulder, swaying to the beat.

I think about how four months on the road brought my family together. How the five of us can dance in a close circle and not feel light-years apart.

I don't know what my future holds with the state of H.M.C. Philanthropies, but Charlie, Jane, Beckett, and Sulli said they'd do anything to help save the charity.

I thought I'd want to protest and tell them *I got it handled.* Maybe I will at some point, but right then, I just nodded. This time, their helping-hands don't feel so much like failure on my part. I don't overthink or read into the deeper meaning I'm grateful that they love me. I love them, and it's as simple as that.

I think about Lao Tzu, a Chinese philosopher who said, *"Being deeply loved by someone gives you strength, while loving someone deeply gives you courage."*

My head turns, and I think about the *someone* who I love deeply. Moments fly past my mind in Technicolor, every second I've spent with Farrow. Vivid. And overwhelming.

My chest swells, and I glance at Janie.

She smiles bright, knowing who I'm thinking about. "Go get him, old chap."

So I leave the dance floor in search of a colossal know-it-all. My shoes sink into grass, and I wave briskly at my grandparents who call my name.

I undo my bowtie, passing wooden tables and wicker chairs.

Easily, I see him. Farrow chats with Oscar at the garden entrance. Where tall hedges form an opening, and cedar stools and barrel tabletops scatter the area.

As soon as I approach, their conversation still continues, but their attention zeroes in on me.

Farrow's eyes descend my body in a hot once-over.

My brain sputters like a fourth-grader. Whatever I fucking planned to say just evacuates. Great.

Before I find any words, Oscar flashes a circular pin at me. Black with rainbow block letters that spell out: *Rainbow Brigade*.

"Your sister recruited us into her little club." Oscar attaches his pin to his button-down.

"Officially," Farrow adds with the raise of his brows.

"And she called me a troll," Oscar tells me.

My lips almost lift. Kinney already gave Tom and me a pin this morning. "She does that," I say and watch his gaze drift to the taco bar and cake.

"Extra security is here," Farrow reminds him.

"Then I'm out for a cake break." Oscar puts a hand on Farrow's shoulder. "See you, Redford." Then mine. "Hale."

Farrow balances his boot on the rung of a stool, his piercings glinting in the warm light. I rest my forearm on the barrel tabletop. Trying to be casual, nonchalant.

He notices, and his smile keeps expanding. "Man, if you have something to say—"

"I heard that you retook the Hogwarts House sorting quiz." Jesus Christ. I couldn't have made a stranger digression from what I actually *want* to say. I end up crossing my arms.

Farrow tilts his head, eyeing me up and down. "Luna wanted me to. She didn't think I was Gryffindor."

Apparently, he got Ravenclaw this time around. My mom freaked, and she's been ordering him some Ravenclaw scarves to add to the Gryffindor paraphernalia she bought him years ago.

I nod. "Cool." I pop a button at my collar, my bowtie already undone.

Farrow looks at me like I've rocketed to Mars and built a colony of one. "Cool?" he repeats, then he checks me out again, which scorches my body. "You look good in a tux, wolf scout."

"Better than you," I say, even though he's only wearing a black button-down, tucked into black pants that fit him too damn perfectly.

Farrow rolls his eyes into a short laugh. "You love your fan fiction."

I shake my head and seriousness slams hard into my chest. "I like my reality."

His chest rises, and he steps closer. But a drone buzzes overhead. Causing him to pause and check over his shoulder. "I think you mean," he says, his gaze returning to me, "that you *love* your reality."

"Almost," I tell him strongly, and words pour out of me. "You know what I was thinking while my parents recited their vows today?"

Farrow shifts his weight like he's bracing for impact. "What?"

"I was thinking that I want a love like theirs, the in-your-face, overjoyed kind of love that knocks you backwards—and what the fuck is stopping me?" I pause. "And I realized the answer is *me*."

Farrow takes a tight breath. "What are you saying?"

"I've been fucking stubborn, but I'd rather be stubborn *with you* than without you." I'm more assured than I've ever been. "I'm not standing in my own way anymore. You've given me the courage to move."

His eyes push through me. *Into* me. Excavating parts of my soul that belong to him.

He's wanted more, and I said *no* out of a moral obligation to protect his privacy. I'm finally ready to let go. I don't want to drag us down when a greater happiness is in reach. All I need to do is move towards it.

So I say, "I know your life will drastically change if we go public. I know the media will hound you. I know your job will be harder. I know there's a chance it could fuck everything up, but I'm willing to take that giant risk with you and only you."

Farrow rubs his mouth, and his overcome smile lights my core. "Damn."

My pulse is racing. "So that's a yes?" I need to make sure he hasn't changed his mind.

He doesn't look away from me. "It's always been a yes." We draw towards one another, no longer stopping, and I take out my phone.

He notices the cell, understanding what we're about to do.

And Farrow cups my face with one hand. I grip the back of his neck. Our mouths a breath apart, he whispers, "Ready, wolf scout?"

Unequivocally, fucking wholeheartedly, yes. I commit a thousand-and-one percent, and our mouths meet, the sweltering kiss zipping through my veins and scorching me. I clutch his hair and remember to click a photo.

He nips my lip, *fuck me*. God, it takes all my energy to lean back, to part for a second. My pulse thumps hard, breath knotted and wanting for more. Deeper and longer. Farrow holds my waist, and we both train our eyes on my phone.

In the picture, his tattooed hand clasps my sharp jaw and my hand grips his black hair. Chest against chest, our eyes stay closed and our lips are pressed together in a cinematic-worthy embrace.

It's too affectionate to be called *fake*.

I already know what to type in the Instagram box. When I finish, I angle the phone to Farrow. Making sure he's alright with this before we upload.

His smile stretches, and with one more glance at me, he presses *post*.

Instantly, our photo pops up in the feed. Only three words beneath the picture. Three words that announce we're a couple. Three words that I'll never forget. Three words that'll change everything.

Lovers Like Us.

His hand returns to my jaw, mine to his neck, and we fucking kiss again. And again. My muscles pull taut, burning for more, and his smile rises against my lips. My back digs into the barrel, and I'm holding him in a strong grip that pulls his firm body against my hard chest. Our breath hot and shallow.

The garden explodes with buzzing. Pinging notifications. Texts and calls.

People realize what's happened, but I'm not looking. I'm not watching them.

We're in our own world.

Our own universe.

No one can have it. No one can break it.

This moment belongs to us.

ACKNOWLEDGMENTS

We always say our books have certain "tones" that change depending on when the book was written in the time of our lives. Addicted to You is an angsty, raw novel because we were twenty-one when we wrote it and about to graduate college. About to head off into the unknown. While we were writing, we truly believed we were fighting for a love, a career. Our emotions bled into the words.

Amour Amour is hopeful. We wrote it when we felt like we accomplished a dream. When writing long-term, full-time seemed well within our grasp.

So when we sat down to write Lovers Like Us, we knew what type of book we would write. Something that swept us away. That was heartfelt, fun, emotional, and full of all the things we love.

This year has been extremely difficult for us, and this book has been our outlet. Our happiness. Each time we put fingers to the keyboards, it was like living and breathing in a world that loved us and we loved it back. This book and Maximoff & Farrow's love story are so very special to us in so many ways. And there are people we need to thank for making this book possible. Because it wouldn't be here without them.

Our mom, there are no words that will do justice to our gratitude. We know this came to you at an incredibly hard time, but you still lent us your editing skills. Our love is boundless for you. We're not sure how we lucked out on having Rose Calloway as our mom, but we did. Thank you.

Our lovely aunt, your energy is like a ball of light. We love you. Thank you for reading those last few chapters for us!

Marie, you are the French goddess that we definitely don't deserve, but we're so lucky to know. Thank you for all your translations. We're so glad that Jane, Maximoff, Charlie and Beckett sound like they really know French, and that's truly all thanks to you.

The Fizzle Force, thank you for being a group of loving readers who fangirl along with us. The Facebook group is one of our most cherished places and without it, this job would be a much more lonely affair. Special thanks to the admins—Lanie, Jenn, Jae, and Siiri—for all that you do. We're grateful for all the support you shower us with. Without you four, we'd be nervous wrecks.

Lastly, thank you, the reader, for picking up this book and continuing with Maximoff & Farrow's love story. Writing their romance was pure joy for us, something we desperately needed. The extra icing on the cake: their romance isn't over. Another book means more banter, more fun, more family and love. We really hope you'll continue on their journey with us.

All the love,
xoxo Krista & Becca

If you or someone you know is struggling with anxiety, depression, or suicidal thoughts, it's important to reach out for help.

National Suicide Prevention Lifeline:
1-800-273-8255